Praise for
MARK FROST's
THE SIX MESSIAHS

"Intriguing . . . A historical thriller with more than
a touch of the supernatural to it . . . Frost expertly
turns up the thrills."
Virginia-Pilot

"Fantasy and horror are augmented by
action/adventure, mystery, and more than a few
appearances of notable historic personages . . . This
book succeeds on any number of fronts and cries out
for translation to the big screen."
Orlando Sentinel

"Extraordinary . . . Plenty of thrills, chills, and
tongue-in-cheek laughs."
San Francisco Chronicle

"*The Six Messiahs* ranks high. Frost has a sense of
humor, can tell a story, and writes action very well."
Palm Beach Post

"Clever . . . terrifying . . . A classical-style,
slam-bang adventure."
Publishers Weekly

"*The Six Messiahs* just gallops along."
Washington Post Book World

Books by
Mark Frost

THE SIX MESSIAHS
THE LIST OF SEVEN
THE GRAND SLAM
THE GREATEST GAME EVER PLAYED

MARK FROST

THE SIX
MESSIAHS

AVON BOOKS
An Imprint of HarperCollinsPublishers

AVON BOOKS
An Imprint of HarperCollins*Publishers*
195 Broadway
New York, NY, 10007

Copyright © 1995 by Mark Frost
ISBN: 0-380-72229-1
www.avonbooks.com

First Avon Books paperback printing: September 1996
First Avon Books special printing: February 1996
First William Morrow hardcover printing: August 1995

Avon Trademark Reg. U.S. Pat. Off. and in Other Countries, Marca Registrada, Hecho en U.S.A.
HarperCollins ® is a trademark of HarperCollins Publishers Inc.

Printed in the U.S.A.

10 9 8 7

For my family
For Lynn

Many thanks to Ed Victor,
Susie Putnam, Howard Kaminsky,
Will Schwalbe, and Bob Mecoy

contents

CONTENTS

THE SIX
MESSIAHS

prologue

THE SCORPION SAT MOTIONLESS ON THE BACK OF THE GAMbler's hand. A tremor racked its ribbed, leathery torso, but the insect's aggressive instincts were overruled by a superior force its simple nervous system had no capacity to question.

It only knew: *Not yet.*

The gambler felt the same power pin him to the ground like a mantle of flat rocks. Spread-eagled, muscles and bones fused. His eyes could still move, wild and wide, and he could see the scorpion but not the humpbacked Preacher Man, pacing behind him, boots crunching in the crusty dirt. Terror sang in the gambler, caterwauling loud as that Eyetalian opera he'd seen in St. Louis. His thoughts melted like spring snow before they could form, the mind he'd labored so hard to educate useless to him now as a dry well.

The Preacher Man came into view, stopped, spat a hot splash of tobacco juice across the gambler's rigid face, and smiled down at the hapless dandy in his vest and spats, pegged taut as a tent in the dust.

"Promise you this; a man cheats at poker with me, friend, and I will favor him with more than a bullet for his trouble," said the Preacher, in his honey-dipped Alabama drawl. "Pay attention now, son, and I will deliver unto you a reward more righteous than a blade through your belly."

The Preacher shook out his arms and felt the Holy Fire rumble up his spine: *Oh yes,* he thought, *this is how the Good Lord rewards his Faithful Servant; my ceaseless pain, the lost years, that black stretch of empty road down the center of my mind all forgotten: I have been sown with the seed of the Prophet! I have been chosen! The Vision coming into my dreams these past months is a gift from God, my destiny set before me, clear as ice: I will lead the multitudes into the wasteland and build a New Jerusalem in the desert. We shall strike the hammer of Salvation down on a wicked world.*

The Preacher sneered contemptuously at the gambler. *And this tinhorn card sharp with the ace down his boot and the derringer in his belt buckle and the rest of these prairie shit-heel peckerheads are just a sea of empty vessels waiting for me to pour purpose into their puny souls. The Archangel lifts me on his wing and fills my soul with the Power!*

As he had trained himself, the Preacher grabbed hold of the Power churning his insides and shot it out across the desert like the sweep of a lighthouse beacon. A dry rattle answered and the sand boiled with life in the red dying light. He peered out, shielding his eyes against the low-lying sun: pincers, scales, spiny claws, a living wave clattering, swarming toward him. Rattlers, centipedes, adders, toads, tarantulas, all caught in the net, the magnetic promise of his Word.

The Preacher twisted his crooked, perpetually stiff neck in mock surprise at the sight.

"Why bless my soul," he whispered, "who would have thought there'd be so many of them out there?"

The swell of scorpions and spiders and snakes rose up and stopped cold an inch shy of the gambler, a wall outlining his body in the dirt. Swaying above him, the column obscured the sunset, but the man's reeling brain could make no sense of what he saw.

The Preacher pushed his hands out and his will flowed into the massed creatures; with one mind the vermin crawled forward and blanketed every square inch of the gambler's body. His feeble breath rasped as it filtered through a forest of busy, scuttling limbs. There the creatures froze, paralyzed as the man beneath them, obediently waiting their next instruction.

The Preacher Man stepped back, folded his arms, and stroked his chin, a parody of an artist admiring his canvas.

"A figure of a man, rendered in insect and reptile. Seems to me . . . we are in need of a title for this fine work, wouldn't you agree, neighbor?" said the Preacher, then, snapping his fingers: "I've got it: *Desert Still Life.*"

A wet laugh bubbled from his lips. Folding his hand around the gambler's thick bankroll in his pocket, the Preacher felt joy wash over him like warm seawater.

Yes. This was better than waking by the side of a road, cold and shaking, without a name, unable to speak, no past or future, a dumb beast trapped in a crevice of time. Resurrected. Born again in His image. Here to spread the Word and begin the Holy Work.

This was so much more . . . *fulfilling.*

The Preacher raised his hands dramatically, a conductor in command of his orchestra. The instruments responded; lifting tails, opening mandibles, baring fangs.

The gambler felt the change around him and what remained of his mind fled like a burglar.

Now.

Discharged, the still life instantly dissolved, scurrying back into the desert, mindless again, separate and fearful.

The Preacher tried to think of some appropriate remarks to say over the gambler's body but lost interest when his gaze slipped past the dead man to the cow town in the distance, its buildings black against the red-and-orange horizon: A lamp in the upper window of the saloon where they had played the poker game winked on.

What do they call this place again?

Texas.

Godforsaken provincial wilderness, this American West; no culture, no theater or coffeehouses. What a waste of perfectly good real estate.

But on the other hand, the people are so much more impressionable.

The Preacher Man tossed a handful of dirt onto the swollen, discolored corpse, turned on his heel, and headed back toward town, silver spurs jangling as his ruined leg trailed half a step behind.

I'm going to have to read the Bible, he realized. *That's the very least these yokels will expect of me.*

book one

THE ELBE

chapter one

WHAT A DAMNABLE NUISANCE ALL THIS HOLMES POPPYCOCK *has turned out to be. That such a cipher of a man, a walking talking calculating machine who displays no more humanity than a hobbyhorse, should inspire such passion in the bosom of the reading public is a greater mystery to me than any I ever dreamt up for him to solve.*

Even as I write this entry, again, this evening at the Garrick Club—my farewell dinner—the subject of Sherlock's untimely death dominated conversation with the boorish, opinionated insistence of an American running for political office. Conceived at a moment when my only concern was putting food on my family's table, this Holm-unculus, this cerebral marionette has assumed a place in their lives more real to some of my readers than their own friends and relations. Shocking: but then if predictability in all God's creations was what the Man Upstairs was after He would have called it quits after putting up the Himalayas.

How naive of me to imagine that giving old Holmesy the heave-ho off Reichenbach Falls would put an end to the ballyhoo and let me get on with my serious work. Nearly a year now since Sheer-luck took the plunge, and the public outrage at his demise shows no signs of slacking off. Indeed, there've been a few occasions where I've felt legitimate concern for my physical wellbeing. That sturdy red-faced woman brandishing an umbrella on a country road near Leeds. A scarecrow of a man with genuine derangement in his eye trailing my carriage around town. The trembling, hollow-eyed boy who approached me in Grosvenor Square with such a stammering surplus of contained violence it seemed likely his head would detonate before spitting out a sentence. Madness!

What drives me to wit's end is the possibility that, as a result of the fanatical devotion engendered by my Baker Street Frankenstein, the rest of my books, the work into which I've poured heart and soul, may never receive the fair hearing every author hopes for in the court of public opinion. Still, I console myself with the thought that if it weren't for Mr. H. the only shelves my so-called personal writing might be lining are at the bottom of my steamer trunk.

But as to the Burning Question put to me so energetically last night, and likewise at every instance where I see fit to present myself publicly (including, appalling circumstance—mouth wedged open, throat exposed, sharp instruments in the hand of my inquisitor—my recent trip to the dentist!), the answer remains, steadfastly:

No, no, and no.

There will be no Resurrection. The man fell two thousand feet straight down into a crevasse. Dashed beyond repair, no reasonable hope for recovery. He is deader than Julius Caesar. Respect to the gods of logic must be paid.

I wonder how long I'll need to remind these people that, not only is he deceased, the man is a fictional character: He can't reply to their letters, he doesn't actually reside at 221B Baker Street, and he can finally be of no help to them whatsoever in solving that lingering mystery which haunts their every waking moment—although my earnest advice to them remains that if Pussywillow has indeed gone missing they should look up a tree. If I had half a shilling for every time I've been asked if he . . . well, come to think of it, I suppose I do.

What awaits me with regard to the death of SH in America? I'm given to understand the passion for Holmes burns even hotter there, although my excitement at the prospect of setting foot on their shore should balance any inconvenience stirred up by Sherlock's leap into the void. The United States and the Americans have captivated my imagination since I was a child; their rambunctious precocity, the driving will that serves as whip hand to the blinding progress of that new republic should act as a strong and revivifying tonic to me.

Five months abroad: My dear wife not nearly as strong as

she would like me to believe, but so determined to see me make the career advancement this journey represents. So be it: The frustration of my inability to ease her discomfort is bringing peace to neither of us. This damned disease will run its inevitable course regardless of my efforts, and the distance between us grows regardless of my whereabouts: The more I move out into the world the further she withdraws from it. For now the energy she spends trying to reassure me will be better spent marshaling her own resources. It is her battle to fight, finally, alone.

No regrets, then. The coming days will pass quickly in that way they always do; I shall conduct my tour of America and be home among my loved ones soon enough. Young brother Innes will make a splendid traveling companion: Two years in the Royal Fusiliers have done wonders for the boy. It occurred to me tonight, watching him leap to my defense at the Garrick, that Innes puts me very much in mind of the hotheaded young snapper I was myself ten years ago, when I briefly traveled in the company of a man the memory of whom remains to this day more vivid and beyond compare than any other I have known in this life.

Our train leaves for Southampton at first light; setting sail at noon tomorrow. Looking forward to a peaceful and uninterrupted week of luxurious relaxation.

Until then, Diary . . .

"Innes, give those bags to the porter, that's what the man's here for; smartly, move along. . . ."

"We've still plenty of time, Arthur," said Innes, lifting a valise.

"No, not the valise; it's got my correspondence, don't let that one out of your sight. . . ."

"I know perfectly well which one is which. . . ."

An elderly porter wrestled their first steamer trunk onto his trolley.

"There's a carriage waiting for us, porter—careful with that footlocker, it's crowded with books." Then, taking Innes aside: "Give the fellow half a crown, not a penny more; these pensioners always make a big show out of struggling with the bags when the truth is they're as fit as a circus strong man—now where the devil is Larry?"

"The train's only just arrived, Arthur," said Innes.

"And he was supposed to be waiting for us here on the platform; drat the man, why send him down a day early if he can't manage to find—"

"Halloo! Halloo, sir! Here we are!"

Larry waving, moving toward them from the station entrance.

Doyle glanced at his watch, grumbling, "We arrived ten minutes ago. On time. Ships have been known to sail off and leave people."

"There's an hour to go yet, Arthur. Look, you can see the ship from here. I honestly think you can relax. . . ." Innes pointed toward the Royal Pier, where the massive double red stacks of the steamship *Elbe* stood plain against the gray, low-hanging sky.

"I'll relax when we're on board, in our cabin, luggage secured in the hold, and not a moment before," said Doyle, checking tickets and passports for the third time since leaving the train.

"You really *are* an anxious traveler, aren't you?" said Innes with the smirk reserved for his older brother's more obviously ridiculous behavior.

"Go ahead and laugh; one day you'll miss your train or your ship, and then we'll see if you think I'm quite so amusing; there's a list of potential mishaps that could keep us from our destination that's as long as a lamplighter's candlestick. Arriving somewhere on time is not a matter of good fortune: it is a sheer act of will. Any attitude to the contrary extends an open invitation to the universe to heap disaster upon you indiscriminately, not that it ever needs to be invited. . . ."

"Here we are, sir!"

"Good Christ, Larry, where have you been? We arrived ages ago."

"Sorry. Absolute devil of a morning, sir," said the short, sturdy Larry, breathless from his upstream swim against the disembarking passengers.

"Oh?" said Doyle, cocking an eyebrow at Innes. "How so?"

"Right; alarm goes off in the hotel at five this morning—bells in your ear, women howling in the halls, all of us mucking about in our woolies—and they won't let us back up to our bunks for nearly three hours; seems some sheik of Araby cooking a curry in his room set the curtains on fire."

"Dreadful," said Doyle, keeping an eye on Innes to chart the impact of Larry's woeful narrative. "What happened then?"

"Everyone late departing the hotel as a result, resultin' in a massive migration down to the station, half an hour's wait to grab a hansom in the carriageway, and even though I precautionarily engaged a driver for the day the bugger can't get his rig within a loud shout of the entrance what with the traffic and my eyes can't pick him out of the mix."

"It's a wonder he didn't split an axle."

"Oh, it was a scrum, all right, a regular rugby match," said Larry, who had never once turned down an implied invitation to elaborate. "My driver's nowhere to be spied; I'm about to abandon ship and let down the lifeboats when finally my fella squirts out of the pack, and we're no sooner clear of that fine mess in front of the Ritz when the next thing you know a beer wagon goes bum over teakettle ahead of us on the High Street and nothing can wiggle an eyelash in either direction for two solid blocks."

"Must have taken half an hour to clear the wagon," said Doyle, glancing sideways again at Innes.

"Half an hour easy before we're clear and we're no sooner on the go again when one of his geldings tosses a shoe in the mud and starts limpin' like a three-legged dog. Now my driver goes into a brown sulk and won't be comforted—he's a Welshman, it should come as no surprise—so I'm left with no alternative but to abandon the wretch in the middle of the street, hike the last half mile here in a driving rain and hack my way through a deranged mob of tourists outside to find another cab. It's a good thing I left an hour before your train was due or I wouldn't have been ten minutes late."

"Thank you, Larry," said Doyle.

Feeling his argument to Innes about the vagaries of fate emphatically settled, Doyle flashed a triumphant smile, but in that way peculiar to younger brothers Innes offered no concession of defeat, staring coolly at the horizon, as if the Great Pyramids occupied a distant hillside.

With the porter behind them, Doyle gave a dry snort and pointed them toward the exit. Strapping young Innes ran interference, plowing a path through the crowd like a cow-catcher on a locomotive.

"You can thank the fact our new driver's a fan of the Adding Machine," said Larry, using one of their coded references to Doyle's famous fictional creation. "Took the promise of an autograph to get him to wait."

Before Doyle could inquire, from under his raincoat Larry produced a *Strand* magazine featuring a vintage Holmes story. Five years in Doyle's employ had produced an almost supernatural ability in the former Cockney burglar to anticipate his master's every need: "Already took the liberty."

"Good man," said Doyle, taking a pen from his pocket. "What's the fellow's name?"

"Roger Thornhill."

Doyle took the magazine from his loyal secretary and scrawled an inscription—"For Roger, The Game's Afoot! Yours, Arthur Conan Doyle"—as they pushed through the station doors.

"Still plenty of time," said Innes calmly.

"Only thing is," said Larry, "with my having to raise my voice above the ruckus for the drivers to hear me I'm afraid word leaked out about your arrival—"

"There he is!"

And with that cry, a crowd of fifty, many with *Strand* magazines in hand, closed in on Doyle as he cleared the doors, an impenetrable clamoring mob between them and their cab—driver Roger standing atop, waving his arms frantically—while in the distance, the tantalizing stacks of the *Elbe,* their ever-so-much-closer-to-departure destination.

"Game, set, and match," said Doyle to Innes, before putting on his public face and wading forward to meet the onslaught, pen at the ready, with a friendly word for every comer and a determination to courteously satisfy every one of their requests, as swiftly as humanly possible.

Between signatures inscribed, greetings exchanged, anecdotes endured ("I've got an uncle in Brighton who's a bit of a detective himself. . . ."), and offered amateur manuscripts kindly but firmly refused, half an hour flew by. A ten-minute carriage ride to the docks passed without incident, filled by their driver's monologue about his astonishing good fortune, variations on the theme: "Wait'll me missus hears about this."

Upon arrival at the customhouse, they jumped so smoothly over every hedge of the bureaucratic steeplechase involved in departing mother country that Doyle felt a twinge of disappointment: He had worked up a terrific head of steam for annihilating the first bureaucrat who tried to obstruct them but he had had no occasion to use it.

Something was wrong; this was too easy.

There Doyle stood, clerk before him—papers in one hand, stamp in the other—one fence away from the finish and the ship's departure still five minutes off, when out of the corner of his eye Doyle spotted and, with the unerring instincts of hunted prey, instantly recognized the lone journalist lying in wait for him, poised like a jungle cat.

"Mr. Conan Doyle!"

The man pounced; pad in hand, rumpled suit, mangled cigar stump, panama hat, and the bounce and confidence of a terrier on a scent. He was a newshound, all right; an American, the most dangerous of the breed.

Doyle glanced quickly around: Damn, Larry and Innes preoccupied with the bags. Penned in by the queue; nowhere to run.

"Mr. Arthur Conan Doyle!"

"You have my attention, sir," said Doyle, turning to face him.

"Fantastic! Off to the States today—your first visit! Any thoughts?"

"Far too many to mention."

"Sure! Why not? Looking forward to it? Have to be! They're gonna love you in New York—great city—huge! You can't believe it; straight up!" He gestured emphatically toward the sky with both hands. "Look at it go!"

The man was insane, realized Doyle. Completely off his squash. Smile, Doyle; always humor a lunatic.

"So! Big plans, huh? Reading tour, fifteen cities. How 'bout that? If you aren't the second coming of old Charley Dickens!"

"One cannot aspire to follow in the immortal footsteps of Boz with anything but the deepest humility."

The reporter's eyes glazed over, but total incomprehension seemed his natural state and troubled him not in the least.

"Sensational!"

"If you'll excuse me, I must be getting on board. . . ."

"Which one do you like the best?"

"Which one what?"

"Holmes story; got a favorite?"

"I don't know, perhaps the one about the snake—sorry, for the life of me I can't remember the name of it. . . ."

The man snapped his fingers and pointed at him: " 'The Speckled Band'; fantastic stuff!"

"I don't suppose you've read any of my . . . other books."

"What other books?"

"Right. Sorry, I really must be going. . . ."

"Okay, now tell the truth, what do you hope to find in America?"

"My hotel room and a small measure of privacy."

"Haw! Fat chance. You're big news, Mr. Doyle: Sherlock mania. It's like a fever, friend. Get used to it. They'll be lining up to take shots at you."

"*Shots?*"

"Everybody and his brother wants to know, see: Who is this guy? What makes him tick? And what kind of a weird, twisted mind can think up stuff like this?"

"How appalling."

"Hey, why do you think the paper booked me on this ship? Get a first look at you, that's the idea."

"Booked you a passage on *this* ship?" Oh, no; too late to change plans.

"Okay, so here's my proposition," said the little man, sidling up confidentially. "Help me out with a few exclusives on the way over and I can make things pretty easy for you on the other side. I got connections in New York. Animal, vegetable, mineral; you name it. Sky's the limit. Silver platter."

The man winked at him. What an extraordinary creature.

The customs agent handed back Doyle's transport papers with a sheepish, gap-toothed grin. "Din't have to kill him, didja, guv?"

"We all have to go sometime," said Doyle agreeably, tucking the papers away and striding quickly toward the gate.

The reporter dogged his steps, holding a card in front of Doyle's face. "Name's Pinkus. Ira Pinkus. *New York Herald.* Think about it, will you?"

"Thank you, Mr. Pinkus."

"Could I invite you to join me for dinner tonight?"

Doyle waved and smiled.

"Or how about drinks? A cocktail? What do you say?"

The guard at the gate stopped Pinkus from following. Could it be? Yes! The man hadn't cleared customs yet. The gap widened; Doyle grinned. Was any human experience more purely pleasurable than escape?

"Say, any plans on bringing Sherlock back?" shouted Pinkus. "Can't leave him buried up there in that Swiss Alp! We want more stories! Your readers are ready to riot!"

Doyle never looked back. A knot of activity ahead: Larry at the trolley, Innes paying the porter. Dock hands shouldered their bags up the gangway. Farther down the pier a row of plain wooden coffins were being loaded from a jitney directly into the ship's cargo hold; bodies going home for burial.

Odd, thought Doyle; the dead shipped home unnoticed on every transatlantic crossing but were usually loaded in the night before, out of the paying customers' sight. Must be last-minute arrivals.

Concerned officers looked down at Doyle from the quarterdeck; one consulted a watch. Two minutes to noon. Along with the corpses, it looked as though they would be the last passengers to board, save Ira Pinkus.

Or, with any luck, excluding him.

"I'm afraid there isn't time for me to see you on board," said Larry.

"We'll say our good-byes, then. Here's this morning's correspondence," said Doyle, handing him a generous packet of letters.

"Right sorry I'm not going with you." Larry stared at his feet and looked as mournful as a bloodhound.

"No more than I, Larry," said Doyle, banging him affectionately about the shoulders. "Don't know how I'll manage without you, but someone needs to mind the home front. No one better than you, old boy."

"Hate to think there'll come a moment you might need me and I won't be at hand, that's all."

"I'm sure Innes will do a bang-up job in your stead."

"Or die trying," said Innes, with a crisp salute.

"We'll write every day. You do the same. These are for the children," he said, handing over a bag of gifts and sweets.

"We'll miss you something terrible," said Larry, lower lip trembling.

"Keep the missus away from the damp, now, there's a good fellow," said Doyle, clutching Larry's arm, his voice husky with emotion. He turned away to hold back the tears. "Here we go, Innes. Onward. Off to conquer America."

"*Bon voyage,* sir," said Larry, waving enthusiastically even though they were only a few feet up the gangway. "*Bon voyage.*"

The purser greeted them warmly as they boarded. The stalwart figure of Larry stood on the dock below, swinging his arm like a pendulum.

Behind him, a darting figure sprinted from customs for the gangway.

Ira Pinkus. Damn.

Doyle walked out onto the upper deck and took a deep breath of bracing salt air, alone for the first time since the tugs had led them from shore. A man of thirty-five, his six-foot-two-inch frame filled out by two hundred pounds of muscle well conditioned by a strict regimen of boxing and gymnasium work. His moustache thick, black, and well-groomed; his face more rounded now, ridged and shaped by experience; his eyes set with an authority justified by a worldly success his dress and manner suggested he had found more than agreeable. Doyle had about him the magnetic, unself-conscious aura of a man destined for great things, but he still considered himself first and foremost a family man and this long separation from his wife and three young children posed a trying deprivation.

The trimmings of fame did nothing to protect one from the plague of life's unhappy little surprises, as Doyle had quickly discovered, let alone the deeper discomforts of loneliness or emotional turmoil, while the daily maintenance of what seemed a prosperous life demanded such enormous expense of capital that the margin between income and outgo was shaved down to the same razor's edge that haunted every man's existence.

Not that Doyle expected sympathy for the trials of new-found affluence, however far short his actual worth fell from people's speculations—a jolly great distance indeed. No, he had made his bed and he was lying in it, eyes like dinner plates. He still didn't understand why the arrival of cash only momentarily preceded its abrupt departure—often for ridiculous objects put right to work collecting dust, neatly disappearing along an orderly line of retreat: closet, packing box, garage, garbage heap—but it did. And this from a native Scotsman, a man with thrift embedded in the fiber of his being, who had labored heroically throughout his life to avoid the unnecessary and extravagant.

No use fighting it: The migration of money must be respected as one of the fixed laws of nature. A man labors to earn enough to satisfy his basic biological needs—warmth, food, shelter, sex—then, in order to reward himself for his backbreaking work, carries right on spreading any surplus cash around for *non*essential luxuries, until the basics are so thoroughly jeopardized it drives him back to start the damn business all over again. As trapped by our genetic destiny as salmon swimming upstream to die.

A week at sea: Good Christ, how he looked forward to it. To leave behind those grinding, commonplace headaches for a while. A fellow never realizes how responsibilities accumulate like stones in his pockets until he takes a swim. A week of his obligatory correspondence alone—sixty letters a day on average—would be enough to sink any ordinary man.

And what a tremendous vehicle for his escape, this grand steamship, an opulent juggernaut cutting through the swell, nearly immune to the vicissitudes of wind and weather; a refined, dignified experience in contrast to the cramped frigates and sloops he'd sailed during his tours as a young ship's doctor. Fifteen years ago now; those long months afloat felt like a dream he'd had a century ago.

He rested a foot up on the rail and watched England recede, telescoped his new spyglass and trained it on the promenade that hugged the Southampton shore below the harbor. Tourists parading on the boardwalk fronting the seaside resorts, taking the air. He pulled focus on the glass, saw the blankets in their laps, the black cloths stretched across the mouths of the consumptives in their rolling chairs. . . .

A stab pierced his chest. Not three months ago, wheeling his wife, Louise, in one of those rollers along a walkway in Switzerland. Cold blue sky. Mountains looming overhead; how he'd resented the majestic indifference of those stolid rocks. Hated how the sanitarium staff treated Louise with their standardized, patronizing cheeriness . . .

Finally, he'd grabbed one of them by the arm, a shovel-faced Austrian nurse, shook her, hard: You're talking to the disease! Talk to *her,* there's a person in this chair! Louise embarrassed, the woman backing away, pale hands fluttering. He hated them all! They didn't know his wife, made no attempt to engage her, not a moment's appreciation for what she'd already endured, this gallant, brave, good-hearted woman.

Why did people turn away from suffering? The ravages of

disease were cruel, hard to witness; how many times had he himself been guilty of retreating behind the mask of a doctor's authority, when what the person before him needed more than medicine was a steadying gaze that looked past their affliction to the heart, where a soul cried out for comfort. His anger at that nurse's indifference had been inspired, in equal part, by his own failings. None greater than his inability to save his wife from a wasting disease for which there was no cure, that carried her farther and farther away from him by imperceptible degrees. How long now since they had truly been man and wife? Three months? Four?

The shipyards of the Portsmouth Naval Base came into view to the southeast. Lord; so many lazy afternoons passed there during his medical apprenticeship, gazing down from his office window to watch the gunboats maneuver in the harbor. When you treat one patient in six months there's not much else to do but sit and watch the gunboats. Nearly ten years since he'd moved there after that business with the Seven. Was it possible?

A flood of memories released: little Innes—only twelve then—working that summer as his hallboy; fresh-faced in his stiff blue suit, eagerly waiting to greet the clients who never arrived. Warm morning sunlight inching lazily across the kitchen wall of their Southsea cottage. The sharp tang of the kerosene lamp on his red maple desk where he sat up nights, writing, writing endlessly, dreaming of the new life his work might bring them. The tiny bedroom where their firstborn, Mary, was conceived and came into the world. Laughing as he carried Louise over that threshold, their marriage just beginning in a bubble of youthful ignorance, sentiment, and blind faith.

The horizon went blurry, his eyes misting over—mustn't think of her now, come on, old boy, put some backbone in it.

Passengers filled the decks below him. Excited chatter. Ship seemed at capacity. Germans mostly. Well-heeled. Only two dozen English had come on at Southampton. The *Elbe,* out of Bremen, a German steamer; the Nordeutscher Lloyd line, an entirely new breed of ship. Nine thousand tons. Twin screws; with a top speed of seventeen knots she cut a fast line through the hard gray chop of the Channel. First-class accommodations for 275, only 50 second-class cabins. An impeccable, disciplined crew. German lines nearly monopolized the North American commercial routes; one expected a high standard of professionalism from the German people: They were a nation on the march. . . .

On a lower deck he caught a glimpse of Innes. Someone pressing in on him, handing him a card, hard to see the man from this angle—good Christ, it looked like Ira Pinkus.

"Heading home or taking leave of it?"

Doyle turned sharply; he thought he'd been alone at the rail. The man stood ten feet away, big-bellied, ruddy-faced. A receding halo of grizzled red hair. Graying muttonchop whiskers. Looked fifty. A lilt of Irish in the voice.

"Leaving," said Doyle.

"Sorrowful partings often precede long journeys," the man said.

Doyle nodded a polite agreement. Yes, Irish. The man shifted slightly, still facing out to sea, and Doyle saw the priest's collar, thick boots, the black beads and crucifix protruding from his pocket. Damn, the last thing he wanted to hear now was some empty, unsolicited homily from a Roman—

"Sometimes the pleasure of sadness is sweeter than the pleasure of pleasure itself," said the priest. "Something new has entered us. We're able to look at the unknown without prejudice or preconception. Welcome it as an opportunity. And we may find in ourselves an undiscovered territory, a place closer to the heart of the terrible mystery of who we really are."

The man's warm tone struck a deep note of authenticity. This wasn't the usual pious blather; real sympathy weighed in behind his words and moved Doyle in spite of his resistance. He found it difficult to respond; how could this priest know so precisely what he was going through? Were his feelings so transparent? The man kept his eyes toward the shore, respecting the borders of Doyle's privacy.

"Sometimes we leave the best of ourselves behind," said Doyle.

"Journeys may have a purpose unimagined at departure," said the priest. "They can save a life. Sometimes they can even save a soul."

Doyle allowed the words to slip in and soothe him; his inner voice went quiet. The lazy rhythms of the Channel captured his eye and a peaceful stillness descended over him.

A fracture of sunlight danced off the water and broke his reverie. He wasn't certain how long he'd been standing since they'd spoken; the shoreline had changed. Open countryside now, rolling hills. Ocean beckoning ahead. He looked over.

The priest was gone.

One deck below where Doyle stood alone, a tall, handsome, smartly dressed man, blond and big-shouldered, walked out of a stairwell leading down to the *Elbe*'s cargo hold. He slipped smoothly into the crowd, speaking casually to people around him in flawless German that bore the clean, clipped aristocratic accent particular to natives of Hamburg. Having effortlessly made himself seem a part of their group without leaving any particularly vivid impressions, his strong features coiled in a mask of perpetual amusement, the man ordered a drink, lit a cigarette, and leaned against a column, studying his fellow passengers.

Intent on the receding shoreline, not one of these self-satisfied burghers had noticed him arrive from belowdecks, the man decided. That was good. No one had seen him in the hold, either. And so far no ship's officer had paid him so much as a passing glance.

Landfall faded from sight; he scanned the passengers carefully as they drifted from the rails. Many moved inside to the bar, turning their attentions to the empty-headed fun they all seemed determined to enjoy on board an Atlantic crossing.

There they were: the two young men—distinctly less well dressed than these vacationing bourgeoisie—in the corner near the lifeboats. The stink of merchants about them, talking in that earnest conspiratorial way he had seen so often while observing them in London; two Jews making an effort to assimilate, but he knew better.

Had they realized they were being watched? Not now. But something had scared them off, alerted the two men in London to make them book this passage so quickly. Assembling his team and following them here on such short notice had not been easy: He had managed.

In the midst of conversation the two men glanced his way; he casually moved his gaze to a passing woman, tipping his hat. When he looked back, their attention had not fixed on him; they were walking away, still absorbed in their discussion.

He watched them retreat. Finding their cabins was next. Then he would involve the others.

He tossed his cigarette over the side and strolled after the two men.

They were making it easy for him.

AT SEA, APPROACHING SAN FRANCISCO

Half a world away, from the deck of another ship—the *Canton,* a squalid tramp steamer, carrying only steerage class, a bucket of rust bound from Shanghai—as it sailed east and entered the straights that opened into another great deepwater port, a man stood quietly alone at the starboard rail, silently intoning a prayer as he watched the rounded headlands of a strange country draw near. A hoard of impoverished, ragtag immigrants swarmed around him, cheering as the mythical land of plenty glided into view. After enduring two weeks belowdecks in a pestilent hellhole of contagion and crime, it seemed for the first time conceivable that the gamble they'd made with their lives might have been worth the taking.

The man stood alone near the center of the pack, yet none of the others pressed in or jostled him. He was of moderate size, unextraordinary appearance, and occupied little space himself, but when he so desired it that space was never violated. Neither young nor old, nothing about him lingered long in one's memory: Even here, in the middle of an alert and agitated mob, his presence hardly registered. This was one of his most practiced abilities; to leave a hole in the air, rendering himself virtually invisible whenever the situation demanded. Yet even then he was left alone; the respect he commanded was granted to him unconsciously.

His parents and natural family were as unknown to him as these strangers on deck; no given name had followed him when he was abandoned in an alley after birth. He had early on displayed such a self-reliant and single-minded strength of will that the brothers of the monastery who had raised the boy from infancy named him Kanazuchi—"the Hammer."

When the ship docked and they passed through immigration in San Francisco, no official would question that he was anything other than what he appeared to be: one of four hundred indigent Chinese laborers from Quongdong province on the Mainland. With his shaved forehead and topknot queue, he knew he could depend on the white man's inability to distinguish one Asian face from another.

That he was Japanese, a race of people still seen only rarely in this country, would not occur to a single one of them. That he was a Holy Man from an ancient monastic order on the island of Hokkaido was unimaginable.

That he was one of the most dangerous men alive he could rest assured was an idea that would never take shape in the mind of a single living being.

Kanazuchi ended his meditation with a grace that pleased his keen sense of aesthetic balance. As the ship sailed closer to America, the visions that had plagued his dreams for the last three months had grown more disturbing than ever before; only these meditations had any calming effect.

The agitation on deck increased; the outskirts of a city drawing closer on the rolling green hills. Shifting the light, oblong bundle on his back, Kanazuchi wondered if he would be asked to open it for inspection as they cleared immigration. Many of the skilled workers on board—carpenters, masons— had carried their tools along with them. Perhaps they would all be allowed to pass without having to display their belongings; if not he would find a way to avoid the authorities.

Kanazuchi was prepared. He had come too far. His mind was closed to the possibility of failure. And he knew that if anyone saw the sword concealed in his bundle, he would have to kill them.

chapter two

"MY NAME IS WERNER. IF THERE IS ANYTHING I MUST do to make your voyage more comfortable, please you will let me know."

"Thank you, Werner."

Doyle made to enter his cabin but Werner blocked his way.

"If I might be so bold: I have read about your famous detective, sir, and I would like to demonstrate that the great Mr. Holmes is not alone in his power of the deductive capability," said the dapper German steward in his crisply accented English.

"Fine. How do you wish to do this?" said Doyle politely.

"I have observed you for only a few moments, you agree, yes?"

"I cannot dispute you."

"And yet I am able to tell you that from within the last year you have traveled to Cherbourg, Paris, Geneva, Davos, Marienbad, back to London, once to Edinburgh, and twice to Dublin. Will I not be correct, sir?"

Doyle had to admit that he was.

"And would you like me to tell you how I have reached this conclusion, sir?"

Doyle was compelled to admit that he would.

"I have looked at the labels on your luggage."

Werner winked, wiggled his little blond moustache, gave a smart salute, and slipped smoothly down the passageway. Doyle had just begun to unpack when Innes rushed into the cabin, knocking off his derby on the doorway overhead.

"Smashing good news," said Innes, retrieving his hat. "I've found someone who'll be of tremendous help to us when we reach New York."

"Who's that, Innes?"

"He gave me his card. Here," he said, producing it. "His name is Nels Pimmel."

"Pimmel?"

"A reporter for the *New York Post*. You'll be ever so amused by the fellow, Arthur. He's what you would call a real 'character.' . . ."

"Let me see that," said Doyle, taking the card.

"And a most agreeable chap. Seems he has the acquaintance of nearly everybody who's anybody in the entire United States. . . ."

"And what did Mr. Pimmel want from you?"

"Nothing. He's invited us to dine with him tonight."

"You didn't accept of course."

"I didn't see the harm in it. . . ."

"Innes, listen to me carefully; you are not to seek out, speak to, or encourage this man's advances from this moment forward in even the slightest way."

"I don't know why; he's a perfectly pleasant sort of bloke."

"This man is not a bloke, chap, or any other sort of regular person; he's a journalist and they are a breed apart."

"So you immediately assume he must be cultivating my friendship only so he can get closer to you, is that it?"

"If this is the man I think it is, be assured he is not remotely interested in your friendship or even your passing acquaintance. . . ."

Two small spots of red appeared on Innes's cheeks and his pupils contracted down to pinpricks—oh dear, thought Doyle, how many times have I seen those dependable beacons of distress before.

"So what you're saying is I'm ridiculous to assume that anyone might take a genuine interest in *me* alone as a human being. . . ."

"Innes, please, that's not what I'm saying at all."

"Oh, really?"

"There are different rules for social intercourse on board ship. This Pimmel or Pinkus or whatever his name is has already accosted me once. Give him one inch of encouragement now before we've left sight of land and the man will be living in our pockets for the remainder of the cruise."

"Do you want to know what I think?" said Innes, bouncing up on his toes, voice rising alarmingly in pitch. "I think you've read too many of your press clippings. I think you think you're better than other people. I'm twenty-four years old, Arthur, and I may never have been on a ship before, but that doesn't mean I've forgotten my manners and I shall speak to or dine with whomsoever I choose."

Punctuating the impact of his outburst with a dramatic exit, Innes turned to go and threw open the door to the closet. To his credit, he kept his composure, gave the contents of the closet the once-over as if that had been his original intent, slammed the door with a satisfied grunt, and swept out of the cabin, knocking his hat off on the overhead again for good measure.

Five months without Larry, thought Doyle. Good Christ, I'll never make it back to England alive.

That evening, Doyle dined at the table of Captain Karl Heinz Hoffner unaccompanied by his younger brother, who took his first meal at the far end of the elegant hall, in the company of Ira Pinkus/Nels Pimmel and the other four pseudonyms under which Pinkus plied his trade for six different New York newspapers. Pinkus/Pimmel expressed glancing disappointment that Innes's illustrious brother would not be joining them, but then a worm doesn't eat its way to the center of the apple by starting at the core.

Infuriated by Arthur's snobbery, Innes experienced no misgivings afterward about the full menu of Conan Doyle anecdotes he trotted out for Pimmel as the meal progressed—what was the harm in it? Wasn't as if the man was openly interrogating him, and he seemed every bit as engrossed by Innes's own escapades with the Royal Fusiliers as he was about anything to do with the life and times of the Great Author. And Pimmel himself proved supremely entertaining on the subject of New York, particularly his intimate and apparently inexhaustible lowdown on Broadway show girls.

Why, no, it wouldn't be any trouble at all to introduce you to some of these gals, Pimmel assured him. Say, here's an idea: Why don't the two of us go out on the town one night with a great big bunch of them? Better yet, we'll throw a party! Let them come to us! Have a little more wine, Innes!

Outstanding fellow, Pimmel.

Realizing he was expected to spend every evening of the cruise with Captain Hoffner—a stolid pillar of a man singularly preoccupied with maritime statistics, shipboard etiquette, and the tide tables, all untainted by the slightest hint of humor—Doyle rolled out the questions he'd dreamed up about the *Elbe* at a measured pace, hoping the Captain's replies might buy enough time to root out other areas of conversational fertility. But Hoffner's answers lacked wind; they were as precise, as streamlined, and about as riveting as an engine manual recited by a myna bird. The man had spent so much of his life at sea he had failed to acquire an opinion on any unseaworthy subject and had apparently never even cracked open a novel. Certainly none of Doyle's, at any rate.

Fellow guests at the table weren't much help, either; a congregation of beer executives from Bavaria and their well-groomed wives, off for a pleasure tour of midwestern American breweries. All in possession of modestly serviceable English that they chose for the most part not to exercise, spending the better part of the meal hanging on Doyle's every word as if each utterance contained hidden religious significance: Sherlock Holmes was Big Business in Germany.

The Famous Author syndrome usually provided sufficient inspiration to hoist Doyle into the saddle of some pet high-horse of his, but tonight every time he rolled up to the edge of a really first-rate pontification the sight of Innes huddling with Pinkus/Pimmel across the room knocked him right off his perch. He felt as dull and becalmed as the glacial Captain Hoffner. As the lapses between exchanges became longer and grimmer, the screech of cutlery grinding on china grew deafening.

"I remember reading somewhere that you have an enduring interest in the occult, Mr. Doyle," said the lone English woman at the table, who had until that moment maintained a watchful silence.

Indeed he had, replied Doyle. An interest tempered by a natural and healthy skepticism, he was quick to add.

Glum faces around the table assumed new life. The burghers' wives ganged up on Hoffner with a hard flurry of German, attempting to prod him to some unknown action involving Doyle. Hoffner held his ground during the brief, one-sided engagement before turning to Doyle with a look of deeply felt apology.

"I have been telling a story last night at dinner as we crossed the Channel," said the Captain. "It seems some of my crew are convinced we are having a ghost on board."

"The ship is haunted," said the English woman.

She roosted on the edge of her chair, small and birdlike, and throughout the meal he hadn't taken much notice of her, but now that she had set foot in her element, Doyle recognized that slightly deranged sparkle in her pale eyes: She was a True Believer.

"I am afraid that I cannot say this is true with any assurance, Mrs. Saint-John," said Captain Hoffner. Then to Doyle, again apologetically: "We have been having over a period of some years on board the *Elbe* a series of strange and . . . unexplainable occurrences."

"Why don't you tell Mr. Conan Doyle about your most recent episode, Captain?" said Mrs. Saint-John, flashing a nervous smile, eyes blinking rapidly.

"This has happened earlier this evening," said Hoffner with a shrug, lowering his voice.

"After we set sail?"

Hoffner nodded sharply. "A passenger hears some strange noises from the cargo hold; a series of shrieking cries, a repeated knocking sound. . . ."

"Any other witnesses?" asked Doyle.

"No; just this one woman," said Hoffner.

"It is a classic haunting," said Mrs. Saint-John, her hands nervously fidgeting her napkin ring. "I'm sure you would agree with my diagnosis, Mr. Conan Doyle; footsteps in an empty hall, thumps, raps, mournful voices. And a sighting of a large, looming gray figure in a cargo hold passageway."

"None of this I am ever seeing myself, you understand," said Hoffner, minimizing; there was clearly no room for a bona fide ghost on his ship.

"Captain, have there been any tragedies aboard the *Elbe*?" asked Doyle.

"This ship is now ten years at sea; I am sailing with her every one of those days. Whenever there is such a regular gathering of human lives tragedy must inevitably, sadly, play a part in the experience," said Hoffner.

"Sadly true," said Doyle, surprised at how near Hoffner's observation had approached eloquence. "Are there any that stand out particularly? Any violent murders or brutally memorable suicides?"

The burghers and their wives seemed slightly taken aback.

"Pardon my bluntness, ladies and gentlemen, but there's no point in our mincing any words; phenomena of the sort described by Mrs. Saint-John usually result from some terrible unhappiness that cannot be wished away by our tiptoeing around the facts in the interest of propriety."

At last, thought Doyle happily, a subject I can take to the bank.

"In former times," the Captain said cautiously, "there have been a few such instances."

"Just so; I shan't trouble you over mixed company at dinner for the details. I'll offer one interesting theory about ghosts, *meine Damen und Herren,* and the most credible to my way of thinking if you credit the phenomenon at all: The specter constitutes the emotional residue of a life that ended unexpectedly or in great spiritual confusion—this is why sightings are frequently related to murder or accident victims, or suicides—the equivalent, if you will, of a footprint left on a sandy beach, a remnant that lives on outside our perception of time, with no more actual connection than that footprint has to the person who leaves it behind. . . ."

"Oh no. No, no, no; what one encounters is the immortal soul of the poor unfortunate itself," said Mrs. Saint-John.

"Trapped between heaven and earth, in a purgatorial void. . . ."

"That is another point of view entirely," said Doyle, annoyed to have been so aggressively knocked off his rails. "One I'm afraid I cannot wholeheartedly endorse."

"But I can assure you, Mr. Conan Doyle, that this is indeed the case. It has been our experience with them time and again. . . ."

"*Our* experience?"

Mrs. Saint-John smiled assuredly at the other guests. "I refer to my companion, largely, and myself to a much more limited degree."

"Companion."

Oh dear; not one of those invisible spirit guides that certain slightly hysterical middle-aged women allege to have trotting around after them like a Pekingese dog. Definitely a nutter, thought Doyle.

"I'm afraid Sophie wasn't feeling well enough to join us for dinner tonight," said Mrs. Saint-John. "She's just completed an exhausting lecture tour of Germany and we're traveling on to America without a stop at home."

"It sounds as if you and your friend are very much in demand," said Doyle, relieved that at least her "friend" currently resided in a human body.

"Yes. We were introduced three years ago, not long after my husband died. I was quite naturally bereft. Inconsolable, really, because I felt then very much like you apparently do now, Mr. Conan Doyle: that my dearest Benjamin was simply gone. And then, in my despair, a close friend insisted that I must meet Sophie. Sophie Hills."

"*The* Sophie Hills."

"Ah, so you are familiar with her."

Sophie Hills was the most celebrated, if not notorious, psychic-medium in England of the moment. The woman claimed to be attended by a vast congregation of disembodied spirits, all with direct links to the central switchboard of the hereafter, which time and again had coughed up on request verifiably accurate information about dead relatives, lost envelopes, missing engagement rings, mysterious med-

ical ailments, and, in one sensational instance, a revelation
about an unsolved decade-old crime in Heresfordshire that
resulted in a confession of murder. Sophie occasionally
demonstrated the peculiar talent of apport mediumship, the
ability to manifest out of thin air three-dimensional objects
as oddly diverse as African bird nests, ancient Roman coins,
and exotic—still flopping—fish. Her puzzling faculties had
been subjected to exhaustive tests by the scientific community and to date not a single reasonable doubt had been confirmed as to their authenticity. In one such instance, before
credible witnesses, while strapped into a straitjacket and
wearing a gunny sack on her head, under the guidance of
Miss Hills one of her spirit guides played "Turkey in the
Straw" on an accordion stashed across the room under a
bushel basket.

Oh yes, Doyle was familiar with Sophie Hills. And more
than passingly interested in a chance to have a whack at the
old girl in action.

"I have proposed to Mrs. Saint-John," said Captain
Hoffner, "that one night during our crossing we might impose upon Miss Hills to give a demonstration of her powers."

"And in so doing put to rest the tormented spirit that
haunts the good ship *Elbe*," said Mrs. Saint-John. "After
hearing that you were to sail with us, it was my suggestion
that we solicit your participation, Mr. Conan Doyle. And if
you were to find such a demonstration of sufficient scientific
rigor, the strength of your reputation could go a long way towards persuading the general public of the goodness of Sophie's powers."

"Perhaps tomorrow night, then," said the Captain. "I
would propose that we do this after dinner?"

"I should be delighted, Captain," said Doyle.

Now if there were only some way to keep Ira Pinkus from
finding out about it. He could just see the headline waiting
for him in New York: HOLMES CREATOR CHASES SHIPBOARD
SPOOK.

CHICAGO, ILLINOIS

Look at yourself, Jacob: What you are doing here? Can there
be any doubt? No, truthfully, I don't believe so. At the ripe
old age of sixty-eight, when most men of your profession
have long ago achieved mastery of their mind and self, you
have taken complete leave of your senses.

You old fool, the best part of your life was just beginning;
remember how you sustained yourself through the striving
and deprivation with the promise that after retirement you
would devote yourself to scholarship? No domestic distractions or professional obligations, alone in your library, a
lifetime's accumulated wisdom lining the walls, peace and
quiet and months without end of metaphysical study and
solitary contemplation. The logical, satisfying culmination
of a life's work and such a joyous time this was going to be!
And with it, within reach, the genuine possibility of enlightenment.

But instead of sitting at your desk surrounded by books,
in your cozy basement office on Delancey Street, a cup of
hot tea with lemon in your hands, here you stand on a railway platform in the pouring rain in downtown Chicago, Illinois, waiting to board a train for—where?—Colorado, God
forbid, where you don't know a soul in the world. And when
was the last time they saw a rabbi in Colorado, I'd like to
know.

Because a dream told you to do it.

All right, not a dream, exactly; a vision, if you like, that's
haunted your sleep for the last three months. A vision powerful and frightening enough to send you careening out of
your rabbit hole into the wilderness like some mad biblical
prophet. The kind of Old Testament, bone-rattling nightmare
you used to read about with such interest. In your comfortable chair. Warm, dry socks on your feet.

Meshugener mamzer! You don't need a one-way ticket to
the wild West; what you need is a doctor. This is probably
the onset of an exotic fever or a galloping mental illness.
There's still time to reconsider: You could be back in New
York without a word of this madness to anyone before your

son gets off the ship. And listen, Jacob, do you have any idea
how disturbed Lionel is going to be when he arrives with the
book he's gone to such trouble to get for you and you've
vanished into thin air? There's a train leaving for New York
in two hours; what in God's name should prevent you from
being on it?

You know perfectly well what's stopping you, old man.

Having dedicated your life to studying the myths and al-
legories of Kabbalah, you know they're more than words on
old parchments handed down through the ages. You know
this earth is a battleground between forces of light and darkness and when you are called to serve in that struggle—you
know in your heart that's what's happened here, Jacob—you
do not wriggle off the hook by reciting a list of your infir-
mities . . . although between your neuralgia and your arthri-
tis, God knows you could make a convincing case.

What did the rabbis tell you when you first took up Kabbalah? Only a man who is married, who has reached the age
of forty with his feet firmly on the ground should study this
strange book. What's inside these covers is far too dangerous for a dilettante. Knowledge is power and esoteric books
are like sticks of dynamite, they said; it takes a special man
to make this commitment.

"I am that man," you told them.

Why, what possessed you? If it was thirst for wisdom,
there were hundreds of less dangerous wells from which to
drink. And twenty-eight years later, here you stand waiting
for a train. Mysterious, isn't it?

Be honest with yourself, old man: Some part of you knew
from the moment you opened the book—the authentic *Sefer
ha-Zohar*—that as a result one day something extraordinary
would happen to you. You *wanted* it to. So really, what's to
complain about? What's so precious about this life you're
living, anyway? Your wife gone six years now, rest her soul,
your son grown. And Jacob, your office in that basement on
Delancey Street? It's not exactly been the sanctuary you'd
imagined. It's boring: There, you said it.

You're going to get on that train to Colorado, Rabbi Stern,
and make this journey to God-knows-where for the same

reasons that brought you to Chicago: because you are a man who believes oracular visions must be paid attention to, even when they come unasked for to sixty-eight-year-old men in less than the best of health who have not led lives you would be tempted to describe as vigorous. Because you've since discovered that part of that vision has already come to pass—the copy of the Tikkunei Zohar *has* been stolen from Rabbi Brachman's temple in Chicago.

Most of all because if you turn your back now and Lucifer does manifest in a desert somewhere and the earth ends up falling into the hands of the Evil One as this dream of yours suggests . . . well, if you feel poorly now, just imagine how rotten you're going to feel then.

Here comes the train. God in Heaven, watch over my son—maybe I should wait for Lionel to arrive before running off. What if he's in danger as well? I could at least write him a letter—

No. That's not what the vision advised. Relax, Jacob. Breathe; still your heart. That's better. There's a wonderful confidence that comes with losing your mind; you don't have to put up with nearly so much second-guessing.

Have you got your ticket? Yes, here it is. If only this old suitcase weren't so heavy; I've never packed for such an unpredictable journey before, who knew how much to bring—

Stop now: What were those words you always used to console the suffering in your temple? All of our problems are temporary, so why be sad about them?

And you can also take some comfort, can't you, from that other part of the vision you don't understand. Those words that keep repeating in your mind.

We are Six.

Don't have a clue what it means. Sounds somewhat encouraging, though, doesn't it?

SAN FRANCISCO, CALIFORNIA

The *Canton* made port in San Francisco by the middle of the afternoon, but night had fallen before the authorities let the first workers off the ship. Better for the city's white citizens not to see so many Asians setting foot on their shores in the light of day, thought Kanazuchi.

As the mob pressed forward to disembark, he made his way to the back of the pack where he could observe activity on the pier. Two Chinese at the base of the gangway shouted instructions in Mandarin as the workers left the ship—straight ahead, no talking, into the building! Guards in black uniforms carrying long sticks framed a loose corridor, and the immigrants massed along it like cattle toward the high entrance of a long processing shed.

Inside the shed, following more barked orders, they obediently fell into lines and produced their papers for a row of white officials sitting on high benches. At wide tables leading to the benches, the workers' belongings were taken by the guards and opened for inspection.

Kanazuchi realized he would have to make other arrangements.

Three slovenly crew members on the foredeck above him were braying about their coming shore leave; using his second sight, Kanazuchi could see the anticipated drunkenness and debauchery already stimulating their lower centers. He slipped back into the shadows as the last of the Chinese were herded down the gangway.

With the steel strength of his fingers, he shimmied twenty feet up a halyard, dropped silently behind the crew members, and waited until one of them broke away, a muscular, bandy-legged engineer's mate, moving to the sea-side rail to empty his bladder. As the mate finished urinating, two hands clamped onto his face with the strength of bear claws; whip motion, a quiet crack, the man's neck snapped. His clothes stripped in thirty seconds, body hoisted and carried over the side on the Holy Man's back.

Kanazuchi used the rail to slide sideways along the ship's bulwark until he reached the anchor line, then lowered himself and the engineer's mate down along the heavy chain to the water, where he gently set the body adrift in the oily bay. Holding his clothes and the bundle that carried his weapons, powders, and herbs dry above the water, he swam a quarter

mile along the pier to an empty berth and scaled a ladder to
the wharf.

The clothes were a reasonable fit. A small amount of
American money in the pockets. So far the gods were smiling, but his journey had only begun. Kanazuchi did not ne-
glect to thank the dead man for the gift of his life and prayed
that he was already enjoying his reward.

He climbed over a fence undetected, slipped the pack that
held the Grass Cutter over his shoulder, and started walking
toward San Francisco. He knew his conscious mind need not
worry about where he was going or how he would arrive:
Sensei had said the vision which had chosen him for this
task would lead him to the missing Book.

> *A dark tower rising from the sand.*
> *A black labyrinth beneath the ground.*
> *Chinese coolies digging a tunnel.*
> *An old thin man with a white beard*
>   *and a round black hat.*
> *We are Six.*

As he walked Kanazuchi repeated the phrase he used to
begin his meditation: Life is a dream from which we are trying to awaken.

BUTTE, MONTANA

"Now they will never return me alive to that cursed black
tower of Zenda! And I have you to thank for my life, my best
and dearest friend, Cousin Rudolfo, and for my return to the
throne of Ruritania!"

Bendigo Rymer dropped heavily to his knees beside the
king's sickbed, and as usual the shock shimmied the moth-
eaten backdrop of the lush, cartoonish Ruritanian Alps.
Rymer windmilled his arms, indicating the depths of emotion he wrestled with; speech, just this once, deserting him.

"Come on, you ridiculous cow, don't flog it to death,"
muttered Eileen, watching from the wings as she waited for

her entrance; she checked the pins in her hair to make sure her cheap paste tiara wouldn't go flying into the orchestra pit as it had last week in Omaha.

"Your Majesty, my work here is finished, I can accept no praise. I am only too happy to have served you in the only way an Englishman knows how: with all my heart and soul," said Rymer finally, before rising and turning across the footlights to the audience. "Sacrifice in the service of so noble a cause is no hardship."

That brawny declaration begged for applause from the men, brought out the ladies' hankies, and once again the good citizens of—where were they, Butte, Montana?—were only too happy to hold up their end; Rymer basked in the snug glow of their uncritical affections.

Eileen snorted in disgust. Even for an actor, a breed not celebrated for their sense of restraint, the man was completely incapable of shame.

"But there is still one way in which I can be of use to Your Majesty. . . ." Bendigo made a dashing beeline north, upstaging the witless nincompoop playing King Alexander before he could counter the move; six months on tour and the moron still hadn't learned how to hold center stage. "I shall return to you the love of your fiancée, Princess Flavia, who has stood by through the darkest hour of your uncertain fate, praying for your return."

Ha! If I was Flavia waiting to marry this bad haircut, thought Eileen, by now I'd've slept my way through a squadron of Royal Mounted Dragoons.

Rymer gestured toward the wing; Eileen gave her bosom a shove to encourage a plump décolletage—getting a little long in the tooth for this ingenue crap, aren't we, dearie?—and pranced ethereally onstage.

"My lord, you're alive! My fondest hope! Heaven bless you!"

She draped herself over King Chucklehead and sniffed experimentally. Good, at least he hadn't been munching green onions while offstage in the tower of Zenda. Then the big kiss—the kid hadn't thrust his tongue down her throat again since she gave him a knee in Cleveland—and

Bendigo's ever so touching turn downstage, shielding his eyes from the indelicate spectacle of watching the woman he loved returning to the king whose life he had saved, as the final curtain fell and predictably brought down the house.

American audiences were pathetically easy to please.

"Eileen, darling, in our final scene together when I declare my, uh, undying love for you, do you suppose you could come back with your line about my ring always being on your finger just a bit, uh, faster?"

Bendigo Rymer was staring at himself in the mirror, at the midpoint of stripping off his shiny greasepaint. Mesmerized as a charmed snake.

What in the world does he think he's looking at? wondered Eileen. Sharing a stage with the man was punishment enough; inhabiting the same dressing room, as necessity required in some of these rural outposts, felt like a prison sentence.

"Bendigo, darling, the point of Flavia hesitating has to do with being torn between her obligation to Kingy-poo and the incredible passion she feels for dear Rudolfo. If she replies too quickly, I'm afraid it suggests you don't hold nearly the same dangerous command of her affections."

She waited for the gears of his mind to engage the idea and could nearly hear them grinding. "That's always been my interpretation anyway," she added modestly.

"If it's played *that* way . . ." he said, stroking his chin; as with every pose he struck having to do with thought, it seemed effortful. "It's rather useful to us, that pause then, isn't it?"

"If Flavia is desperately in love with you, it's probably best to let the customers in on the secret."

"How right you are!" he bellowed, jumping to his feet. "Bless you, my dear! I have always maintained you are a genuine asset to my company!"

Bendigo tilted his head back and showered his mouth with a deluge of the McGarrigle's Throat Comforter he kept in the atomizer on his table.

Oh God, that means he's going to kiss me.

Rymer's breath generally gave the impression that he'd recently devoured an embalmed cat; the McGarrigle's only succeeded in making it seem as if the cat had been marinated in cheap cologne.

Rymer loomed over her. Eileen skillfully, and somehow graciously, offered him only the top of her head; grease smeared her hair as his lips struck a glancing blow. Then Bendigo was off pacing the room, running his hands through his long dyed locks, simulating the look of a man in the frenzied grip of inspiration.

I'm living a nightmare, thought Eileen Temple, not for the first time. Not even the first time that night. When she'd set sail for America ten years before on the wings of hope and youthful ambition, who could have imagined her star would plummet so far below the visible horizon?

Bendigo Rymer's Penultimate Touring Players. (She'd never had the heart to ask him if he knew the actual definition of "penultimate"; her guess was no.) Former matinee idol Bendigo Rymer—Oscar Krantz from Scranton, Pennsylvania, truth be known; she'd come across his birth certificate once in the company strongbox—was pushing fifty, if it hadn't toppled already.

If only I hadn't slept with him that one time in Cincinnati, thought Eileen: A moment of weakness early in their tour; she'd sipped too deeply of the *vino blanco* and the poor sod could still look half-handsome—his good side, anyway, the one he unfailingly tried to present—in the right light, for instance the pitch darkness of a mine shaft.

And after all, she reminded herself forgivingly, you're only human, ducks, and loneliness does make strange bedfellows. Rymer's subsequent attempts at seduction had been pathetically easy to fend off; he was far too preoccupied with himself to sustain an enduring interest in another human being—and the occasional conquest of some adoring, doe-eyed plain Jane as they trooped their way west seemed more than enough to satisfy his somewhat, how should she put it kindly, meager masculine needs.

What about my needs, then? Eileen asked herself. Life on the stage had fallen so short of the land of milk and honey she'd grown up hoping for. Oh, there had been some thrilling early days in New York: every light on Broadway sparkling with the promise of fame, riches, and an endless supply of fabulously attractive men. That lasted about a week. And the theater was a harsh mistress when a girl hit the downhill side of thirty. Thank God for makeup, long, thick hair, decent bone structure, and a body that didn't run to fat or she'd've been out of a job years ago. Eileen was grudgingly a realist of both the heart and mind, a distinct handicap in a profession full of dreamers and losers. In reality, the best parts usually fell to some younger, hungry-eyed girl, and all most of those stage-door johnnies were looking for was a weekend furlough from dreary marriages they were only too eager to bore you to death about over bottles of rotgut champagne.

Lord, what these upper-crust American wives knew about sex you could engrave on the head of a gnat. Why else would their husbands be out every night baying at the moon? Eileen kept an up-to-the-minute inventory of her shortcomings, and lousy in bed wasn't one of them: Shame she couldn't make a living at it. Not that she hadn't considered the idea—she'd heard generous enough offers—but although she would on occasion accept with good grace extravagant trifles from her admirers, she'd never allowed their more explicit proposals to jeopardize her standing as a gifted, enthusiastic amateur. No, turning sex into business would only suck all the fun out of it, and fun was in short enough supply in her life. Nor did she have any intention of turning into one of these rumpot wardrobe mistresses who creaked around backstage half-swilled, mumbling about the good old days: playing opposite so-and-so, wearing such a glorious dress.

But what had she planned for the inevitable day when even the Bendigo Rymers of the world didn't want her for a third-rate provincial tour of *The Prisoner of Zenda*? She hadn't exactly socked away a nest egg over the years, what with maintaining a well-accessorized wardrobe to keep the gents half-interested. . . .

Don't think about the future, love: Get through tonight

and let tomorrow take care of itself. One more show in Butte, then on to Boise, Idaho. Three more weeks on the road, working our way south into ever deeper obscurity. Bendigo had just added another city near Phoenix that she couldn't even find on a map; some sort of religious settlement, he said, like the Mormons in Utah. Didn't matter to him who the pikers worshiped, as long as they paid cash to park their behinds in the seats.

Amazing the disappointments to which you can accommodate yourself in life, she thought, watching Bendigo pace the floor, flinging his arms about like an angry monkey. What was he raving on about now?

". . . he had no legitimate *reason* to let me go! I was *brilliant* in that role. Brilliant! I modeled my performance after Kean: Shakespeare played by flashes of lightning! It was only the damn-ned jealousy of Booth himself. . . ."

Ah, the Edwin-Booth-fired-me-at-twenty-six-threatened-by-my-genius-single-handedly-destroyed-my-reputation-preventing-my-career-from-reaching-the-Olympian-heights-which-had-always-been-my-destiny routine. No wonder my mind wandered. Look at him fume, the fossilized clown. Shame he hasn't any talent to complement his epic self-esteem. But then if it weren't for delusions of grandeur, he'd have no grandeur at all.

Yes, well, on the other hand, Miss High and Mighty, look who's sharing the short end of his Butte, Montana, dressing room: Is your common sense any more use to you than his delusions are to him? They tossed gold nuggets on the stage when the great Adah Isaacs Menken toured the West. Bendigo still snags the occasional threadbare bouquet on opening nights. You're so grateful for a wilted handful of daisies from some lovesick high-plains Romeo, offered with dumb, stuttering sincerity as you slip out the stage door, that it reduces you to tears.

Not much of a life, finally, but your own, dear. No husband to order you about with his sweaty socks to mend. No bawling babies crawling up the drapes. New places to see. New people to meet. Always the chance something sunny and surprising might lie around the next bend. And how many girls can wake up to that thought every morning?

The triumph of hope over experience.

After I've strutted and fretted my hour on the stage, she thought, let them carve that on my tombstone.

chapter three

GERMAN FLAGS ON THE TABLES. GERMAN SONGS FROM THE Bavarian band in the dining hall. German wines and beers and German food from the German waiters, speaking German to the German passengers. It was getting to be all so, well, Germanic, thought Doyle. And the decor: Prussian banners, double-headed eagles, heraldic shields on the walls. All that's missing is Kaiser Wilhelm. At least the good burghers of Frankfurt and Munich didn't throw their noses out of joint when we retaliated in our good-natured way; Innes planting his hand-fashioned Union Jack on the table, me commandeering the band's tuba, playing my oompah version of "God Save the Queen."

Innes even clapped me on the back after I hijacked that tuba. Seemed almost proud of his old brother. Warmed my heart. Come to think of it, Innes had been civil enough all afternoon, executing his secretarial duties briskly, efficiently. And the name of Pinkus/Pimmel not even mentioned since dinner. Perhaps I shouldn't give up on the boy just yet.

The brothers' patriotic counterattack cheered the hearts of the few English souls on board and Doyle realized he needn't have worried that the Germans would take offense; he'd always found them a jovial, high-spirited people—although he occasionally suspected that if one were shipwrecked alone on a desert island, he would eventually begin to lunge about and brandish a club. But their applause after his performance had seemed sincere enough; a smile even cracked the granite face of Captain Hoffner. Doyle had noted this loosening of inhibition often during previous voyages; the farther people ventured out to sea, the less encumbered they became by their landlocked identities.

But what had that disagreeable incident before dinner been about? A half-whispered confrontation outside the bridge: Captain Hoffner and two anxious young men; American accents, Jewish, one of them wearing a Star of David. Voicing heated concern about shipboard security and where a certain item was being stored: something about a book?

The younger of the two men—thin beard, sandy moustache—looking confused, genuinely frightened. Hoffner polite but strained, clearly put upon. Conversation dying instantly as Doyle came around the corner. A complicated look to Doyle from the second of the men—the senior of whatever partnership they represented: recognition, rising expectation, relief. Hoffner nodding to Doyle, waiting for him to pass before taking up with them again, impatiently, wishing this problem would go away.

Doyle kept an eye out for them but the two men had not made an appearance during dinner—no, wait, there was one of them now, the older one, standing in the passage outside the dining hall doors, up on his toes, searching through the dispersing crowd.

Probably for me, Doyle concluded. But no time to deal with the man now; he was already late for the evening's entertainment.

Sophie Hills had a square, sensible face and the no-nonsense manner of a beloved nanny or the neighborhood grocer's wife. Short, graying hair. No concessions to fashion. Eyes clear and alert. Her handshake as firm as an admiral's. Wearing the corsetless clothes of a suffragette, she exhibited none of the vaporous affectations so common to those in the spirit-raising trade. After being introduced to Doyle, she clapped the séance to order as if it were a meeting of a Wimbledon gardening club, crisply taking her seat in front of five rows of chairs crowded into the ship's library. The audience settled in.

No round table, hand holding, or candlelight for Miss Hills: right down to business. One chair reserved beside her from which Mrs. Saint-John could administrate. Doyle took a seat in the front row to their left, surrounded by his companions from the Captain's table. Neither Innes nor the American reporter in view; he hadn't mentioned the event to his brother and word had apparently not trickled down to Pinkus from any other direction. Doyle noticed the red-haired Irish priest settle in behind him to his right. Hadn't seen the man since yesterday afternoon on the top deck. They acknowledged each other with a polite nod.

Mrs. Saint-John led them through the usual preséance disclaimers: Sometimes the spirits follow their own prerogatives, their behavior nothing if not unpredictable and as far as their statements were concerned no guarantee could be given for complete authenticity. . . .

"Sometimes the spirits are as downright pigheaded and ridiculous as any living human being. Particularly our closest relations," said Sophie.

A good laugh. Ice broken. Smart. Remarkably relaxed atmosphere, thought Doyle. Completely free of hokum or mumbo-jumbo. So far. Doyle glanced around. . . .

There was the young man from the bridge, edging into the back of the room. Their eyes met briefly; he slipped into one of the few remaining seats. What does he want? Doyle wondered; well, I'll find out soon enough. . . .

Wait: two more figures crowding in behind the young man.

Innes and Pinkus, in that ridiculous hat.

Rats.

"Now if we could have complete silence, please," said Mrs. Saint-John.

Sophie Hills smiled, waved—like a child's bye-bye—closed her eyes, and began a series of deep breaths. Her body slackened gradually, then without warning snapped into an awkward pose completely unlike what she'd maintained before the onset of her trance: fingers locked, hands joined in front of her as if folded into the generous arms of a dressing gown, elbows thrust straight out to the side. Head perched on an elongated neck, wobbling gently side to side as if balancing on a spindle. Wide, enigmatic smile. Eyes open but creased horizontally . . .

There was no other way to say it, thought Doyle: She looked Chinese.

A golden, tinkling laugh bubbled out of Sophie Hills.

"Look at all the friendly faces here," she said—the voice masculine, high-pitched, tonally distinct from her own—and yes, the accent was Mandarin. She laughed again.

Her audience giggled in return; an involuntary response.

"Everybody happy on a ship. Everybody leave their troubles at home!" she said, laughing again, her irrepressible good nature filling the room; the air felt lighter, invigorating as sweet springwater.

Why, I feel better myself, thought Doyle, chuckling. What sort of a trick is this? Infecting people with happiness? New one on me.

"Nobody seasick?" she said.

A collective groan and more laughter. One raised hand from a woman in the middle row.

"Oh, too bad for you, lady. You sit back there, okay?" Some people were holding their sides, doubling over with laughter. "How the food on this ship? Pretty good?"

Yes, the food was good, answered the audience.

"Lady, you really missing out!" she said to the seasick woman. "We really miss food. We got no food over here."

We're certainly eating out of your hand tonight, thought Doyle. Séances usually turned up dour, gloomy spirit personalities, the sort that suggest suicide had played a part in their passing; this was unquestionably the happiest soul Doyle had ever seen a medium manifest. No wonder Sophie was such a crowd pleaser.

"My name is Mr. Li," said Sophie. "But you can call me . . . Mr. Li."

Even his stupidest jokes sounded funny; maybe Mr. Li had been a court jester in his former life.

"We got all sorts people over here. Lots and lots of peoples. All happy, friendly; if not they are after they meet Mr. Li. Same for you. Mr. Li say, Life should make you happy. Why so serious? Not so bad. Look at you: on ship. Good food. No seasick. Except for one lady. Don't sit too close to her!" She laughed again and the crowd laughed right along with her.

Extraordinary talent for mimicry, thought Doyle: I'm completely persuaded that I am looking at a jolly old Chinese man, not the sort of sturdy, middle-aged English woman you find striding through Hyde Park on a Sunday afternoon. But nothing necessarily supernatural at work yet.

"All sorts of peoples here tonight. Somebody there want to talk to somebody over here, you tell Mr. Li. If they over here, Mr. Li go find, okay? Mr. Li like, uh, like tele-phone operator."

Standard enough procedure to kick off a reading; now let's see how "Mr. Li" delivers, thought Doyle, studying her every move.

"If I could have a show of hands, please," said Mrs. Saint-John. "We'll try to get to everyone, time permitting."

Audience members began to ask Sophie questions about dead uncles and cousins and husbands, and she relayed straightforward detailed answers that seemed to more than satisfy them. Bringing to bear all his observational skills he could spot none of the usual flaws in her presentation; possible confirmation, thought Doyle, for his theory that mediums somehow tap into the mind of the questioner for their desired information, an easier explanation to swallow than a sea of disembodied spirits hanging about an interdimensional switching board.

But Doyle still had his trump card to play. He took out his pen and wrote a name on a cocktail napkin.

Jack Sparks.

When Mrs. Saint-John pointed to him, he handed her the napkin.

"This is the departed you wish to speak to?" asked Mrs. Saint-John.

Yes, Doyle replied. That was the man. The same test he had applied to every medium he had investigated over the last ten years since Jack had died. The test every one of them had failed.

Mrs. Saint-John leaned in and whispered the name to Sophie. A pause. The brow of "Mr. Li" furrowed; he craned his neck, closed his eyes. Finally he shook his head.

"That man not here," she said.

"So you are unable to contact him?" asked Doyle. Curious; he usually received a parcel of lies; never this response before.

"No. He not here. So sorry."

"I'm sorry, I don't understand."

"What you don't understand, mistah? You pretty smart fella, huh? I think so. Listen to Mr. Li: Man not here. Man not dead."

"Not dead? That's impossible."

"Oh, now you think Mr. Li a liar, huh? Well, you know, Mr. Li been called worse before. . . ."

Doyle felt absurd; here he sat arguing with an English-woman masquerading as a Chinaman in front of a crowd of German tourists—and one American reporter—about the death of a man who had plunged off a waterfall locked in a mortal struggle with his brother, as seen and described by Larry his trusted secretary. Fine way for a distinguished author to behave.

On the other hand, all every other medium he'd asked about Jack had ever been able to provide were patently phony bromides that bore no relation whatsoever to the man himself. . . .

Crack!

Doyle's first thought: a gun shot. No, a light bulb had burst, one of the ceiling fixtures, over their heads. A shower of sparks cascaded softly over the audience.

"Look what happen, mistah, see? Now you make spirits mad!"

Mr. Li laughed again, alone this time, the audience taken aback: This Mr. Li was less friendly, his voice assuming a more remote Otherness, metallic and cold. The temperature in the room dropped as his warmth retreated; queasy, ill-fitting. Some shivered and drew their wraps close around their shoulders; a woman moaned inadvertently.

The air around Sophie Hills grew dense and bright, making her suddenly harder to see. Mr. Li's laughter stopped dead; Sophie choked, breath catching in her chest. Her eyes opened wide; she looked panicked. "Mr. Li" was gone. Mrs. Saint-John froze where she sat, alarmed.

This is not part of their program, thought Doyle, rising from his chair. No one else in the room moved; Pinkus pinned against the wall, primal fear. He saw Innes take a step toward the two women. . . .

Crack!

Another light bulb burst. Frightened cries. People scrambling to avoid sparks.

Doyle felt a hand on his shoulder: the priest.

Sophie fell to her knees; her body shuddered uncontrollably but her eyes remained clear and full of appeal, wrestling against something unseen and turbulent, some force trying to enter her?

The priest moving quickly toward her.

"Someone in this room!" said Sophie, terror warping her voice. "Someone not what they seem! There is a liar here!"

Innes was the first to reach her; he took hold of an arm. At that moment, Sophie Hills lost whatever battle she was fighting; her eyes closed, her body went rigid as an oak. She turned to Innes and her eyes opened—she shook her arm and Innes flew off her as if he'd been struck by a runaway horse, crashing into the first row of deck chairs six feet away.

Doyle lowered a shoulder and threw his full considerable weight into the woman; she yielded hardly an inch, hitting a wall. He slid around to the back, clamped a bear hug on Sophie Hills, pinning her arms and held on. The priest thrust a crucifix before her face; she stopped struggling, eyes fixed on the cross. Innes scrambled back resiliently and from behind locked his arms around the woman's shoulders. She offered no resistance but a ferocious energy coursed through her body; both brothers agreed later it felt as if they were holding a Bengal tiger.

The priest didn't waver.

"In the name of all that is Holy, I command you, Unclean Spirit, to leave this body!"

The woman looked at him. Placid, serene. Smiled angelically.

"Do you remember your dream?" she asked the priest; a woman's voice again; low, intimate, melodic. But not Sophie's.

The priest stared at her in amazement.

"There are six. You are one. Listen to the dream."

What the devil was this?

"You must find the others. There are five. You will know

them. If you fail, hope dies with you. This is the Word of the Archangel."

The voice so quiet no one else heard it: only Doyle, Innes, and the priest. Her smile faded and the woman went limp in their arms. Doyle laid Sophie gently to the ground. Slow, shallow breathing. Unconscious.

Air in the room clear again. Time, which had felt suspended, began again. Mrs. Saint-John collapsed; Innes caught her before she hit the floor.

Captain Hoffner appeared next to Doyle, his smooth facade ruined. *"Mein Gott. Mein Gott."*

"Get them to their beds," said Doyle.

Hoffner nodded. Crewmen appeared. Sophie Hills gently carried off. Innes fanning Mrs. Saint-John back to woozy life. That sobering relief particular to accident survivors washed through the crowd; some stunned, not moving off their chairs, others slowly leaving the room, clinging to each other.

The young man from the dining hall, still as eager as before, caught Doyle's eye again. A respectful, urgent appeal: now, sir? Doyle nodded to him: yes, in my cabin, half an hour. He wanted to talk to the priest first—where did he go? Doyle turned: no sign of him.

There was Pinkus in the corner. Throwing up into his hat.

So the evening shouldn't be a total loss.

Innes rushed back into Doyle's cabin.

"Miss Hills is resting comfortably. . . ."

"And the priest?" asked Doyle, looking up from a book in his hand.

"Nowhere on deck. I tried to page his cabin from the steward's office, but no one seems to know which cabin he's in. The dining room staff says his name is Devine; Father Devine from Kilarney. . . ."

A soft knock at the door. Doyle nodded. Innes admitted the nervous young man; mid-twenties, medium height, high forehead, large owlish eyes, thinning curly brown hair, posture slightly stooped—the apologetic air of a man perpetually exuding self-effacement. Dark circles under his eyes provided the only shading in his ghostly pallor.

"Mr. Conan Doyle, thank you, sir, thank you so much for seeing me. I'm really sorry for the inconvenience. . . ." American: traces of New York. The man glanced at Innes, uncertain if he should continue.

"My brother will not violate your confidence, sir. Who are you and how may I help?"

"My name is Lionel Stern. I came on board when you gentlemen did. Traveling with a business associate of mine. I wanted to speak with you, sir, because we have reason to believe someone on this ship intends to murder us before we reach New York."

"You've taken this up with the Captain." The conversation overheard on the bridge.

"At some length. He maintains his ship is safe, every reasonable precaution taken; he was unable to offer us any additional guarantees."

"What did you offer him to authenticate this threat to your lives?"

Stern appeared taken aback. "We were followed all the way from London to Southampton. . . ."

"And, you believe, onto this ship."

"Yes."

"Have any direct actions been taken against you?"

"Not to date, but—"

"Have you seen or had any contact with the person or persons you believe are planning to kill you?"

"No." The man looked at them both sheepishly; this seemed to be the limit of his hard evidence. No mention of the "book" Doyle had heard them talking to the Captain about. Doyle gave Innes a look—back me up on this—then moved to the door, opened it, and gestured firmly to Lionel Stern.

"I will ask you to leave my cabin, sir."

Stern's jaw dropped. He looked ghastly. "You're not serious."

"I cannot be expected to help you, and I would resent this unwelcome intrusion from any man unless he is willing to part with the truth. You will please leave at once."

Whatever force of will had been holding Stern together dissolved; his plain features fell. He collapsed into a chair and cradled his head in his hands. "Sorry. You don't know the strain I'm under. You can't imagine. . . ."

Doyle closed the door, walked over, and studied Stern for a moment. "You were born and raised on the Lower East Side of New York City. The oldest son of Russian immigrant parents. You are a secular Jew, thoroughly and willfully assimilated into American culture. That you have rejected the religious observances of your father has been a matter of no small dispute between you. You sailed to London approximately six weeks ago from Spain—Seville, I believe—where, over a period of at least one month, in partnership with the man who accompanied you on board the *Elbe*, you negotiated a complicated transaction involving the use or purchase of an extremely rare and valuable book, which you are now transporting to America. A book of some profound religious or philosophical significance. This book is the cause for these well-founded concerns about your safety, Mr. Stern, and I will enjoy your complete candor in this matter from this moment on or we will proceed no further."

Stern, as well as Innes, stared at him uncomprehending, mouth agape.

"Have I left anything off?" asked Doyle.

Stern slowly shook his head.

"How in the world . . ." began Innes.

"You wear a Star of David around your neck at the end of that chain."

Stern lifted the medallion, as described, from under his shirt.

"But how did you know he was Russian?" asked Innes.

"Stern is a fairly common diminution—Americanization, if you will—of an entire subgroup of Russian surnames. You display none of the obvious outward signs of a devout, Orthodox Jew—it's likely your father, who was undoubtedly part of the first wholesale immigration from Russia to New York a generation ago, is more avidly a practitioner—in spite of which you wear a religious symbol concealed around your neck, indicating some self-division about your

status; a conflict not uncommon in the relationship between
a father and his eldest son.

"The uppers of your shoes—relatively new as indicated
by the lack of wear on the edge of the soles; purchased
within the last few weeks—are a distinctive Spanish leather
particular to Seville. Your stay in that one city was of sufficient length to have this pair of shoes crafted to order—three
weeks to a month usually—which suggests you were probably there on business. And this afternoon I happened to
overhear a portion of your conversation with the Captain
about the safekeeping of a book."

Stern let them know all of Doyle's conclusions were accurate, save two: His shoes had been purchased from a boot-
maker on Jermyn Street in London, where his recent
business had been conducted—he'd never set foot in
Spain—but yes, the leather had been sold to him as a product of Seville, and the book in question was indeed of Spanish origin.

Innes shared but did not disclose his equal astonishment,
unwilling to indicate either undue admiration of or a lack of
solidarity with his brother. He knew Arthur had consulted
with the police from time to time, and of course he'd written
those detective stories, but had no idea his detective skills
were sharpened to such a remarkable edge.

"So, Mr. Stern," continued Doyle, standing over the man,
hands folded magisterially behind his back, "now you had
better tell us about this book the parties allegedly following
you are so interested in and how it came into your possession."

Stern nodded, running his pale, slender hands back
through his unruly hair. "It is called the *Sefer ha-Zohar,* or
Book of Zohar, which means 'The Book of Splendor,' a collection of twelfth-century writings that originated in Spain.
They are the basis of what is known in Judaism as Kabbalah."

"The tradition of Jewish mysticism," said Doyle; he
searched his mind, finding his hard knowledge of the subject
frustratingly scant.

"That's right. The Zohar has been for centuries a restricted document, studied only by an eccentric line of rabbinical scholars."

"Well, what is it?" asked Innes, lost as a motherless calf.

"Kabbalah? Hard to describe, really; a patchwork of medieval philosophy and folklore, scriptural interpretations, legends of creation, mystical theology, cosmogony, anthropology, transmigration of souls."

"Oh," said Innes, feeling sorry he'd asked.

"Most of it's written as a dialogue between a legendary, perhaps fictional teacher by the name of Rabbi Simeon bar Yochai and his son and disciple, Eleazar. The two supposedly hid in a cave for thirteen years to avoid prosecution by the Roman emperor; when the emperor died and the Rabbi came out of seclusion, he was so disturbed by the lack of spirituality he saw among his people that he went right back into the cave, to meditate for guidance. After a year, he heard a voice that told him to let ordinary people go their own way and to teach only the ones who were ready. The Zohar is the record of those teachings, written down by his followers."

"Not unlike the Socratic dialogues of Plato and . . . er, what's his name," said Innes, not wanting to appear entirely ignorant, although he still had only the dimmest idea of what the fellow was talking about.

"Aristotle," said Stern and Doyle.

"Right-o."

"Did those original manuscripts survive?" asked Doyle.

"Perhaps; the Zohar was written in Aramaic, the language of second-century Palestine. Authorship of the original remains in dispute, but it is most often attributed to an obscure thirteenth-century rabbi who lived in Spain, Moses de Leon. Only two surviving manuscripts of De Leon's original work have been found; one is called the Tikkunei Zohar, a short addendum written some years after the main book. The Tikkunei was obtained last year from Oxford by the University of Chicago for study by a group of Jewish-American scholars—among whom my father, Rabbi Jacob Stern, as you correctly surmised, Mr. Doyle, is one of the foremost.

"After long negotiations, my partner and I have just secured the temporary loan of the oldest complete handwritten manuscript of the Book of Zohar. Called the Gerona Zohar; it dates from the early fourteenth century and was discovered years ago at the site of an ancient temple near Gerona, Spain. There's been tremendous controversy among experts about the Gerona Zohar's authenticity; my father and his colleagues hope that with both books in their possession they can compare them side by side and resolve these questions once and for all."

"Right, so what's so special about this old Bologna Zohar?" asked Innes, stifling a yawn.

"Gerona. To be honest, I've never studied it myself. I'm a businessman, rare books are my trade not my passion; I have no training or interest in such an academic undertaking. But my father, who's studied the Kabbalah for close to thirty years, would tell you he believes this book, if successfully decoded, will provide man with the answer to the mystery of creation, the identity of our creator, and the exact nature of the relationship between us."

"Mmph. Tall order, that," said Innes, displaying his natural gift for understatement.

"No one's managed it yet, have they?" said Doyle.

"It's all Greek to me," said Stern. "I wouldn't know what the mystery of creation was if it jumped up and stole my hat; all I'm told is that among the men my father keeps faith with, the Book of Zohar is reputed to contain the hidden key that will unlock the secret meanings of the Torah. . . ."

"The first five books of the Old Testament," said Doyle.

"Genesis, Exodus, Leviticus, Numbers, and Deuteronomy," said Innes, counting his fingers to remember—behind his back—as he'd been taught to do in Sunday school.

". . . and that the Torah was allegedly transcribed directly from the teachings that Moses supposedly received from God on Mount Sinai."

"Allegedly; supposedly."

"As you also correctly observed, Mr. Doyle, I am not by temperament or inclination in even the slightest way a religious man. If there is an all-powerful, all-knowing God, and if He had intended for man to solve the riddle of his own creation, I seriously doubt He would have gone to all the trouble of hiding the answer in the pages of a musty old book."

"A book which, nevertheless, you now believe someone is willing to kill you for."

"I didn't say the book was without earthly value: before taking possession of it we had the Gerona Zohar insured by Lloyd's of London for a sum of two hundred and fifty thousand dollars."

"Preposterous!" snorted Innes. "Who'd pay that much for a book?"

"There are private collectors the world over who would consider it a priceless addition to their libraries," said Doyle. "Men for whom money is no object and who might be more than willing to commission the theft of such an item."

"Commission the theft? Fiddlesticks; from whom?"

"Well, thieves, naturally." Good Christ, the boy was thick sometimes.

"You have arrived at the root of my fears exactly, Mr. Doyle," said Stern. "As I said, neither my associate nor I—his name is Rupert Selig, by the way; he manages European accounts and works out of our London office—neither of us can point to any direct evidence of someone stalking us. But ever since we arrived in London with the book, we have both experienced the uncanny feeling that we were being observed. The feeling grew steadily worse as we made our way to Southampton and onto the *Elbe*. I don't know how else to describe it: a crawly feeling up the back of my neck, small sounds that stay just out of earshot when you stop to listen, shadows that seem to move from sight as you turn. . . ."

"I am familiar with the sensation," said Doyle.

"Bloody spooks at a séance don't help much," said Innes.

"Absolutely; I don't know about you but I found that business tonight terrifying," said Stern. "And I can't tell you why but I felt that what we saw tonight and what I've been going through are somehow related. I consider myself a logical man, Mr. Doyle; I hope you will never hear me utter a more perfectly illogical statement."

Doyle felt his responses to Stern softening; once the man

unburdened himself of his initial reluctance, his honest modesty and intelligence grew considerably more appealing.

"When such a feeling comes from deep levels of the intuition, I advise anyone to pay attention to it," said Doyle.

"That's why when the Captain said he could not help us I turned to you: I've read newspaper accounts of your assisting the police on a number of mysterious cases. You also strike me as a man who is not afraid to take a stand for what he believes in. . . ."

Embarrassed, Doyle waved off the compliment. "Where is your copy of the Gerona Zohar now, Mr. Stern?"

"Under lock and key in the ship's hold. I checked it this afternoon."

"And your companion, Mr. . . ."

"Mr. Selig. In our cabin. As I told you, Rupert's concerns for our safety have been even greater than mine. Since we sailed, he's refused to go out on deck after dark. . . ."

Innes snorted contemptuously—in the tradition of the Royal Fusiliers—then realizing the inappropriateness of his response, disguised it as the onset of a protracted coughing fit.

"Must be the goose feathers in my pillow," said Innes.

"Perhaps we should have a word with your Mr. Selig as well," said Doyle, not stooping to dignify Innes's outburst with even an evil eye.

Lionel Stern knocked softly on the door to his cabin: three rapid knocks, then two slower ones. Innes was appalled at the lack of luxury in this second-class passageway, but in mixed company decided such an observation was best kept to oneself.

"Rupert? Rupert, it's Lionel."

No reply. Stern looked at Doyle, concerned.

"Asleep?" asked Doyle.

Stern shook his head and knocked again. "Rupert!"

Still no answer. Putting his ear to the door, Doyle heard a creak of movement inside, followed by a slight click.

"Your key?"

"Left in the room," said Stern. "We decided it was best not to go walking around the ship with it."

Innes rolled his eyes skyward.

"We should ring for the steward," said Doyle. "Innes?"

Doyle gestured him off with a toss of the head. Innes sighed and idled down the hall in search of a steward, thinking they must be a rare sight down here among the unwashed.

Stern rattled the door handle. "Rupert, please open the door!"

"Keep your voice low, Mr. Stern. I'm sure there's no reason for alarm."

"You told me to pay attention to my intuition, didn't you?" He banged his fist on the door. "Rupert!"

Innes returned with a steward, who absorbed a quick explanation before opening the cabin with his passkey. The door jerked to a halt at six inches, stopped by a taut security chain.

The steward began explaining the chain could only be removed by someone inside when Doyle raised his boot and gave the door a mighty kick; the chain snapped, the door flew open.

The cabin long and narrow. Double bunks bolted to the left wall. Closed and locked porthole over a washbasin at the far end.

Rupert Selig lay on the cold steel floor, legs fully extended, arms raised to the level of his shoulders, fists clenched, mouth and eyes frozen open in as perfect an expression of ungodly terror as Doyle had ever witnessed.

"Stay back," said Doyle.

The steward ran for help. Stern slumped against the wall; Innes propped him up with a free hand. Doyle stepped cautiously over the bulkhead, pausing to absorb as much detail as possible in a room that he knew within minutes would be trafficked beyond usefulness.

"Is he dead?" whispered Stern.

"Afraid so," said Innes.

Stern's eyes rolled back in his head. Innes directed his inert form gently down to the floor of the passage outside the cabin.

Doyle knelt beside Selig's body to examine something

faintly scrawled on the wall. His eye moved to a small clot of mud on the tiles by the door. Traces of the same mud were visible beneath the nails of his right hand.

"Try to keep them out of the cabin for a while, would you, Innes?" said Doyle, taking a magnifying glass from his pocket.

"Certainly, Arthur."

"There's a good fellow."

ROSEBUD RESERVATION, SOUTH DAKOTA

The moon was one night from round. The first cold breath of winter rode in the pocket of the wind. Leaves already turning. Geese overhead, flying south, away from the motherland. She looked back from the rise at the tumbledown houses and huts on the reserve and wondered how many more of her People would be taken when the snows came? How many would be left to welcome the spring?

She hugged the blanket tight around her shoulders. Hoped one of the patrols would not find her out here beyond the walls and send her back onto the reserve. So much sorrow: disgusting food, whiskey, the coughing sickness. The blue coats' repeating rifles. Sitting Bull murdered by one of his own. Whites with their lying treaties, ripping open the belly of the sacred black hills for their gold . . .

And she was afraid to sleep because of a dream that the world was ending? How was that any worse than what she saw when her eyes were open?

She knew the world of the Dakota, their Way, was gone forever. One trip to their city of Chicago had shown her that. The whites had built a new world—machines, straight lines, squared corners—and if it was that world she saw ending in the dream, why should she lose any sleep? If the world of the Dakota, the first human beings, could be destroyed in one generation, then no world could be made to last; surely not one built on the blood and bones of her People.

This dream was not a curse wished on the whites, although many had passed her lips. They had killed her mother and father, but this was no vision of revenge. This dream had crept into her sleeping mind unwelcomed, and in the three months since, it had become a nightly torment from which she could find no relief. Driving her to stand out here on the flats beyond the reserve and ask her grandfather for an answer, which still had not come after seven nights of waiting.

There was proud, strong medicine in her family, and she knew when a dream-quest came she must follow wherever it would take her. This vision held no medicine she knew—a dark tower rising into burning skies above a lifeless desert, tunnels carved beneath the earth, six figures joining hands; out of a hole in the ground the Black Crow Man rode a wheel of fire. The images reminded her of what the Christians called Apocalypse, but if it came to that she was not afraid to die: When the fighting began, and she was called upon as in the dream, her only fear was that she might fail.

Thirty summers. Many suitors; never a husband. Hard to accept a man who had never ridden the hunt, a no-fight man, a touch-the-pen who'd given up their Way. But the whites killed all the strong ones and whiskey took the rest. So she had learned to ride and shoot and skin, made herself a warrior in body and in mind. She went to the white school as law required, learned to read their words and understand how they lived. They baptized her—one of their many strange rituals; and they thought *her* people were primitives—and called her Mary Williams.

When it suited her, she would answer to that name, wear their clothes—these skirts, these uncomfortable binding stays—and make herself handsome with their paints, but she took a lover only when she wanted one and even then always held herself apart. She had known since she was small that she was making ready for a life of power. When the dreams started, she knew that her time had finally come. No more preparing.

An owl circled the rising moon. Grandfather had taught her about the spirit of the owl: He had such powerful medicine. More than any of the big bellies left alive in the Hunkapa or Oglala families. What would he counsel if he were with her now?

The owl landed softly on the branch of an overhead pine, settled his wings, looked sharply down at her, and through his ageless eyes she felt the presence of her grandfather.

Go back to your bed and sleep and wait for the dream. The dream is the question and the answer. The dream will tell you what to do.

The owl blinked twice then swooped off into the night.

She remembered something else he used to tell her: *Be careful what you ask the gods for.*

Walks Alone walked back inside the walls of the reserve. Sleep would come for her quickly after so much time.

THE NEW CITY, ARIZONA TERRITORY

Cornelius Moncrief had a king-size headache, and prospects for improvement looked dim; there wasn't a man jack, or woman, in the West he couldn't persuade to see things his way—that was his *job*—but he found himself starting to wonder if the Reverend A. Glorious Day was going to come around. Shit. Nobody ever won an argument with the railroad and who was Cornelius Moncrief if not the railroad personified?

Lord knows I laid it out for him plain as day—polite, too, first time through, like always, that's company policy—but this white-eyed, Bible beatin' hunchback in the black frock coat with that scraggly hair and his Holy Roller attitude don't seem to grasp the nature of my authority. What is wrong with this jasper? I'm here to dictate terms and he's rantin' and ravin' at me like I'm some sinner in the market for salvation.

Give him this much, the fella must preach a mean sermon: One look at that cadaverous face'd suck coins into the collection basket right out of my pockets. That mug belongs in a box with the lid nailed shut. Somethin's gone sour in this fella's pickle barrel, 'cause I know this much: I know there's nothing wrong with Cornelius Moncrief.

'Course none of the Reverend's soul-saving flapdoodle was going to put Cornelius off his feed. He'd worked some

of the diciest backwaters in creation during his fifteen years
on the western circuit; murder, rape, casual violence:
Couldn't expect people on a frontier to behave any other
way. But somebody had to enforce the will of the railroad
and Cornelius was the syndicate's number one trou-
bleshooter: labor disputes, runaway coolies, accounts in ar-
rears, they sent him in to settle up when all other options fell
short. Cornelius carried a Sharps buffalo gun in a custom
valise and a mother-of-pearl-handled Colt .45 with a Bunt-
line barrel in his belt. At six foot four, 285 pounds, with his
Sharps and that hogleg Colt, he'd never run into nothing yet
he couldn't handle.

But Cornelius had felt the heebie-jeebies crawling over
him like bad violin music from the moment he jumped off
his horse in this hick burg.

Why you call this place The New City? Cornelius wanted
to ask the Reverend. Was there an "old" one? What's the
"the" for? And what's with the slaphappy grins on these ya-
hoos? He hadn't heard a single contrary word from these
citizens—spades, Indians, chinks, Mexicans, whites, all
mingling together, everybody so nice and friendly to him
you'd think he was Gentleman Jim Corbett come to town for
a heavyweight championship bout. What did these puddin'
headed dirt farmers got to be so damn giddy about? Living
in a rat's nest of half-assed, fly-infested shanties fifty miles
from nowhere in the middle of the Arizona desert? Road
goes straight through Hell Valley, then takes a turn up Skull
Canyon; even the goddamn Apaches had more sense than to
put down wigwams this far out in the sand. No running
water, electricity. Sweet Jesus, they ain't even got a proper
saloon: The New City's a "dry community," they're so
pleased to tell you with their pea-brain smiles.

They built an opera house, though, right there on Main
Street. Theatrical companies coming in to put on shows; if
they die out here it won't be for lack of entertainment. But
not another building in town off the Main Street with more
than four walls and a planked floor 'cept that big black
church on the edge of town.

What'd the Reverend call it? The "cathedral."

Now Cornelius had been to St. Louis and New Orleans and San Francisco, and this didn't look like any cathedral he'd ever clapped eyes on: towers, spires, black stones, not a single cross in sight, staircases twisting this way and that. Looked more like a castle in one of those short-pants fairy tales. Big enough to fit into any one of those cities, though. Going up fast, a whole hive of worker bees—and there was demolition going on underground, too; he'd heard muffled explosions round the clock since he arrived. Must be mining something in those high rocks behind the tower; quartz, maybe silver or gold. Some kind'a fresh money was bankrolling this crazy tank town.

Cornelius was getting steamed. First they kept him cooling his heels in the Reverend's parlor half the morning without offering so much as a root beer to cut the dust. Finally, he gets a sit-down in the same room with the head rooster and he's barely said hello before the Reverend rips into a tub-thumpin' filibuster on the evils of man, how it's the foretold destiny of The New City to rise out of the desert and create a world without sin—which is why he can't allow the railroad to bring the foul taint of civilization into their Garden of Eden.

Right from the git-go, Cornelius wants to cut in: Save your breath, pal; I don't even pray to your God, though I've sent a Chinaman off to meet Him from time to time. But try as he might, Cornelius can't find an opening to slip into his pitch 'bout how no-body in their right mind turns down the railroad. . . .

Come to think of it . . .

A team of coolies deserted construction on the north/south Arizona spur line three months ago; pinched a ton of supplies when they skipped, too; explosives and such. Not a hundred miles from here. And he'd seen more than a few chink faces in that crowd when he arrived . . . this little excursion might be worth the trouble after all.

But as I sit here and listen to this padre jabber, not that I'm half-interested in what he's flapping his gums about, there's some odd thing about the Reverend's voice makes it hard to break back in to my pitch: some sound buzzing in the room, like horseflies or a bunch of bees. . . .

What's that on the Reverend's desk?

Looks like a . . . a box of pins. That's it. Pins. Open box of pins. Never seen pins look like that before. Shiny. Long. Look new. Must be new. What is it about 'em? Are they new?

"That's right, Mr. Moncrief. Shiny new pins."

"Excuse me?" said Cornelius, without taking his eyes off the box. Not that he wanted to. He felt good; warm inside, better than he'd felt since he got here . . . when was it, yesterday?

"You go right on ahead and look at them. There's no problem with looking at the pins, is there, Mr. Moncrief?"

Cornelius slowly shook his head. Heat spread through him deep and fast like Kentucky bourbon from a cool glass. He could relax. There was no problem with looking at the pins.

"Take all the time you need. That's fine."

Reverend Day didn't move. Standing behind the desk. Couldn't look at him. Eyes going soft . . .

The pins stirred in the box. There was life in them. Yes, he knew it. They shifted, tumbling over each other, and then fast, one by one, the pins stood up out of the box and hung there before him in the air. Shining like ornaments, Christmas tinsel—no, the light flickering off them, reflections tossed high around the room: like diamonds. By the handfuls.

"Beautiful . . ." whispered Cornelius. "So beautiful."

Sounds around him. Clear bells. Birdsong. Whispery voices.

"You watch them now, Cornelius."

He nodded again. So happy. The Reverend's voice blended sweetly with that bell tone. Other voices clearer: a church choir.

The pins formed a curtain, dancing, shimmering before his eyes: Pictures swam in and out of its surface. Silver fields of tall grass, waving in the wind. Sun jumping off a snowpack. Bright, clear water tumbling down a meadow of yellow flowers . . .

Life: so much life. Fish in a stream, horses running free down a lush box canyon. A mountain cat moving peacefully through herds of grazing antelope and deer. Hawks wheeling in a cloudless sapphire sky. And there far down below, near the horizon, what was that? What complete perfection of line, color, and shape dazzled his eye?

A City blooming out of the desert like a hothouse orchid. An oasis around its towers, rising up a thousand feet to meet the heavens. Towers of glass or crystal, red, blue, amber, twinkling in the brilliant sunlight like a canopy of jewels.

Tears flowed down Cornelius's cheeks. His lips blubbered with inexpressible joy. He felt a deep loosening in his chest; his heart opened like a night jasmine.

Through the translucent walls of the City, he saw some greater radiance illuminating its interior. A whisper of a thought and he glided toward the light, drifting through the walls as if they were an insubstantial mist. There were people below, a great mass of them, gathered peacefully on a tree-lined green around a raised platform from where the light originated. Hovering over the crowd now; he'd never seen such peaceful, welcoming faces. They held up their hands to him, guiding him gently down into their warm enveloping embrace.

Love. They loved him. He felt it flooding his senses, filling every corner of his mind. Pouring out of this crowd and into him; oh, the powerful feelings he felt in return . . .

He loved them all so much.

The crowd around him turned as one to face a figure of light standing above them on the central column. He gasped: The light came from within a beauty unearthly. Form obscured, features indistinct—golden, burnished—emanating from within a halo of perfect love and generosity and peace.

The figure titanic. Wings spreading out beyond the eye's capacity. No way to measure their span.

An angel.

Eyes found him: great round disks of sky. His angel, there for him and him alone. Eyes held him in the embrace of their gaze. Loving him. A smile; a blessing. The angel spoke without words: He heard them in his head.

"Are you happy here, Cornelius?"

"Oh yes."

"We have been waiting for you."

"Waiting for me?"

"Waiting for the longest time. We need you, Cornelius."

"You do?"

"The time is drawing near. There is so much for you to do."

"I want to help you."

"You've been treated very badly by those people; those people out there."

Tears ran from his eyes. "Yes."

"They don't understand you at all, do they? Not like we do."

"No."

The angel's immensity filled his field of vision; its voice echoed deeply through every fiber of his body.

"Do you want to stay here, with us, Cornelius?"

"I want to, yes. I want to so much."

The angel smiled. Wind ruffled back Cornelius's hair with a sound like a thousand muffled drums. Hands folded in silent prayer, the angel flapped its wings again and ascended from the platform into the firmament. All eyes turned skyward, watching the departure. Music rising to a grand crescendo, drowning out the blissful murmuring of the crowd.

Cornelius smiled, sharing now in their secret knowledge: He was home.

chapter four

DEAD SEA AROUND THEM. BLACK, OILY WATER, BECALMED: a false peace and a certain promise of violence. Vague, evil shapes flickered along the surface. Squall lines hanging black curtains across the northern horizon. Drab light from the west, yellow, greasy on the scummy foam. A full moon rising soon behind them, precise counterweight to the setting sun.

Doyle stood at the aft starboard rail. Tried to roughly calculate their position at sea; nearing the 30th parallel, 50 degrees north. Nearest landfall the Azores, a thousand miles south. He heard the whine of the screws below. Engines laboring. Innes would be along any minute; no one would overhear them at this end of the ship.

Doyle stared at the sketch he'd made of the scrawl on Selig's wall, aching to make sense of it. He had worked throughout the day on the whole problem, agonizingly close to unraveling the mystery, but the last piece that would complete the puzzle remained just out of his reach. And still no sign of that priest, Father Devine. He felt reluctant to approach Captain Hoffner with only his current conclusions, but the danger was unmistakable; if he didn't, Lionel Stern might not live through the night.

Here was Innes.

"Aside from what they stowed in their cabin, Rupert Selig and Stern brought four pieces of luggage," said Innes, producing a list. "Steamer trunk, two valises, one crate. Saw them myself; sitting in the hold, undisturbed." Doyle raised an eyebrow. "I slipped this bloke in the engine room a fiver."

"Good work."

"Crate's sealed with an intact customhouse band. About the size of a large hatbox. Figure that for the Book of Zohar, what?"

Doyle said nothing.

"Where's Stern now?" asked Innes.

"Captain's cabin, well looked after for the moment. There's an inordinate amount of paperwork to sort out a civilian death at sea."

"Never even occurred to me: What do they do with the body?"

"Refrigerated lockers. Necessity on any cruise liner with their older clientele: a good many of them overfed, apoplectic, sclerotic . . ."

Innes shivered involuntarily. "Not too near the kitchen, I hope."

"Separate area. Nearer the hold, where they store those coffins we saw them loading in port."

"Put a man right off his mutton."

"Listen: The ship's doctor insists on labeling Selig's a natural death," said Doyle.

"He can't be serious."

"All outward signs indicate Selig died of acute coronary failure. I can't dispute that, and that's surely what his killers would like us to believe. There's no facility to conduct a proper autopsy on board; if there were, I'm not sure the results would contravene. And the last thing the Captain needs on board his luxury liner is idle talk about the murder of a passenger."

"But of course that's exactly what we think it is."

"Frighten a man to death? Send an excess of adrenaline racing through his system and literally explode his heart? Yes, I'd call that murder."

"What could have set him off?"

Doyle shook his head.

"Maybe he caught a glimpse of the ship's ghost wandering around belowdecks," said Innes.

"Good Christ." Doyle stared at him, wide-eyed, as if he'd been struck with a mallet.

"Are you all right, Arthur?"

"Of course; that's it. Well done, Innes."

"What did I do?"

"You've cracked it open, old boy," said Doyle, walking him rapidly toward the nearest hatchway.

"I did?"

"Call back that engineer of yours. Have him fetch a fire-man's ax, a hammer, and a crowbar. It's time we had a few words with Mr. Stern and Captain Hoffner."

The engineer flashed the beam of his lantern into the dark recess of the storage bay, picking out a sealed, rectangular shipping crate from among the forest of cargo.

"Is that your crate, Mr. Stern?" asked Doyle.

"Yes, it is."

"I'm sure we are all most interested, Mr. Conan Doyle," said Captain Hoffner with chafed civility, "but I'm afraid I am not seeing the point of this exercise. . . ."

Doyle raised the ax and with one short, economical blow smashed the cover of the crate to pieces. Stern gasped. Doyle reached down, picked through the splinters, and ex-tracted the contents of the box: a large square sheath of blank white paper.

"Equivalently weighted to approximate your Book of Zohar," said Doyle to Stern, balancing the stack in his hand.

"I didn't know; I swear," protested Stern. "I mean I saw them; I was there in London when the Book was crated."

"It seems your late partner Mr. Selig had other plans, which may account for his disinclination to leave your cabin."

"What is the significance of this, please?" asked Hoffner.

"Begging your patience for the moment, Captain, I will attend to that presently," said Doyle, dropping the paper and hefting the ax over his shoulder. "Now if you would be good enough to accompany us to our next destination. Innes?"

Innes gestured and the little engineer—secretly thrilled at the spectacle of his rigid, disciplinarian Captain kowtowing to this crazy Englishman—led the way through a maze of passages and hatches to an adjacent hold: a frigid, uninvit-ing room dominated by a row of square steel-hood-handled vaults. Rows of bare light bulbs hung from the ceiling, their pale auras failing against the odors of decay that permeated the air.

"May I be permitted to ask what we are doing in the morgue?" asked Hoffner.

With Innes holding up a lantern, Doyle cracked open one of the refrigerated lockers and rolled out its enclosed metal tray, introducing the rigid enshrouded outline of a corpse. He pulled the sheet away from the face and dispassionately yanked down the lower eyelids of the late Rupert Selig, revealing congested spiderwebs of blue and purple capillaries.

"Contrary to your ship physician's opinion that he was in perfect health for a man his age, Mr. Selig suffered from heart disease and severe high blood pressure, evidenced as you can see by these massively ruptured vessels in the soft tissue under his eyes—a condition he kept secret even from you, Mr. Stern. You were not aware of it, were you, sir?"

Stern shook his head.

Doyle showed them a small glass vial of medicine; round, white pills. "Mr. Selig carried this homeopathic remedy—a mixture of potassium, calcium, and tincture of iodine of no small popularity but little established benefit—in a hidden pocket sewn into the lining of his jacket."

"All very well and good, Mr. Doyle; it supports in fact my doctor's conclusion that a heart attack was being the cause of the gentleman's death, but what does it have to do with—"

Doyle raised a hand, cutting Hoffner off again. "One point at a time, Captain; there is a design at work here, if you will trust me to bring it to light in the appropriate sequence." Doyle tossed the sheet back over Selig's gray face and gave the tray a shove, and it slid home with a metallic clang that echoed through the grim room.

"Innes, if you please . . ." said Doyle.

Innes took the torch from the engineer and illuminated the far corner of the room; an orderly row of coffins lined the floor next to the wall.

"You accepted these five coffins as cargo in Southampton, isn't that correct, Captain?"

"Yes, so?"

"All from the same shipping agent, I trust."

"That would be customary."

"I shall in short order wish to examine the bill of lading for them," said Doyle, accepting the hammer and crowbar from the engineer. "There was only one insurmountable difficulty in the resolution of my theory; as we saw while boarding the ship, security was airtight—which is more than I can say for this casket." Doyle shimmed the crowbar with the hammer into a gap beneath the mahogany lid of the first coffin.

"*Mein Gott,* sir, think what you are doing. . . ." Hoffner moved to stop Doyle from proceeding with the exhumation: Innes clamped a strong hand on his arm, holding him back, as Doyle continued.

"If a band of professional assassins have found their way onto the *Elbe*—and I assure you, Captain, that is exactly what we are dealing with here—they had to have managed it by some less conventional means than strolling up the gangplank in plain view—"

"I must order you to stop this at once. . . ."

"You'll recall one of your passengers heard the cries of a 'ghost' from somewhere in the hold our first day out of port. . . ." Doyle heaved at the crowbar; with a piercing shriek of protest from its nails, the coffin lid separated and lifted an inch from the sides. The shriek echoed hauntingly down the steel passageways around them. Doyle took a strong grip on the exposed edge of a coffin lid and pulled it open the rest of the way.

"This is a desecration. . . ." Captain Hoffner broke free of Innes and rushed forward to discover that the plush pink satin-lined interior of the coffin was completely empty. Hoffner stared at Doyle, mouth agape.

"The 'ghost's' cries were followed shortly thereafter by a loud, rhythmic knocking."

Doyle dropped the lid shut and hammered the nails back in.

"Look closely and you can see the indentations made when they hammered the nails back in," said Doyle, beckoning Hoffner closer to the box. "Your cargo hands have assured me that each coffin carried the full, shifting complement of a body weight when they were carried aboard. If you examine them closely down here as well, Captain, you can see that minute holes were drilled in the corners for the circulation of air."

Hoffner ran a finger over the perforations. "I do not know what to say."

"An apology to Mr. Stern might be a prudent beginning. And the next time one of your passengers approaches you with concerns for their personal security, regardless of their religious or cultural persuasion, one hopes you will respond with a generosity more befitting your position."

Hoffner's face turned crimson; he grabbed the hammer and crowbar from Doyle; three minutes and four more open empty coffins later, a winded, chastened Hoffner laid down the tools.

"Mr. Stern," he said, standing tall. "Please accept my deepest and most sincere apologies."

Stern nodded, avoiding the Captain's eyes.

"You have five stowaways on board, Captain. There are dozens of places to hide on a ship this size. I don't need to suggest that you take all appropriate actions."

"No. Yes, of course. We shall conduct a search of the entire ship at once," said Hoffner, wiping his brow, mind racing. He considered himself a man of reason, above all, and second-most, a man of action.

"A concerted effort to find the Irish priest Father Devine would also be in order," said Doyle.

"Why is that?"

"Because this man is not a priest. He is their leader."

That's when the lights went out.

SAN FRANCISCO, CALIFORNIA

To call this place the Devil's Kitchen does not do it justice, thought Kanazuchi, watching a rat chase a cockroach. He lay on a lice-infested blanket covering a wooden pallet he had secured the use of for the princely sum of two pennies a night. The beds of twenty other vagrants crowded the fifteen-square-foot room, one of four equally congested flops on the third floor of a five-story tenement in the middle of Tangrenbu, the twelve-square-block area of downtown San Francisco that the whites called Chinatown.

An opium den occupied the basement, and rumors circulated among these poor and illiterate peasants, many of them migrant farm workers who flooded the city each autumn when the central valley's harvest ended, that a demon roamed the hallways at night, tracking down souls to devour. The bodies of three men had been discovered recently in the alley behind the tenement; throats slashed, hearts ripped from their bodies. Offerings left in shrines outside their doorways, what little money these Chinese could scrape together, collectively appeared to placate the monster. Each night they heard it prowling outside their doors and each morning the offerings were gone. But no one else had been killed in the week since the offerings began.

Of the four hundred men living in this building, only one had seen the demon and lived to tell about it: the building's trustee—a pockmarked, thick-necked bully in charge of gathering each day's rent and, more recently, the money for the offerings. This demon had the head of a dragon, a thousand eyes, and ten ravenous mouths, he testified, a first-rank demon, one of the ten thousand that figured in their complex belief system. He had watched it use its hideous talons to rip open the chests of the men found in the alley, as easily, he said, as if it were peeling an orange.

Each room was now locked by the trustee at night, but even if they had been able to, none of these men would dare venture into the halls after dark, which left personal sanitation a concern to be attended to locally. There were times when Kanazuchi wished his senses were not honed as sharply as the Grass Cutter that lay beside him in his bundle; the ripe stink of these unwashed provincials occasioned one of those moments.

Amid such fear, squalor, and destitution, Kanazuchi knew that since his arrival the day before no one had taken notice of him, but not being able to move freely at night was unacceptable. Sighs, guttural snoring, the whimper of a troubled dreamer, underscored the darkness around him. He did not want to leave the room until its occupants were sound asleep, and the thin man with the fever two beds down was still tossing and turning.

Kanazuchi had been visited by his dream again last night; one image leaped out with the solid clarity of a lead worth pursuing.

Chinese faces working in a tunnel.

His first two days in Dai Fow, the Big City, New Golden Mountain—what these Chinese called San Francisco—had failed to shed light on this mysterious image. Menials like these ignorant slum dwellers were of no use. He had considered cultivating the local merchants, but they spoke a more cultured dialect than the guttural Mandarin of the peasants he'd made the crossing with; it would take another week to master its nuances and they were notoriously tight-lipped to anyone outside their social tongs. His other option was to move beyond the ghetto into the white sections of the city, but every person he had spoken to in Tangrenbu had warned him not to. A wave of anti-Asian rage had swept through America in recent years; in Chinatowns up and down the western coasts, crimes of violence against Asian immigrants had grown steadily worse—murders, riots, lynchings. Whenever the whites needed someone to scapegoat for their economic misfortunes, the "yellow peril" was emphasized in public sentiment and these acts of racial barbarity inevitably followed. What more could you expect from such uncivilized people? Kanazuchi was hesitant to go into white areas, not for fear of being attacked, but only because killing any white men in public would trigger unnecessary complications.

First things first: A more direct path to the information he sought might lie right in front of him.

The man two beds down had settled, breathing strained but slow and regular. Kanazuchi shouldered his bundle and stepped between the sleepers, careful to avoid the four creaking floorboards. He stopped at the bed of the trustee next to the door. Using the tip of his *wakizashi*—his long knife—he delicately slipped the room key undetected from under the trustee's pallet. A length of rawhide secured it to a slat; he slit it with a flick of the wrist.

One minute later, he stood in the hallway, eyes already conditioned to the darkness. The air pungent with the smoke of the joss sticks burning on the shrines; each one still packed with fruit and coins. Kanazuchi examined the dust on the floor; no one had moved through the hall since their doors were locked at midnight, two hours before. He drifted to the center of the hall near the stairs, blended into the shadows, stood still, and listened.

Sleepers breathing in the four rooms on his floor. In the rooms above and below. Cockroaches scuttling behind the walls. He pushed the reach of his extraordinary senses further out; an old, familiar exercise, slipping into it as easily as a well-worn garment.

An alley cat tipped a trash can outside. Rats foraging. A carriage clipping by. Drunks laughing. The shrill negotiations of a prostitute. Horses shifting, stamping their feet, snorting in the stables next door.

Footsteps; nearer.

He reeled the net of his senses back in and cast it down to the tenement's first floor.

One man entered. Heavy. Tall, by the length of the stride. Western leather boots. A sack dragging on the ground behind. Rattling, hissing like a snake. A soft scoop, then the clink of coins falling together. Banging sounds; a clash of tinny cymbals.

Sleepers waking on the lower floors. Fearful whispers. Cowering. No one moving from his pallet.

Footsteps climbed the stairs. Second floor. Drumbeats, cymbals louder: hissing and rattling. More coins collected: moving closer.

Terror spread through the building. Prayers mumbled, worry beads clacking frantically. Kanazuchi turned his mind away from the chattering peasants and toward the leaden footsteps coming up the stairs.

The demon turned at the landing. A bulky, intimidating figure; dragon's head, feathered limbs, avian claws clutching a tambourine that banged against its hip. Large burlap sack behind, bumping up the risers.

As the demon reached the third floor, a coin dropped at its

feet; it stopped, looked down. Gold; the demon reached for it. A shadow moved; the demon's mind registered confusion and a flash of something silver moving toward him in the instant before consciousness ceased. The sword cut so quickly the demon's eyes were still sending information to its brain—the room spinning out of control—as its head tumbled backward down the stairs away from the still-stationary body.

Kanazuchi cut up at an angle so the demon's body would shoot no blood onto his clothes. He sheathed Grass Cutter, reached out in time to lower the body silently as the arteries began to pump onto the floor. He jumped lightly to the landing, and pulled the demon's head out of the cheap paper dragon costume—eyes and mouth caught wide open in surprise; the flat, stupid face of a common thug.

Kanazuchi pulled the flute from his belt and headed back toward his room.

When the trustee heard the demon stop outside, he reached for his key, then for his knife when he found the key was missing. The knife was gone, too. Just then the door swung open and he heard the hollow, reedy whistling of an evil wind. The rest of the men in the room huddled under their blankets.

The bright paper dragon head peeked around the corner of the open doorway. A clawed finger pointed at the trustee and beckoned him forward.

What the hell was Charlie doing? thought the trustee. This is not how things are supposed to work.

Annoyed, the trustee walked out into the hall. The wind stopped suddenly; the door closed behind him. A sulfurous white cloud of smoke billowed before him in the hall, and in a flash of light he saw the head and body of his cohort, Charlie Lee, laid out on the blood-soaked floor. Before his legs could run, an iron vise grabbed him around the throat and lifted him straight off the floor. His captured breath swelled in his chest like a balloon.

"The gods are unhappy with you," said a harsh whisper in the trustee's ear.

What a horrible voice! He kicked his legs futilely and

struggled for air: Nothing moved inside him. Surely he was about to die. . . .

"They have sent me to punish you with the death of a thousand torments."

Heaven protect him: a real demon!

"Maybe you don't deserve such mercy. Maybe I should just eat you one piece at a time."

The demon shook him like a helpless kitten.

"Lucky for you I am in a good mood. Return the money you've stolen from these men and maybe I will let you live."

The trustee tried to nod his head: anything! A trickle of breath slipped through the demon's grip, keeping him on a thin edge of consciousness.

"Tell me: Do you steal this money for yourself?"

The trustee frantically shook his head no.

"Really? Then who told you to steal this money?"

The grip relaxed enough for him to croak out an answer. "Little Pete."

"Little Pete? What sort of name is that for a civilized person?"

"Real name is . . . Fung Jing Toy. Chinatown boss."

"Which tong does he lead?"

"Sue Yop Tong."

"Where will I find Little Pete?"

"On Leong Society Building," croaked the trustee.

"The Chamber of Tranquil Conscientiousness?"

The trustee nodded again. For a Chinese demon, this one spoke pretty good English, he thought, just before its grip tightened on his neck like a band of iron; another blinding flash in the air. The trustee blacked out.

When he came to, a crowd of men from all the building's rooms milled around the decapitated remains of well-known neighborhood tough Charlie Lee. The trustee scrambled to his feet, sharing their happiness that the reign of terror had come to such a satisfying end: It wasn't a demon after all! Picking up the extortionist's grab bag, the trustee began to distribute its coins to the residents: What a stroke of fortune! He took none for himself; a change of heart had come over the trustee, a spurt of generosity that might last as long as another two days: The demon had let him live!

In his elation, the trustee took no notice of the slender, quiet man who had come in the day before, the last to leave his pallet and step into the hallway with the others. The man stood near the back of the crowd, apart from them, his bundle over his shoulder. Ready to go.

Fung Jing Toy noisily sucked out the marrow between the webbing of the pickled duck's foot. A delicacy his lower-caste family could never afford, duck's feet served every afternoon was one of the more genteel ways in which Little Pete reminded himself of the good fortune that twenty years of backbreaking work and self-sacrifice had given him. Although of modest stature befitting his nickname and an outwardly mild disposition, Little Pete was in his basic nature a man of ravenous appetites, and he rarely obeyed any impulse to hold them in check.

He was the only tong leader with whom "Blind Chris" Buckley and the corrupt white political establishment of San Francisco could negotiate comfortably; the rest of these top-dog Chinamen acted too high and mighty by half for their taste. Little Pete was the only one of them who laughed at the insults they casually tossed in his face, a clown who bowed and scraped in a manner reflecting his inferior racial status.

But Chris Buckley and his cronies recognized in Little Pete a man fiercely dedicated to an objective dear to their own hearts: the perpetual containment, subjugation, and enslavement of the city's Chinese population. The residents of Tangrenbu lived in mortal fear of Pete and the vicious henchmen of his Sue Yop Tong. Although five other criminal tongs owned significant holdings in Tangrenbu, Little Pete's On Leong Society controlled the flow of opium into the quarter. He owned many of the sweatshops where addicts slaved away for the pennies they spent to fill their bowls every night and most of the verminous flophouses where they slept it off.

In trade for their cooperation with the political machine, the six tongs had been granted sole responsibility for the importation and regulation of all workers from mainland China. And through Buckley's cozy association with the powerful railroad barons of San Francisco—Hopkins, Huntington, Crocker, and Stanford—Little Pete had become chief supplier of "coolie" labor for the expansion of the western lines. In Mandarin dialect, *kuli* signified "bitter strength."

So for the privilege of resettling in this land of opportunity, once a lower-caste worker passed through the sheds at the embarcadero he was chattel, owned and exploited to the grave by Little Pete and the Six Companies. At which point one of Pete's funeral parlors would perform the cremation and turn a tidy profit on shipping the ashes—by no means necessarily those of the worker—back to the departed's family in China.

Bitter strength, indeed.

Little Pete was a creature of habit. One of his established routines: hearing requests from his constituents during the business day lunch hour on the second-floor balcony of his Kearney Street town house. Little Pete liked to stuff himself heartily while his workers and shopkeepers humbled themselves before him. On occasion, if a request was sufficiently innocuous or inexpensive enough, he would demonstrate his rare and therefore legendary magnanimity.

But here it was half past noon; already on his third helping of duck's feet and no one had yet arrived to petition him with their stupid problems. He yelled out to his houseboy, Yee Chin: Why is no one here? If they have been left waiting downstairs, someone will be punished!

No answer. He threw down the bones on his plate and demanded more food. No one appeared. Now he was angry: His kitchen boys had orders to stand by inside the balcony with extra helpings to bring out the moment he called; they had all felt his crop on their back when a dish landed on his table cold. Little Pete rang the little porcelain bell he kept by his plate and shouted again.

Nothing. Yee Chin would catch unholy hell for this incompetence.

Little Pete wedged his bulbous stomach from behind the table, lifted his generous behind off the silk pillows on his hand-carved Tang dynasty chair, picked up his riding crop, and waddled into the sitting room, thinking of creative new ways he was going to punish these useless domestics.

A silver dome covered the serving that waited for him on the cart inside the door. If his next course had gone cold, heaven help Yee Chin. He lifted the dome off the tray. . . .

Little Pete fell to his knees and violently retched up his lunch, mind blanked, senses obliterated; blind, deaf, and dumb.

There were feet on the tray.

Human feet.

Little Pete crawled quickly away on hands and knees, instincts for survival surfacing. Where were his bodyguards? Four on duty downstairs around the clock; someone got past them. The attack could come from any direction, at any moment. He would have to defend himself. There had been a time when no one bested him with a knife, but he hadn't been in a fight that mattered for over ten years.

A pistol in the top drawer of that table. Little Pete scampered over, pulled the gun out, hands shaking wildly, gripping onto the table for support. He wiped the drool from his lips with the sleeve of his gun hand, tried to summon enough voice to call out for his guards, but the words died in his throat; heart beating too hard, tongue cottony and sluggish.

Slow, slow down now, Pete. This is a good place. You can see every door and window from here. Steady the gun with both hands. Wait until they come close: Don't waste any bullets. . . .

A tremendous force slammed his head down from behind onto the tabletop. The layer of thick glass covering its hardwood surface cracked, his face locked in place motionless against it; Little Pete felt heat run down his face, saw his own blood flowing freely into the splinters. His arm wrenched backward and the gun was taken from his hand like a rattle from a baby.

"You understand how easily I can kill you," said a quiet voice.

"Yes," croaked Little Pete.

"Your guards are dead. No one is coming to help you. Answer my questions; don't waste time and you will live."

The voice spoke flawless, unaccented Mandarin. He didn't know this man. Little Pete tried to nod in agreement, grinding the shattered glass deeper into his face.

"You sell workers to the railroads," said the voice.

"Yes."

"Tunnel men. Chinese. Good with explosives."

"Yes, a few . . ."

"There can't be many of them."

"No, not good ones."

"You would know who they are, then, the good ones."

What in heaven's name was this about?

"Yes. If they're demolition; they used to be miners mostly. They came here for the gold rush. . . ."

"You sent some out to the desert."

Little Pete's mind raced: There weren't many Chinese demolition men left, the good ones were always in demand—hard to think now. . . .

"Answer or I'll kill you."

They worked in teams; his offices handled sale and shipping of dynamite as well. Couldn't remember; he would have to check his ledgers—that would take time—would this man let him live long enough to do it?

Wait. Something coming back; *yes.*

"SF, P and P."

"What is that?"

"Santa Fe, Prescott and Phoenix Railroad. One team."

"When?"

"Six months ago."

"Where exactly did you send them?"

"Arizona Territory. Working the line west from Tucson. From Stockton, they come from Stockton, California. I don't remember anything else; I don't know their names but I could find out for you. Four men . . ."

The man's hand palmed Little Pete's head and rammed the soft center of his temple against the table edge. Little Pete slumped into a pile on the floor, unconscious.

Kanazuchi walked to the balcony, rapidly scaled a trellis up to the roof, and faded away. No one had seen him enter; no one saw him leave.

By the time Little Pete came to his senses and the uproar over the murders in his town house spread through Tangrenbu like a grass fire—the feet of one of his bodyguards had been severed and served as Little Pete's lunch *and he was forced to eat them,* according to more extravagant versions—Kanazuchi had already moved well beyond the San Francisco city limits.

Eerie silence belowdecks: The ship's engines had died along with the lights. The *Elbe* sat dead in the still water. The hold seemed as dark and inhospitable as the belly of a whale.

"Gott im Himmel—"

Doyle shushed him. They stood and strained to listen. . . .

Someone was moving down the passageway toward the bay forty feet below the water line where the five men stood beside the empty coffins.

Doyle took the crowbar from Captain Hoffner, grabbed the lantern from Innes, and closed its shutters, plunging them into darkness.

"Stand against the walls. Away from the door," he whispered to the others. "Not a word from anyone."

They waited and watched. A small flame flickered to life fifty feet down the passage; a match igniting. It bobbed toward them, died out, then another took its place and continued forward. Doyle tracked the progress of the shuffling footsteps, and as the advancing figure reached the hatch to the hold he stepped out and uncovered the lantern right in the face of the man, blinding him. The man cried out, dropped the match, and shielded his eyes.

"For crying out loud, what'd you have to go and do that for?"

"What are you doing here, Pinkus?" said Doyle.

Ira Pinkus bent over, trying to rub the dancing spots away from his field of vision, too disoriented to organize a lie.

"I was following you," said Pinkus.

"You've picked a very inopportune time—stand away from the door, Pinkus; someone might shoot you," said

Doyle, maneuvering the little man against a bulkhead and closing the hatch behind him.

"I was halfway down a flight of stairs when everything went black. . . ."

"And keep your voice down."

"Okay," whispered Pinkus. "Jesus, I can't see a thing: Everybody looks like a light bulb—so anyway, what gives with the skull and crossbones stuff, Mr. Conan Doyle—oh, hello, Innes, nice to see you again."

"Hello."

"What's your name, friend?"

"Lionel Stern."

"How are ya? Ira Pinkus. And this must be Captain Hoffner; very pleased to meet you, sir, been looking forward to it; very fine ship you have here—Ira Pinkus, *New York Herald*. . . ."

"Why is this man following you?" asked Hoffner of Doyle.

"I'm writing a series of articles about transatlantic steamship travel, Captain, and I would greatly appreciate an opportunity to interview you. . . ."

"Pinkus," said Doyle ominously.

"Yeah?"

"Be quiet or I'll be compelled to throttle you."

"Oh. Sure, okay."

The silence that followed was broken by a series of kicks and shuddering metallic groans from somewhere aft and above them in the ship.

"Emergency generator," said the engineer.

"Trying to restart the screws," said Doyle.

Hoffner nodded. They listened.

"But it's not working," said Innes.

"That generator was inspected and fully operational before we left Southampton," said Captain Hoffner.

"But then, I assume, so were the engines," said Doyle.

Hoffner stared at him. "You are not suggesting . . ."

"Sabotage?" piped in Pinkus, somewhat gleefully.

The word hung in the air. Pinkus looked back and forth from Doyle to Hoffner like a man watching table tennis.

"What is your standard procedure in such a situation?"

"The crew will distribute lamps and escort all passengers who are abovedecks back to quarters."

"How long will that take?"

"Twenty minutes, maybe half an hour."

"And all passengers are then expected to remain in their cabins."

"Yes, until power is restored."

"Captain . . . does anyone else know we're down here?" asked Doyle.

"My first officer," said Hoffner. "Whoever else is on the bridge."

"Are they after me?" asked Lionel Stern glumly.

On the verge of answering, from the corner of his eye Doyle caught Pinkus's puppy-dog eager expression. "Mr. Pinkus, would you please be good enough to go over there and stand in the corner for a while?"

"Really? What for?"

"This is a private conversation," said Doyle, lighting the way for him with the torch.

Pinkus shrugged congenially and followed Doyle's beam to the far corner, with an uneasy glance at the vacant coffins.

"You want me to face the wall?"

"If you would be so kind."

"Hey, no problem at all," said Pinkus. He gave a friendly, overfamiliar wave and turned away.

Doyle gestured for the others to form a tight ring around him; he held the torch under his jacket and the five faces pushed into the faint glow.

"These men have every intention of killing you, Mr. Stern," said Doyle, his voice a barely audible whisper. "If doing so will bring the Book of Zohar into their possession."

"Why don't we just give it to them?" said Hoffner.

"But we have no idea where it is. . . ."

"It is in my cabin," said Doyle.

Astonished exclamations.

"Gentlemen, please," pleaded Doyle, shining the light over to Pinkus just as he whipped his head back around to face the wall. "There will be time for explanations when we

are in different company, unless you'd prefer to read about
them on the front page of a newspaper."

"I could not agree more," said Hoffner.

"Since they seem perfectly aware that the Book of Zohar
was not in its crate in the hold, our stowaways presumed it
was still in your cabin, Mr. Stern, where they originally tried
to take it from Mr. Selig. Your cabin is where they plan to
strike again now under this cover of darkness."

"But why now? Out here, in the middle of the ocean?"
asked Stern.

"As opposed to a day away from shore, when their
chances of escaping undetected would be that much
greater?" said Doyle, about to elaborate.

"Because they've realized we know they're on board and
they can't afford to wait any longer. Obviously," said Innes.

Jolly good, Innes, thought Doyle.

"How could they know this?" asked Hoffner.

"A breach in security," said Doyle. "On the bridge."

"Impossible."

"Not one of your men, Captain. One of theirs."

"In uniform?"

"You may regrettably discover that one of your officers
has gone missing."

"*Mein Gott,* then we will scour the ship top to bottom, we
will find these men. . . ."

"We shall do even better than that, Captain, but we need
to act without delay, we have less than thirty minutes."
Doyle turned to the engineer. "Do you have any red phosphorus on board?"

The engineer turned to Hoffner, who translated the question.

"Yes, sir," answered the engineer.

"Good. Bring as much as you've got to us here at once."

The stout little engineer, whose incomplete command of
English had left him utterly perplexed by these develop-
ments, felt enormous relief at having such a straightforward
task to discharge. He saluted smartly and marched out of the
cargo bay.

"Captain, can you secure us some firearms?"

"Of course; they are kept under lock and key on the bridge—"

"Without alerting any of your officers?"

Hoffner tugged down on the edge of his tunic and screwed up his Teutonic pride to its fullest measure.

"I believe I can manage this much."

"What are we going to do, Arthur?" asked Innes.

"Set a trap," said Doyle.

"Really? Tremendous! Can I help?" asked Ira Pinkus.

Doyle turned the light on him; Pinkus had crept within five feet of them, and had been huddling there for God knows how long.

"As a matter of fact, you can," said Doyle.

Twenty minutes later. Velvety moonlight through the porthole and unearthly quiet inside Stern's cabin.

The first sound: a pick sliding smoothly into the keyhole. Scratching as it worked its way through the pins, each one freezing until with a barely audible click the lock yielded, the handle turned. The door opened slowly, a fraction of an inch at a time, until it met resistance from the reattached chain. Wire cutters moved through the gap and gripped the chain; a steady increase of pressure until the pincers sliced through the last link. A gloved hand caught the strands of the chain before they could fall back to scrape against the metal door and laid them to rest.

Now the door swung open just wide enough to admit the first blackclad figure; black from head to toe, crepe-soled shoes, a mask taut over its head. The figure took stock of the room, looked at the stationary form lying in the lower bunk, then held the door for a second identically dressed figure to enter. It moved slowly and purposefully to the edge of the bunk; a thin sliver of steel in its hand gleamed in the moonlight pouring through the porthole.

Now, thought Doyle.

As the figure in black reached for the blanket, a ghastly cry came from the corridor outside; a miserable moan of torment, rising in pitch and volume.

Easy, don't overdo it.

Both men turned to the door; a third identically dressed figure stuck its head in, beckoning them over. They glided outside and looked down the passageway at the strangest spectacle.

The incandescent outline of a ship's officer illuminated the far end of the dark corridor. A glowing, ethereal outline of a man, chains draping its tattered uniform, its eyes black holes recessed in the green-gray plane of its lamentable face. The disturbing specter moaned again, rattled its chains, raised its arms menacingly, and took a step toward the three men in black.

The figures balked, momentarily distracted.

Doyle threw off the blanket, sat up in the bunk, and leveled a shotgun at the three men in the doorway.

"Don't move," ordered Doyle.

At the sound of his voice, the door directly across the hallway flew open: Innes holding a pistol. . . .

One of the figures dove and rolled at Innes's knees, chopping him to the ground; his pistol discharged, the bullet pinged off the metal ceiling and died into the carpeted floor. By the time Doyle pulled the trigger, the other two figures in black had with incredible speed bolted down the passage in opposite directions; the shot ricocheted harmlessly off the bulkheads. Doyle raced to the doorway. One of the fleeing assassins ran into and leveled the "ghost" of the *Elbe*—Doyle saw its luminescent form go tumbling ass-over-teakettle—and disappeared around a corner. The second intruder was sprinting directly toward the hatchway where Captain Hoffner, Stern, and the engineer were laying in wait.

The third assailant jumped up out of the opposing doorway to follow the others; Innes reached out and grabbed hold of his ankle. The man turned and cracked his free foot down on Innes's left wrist; Innes cried out, releasing his grip just as Doyle raised the butt end of the rifle and clubbed the figure across the back of the head, slamming him face first hard into the far wall, but instead of collapsing the man spun out of the collision and mule-kicked Doyle in the midsection, propelling him back through the open doorway where he collided rudely with the unforgiving frame of the bunks.

As the man in black kicked, Innes swept a leg under him; the man went airborne and met the floor with a thud. Innes scrambled to his knees and landed a crushing punch to the man's head. Doyle rushed back into the hall, pinned the barrel of the rifle against the prostrate man's chest, and jacketed a live round into the chamber.

"Move and I'll shoot," said Doyle, wheezing to recapture his wind.

The figure lay still. Doyle gasped for air: thank God Innes was so handy with his fists. Cool under pressure, too. The Fusiliers had taught him well.

"Did we get him?" asked the ghost of the *Elbe*, standing cautiously ten feet away in the hall.

Startled, neither of the brothers could react quickly enough as in one move the figure in black produced a derringer from a sleeve, drew it directly to the side of his own head, and fired.

"Oh, my God. Oh, my God, is he dead?" said the ghost.

"Of course he's dead, Ira," said Innes, thoroughly annoyed. "He shot himself in the head."

"Well what in bejesus would a fella go and do a crazy thing like that for?" said Pinkus, leaning back against the wall, absentmindedly wiping the compound of phosphorus off his gloves.

"You're the reporter," said Doyle, equally irritated. "Why don't you ask him? Stay here, Innes. I'll be back."

Doyle moved quickly away down the corridor to their left.

"Jesus, Mary, and Joe-seppie, I was spooked something fierce, Innes, and I don't mind saying it. I think I even scared myself," said Pinkus, fanning himself with his luminescent hat. "Say, how'd I do? I do okay?"

"If all else fails, you could always find work haunting a house."

"Gee, that's terrific, thanks."

"Give me a hand. We should stow him out of the way before the tourists get wind of this."

"Sure, pal, whatever you say."

Pinkus reached down and Innes got a closer look; the clotted rivulets of phosphorescent sweat running off him made it look as if his face were melting. "Probably a good idea if we stow you out of sight as well."

Doyle found Lionel Stern and the engineer kneeling in the dark outside the hatch at the end of the corridor, attending to Captain Hoffner, who clutched a wounded arm.

"We heard the shots," said Hoffner. "*Mein Gott,* he was on us so quick I have had no time—"

"Like a shadow," said the engineer.

"He ran right through us," said Stern. "Everything happened so fast I couldn't even tell you which way he went."

"That's all right," said Doyle, bending down to examine the deck. "He'll show us himself."

He pointed to the walkway and the thin layer of phosphorus he'd laid down when they finished coating Pinkus. Doyle instructed Stern to stay with Hoffner, and along with the plucky little engineer, who clutched a huge monkey wrench in both hands, they followed the path of glowing footprints leading away from the phosphorus out into the void of the open deck.

The moon drifted behind an advancing cloud bank, and the darkness rendered the glow of the man's tracks even easier to read. Rolling heavily amidships with no power to steer into the heavy swells of the approaching storm, spray dousing her deserted decks, taut lines twanging like harp strings in the whistling wind, the *Elbe* felt less like a luxury liner and more like a steamship version of the doomed *Flying Dutchman.*

"Dis man," whispered the engineer, as they paused before cautiously rounding a corner. "He is like *der Teufel.*"

"The Devil," said Doyle. "Yes. But he is also just a man."

As Doyle bent to examine another footprint, he heard a faint, steady metallic tapping, then noticed the wrench, shaking in the engineer's hands and knocking against the rail.

"What's your name?"

"Dieter. Dieter Boch, sir."

"You're a good man to have around, Dieter."

"Tank you, sir."

They traced the steps up a flight of stairs to the rear deck,

and through the clabbering gloom ahead Doyle thought he
could make out the shape of a large man standing at the far
end near the stern rail. Doyle reached for his pistol but the
ship yawed severely as it dove down into the trough of a
wave. Both men staggered to hold their balance; when
Doyle looked up again, the figure at the rail was gone. He
questioned his companion; the engineer had seen nothing.
They pressed on. Lengthy gaps between their quarry's footprints indicated the man in black had continued to run; the
prints led right up to the edge of the top deck and ended
abruptly.

"*Er ist* going overboard?"

"So it appears," said Doyle.

"Into *dis wasser*?" asked Boch, looking out anxiously at
the towering crests of the waves. Like so many other seago-
ing men he lived in constant terror of the ocean. "Why
would dis man do such a thing?"

Why, indeed? thought Doyle: Why would two men take
their own lives rather than face capture?

For the theft of a book?

They moved the Gerona Zohar from a hidden compartment
in Doyle's steamer trunk to the safety of the ship's vault and
placed it under twenty-four-hour guard. His injured arm in a
sling, Captain Hoffner returned to the bridge, rallied his officers, and initiated a room-by-room search. As Doyle had
predicted, the ship's first lieutenant could not be accounted
for, although many swore they had seen him—a young,
handsome blond man—in uniform on the command deck
since the storm began.

Mechanics swarmed over the engine room, finally coax-
ing the emergency generator into operation; with running
lights on and one quarter power restored to the screws, the
Captain ruddered the *Elbe* into the teeth of the squall as it
closed its jaws around them. While the crew redoubled efforts to repair the primary generator, passengers remained
confined to cabins, rules of emergency in force, with strict
instruction to lock their doors; the storm and complications
posed by their loss of power were convincingly given as the

rationale for these impositions. No mention made of the assassins still presumed to be at large somewhere on board the troubled ship.

Guards posted outside the door, the corridor in either direction cordoned off-limits to passengers, Doyle, Innes, Stern, and Pinkus—with whom they were now saddled, more reluctant to let him out of their sight than to endure his company—huddled in Stern's cabin around a kerosene lamp and the body of the black-clad suicidal assailant.

Removing his mask revealed a man of about thirty with clipped, straight black hair and a brown, broad-browed face—Javanese, perhaps Filipino, thought Doyle. A small distinctive tattoo of abraded skin discolored the hollow of the man's left elbow: a broken circle, penetrated by three jagged lines. This design matched exactly the drawing on the piece of paper in Doyle's pocket, sketched from the scratchings on the wall near Selig's body. Upon examination, Doyle realized the mark was not a tattoo but a severe burn. Of the sort one would find on branded cattle.

The man's clothes were fashioned from plain black cotton. Six weapons concealed on his person: knives holstered up each sleeve and pant leg, the suicidally employed double-barreled derringer, and a thin length of wire around his waist—a deadly garrote. Scars crisscrossed his burled knuckles and callused palms, knife wounds; a seasoned warrior. The bruises Innes and Doyle wore from their brief engagement with him bore vivid testimony to the man's mastery of hand-to-hand combat. Conclusion: a cold, efficient killing machine. They had no compelling reason to believe his surviving accomplices would be any less deadly.

Doyle dropped a sheet over the corpse. All four men had to continually brace themselves against the bulkhead or bunks to fight the grinding up-and-down gyrations of the storm.

"You still haven't explained, Mr. Doyle," said Stern. "How did the Zohar end up in your cabin?"

"Along with the pills sewn into the lining of Mr. Selig's jacket, I found this key," said Doyle, holding it up for display. "Obviously not the key to your room or any passenger cabin, although it bears the identifying stamp of the *Elbe,* here. . . ." He pointed out a minute version of the ship's insignia.

"What's it for?" asked Pinkus impatiently.

"I applied the key to every lock I could find convenient to this room. There is a seldom-used storage closet behind the gymnasium—you'd never see it unless looking for it; its entrance is obscured every morning and night by stacks of lounge chairs and seat cushions. This key opened that door. Inside this shallow closet, I found a recessed panel in the wainscoting; a neglected and no longer serviceable fuse box. Mr. Selig moved the Zohar from its original hiding place here—a simple hole cut into his mattress, by the way; small wonder he was so reluctant to leave the room—to this other location yesterday evening, after the Captain refused your request to use the ship's safe, the conversation I overheard."

"I had no idea . . ." said Stern.

"No. He must have made the transfer while you were attempting to reach me before the séance last night, about an hour before the murder."

"And how did his killers manage that without laying a hand on him?" asked Innes.

Doyle produced two small packets of paper from his pocket and opened them for the others to see. "When we discovered Mr. Selig's body last night, I found a small clump of clay just inside the door. I removed this second identical sample this evening from inside one of the coffins in the hold; a good amount of it, over a pound, but only in one coffin."

"Okay, fine, Doc. So what's a little dirt got to do with the price of beer?" asked Pinkus, with all the impartial tact of a seasoned journalist.

"Mr. Selig was a more devoutly religious man than yourself; is that a fair statement to make, Mr. Stern?" asked Doyle.

"Yes."

"So am I correct in assuming as a practicing Jew he would have been conversant with aspects of Judaic history and mythology?"

"Absolutely: Rupert studied for many years."

"Would it also be fair to say Mr. Selig took what those studies might have given to him very close to heart; one might almost say as gospel?"

"Definitely—what are you driving at?"

Doyle lowered his voice and leaned in over the lantern, the light from below setting off his features in a dramatically sinister way. "Are you at all familiar, Mr. Stern, with the legend of the golem?"

"The golem? Yes, of course, I mean, in a passing way; as a boy my father told me the story many times."

"Golem? What's'zat?" said Pinkus, who still emitted a faint sickly greenish glow in spite of an hour's scrubbing with a stiff steel brush.

"The word *golem* derives from the Hebrew for fetus, or unformed life," said Doyle. "Said to be the name that Jehovah gave Adam when he breathed life into the figure he molded from the common clay of Eden."

"Jehovah?" asked Pinkus, popping his chewing gum. "You mean . . . jumpin' Jehovah?"

"Jehovah is the Hebrew name for God," said Stern, amazed at the depths of the man's blockheadedness.

"But the story of the golem that is more relevant to this discussion," said Doyle, turning to Stern, "begins in the Jewish ghetto of Prague in the late sixteenth century. A campaign of bloody pogroms was brought against the Jews of Prague, as there had been throughout Eastern Europe. But the attacks in Prague were particularly vicious and bloodthirsty. One of the elders of the temple was a scholar by the name of Rabbi Judah Low Ben Bezalel, a gentle, almost saintly figure. Rabbi Low desperately sought a way to protect the Jews in the ghetto from this deadly persecution. He spent years searching through the old temple libraries looking for an answer. One day, so the story goes, buried deep in the cellar of the Great Synagogue he found an ancient book of great and mystical power. . . ."

"Not the Book of Zohar, by any chance," said Innes.

"The name of this book is not specified, but a copy of the Zohar would surely have been in the synagogues of Prague;

a man of Rabbi Low's learning would certainly have known of it. In any case, as he read through this book, the Rabbi allegedly stumbled across a passage that contained a secret coded formula that with his incredible scholarship he was able to decipher. . . .

"The entire Zohar, by the way, is supposedly written like that, every sentence hiding some metaphysical mystery," added Stern.

"So like what are we talking about here, some kind a' turning lead into money-type deal?" asked a wide-eyed Pinkus.

"This passage revealed to Rabbi Low nothing less than the formula for bringing human life out of base earth that Jehovah used for the creation of Adam, the first man."

"You gotta be kiddin' me," said Pinkus.

"It's . . . a *legend,* Pinkus," said Doyle.

"How did he allegedly do it?" asked Innes.

"Using pure water and clay from a pit dug in sanctified ground, he crafted the limbs, head, and torso of a giant figure crudely resembling a man. Then, according to the precepts of the ritual, he connected the pieces together and wrote a sacred Hebrew word on a slip of paper which he inserted under the figure's tongue. . . ."

"What word was that?" said Innes.

"You'd have to ask Lionel's father about that, I'm afraid," said Doyle.

"So did the golem come to life?" asked Pinkus anxiously.

"The next thing he knew, the golem, as he called it, sat up and began to move. When he spoke to it, the golem did exactly as he ordered; Rabbi Low realized he had created a servant that would follow his instructions to the letter. Eight feet tall, powerful arms and legs; small rocks in place of eyes, a crudely fashioned mouth. He used the golem for household labor until his confidence about its obedience grew; then Rabbi Low began to send the golem out into the night, frightening away anyone who might come into the ghetto to harm the Jews.

"Every evening he would insert the paper, giving life to the monster. When its work was done at dawn, the golem returned home, the Rabbi removed the paper, and the golem lay like a statue in the Rabbi's basement. And people were so terrified of this horrible being roaming through the night that violence against the Jews in the ghetto came to a halt."

"Not a bad yarn," said Pinkus, holding on to the bunk beds for dear life. "Kind a' like that whachamacallit, that Frankenstein guy."

"It's been suggested that Mary Shelley derived a large part of her famous work from the legend of the golem," said Doyle.

"No kiddin'," said Pinkus, with not the slightest idea who Mary Shelley might be.

"There's more," said Doyle. "One Sabbath morning, when Jews make their religious observances and must stop all manual labor until sunset, Rabbi Low forgot to remove the slip of paper from the golem's mouth."

"Uh-oh," said Pinkus. "I smell trouble."

"You would be right, Mr. Pinkus. With Rabbi Low's control over the golem lost, the monster went on a terrible rampage. Block after block of shops and houses broken and ruined; many innocent people killed, most of them Jews, crushed and trampled by its mindless fury. Nothing could stop the golem until Rabbi Low finally tracked it down and removed the paper, saving the rest of the ghetto from certain destruction."

The others were silent, hanging on every word.

"The myth of the golem has always seemed to me to be a perfect metaphor for the apocalyptic power of unchecked human rage, as well as a wonderful parable about the life-affirming compassion of the Judaic tradition," said Doyle.

Innes and Pinkus glanced sideways at each other like mystified schoolboys, both drawing a total blank.

"Well, jeez," said Pinkus.

"So what happened to the golem?" asked Innes.

"The body of the golem was carried by Low and his friends to the cellar of the Great Synagogue of Prague, where it supposedly lies buried to this day, waiting for its life to be restored."

Struggling to keep his balance as the battered ship took a

particularly nasty twist, Doyle took out another piece of paper. "Gentlemen, I have here the ship's copy of the agent's manifest for those five coffins in the hold. Would you like to hazard a guess as to their port of origin?"

"Not Prague," said Innes.

"Exactly," said Doyle.

"You gotta be joshin' me," said Pinkus.

"Please, Mr. Doyle. You're not seriously suggesting that the golem of the ghetto of Prague was in one of those boxes," said Stern.

"Or that an eight-foot-tall clay monster is still roaming around somewhere on board the ship," said Innes.

"I suggest this," said Doyle. "If you're trying to obtain something from a man on board a ship in the middle of the ocean and you wish to attract no undue attention to yourself—"

"Eight-foot-tall clay monsters are a choice idea," said Pinkus smartly.

"—and you're aware that the man from whom you wish to obtain this object has a history of heart trouble and that he's aware of a legend about an eight-foot-tall clay monster that may be connected to the object you're attempting to steal and that you need to kill this man in order to get it but circumstances demand that his death not appear to be an obvious murder . . ."

"You scare him to death," said Innes, the pieces falling into place.

"Smuggle four men and one coffin full of clay covering an armature of some kind on board. Label the coffins as coming originally from Prague, to support the superstition. Remember: The passenger who heard the 'ghost' shriek also saw a large gray figure roaming in the hold and these second-class cabins are only two flights of stairs away; when the knock came at Mr. Selig's door last night and he opened it as far as the chain would allow . . . I believe it was the sight of this 'golem'—being held by these two men—standing outside that precipitated his fatal heart attack."

"How about that?" said Pinkus.

"If that was the case, then what prevented them from

going right in and stealing the book?" asked Stern. "The chain wasn't even broken."

"Our sudden arrival interrupted them," said Doyle. "And what's the harm? They waited for another opportunity: Who was going to suspect he died of anything other than what it appeared to be?

"Except that Mr. Selig bravely marshaled his resources in the last moments of his life: Grabbing a handful of the clay from the monster—some still remained under his fingernails—he used it to trace an outline on the wall of this tattoo he had seen on one of his assailant's forearms."

"How 'bout that?" said Pinkus, falling back again on what he always said whenever he had nothing to say.

"I guess it all makes a kind of sense, except how could they know Rupert had a heart condition?" said Stern. "Even I wasn't aware of that."

"Mr. Selig lived in London; presumably they obtained the information from his doctor's office," said Doyle. "He told you he was being followed while you were there; how difficult could it have been?"

Stern weighed the possibilities; after the recent events he'd been through, he was hard pressed to dismiss the idea out of hand.

"Still seems like an awful lot of bother to go to just to get an old book," said Innes, slightly petulant that his brother had failed to confide any of these conclusions to him earlier and in private.

"As Mr. Stern has told us, the Zohar is priceless and whoever hired these men is obviously willing to go to any lengths to obtain it."

"I'd always thought it was nothing more than a collection of superstitious nonsense," said Stern. "What if the Zohar actually does contain some secret formula about the creation of life. Or its meaning . . ."

"Then priceless isn't good enough by half," said Doyle.

"Yeah and besides," said Pinkus, eyes squinting, snapping his gum violently while he wrestled a tremendously obscure inner line of reasoning to the ground, "if they ain't even stole the book yet, how'd they get this monster to walk around by itself anyway?"

Try as they might, to a note sounded from such a bottomless depth of stupidity, no one could respond.

Doyle left Innes and Pinkus to oversee removal of the assassin's body, delivered Stern into the care of officers and trudged back to his cabin alone by the feeble light of an oil lamp. Gripping hard to the rails as he fought the pitch and roll of the decks, Doyle realized a mid-Atlantic storm by itself would be hardship enough for most, although he had lived through many more perilous nights aboard smaller ships on the open sea. He was more deeply troubled by the lingering uncertainties he hadn't shared with the others of his company, details that no one else had lit upon and pursued.

If one of those coffins had been carrying a large clay figure, that left room in the others for four men to steal aboard. One of those dead by his own hand; a second gone overboard; the third member of the attack team had escaped past Pinkus in the second-class passageway. The fourth had most probably killed and then assumed the place of that young lieutenant on the bridge. That left two of them still on the *Elbe*, unaccounted for. And their leader, the man who had called himself Father Devine.

Five men. Four coffins.

The question: How did this Father Devine get on board the ship? He wasn't listed as a passenger, and the ship's staff could find no trace of him. Doyle had been close to him that first day on deck and again at the séance; his age and girth didn't make him for one of the men in black, and that unfortunate lieutenant had been only twenty-three years old; Devine could never have replaced him on the bridge convincingly. And Doyle had encountered the man within an hour of their departure from port, not nearly enough time to have removed himself from a coffin in the hold; the hammering sounds from belowdecks hadn't been heard until that evening.

Think, Doyle: A priest mingling among a busy ship full of

departing passengers would raise no eyebrows; suppose he drifted up the gangway amid a group of people as if to see them off, then simply removed himself from view until they'd sailed from harbor. Yes; that tracked.

There was also the matter of the design engraved on the dead man's arm. Doyle felt almost certain it had some hidden meaning, but try as he might he couldn't crack it. . . .

Let the unconscious mind work on this, he counseled himself. Effort won't help; the answer may bubble up to the surface when I least expect it.

As the ship climbed up and down the canyons of the waves, Doyle struggled to unlock and open his cabin door. Darkness inside; the door flapped back and forth with the rocking.

Someone inside.

Doyle slowly drew the pistol from his belt.

Light from the lantern penetrated the room: A knife pierced the floor near the bed, pinning down a note written in large red block letters.

"NEXT TIME WE'LL KILL YOU."

"Close the door," said a voice.

Father Devine stood motionless in the corner of the room, arms folded, obscured in the crease of a shadow. The ship rolled to starboard and seams in the walls groaned with the strain. Doyle closed the door, cocked the hammer of the pistol, covered Devine, and lifted the lantern higher.

A body lay twisted grotesquely at the foot of the bunk; a figure in black, still wearing a mask. One of the assassins. Strangled with his own garrote. Three men killed; only one of them left alive.

"What do you want?" asked Doyle.

Father Devine took one step forward, did not shield his eyes from the light, and Doyle saw him clearly, head on, for the first time since they'd boarded the ship; saw the jagged ivory scar along his jawline, saw the light in the man's eyes he hadn't taken in before, and it pummeled the breath from his lungs.

The priest smiled thinly, looking down at the body on the floor.

"This one was waiting for you," he said, all the Irish in him gone. "He died before I could learn anything useful."

It wasn't possible.

Good Christ. Good Christ, yes it was. It was him.

Jack Sparks.

book two

NEW YORK

chapter five

SEPTEMBER 23, 1894

*D*ISCRETION IS REQUIRED IN DESCRIBING THE EVENTS OF THE *last few hours. A request has been made to me for assistance. Having served the interests of the Crown on more than one previous occasion, I have remained ever willing to lend my services to that royal office again in whichever way circumstances describe. Suffice it to say that should the Queen herself have appeared in my cabin to make this appeal, it would have carried no greater influence upon my sympathies.*

The facts are these: A book has been stolen. A book of enormous significance to the Church of England and consequently the throne. The Latin Vulgate Bible, the oldest biblical manuscript in the Anglican Church. Vanished from the Bodleian Library at Oxford six weeks ago. Public announcement has been withheld; the Vulgate was kept in a vault, not on display—the only persons likely to miss it to this point are scholars. It is hoped the manuscript can be recovered before such an announcement becomes necessary; however, as yet no requests for the ransom of its return have been received. As more time passes, it seems increasingly unlikely that a ransom is the thieves' objective. A secret investigation by a friend of mine on behalf of the Crown has been under way since the crime occurred and it has led him to this same ship making its crossing to America.

That this incident is central to the difficulties we have experienced since boarding the Elbe is unmistakable. I have set down elsewhere the events of the past few days surrounding Lionel Stern, the attempted robbery of the Book of

Zohar, and the murder of Mr. Rupert Selig. Three of the men responsible for those crimes are now themselves dead; a fourth man has either flung himself overboard, as did another of his accomplices, or is still in hiding somewhere on board; an exhaustive search is even now under way. The sabotage these men brought against the ship's engines has been discovered—an explosive charge detonated in the electrical generators—and thanks to the due diligence of the engineering crew its damage already repaired. We will arrive in New York tomorrow only hours later than originally scheduled and that due as much to the rough weather we have passed through as to the sinister efforts of these villains.

The man I mistakenly took for their ringleader was, as I suspected, posing as a Catholic priest—this concluded from observing an accumulation of small, troubling details: odd boots, rosary beads hanging off the wrong pocket, a ring bearing a Masonic design—but neither is he a criminal. He is, in fact, a man previously well known to me, whose credentials as an agent of the Crown are, or at least once were, beyond reproach.

We have spoken only briefly, and that has been taken up with the urgencies of our situation: His unexpected appearance foiled a potentially deadly attack against me by turning the assassin's own weapon against him. No opportunity for us to discuss the events of the ten years passed since we last saw one another has presented itself; he seemed reluctant to part with any details during the short time spent together; we have agreed to find time for that discussion once the ship has made port. In the interim, I have confided in no one, not even Innes, about his true identity.

The rest of our passengers remain uniformly unaware of the difficulties we have been through on the Elbe, due in part to the storm which confined them to quarters during the critical hours, and not a little to our effective muzzling of the American newshound Pinkus, who remains at this hour under something approaching house arrest. My friend is even now visiting privately with Pinkus to ensure his silence on these matters after we reach New York. A daunting task

*given Pinkus's propensity for blab, but if any man could per-
suade Pinkus to, as they say, keep his trap shut, my money is
on JS.*

*I am saddened to report that my friend is dreadfully al-
tered since I last saw him. In truth, even beyond the effec-
tiveness of his disguise, he is hardly recognizable. Whatever
damage he has endured, whatever dark corners of the
human spirit he has visited, I am afraid the effect has not
been at all to the good.*

*In this instance, I fervently hope the keenness of my ob-
servations, a habit of mind which he helped so much to in-
still in me, is entirely wrong.*

A dense, multispired skyline poked through the morning
mist and announced to the brothers Doyle their first glimpse
of New York; from this vantage point, the city threatened to
burst the seams of the slender island on which it rested. The
Elbe's passengers clustered around them on the upper deck,
marveling at the wonders of this muscular continent.

What prodigious energy, thought Doyle. What enormous
concentration of ambition. And what proud testimony it offered to the potential of man's creative vitality. He wiped a
tear from his eye, stirred to his soul by the magnificence of
imagination that could result in such a city.

Completely unaware of the depth of his brother's feeling,
and loathe to appear the bumpkin, as they sailed by her Innes
feigned indifference to the epic dimensions of the Statue of
Liberty, although his heart secretly raced with hormonal agitation at the irrational image she inspired; an entire nation
populated by towering, voluptuous women wearing nothing
but diaphanous, loosely draped robes.

When Pinkus finally appeared on deck in the company of
Father Devine, Innes thought he looked remarkably sub-
dued, shaken really, his bouncy canine readiness displaced
by a pale, apologetic rue.

"What's the matter with old Pinkus?" he wondered.

"I don't know," said Doyle. "Perhaps he found confession
to be bad for the soul."

A stately turn up the Hudson brought the *Elbe* into the

company of tugboats flocking to nose her gently into moor-
ing at the West Side docks. Captain Hoffner invited Doyle
onto the bridge for the final approach, taking him aside to
offer formal thanks and to let him know their search of the
ship had failed to uncover a fourth assassin. The five coffins
had been confiscated and extra security arranged at the customhouse to ensure that this last man, if he was still on
board, did not slip off in the guise of an officer or passenger.
Doyle once again politely turned away the Captain's inquiries about Father Devine, saying only that in the heat of
the moment his original negative assessment of the man had
turned out to be unfounded. With that they shook hands, respected equals, and exchanged their good-byes.

As Doyle and Innes cleared customs and stepped through
the doors into America, a brass marching band stationed in
the foyer ripped into "For He's a Jolly Good Fellow." Fes-
tively decked out in red, white, and blue bunting, the entrance hall sported a field of hand-painted signs welcoming
the famous author—many of which seemed to have been
crafted with the impression that Doyle was, himself, Sherlock Holmes—dancing above the heads of an alarmingly
large and demonstrative crowd.

*Good Christ; they're chanting my name as if I were a
football team.* The epidemic of overfamiliarity in individual
Americans had never troubled Doyle before, but encountering it at this mob level gave it the appearance of a prelude to
human sacrifice.

Arrayed in front of police department sawhorses that re-
strained the masses was a constellation of greater and lesser
lights from the firmament of Manhattan celebrity—luminar-
ies from the publishing and newspaper worlds, dashing
matinee idols, plump haberdashers, slick-haired restaura-
teurs, and a squadron of obscure city officials, interwoven
throughout by a comely brood of decorative chorus girls; apparently Pinkus had not overstated this one critical aspect of
his story, realized Innes ecstatically.

A gigantic, loose-limbed mountain of a man in riding
boots, jodhpurs, a canary-yellow cutaway jacket, and a
beaver hat perched on a shaggy head half the size of a buf-

falo's broke out of the pack and clapped a smothering bear hug onto Doyle before he could defend himself.

"Bless my soul! Bless my soul!" bellowed the man in a deep, creamy Virginia accent.

I must know this man, thought Doyle, thoroughly panicked. Considering the way he's greeting me, we must be first cousins at the least.

The giant stepped back and shouted into Doyle's face, "Proud, sir! It does my heart proud to see you here!"

Doyle searched desperately for some clue to his identity—surely he would have remembered someone this size. Over the giant's shoulder, he caught a glimpse of Innes, who had decided his dress-blue Royal Fusiliers uniform the only appropriate outfit for their arrival, being sucked into a cloud of perfume, feminine ruffles, and gargantuan floral hats.

"Didn't I promise you a fine how-do-you-do in New York? Did we not do it up right for you?" said the giant, his smile exposing a piano's worth of unnaturally gleaming white teeth.

"I'm afraid you have the advantage of me, sir," said Doyle, uneasily eyeing the battalion of celebrities bearing sharply down on them.

"Why it's Pepperman, Mr. Conan Doyle," said the man, doffing his hat gallantly. "Major Rolando Pepperman. Impresario of your literary tour; at your service."

"Major Pepperman, of course, do forgive me. . . ."

"No, not at all. It is I who have failed you, sir, by not providing in my cables a more detailed description of my person."

His startling blue eyes sparkled, the muscles bulging his jacket crackled with excess energy—everything about the man seemed built to an incredibly overscaled set of plans: America's exuberant essence distilled down into one gigantic prototype.

Pepperman shot an arm around Doyle's shoulder and turned him to face the crowd: "I give you Mr. Arthur Conan Doyle, the creator of the great Sherlock Holmes! Welcome to New York!"

Pepperman thrust his hat up into the air; the crowd shifted

into an even higher gear of frenzy as the band dueled them for control of the audible threshold. A battery of photographers' flash powder exploded in Doyle's wide-open eyes, leaving black spots dancing in place of the faces of the New York elite as they pressed in around him.

Doyle shook fifty hands and received as many business cards; the cacophony swallowed their bearers' shouted messages but Doyle retained the impression that every one of these somebodies wanted him to either eat at their restaurant, appear in their magazine, attend their latest theatrical triumph, or reside at their deluxe hotel. The disquieting phrase "in exchange for a commercial endorsement" often followed hard on the heels of these flattering offers.

The only desire in the crowd that remained unclear to Doyle was exactly what the spectacular show girls wanted from him, although Innes, the axis of a cluster of them orbiting nearby, interpreted their giggling avoidances of his overtures as a solid basis for indulging his eager repertoire of wishful thinking.

Pressed into Doyle's possession by a hierarchy of politicians were a scroll proclaiming an official welcome and a hefty be-ribboned brass object he guessed must represent a key to the city, but which seemed to have greater utility as a weapon. Before any further business could be conducted, or Doyle was prompted to beat back the hordes with his key, Pepperman led his author past the sawhorses to the street through the solid block of humanity and a waiting fleet of carriages.

In the event he would be called upon to deliver an impromptu response—he had been warned Americans loved nothing so much as giving and receiving speeches—Doyle tried to assemble a string of suitable thoughts to express to these people, but as he climbed up beside Pepperman on the running board of their carriage, the rank and file demonstrated no visible interest in anything other than continuing to scream their lungs out in his general direction. Doyle waved to them, then waved some more, then finally followed Pepperman's earlier example and thrust his hat into the air, apparently a signal peculiar to American audiences to behave as if they had entirely lost their minds.

Scanning the back of the crowd as the hysteria played out, Doyle spotted a solemn Lionel Stern leaving the customhouse doors. A plain coffin carrying the body of Rupert Selig was being loaded into a nearby hearse. Supervising the effort, still in priest's cassock, stood Jack Sparks.

Right, then, thought Doyle, as his carriage drove away; no reason to fret over Stern's safety for the moment; if this skirmish turns out to be typical of the treatment I can expect from the average American crowd, it's my own skin I need to worry about.

When the two dozen members of the New York Police Department left the *Elbe* later that day after their exhaustive search of the ship for the last fugitive came up empty-handed, no one took undue notice of a tall, blond, good-looking officer in their midst, badge number 473. No one remembered speaking to him afterward, and most of them didn't even realize badge 473 was missing until three hours after they arrived back at the precinct house.

Three more days would pass before they found the naked body of the badge's original owner, a patrolman named O'Keefe, shoved into a burlap bag in the meat locker of the *Elbe*'s kitchen.

DENVER, COLORADO

Who is that odd-looking old man? wondered Eileen. What a sight: funny round hat, floor-length fur-trimmed black coat, a ribbon around his waist, the strange formal cut of his collar and tie. Thin as a darning needle, hardly strength enough to lift that suitcase. But what a sweet smile he's got, talking to those Negro porters, lifting his hat to thank them. They've pointed him over this way; he must have been asking directions. Can't be easy to travel at his age, poor thing; your heart goes out to him. He looks so vulnerable and out of place, everybody staring at him. Doesn't seem to mind the attention, though. Doesn't even seem to be aware of it actually. He looks like someone . . . who is it? Someone really familiar. God, that's it: Abraham Lincoln, although the beard's much longer, and his hair's gone to gray. But he has the eyes, those same sad puppy-dog eyes.

"Will wonders never cease?" said Bendigo Rymer, giving her a nudge and a big nod in the direction of the approaching man. "A Hebrew in the middle of the Denver train station."

"He looks nice," said Eileen, as she finished rolling a cigarette and struck a match off the bottom of the hard wooden bench. "He looks like Abraham Lincoln."

"By my stars," said Rymer. "He does at that. Imagine: Lincoln as Shylock. What a monumental miscasting."

The man reached the section where the Penultimate Players were stretched out with their luggage, set down his suitcase with a sigh, and pulled out a long white handkerchief to mop the sweat from his forehead. The rest of the Players, those few who weren't doing penance for their excesses of the previous evening, lay on their benches and stared at this exotic creature with the idle curiosity of jaded sophisticates. The man looked around, absorbed their diffident attention, and smiled pleasantly.

Tired, yes, but in good humor. A generous face, thought Eileen, as she smiled back at him.

"There is a rumor going around," said the man, gasping to catch his breath, "that this could be the area to catch the train for Phoenix, Arizona."

"Indeed, sir, you are well informed," said Rymer. "We are bound there ourselves, a poor company of players, but the best actors in the West, either for tragedy, comedy, history, pastoral, pastoral-comical, historical-pastoral, tragical-historical, tragical-comical-historical-pastoral, scene individable or poem unlimited."

"Laying it on a bit thick," said Eileen sideways to him as she smiled.

"To hear the words of the great Shakespeare spoken in such an unexpected place, and with such obvious skill, is not only a pleasure to the ears but a comfort to the mind," said the man.

Rymer grinned like an idiot and blushed beet-red; compliments of any sort completely leveled him. You half expected him to roll over so the man could scratch his belly.

"Why don't you sit down, mister?" said Eileen.

"Most kind, thank you," said the man, settling onto a bench directly across from her.

"My name is Bendigo Rymer, sir, and you are most welcome to join our assembly. We are the Penultimate Players, sir; having just completed, if I do say so, a more than modestly successful engagement in this thriving metropolis, you do find us en route to the city of Phoenix, carrying culture to the desert like water to the gardens of Babylon."

"That's nice," said the man. He smiled at Eileen, a twinkle in his eye just short of a wink.

There's wisdom in this man's eyes, thought Eileen, and his actions; instant recognition of what an irredeemable jackass Rymer is and kindness enough not to take offense. She hadn't seen a face this full of honest-to-goodness humanity since she left New York.

"And what clarion call beckons you, sir, to the land of the sagebrush and the redskin?"

"Nothing nearly so glamorous as you people, I'm afraid," said the man. "Just a little business."

"Ah, *business*," said Rymer, as if it were a secret password. "The wheels of commerce, ever turning."

"My name's Eileen; what's yours?"

"Jacob. Jacob Stern."

"Are you a diamond merchant, Mr. Stern, or perhaps a dealer in furs or exotic metals?" asked Rymer, falling back on his exhaustive inventory of cultural stereotypes.

"I'm a rabbi."

"I should have known it; a man of the cloth, come to shepherd his flock. You have that look about you; that self-forgetful devotion to the life of the spirit. Splendid. I wasn't even aware that there was an Israelite temple in Phoenix."

"Neither was I," said Stern.

"Imagine that, Eileen; one of the Twelve Lost Tribes returning to the desert," said Rymer. "History is being written all around us, if only our eyes were not too poor to see."

Eileen cringed; she was already formulating an excuse for abandoning Rymer in order to sit next to Stern on the train.

If my dreams are any indication, Mr. Bendigo Rymer, you have blundered a lot closer to the truth than you could imagine, thought Jacob. He shifted his weight, trying to find comfort for his bony hips on the bare wooden bench. His back pulsed with pain, his knees ached as if they'd been hammered by a blacksmith, his lungs burned, his ears rang, he was hungry, thirsty, and he needed to empty his bladder.

I'm a wreck. Thanks to God: What an invaluable reminder that we are spiritual beings and if we dwell on the physical, our only reward will be pain. On the other hand, if a hot bath and a bowl of soup were to materialize before me now, I wouldn't complain.

Maybe he could sleep on the train. The same dream had come into his mind with greater intensity the farther south he traveled, additional details of its peculiar landscape coming clearer with each immersion. Throughout the trip from Chicago, Jacob had physically willed himself to stay asleep—not just for the rest, although he felt no less exhausted for it—but so that more of the dream might be revealed.

Consistently now, he experienced while sleeping the unsettling sensation of full waking consciousness, completely aware that he was moving through a dream. Although unable to control the dream's flow of events, he had learned to shift the focus of his attention and see more of what was happening around him. The explicit content of the dream itself was not on the face of it so frightening, but there crept in around its borders an aura of menace and a potency of light and sound and color so overwhelming that each night he had woken out of it in a pool of sweat, heart thundering, eyes raw and stinging from involuntary tears.

The Lost Tribe.

In the dream, he came upon a tribe of people—in the logic of the dream that seemed to be their essence—gathering in an open plaza, all in white, worshiping something mounted on an elevated platform that gave off a tremendous amount of light . . . but each time the object of their veneration remained frustratingly just out of his sight.

Other now familiar images:

An immense black tower casting shadows over waves of white sand. An underground chamber, a crypt or temple carved out of rock. Five other people, faces and forms obscured. An ancient leather-bound book lying in a silver casket. The book in Hebrew. Reaching toward its pristine pages, a hand: talons, scales.

The phrase in his head.

We are Six.

For now that was all he had to go on.

Jacob had no plan. His body felt frail, his skin hardly durable enough to hold every ailing part of him together, but his mind remained clear and his strength of purpose had grown more resolute with every passing mile. Why Phoenix? What was guiding him in that direction? Pure instinct: The dream took place in a desert so he kept moving toward the biggest one anyone seemed to know about—western Arizona, they told him—and he would continue on until he came across something that conformed to his vision. Then . . . who knew? Undoubtedly something else would happen. Or perhaps not. Maybe he would have a nice vacation and the desert air would do wonders for his lungs.

" . . . we played an entire week in Minneapolis, in front of packed houses, every night; they appreciate fine theater in that town, a hearty Scandinavian people, used to sitting for long periods of time—it's the winters, you see, the long winters pacify 'em—that has been my experience many times over, a most patient and receptive audience. . . ."

With Rymer lost in his self-absorbed monologue, Jacob was able to rest and feel his heart settle into rhythm again. He was forced to admit that, for a man in such miserable condition, he felt surprisingly good. After fifty years cooped up with his books, to travel around in such a spontaneous, unrestricted way felt like a revelation; eating sandwiches, watching the spectacular American countryside roll by outside the windows of the train. How exhilarating! Fields and rivers, evergreen forests, the sunset-red Rocky Mountains in the high distance; he'd never been near such exquisite natural beauty before. The world seemed so huge, expansive, and made all his attempts to philosophically encompass it seem laughingly inadequate. A sense of humiliating foolishness about his journey came over him, but he had regularly suffered the same feelings while standing on a street corner or walking to the butcher. Generalized shame is an inescapable part of the human condition, he reminded himself. May as well keep moving forward.

And if the whole mishmash turned out to be born from some crazy defect in his mind, with no horrific calamity awaiting him at the end of the trail, why then, that qualified as good news, didn't it? This spur of the moment train trip to the Wild West would simply pass into the mythology of his circle of friends as the most celebrated example of Jacob Stern's already well-certified eccentricity.

He was certain of only this: Within the hour, the conductor would whistle them onto the train to Phoenix. The actor would continue to talk about himself, unprovoked, until their train arrived or the world ended, whichever came first. And to pass the time until then in the company of such a beautiful woman as this one across from him was not such a terrible fate.

Maybe she would sit next to him. He could think of worse things.

"Deerstalker hats have become all the rage."

"You don't say."

"I'm told there's even been a run on magnifying glasses and meerschaum pipes."

"Honestly? Well, I never."

"I attended a costume party at the Vanderbilt mansion some few weeks ago and I would hazard to say that no less than every third man there came dressed as Mr. Sherlock Holmes," said Major Pepperman, sipping the hotel's complimentary champagne and idly tinkling on the grand piano that sat before the picture window looking down on Fifth

Avenue, its lights twinkling to life as night settled slowly over the city.

"How extraordinary," said Doyle.

How mind-numbingly terrifying, he thought.

Seated snugly in the sitting room of his suite at the Waldorf Hotel—a room considerably larger than every entire flat he had ever lived in until recently—Doyle picked grapes from a courtesy fruit sculpture the size of Rodin's *Balzac* while paging through a stack of the daily tabloids; in all but one of the rags his arrival had rated front-page news. But no stories in the *Herald* under the byline of Ira Pinkus, or in any of the other papers under his various noms de plume, and nothing within the existing write-ups referred remotely to any nefarious events on board the *Elbe*. Whatever pressures Jack had applied to Pinkus had silenced his bark, realized Doyle, allowing himself a private sigh of relief.

"Perhaps that strange fellow we met in the lobby had been at your party as well," said Doyle.

A frumpy pear-shaped man in full Holmes regalia and two equally suspect accomplices had staked out the Waldorf entrance, jumping into Doyle's path as they arrived: "Conan Doyle, we presume?" Then, with stone-faced ceremony, they handed him an engraved plaque—COMMEMORATING MR. ARTHUR CONAN DOYLE'S FIRST AMERICAN VISIT, COURTESY OF THE OFFICIAL NEW YORK CHAPTER OF THE BAKER STREET IRREGULARS—an organization Doyle had never heard of, which according to Pepperman had spontaneously sprouted out of Sherlock mania like a wild toadstool.

This Holmes impersonator then insisted on delivering a rambling, poorly memorized soliloquy in the most wretched simulation of an English accent Doyle could remember hearing, presumably, although it was difficult to tell, as the character of Holmes paying tribute to his creator. This paralyzing assault went on for nearly five minutes, during which time the smile pasted on Doyle's face began to cramp painfully. In the awkward aftermath, it took all Doyle and Pepperman could do to dissuade the sorry trio from following them into the elevator.

An awful thought struck Doyle: What if Jack were to materialize in the middle of such a scene?

"So . . . tell me, is he really dead?"

"Who?"

"Why, Mr. Sherlock Holmes."

"Oh, good God, man, he fell a thousand feet into a waterfall."

"There's one school of thought thinks he might have found some way to survive."

"I can't believe people are honestly walking around thinking about such things."

"As I tried to communicate to you in my cables, Mr. Doyle, you have no idea the powerful impression your stories have made on readers over here," said Pepperman. "A continuing series of mysteries featuring the same characters is just so plumb bob audacious, it's a plain wonder no one ever dreamt it up before. Honestly, sir, I've never seen the like; I used to promote a traveling circus so I've got a sense of the way things catch on, the common touch, how folks want to spend their hard-earned buck. I don't believe you can as yet fully appreciate what Sherlock means to these people."

Doyle smiled absently, feeling it would be impolite to ask but hoping Pepperman would leave soon so he could unpack. He reached for and opened another package off the Matterhorn of ornately wrapped gifts that they'd found piled inside the suite.

A lurid red satin pillow needlepointed with the inscription THOUGH HE MIGHT BE MORE HUMBLE, THERE IS NO POLICE LIKE HOLMES.

"I'm beginning to get a grasp of it," said Doyle, heart sinking as he realized he was now obliged to favor each gift-giver with a reply as etiquette required.

With his obsessive devotion to order, he could already visualize the assembling of the cards and addresses, the infinite tedium of personalizing each and every thank-you—good Christ, it could take weeks. This trip was supposed to be a break from all that, a lark, an excursion. If Larry was along, they might have managed it, but Innes would only make royal hash of a job this logistically complex. And now that he had caught the scent of that herd of dancing girls, the boy would be absolutely unfit for duty. Where had he gotten himself off to now, for example? Doyle hadn't seen him since they checked into the—

"I don't recall if I mentioned it to you, but Grover Cleveland has on more than one occasion stayed in this very same suite," said Pepperman.

"Grover who?"

"Grover Cleveland. The President."

"Of? Oh, the president of your *country*."

"Yes, sir. Right here in the Presidential Suite. On more than one occasion."

All three-hundred-plus pounds of him—oh dear, thought Doyle, perhaps I'd better check to see if the bed's broken. He caught a glimpse of the eager-beaver expression on Pepperman's face and chided himself: Here I am prattling on about my petty ordeals, wondering why the man won't leave, and the poor fellow's only waiting to hear how terribly pleased I am at all the fuss he's made.

"You know, Major, I am so truly grateful beyond my ability to express to you for all the effort you've made on my behalf," said Doyle.

"Really?" Pepperman's face lit up like a full moon.

"I can't tell you how much I appreciate everything you've done; I couldn't be more certain that our tour will be the greatest success for us both, financially, artistically, and in every other way imaginable."

"Why I'm most pleased to hear you say so, sir," said Pepperman, rising and shaking his hand, flashing his blinding teeth again. "Most pleased. Now I should leave you to get yourself more settled in. . . ."

"Oh no, it's quite all right—"

"No, now I'm sure you could use an hour or two of peace and quiet; we'll be setting quite a pace while you're here, it may be the last chance you have for quite some time."

"Perhaps you're right. . . ."

"So if it's convenient, sir, I will call for you at eight with the carriage and we'll go straightaway to your publisher's reception."

With that, the good-natured giant took his leave and Doyle embarked on an exploratory tour of the three-bedroom Presidential Suite, calculating the staggering cost of the place; Italian marble floors and mantels, Persian rugs the size of a cricket pitch, immense Egyptian urns, and paintings of Dutch landscapes with enough spread of canvas to sail an easterly wind halfway back to Britain. The force of water pressure exerted by the overhead shower in the bathroom he found astonishing, if not physically dangerous. He had just finished verifying that the bed had survived the challenge of President Cleveland's amplitude when a knock summoned him to the front door, which in the immensity of the place took an anxious minute to find.

No one there. He walked back into the sitting room.

"Sorry," someone said, as Doyle jumped half a foot.

Jack Sparks stood by the piano near the window. Father Devine's priest's garb had been abandoned, along with the thinning red hair, whiskers, and paunch. Doyle had nearly forgotten the man's genius for disguise and with a jolt remembered he had given that same chameleon talent to his detective; here he was, face-to-face with Sherlock's inspiration.

He looks roughly the same; a decade older, of course—so are we all, thought Doyle, but the mind manufactures an allowance for the erosions of time, keeping pace with the subtle changes one never notices in that face we study in the mirror. He still wore black—neutral, ascetic trousers and shirt—a leather coat, and the same soft leather boots. His hair shorter, clipped closer to the skull, going to gray. The scars Doyle had seen earlier on Father Devine had not been the work of makeup; a stark band of white along the left jaw, an indentation on the forehead running just below the hairline. As if he'd been fractured and reassembled, thought Doyle, dimming his charismatic handsomeness; something harder and more forbidding emerging from his interior.

His eyes had changed most of all, and yet they were the first thing about him Doyle had recognized; he remembered seeing in them this same haunted, spiritually disrupted look during their most troubled times together: Now it seemed a constant presence, deeper set, withdrawing from life. Impossible not to notice eyes like those and be disturbed by them.

A cruel irony, thought Doyle; here I am, an honored guest in this palatial suite, celebrated beyond all reasonable proportion for the exploits of a fictional character, and here its principal inspiration stands before me, a sorrowful, reduced shadow of the man I had known. Over the years, Doyle had wondered hundreds of times how it would feel to see his friend again. The one emotion he had never anticipated was the one he felt now.

Fear.

Perfectly natural. I thought he was long dead; it's a bit like encountering a ghost, isn't it?

Jack made no move toward him, offered no hand in greeting. Nothing warm or welcoming in his look or manner, only a dull glare of rectitude and regret.

"The reason why no approach was made to you on the ship," said Sparks, his voice flat, deflated.

"You knew I was there from the day we sailed, why didn't you? . . ."

"Didn't want to involve you."

"It wouldn't have troubled me. . . ."

"Not your affair. Wasn't aware you were going to be there. Taken aback. Stern or his book either, for that matter. Couldn't be helped."

"I'll take you at your word." Why was he so cold?

"Suspected those four men were on board. Suspected they were involved in the other business."

"The theft from Oxford; the Vulgate Bible."

Sparks kept his hands folded behind his back, offering no nods or shrugs, a complete economy of movement and gesture, with no concession to the comfort of the other.

"Sorry to see you there," said Sparks.

"No reason to be . . ."

"Caused enough trouble in your life."

"Nonsense, I would have been happy to know you were alive. . . ."

Jack shook his head once, with emphatic vehemence.

"I'm *not*."

Doyle's heart tripped. Sparks wouldn't meet his eyes.

"Not in the way you suppose when you say it. Not in the way you assume."

"Of course I had no way of knowing that, did I?" said Doyle.

"That woman. On the ship."

"The medium? Sophie Hills?"

"You asked her about me."

"She said that you weren't dead."

"She was wrong. I did die. I stayed in this body and I died."

"But Jack; you are alive, the fact remains you're standing here. . . ."

"Life . . . does not mean . . . the same thing . . . it does to you. There is no way . . . this can be described . . . that would make you understand. Not any way . . . that would have made you . . . *happy*."

Jack spoke like an automaton, face drained of expression; unreachable. Spitting out the last word like a bitter seed. He was right about this much: He didn't seem human. And using the skills Jack had taught him to now analyze the man himself made Doyle feel vaguely treacherous.

A long silence. Jack turned away, looked out the window. Doyle's skin crawled, palms moist. But he waited for Jack to elaborate. *You'll find I'm not the same man either now, old boy; I don't intimidate so easily.*

"Didn't want you to see me like this," Jack said finally.

Was there a trace of shame in his voice? For the first time, Doyle noticed Jack's hands folded behind his back; they were scored with angry red and white scars, fingers crooked, mangled. The fourth and fifth fingers of the left hand were missing. What had happened to him?

"Larry told me about it," said Doyle. "Found me in London. Nearly ten years ago now. How the two of you followed your brother's trail to Austria. Finding Alexander at the waterfall. Your fight. How you fell."

"Yes. I read your story," said Jack dryly, staring down at the city.

"And I'll make no apologies for writing about a man I thought long dead," said Doyle, his back bristling; then, softening his tone: "I went there, years afterward. With my wife: I'm married now. To Reichenbach Falls. I didn't see how anyone could have survived but someone said it had happened before. It was possible. But I never heard from you. . . ."

Doyle trailed off; no response.

"The Queen sent for me," Doyle went on. "Months after our business with the Seven. An audience with Victoria herself: There I was, twenty-five years old, chatting with the Queen. She confirmed what you'd told me was true, that you'd been working for her all along. She never mentioned anything to suggest you might have survived. . . ."

Why was he telling him what he must already know? Doyle realized he felt a compelling need to fill this gulf of silence between them with words and somehow bridge it, to find a way back to knowing him.

"She calls on me from time to time. Asks my opinion on one thing or another—I've never told anyone of our arrangement, at her request. But I continue to make myself available. Least I could do."

Sparks kept his back to Doyle, offering no reaction.

"And Larry works for me; five years now. Soon as I made my way in the world, I sent for him. He's a splendid secretary. Indispensable to me; you'd be proud of him, Jack. He owes it all to you, leaving that criminal life behind. I know how much he'd love to see you."

Jack shook his head, dismissing the possibility. Doyle had to rein back his anger again.

"But you're obviously still working for the Crown," asked Doyle.

Finally he spoke, slowly, almost disembodied: "Three years ago . . . found myself outside the British embassy in Washington. Been in America for . . . a while. Had them send a cable; coded message only I could have sent. Made its way through channels to . . . the highest level. Response came back: Give this man whatever he needs. Stared at me like some new species pulled from the bottom of the sea."

Why was he so frigid and ungiving? With all his observational acuity brought to bear, Doyle could not penetrate the man's veil of silence. Perhaps a more emotionally straightforward approach.

"You've never been far from my mind, Jack. After what Larry told me, I thought you were lost to us. You never knew how much you meant to me, how my life changed for the better from knowing you. If there was some small chance you'd survived, I thought surely you would have found a way to let me know. . . ."

"You would never have known," said Sparks sharply. "Not from me."

"Why?"

"This was circumstance. Unfortunate but unavoidable. Better you'd never seen me again."

"Why, Jack?"

Sparks turned to him, angry, the glassy scars on his face stark against his pale skin.

"I am not the man you knew. Put him out of your mind. Don't speak of him to me again."

"I must know what's happened to you. . . ."

"Put a headstone over that memory. Move on. If you can't, there is no way for us to proceed: I'll leave and you will never see me again."

Doyle struggled to contain his frustration. "If there's no other way."

Sparks nodded again, satisfied for the moment. "Saw you on the ship, hoped you wouldn't get involved; still a chance you could avoid it. . . ."

"Why should I now when I didn't before?"

"You are a man of position and reputation now. You have a place in this world. A family. More for you to lose."

"Involved in what exactly? And how would anyone find out about what part I've played in this?"

"The fourth man escaped the ship when we reached port. . . ."

"That seems unlikely. . . ."

"No one found him."

"Perhaps he threw himself overboard like the other one."

"He was the last one left alive; his primary responsibility would have been to survive—"

"And report back to whoever hired them."

Jack nodded. "This fourth man will tell them of your involvement."

Doyle's anger flared again. "So you suggest I'm now in danger."

"Greater than you imagine . . ."

"Then for God's sake, stop talking in riddles and answer me plainly: I've had as much of this as I can swallow—I nearly lost my life a dozen times following your lead ten years ago, I'm under no obligation to prove myself to you again. You turn up out of nowhere like Marley's ghost with your secrets and mysterious connections and never a word in the last ten years, and you're right, Jack, I have gotten somewhere in the world, and I've a lot less patience for half-truths and pointed evasions, particularly where my personal safety is at stake. You can be blunt about what you're on about here or be damned as far as I'm concerned."

The silence hung heavy between them. Neither man gave an inch.

"So when you say 'they,' " said Doyle, "who exactly do you mean?"

Sparks stared at him, unblinking, seemingly unmoved, but after making a decision behind his impassive gaze, he took a piece of paper from his pocket and handed it to Doyle.

A lithograph of a woven coat of arms, an interrupted black circle on a field of white, three jagged red lines darting through the circle like lightning bolts.

"I've seen this design before," said Doyle, as he took out the sketch he'd been carrying in his pocket and gave it to Sparks. "Scrawled on the baseboard of Selig's cabin wall. I believe he saw it on the arm of one of his assassins—a scar or tattoo—and wrote it himself just before he died."

"Do you know what it signifies?"

"Haven't the faintest. Do you?"

"For centuries something similar to this served as the official seal of the Hanseatic League."

Doyle rummaged through his schoolboy memories: "The Hanseatic League was an alliance of German merchants. Medieval. Formed for protection of their cities and trade rights in the absence of a central government."

"Their influence eventually spread to every court in Europe. They raised a mercenary army, fought wars to assert their authority. The city of Lübeck, now in Germany, was the seat of their power, which reached its peak in the fourteenth century when they were as strong a force as any sovereignty."

"But they were finally defeated."

"By 1700 the League had all but disappeared, although Lübeck, Hamburg, and Bremen even today are still referred to as Hanseatic cities."

"Why would their seal turn up in the middle of this business?"

"There have for the last two hundred years been persistent rumors that the League did not die out with the consolidation of Germany as originally believed. That a form of the League survived as a secret society, with its resources and objectives intact."

"Who would have been responsible for that?"

"The merchants themselves initially. After the League dissolved, they still needed to protect their ships and caravans so they formed a militia, a private police force. And lacking the skilled men required for that work, they began to recruit criminals and thieves from port cities around the world, training those members rigorously, making them expert in arms, munitions, killing techniques.

"Through the years, this rogue branch began to prey on its employers and finally seized outright control of the organization. This renegade form of the League has survived to this day, headquartered in Eastern Europe."

"An international guild of thieves," said Doyle.

"Smuggling. Pirating. Trafficking in contraband. Stealing for themselves or as commissioned."

"And you suspected them in the theft of the Vulgate from Oxford prior to our sailing."

"Yes."

"And you think the same men, or elements of that organization, are after the Book of Zohar as well."

"Yes."

"But as to the question of who they might be working for or why . . ."

Jack shook his head.

"Someone in America," said Doyle.

"Yes."

"The Vulgate Bible would have been transported here as well. On an earlier ship."

"Correct."

"But we don't know where."

Jack shook his head.

Doyle felt a satisfying and familiar meshing of the gears of their thought. This felt more like the old Sparks, the two of them alternatively sprinting ahead of each other on a chase for buried truth.

"Then we must trace these thieves back to whoever commissioned the crime," said Doyle.

Sparks raised an eyebrow. "How would you do it?"

"Let them steal the Book of Zohar—or think they have—and follow them."

The slightest smile appeared at the edge of Sparks's mouth. "Yes."

"You'll need the full cooperation of Lionel Stern—"

"I have it."

"You'll have mine as well."

"No. You're here on business. Couldn't expect you to—"

"Jack. You know me better than that."

They looked at each other:

And I know you better than you think I do, my friend, thought Doyle. I'll go along with this if only to get to the bottom of what's happened to you.

"We'll start tonight, then," said Sparks, moving toward the door.

"I have an obligation."

"Afterward . . ."

"Where shall we meet?"

"I'll come for you."

Sparks left the room, silent as a cat.

BETWEEN DENVER AND PHOENIX

"In Hebrew *Kabbalah* means 'to receive,' as in the receiving of wisdom. . . . I don't wish to burden you, are you sure you want me to explain all this?" asked Jacob Stern.

"Absolutely," said Eileen. "I'm fascinated."

"Well, it's a long train ride. In Kabbalah it is written that God created the world along thirty-two paths of secret knowledge; these are represented by the numbers one through ten and the twenty-two letters of the Hebrew alphabet. Each number has a secret spiritual meaning that corresponds to one of the ten power centers in the physical body. Each one of the twenty-two letters has a numerical value and a visual significance in the way it is drawn, in addition to its sound that forms language. Each of these different paths to knowledge is of equal importance in deciphering the mystery that lies behind creation. Do you follow?"

"I think so," said Eileen without much assurance but encouraged to try by the man's soft, infectious happiness.

"The student of Kabbalah uses the *sound* of certain powerful words in meditation to create a higher consciousness in himself; the *numerical* significance of its letters is analyzed according to numerological values which reveal hidden meanings; the *shape* of the letters provides a basis for studying visually coded information, like the mandalas of the Hindu. Each discipline exercises a different area of the mind but all are equally valid ways for the aspiring student to move closer to enlightenment."

Night was falling rapidly outside the windows of their moving train; the lights of Denver fading behind them as they snaked through the sparsely settled foothills to the south. Even in the dwindling twilight, one could sense the ponderous weight of the Rockies lying to the west; Eileen wasn't sure which seemed more dense and impenetrable, those mountains or the response she'd gotten from Jacob Stern to her simple query: What is it you do, exactly?

"There are only two qualities of reality that we as human beings can experience: One is physical matter, the other is information." Stern held up a bright green apple. "There are the atoms or particles that make up the form of an object: matter. There is the idea of the object that exists only in our minds: information. One has no meaning without the other but the combination of these two qualities is life. An apple, for instance." He took a big bite and chewed vigorously, smiling. "Would you care for one?"

"Thank you," said Eileen, taking the apple he offered from his bag.

"They are called Granny Smiths; isn't that fantastic? What an image; this wiry old grandmother running around the orchard."

Eileen laughed; he could go on talking about anything he liked as long as he made her laugh.

"It is the same with these old books I study," he said, pulling a leatherbound volume out of his valise. "To a person who has no experience of them they are nothing but funny symbols printed on pages bound together and wrapped in a cover. A primitive could make no sense of this object!"

"Neatly summing up how I felt about schoolbook Latin," said Eileen.

"Of course; because they couldn't convince you of its relevance to your fifteen-year-old existence. But to a scholar whose whole life has been spent preparing, or even better to a prophet whose mind is not clouded by the influence of the physical or animal soul . . ."

At which point Bendigo Rymer, who had been straining to eavesdrop from the seat in front of them—outraged that Eileen had abandoned him for this interloper—fell into a heavy, untroubled sleep.

". . . a great holy book is not just a document for the study of God or even an instrument for the communication of the will of God. It is *in itself* the divine body of God, embodied in a form which allows the person who studies it to penetrate and merge with the book, and in this way enter the secret heart of our Creator."

"You're saying these books are somehow alive," said Eileen.

"In a way, yes. This is complicated. Are you familiar with how a telephone works, my dear?"

"Not exactly."

"Neither am I. But as I understand it, there is a mysterious substance in the little part that you hold and speak into. . . ."

"The mouthpiece."

"Thank you; a substance that when we speak into this mouthpiece vibrates and turns our words into an electrical signal which runs along the wires to the other person—don't ask me how—where there is more of this magical substance in the part they listen to—the earpiece, yes?—that also vibrates and turns these signals back into the words we spoke over here so they can understand them. Isn't that fantastic?"

Three feet away, Bendigo Rymer began to snore, a foghorn cutting through the clacking of the train.

"So holy books are like this substance."

"Yes. The word of God has been received by them on their pages, translated into words and numbers and sounds so that someone who approaches with the proper education can eventually decipher and understand. God speaks in one end; we listen on the other."

"If that's the case," asked Eileen, taking another bite of apple, "why isn't everybody in on the mystery?"

"Not everyone is ready. A person must achieve a high degree of purity before studying this material or the power of the information would rip them apart like a hurricane. There is a saying: The vessel must be made strong for the passing down of wisdom."

With a thud, the silver flask he'd been sipping from slipped from the sleeping Rymer's seat to the floor at Stern's feet. Eileen tucked the flask back under Bendigo's arm, grateful that she hadn't been drinking tonight; she'd indulged altogether too much recently, comfort in place of company, and it was time she tapered off. She rested her head against the seat, more relaxed than she could remember, tranquilized by the gentle rocking of the train and the steady sound of Jacob's voice.

"This has traditionally been the role of the priesthood, in every religion: to help men and women prepare for the receiving of spiritual information from the higher realms."

"All my priest ever did for me was try and stick his hand up my skirt," said Eileen, instantly regretting it.

"Well, that is the great challenge of living, isn't it?" said Jacob, not at all embarrassed. "Humans are divided beings attempting to reconcile our two natures: the spiritual and the animal. That's why I wear this ribbon around my waist, by the way; it is called a *gartel*, symbolically it separates the higher and lower parts of our nature and serves as a constant reminder to me of our ongoing struggle. We are all, in our own way, trying to make this *tikkun*, this healing or repair inside, to reconcile our divided selves. Every individual is responsible for making the *tikkun* in his own life; it is the primary responsibility of living. They say if enough people are able to do this work, one day such a healing may come for the entire world."

"Think the world's fallen from grace, do you? We're all hopeless sinners and the like."

"You are English, are you not?"

"Dear me, is it still so obvious?"

"Only in a most delightful way. But let me ask you: Is there any doubt in your Church of England that man is a completely wicked, sinful wretch?"

"Of the worst sort. And my experience with men bears that out."

Jacob laughed. "This is the feeling most people have about their life, you know. That they have failed their God, or themselves, in some fundamental way."

"Is that what you feel, Mr. Stern?"

Stern looked at her, his blue eyes as bright as shiny buttons, joy radiating from him as steadily as heat from a coal fire. What an attractive younger man he must have been, thought Eileen, instantly deciding how wonderful her life would be now if she had met him then.

"There is no question," said Stern, "that we human beings are sad and broken creatures. Look around; it requires no great vision to see that things are not as they should be. If there was perfection in the world, why would man and woman be separate beings, for instance? Why are there differences of color or religion, country or family that cause such blind hatred and bloodshed? The most unimaginable cruelties seem never to fall outside the capabilities of man."

"Yes. It's all quite hopeless, isn't it?" she said, staring dreamily into his eyes.

"They say that in every creation the creator reveals his personality; if so then the Creator of this world must Himself be a terribly wounded and incomplete being. In this way, perhaps we do resemble our God. And if there is such a God, surely he must be in exile with us, suffering as we do, struggling on his own path toward spiritual perfection. The path we are all stumbling along. The history of humanity tells us there is an undeniable progression in spite of all our violence and pain, a slow, gradual moving toward the light—in Hebrew 'light' has the same numerological value as 'mystery.' Perhaps one day we will all achieve this 'enlightenment.' "

Eileen tried to disguise a yawn. Jacob smiled.

"One of the great disadvantages of growing old; you think you know so much but nobody else has the endurance to listen to you."

"No, it's quite interesting, really," said Eileen. "I just haven't had any reason to think about such things for the longest time."

"Who does? Only crazy old men locked in their basements with a thousand books. Real life, families, making a living; who has time to worry about suffering when suffering takes up so much time?" said Stern, laughing.

"You really are the most wonderfully peculiar man," said Eileen.

"This is a compliment?"

"I mean it to be. Different. Unusual. Out of the ordinary."

"Some of my most outstanding qualities," said Stern, laughing again.

"Well, I approve of them, Mr. Stern. You're a fine old fellow."

Stern took a satisfying breath and looked out the window, moonlight gleaming off the luminous snowcap of a distant peak. "It is a most amazing world, in any case," he said. "Such a shame we can't appreciate it more."

"I suppose you just have to take advantage of those moments when they come your way," said Eileen, a delicious sleepiness creeping into her.

A dreamy look came over Stern, transparent and fine; he looked years younger suddenly. "Nothing is lost. Nothing's destroyed. There are no divisions. No disharmony. Everything returns."

No, this isn't possible, thought Eileen, a familiar stirring quickening her heart. Ridiculous. She hunted down the feeling, examined it, produced it, tested it; and then had to admit there was validity to it, however absurd.

She was falling in love with him.

chapter six

THEY GATHERED UNDER THE HEROIC ARCH IN THE GREAT hall of the Metropolitan Museum, Fifth Avenue's northern-most outpost of downtown civilization, a glittering multi-tude of bosomy dowagers and their consorts, society's finest—they called themselves the Four Hundred, someone explained to Doyle, the exact number of people who could fit into Mrs. Vanderbilt's ballroom—paying homage to their distinguished visitor from England. Doyle felt overmatched at first sight of the prestigious throng, but he had watched the Queen handle a few receiving lines over the years; the moves were as ritualized as dance steps and he had learned from a master.

Repeat the person's name when it's spoken to you, shake their hand—unless you're the Queen; one notable perquisite of royalty—accept their obligatory compliment with mod-esty and a poised facial expression suggesting an abstract fascination with the person, offer brief thanks and a neutral see-you-later: Next please. He'd been through the drill many times at home, although as with everything else he'd en-countered during his first day in New York, never on such a colossal scale. By the time Doyle had dutifully worked his way to the end of this wave of wellwishers, his palm throbbed like a beaten timpani; what strange custom led these American tycoons to believe that crushing the bones of a stranger's hand would be interpreted as a sign of friend-ship?

After the first hour, the crowd merged into one bejeweled and black-tied thousand-headed beast, which put him at a distinct disadvantage as he circulated the floor; it seemed that once you'd been introduced to a person in this country, he could just walk right up and start talking to you. How ghastly! Flanks unprotected, vulnerable to attack from every direction, he felt like a partridge flushed into an open meadow.

And why weren't they sitting down to eat a proper dinner? Another American innovation, Innes explained, as they ducked behind a pillar: no big meal. Only enough champagne to float a gunship and an open field of raw mollusks. More circulation of the guests, less outlay of cash, and this way multiple affairs could be scheduled on the same night and the same four hundred socialites could attend them all without offending anyone by taking an early leave. What did it matter? thought Doyle. They'll all see each other an hour later at the next party, anyway. What an exhausting schedule to maintain; half their time spent dressing up to go out, the rest in transit hurtling through the night perpetually troubled by the nagging possibility that somebody somewhere else might be having a better time.

"Sorry about Pinkus, by the way," said Innes. "The way I behaved on board. Afraid I was quite taken in by him at first. My fault entirely."

"Quite all right," said Doyle, secretly delighted. "Happen to anyone."

"Visions of show girls dancing in my head; quite the silly ass—look lively, Arthur, trouble off the starboard bow."

Innes drew his attention to an approaching flock of matrons who had him locked directly in their sights, ravenous admiration firing their eyes; Doyle pretended not to notice their advance and took flight while Innes waded into their midst to stage a rearguard delay.

But in his haste to escape, Doyle strayed into a boxed thicket under a flight of stairs and found himself penned in by a wedge of sweaty faces, glowing with sun and unnatural health. Where was Pepperman? The Major had kept pace with Doyle as they made the rounds, repeating the name of each assailant as they closed in on him—why couldn't they wear little buttons printed with their names instead of these silly boutonnieres?—but he had been swept aside by the rush of some mad Italian tenor. Doyle could see the Major's shaggy head poking out of the fray nearby beyond his reach and he realized he would have to fend off the pugnacious,

buck-toothed predator at the head of this pack alone. What
was the man's name again?

Roosevelt? That was it. "Theodore: call me Teddy."
Ruling-class family—although there weren't supposed to be
any in this land of the free, it would take an idiot only one
glance at this room to know differently. Roughly Doyle's
age. Blunt and stubby as that fat cigar in his mouth, packing
enough fearless will in his eyes to stare down a rhinoceros;
fanatical eyes, magnified by thick lenses, jutting out of a
perfectly square head.

Roosevelt had been introduced as the Commissioner of
Something or Other, Parks or Commerce or the Interior of
the Exterior. Americans made a national pastime of bestow-
ing on each other titles that strung together tike railroad cars,
ripe with redundancy and a dearth of imagination. Vice Su-
perintendent of the Assistant Commissioner's Office for
Health and Safety Regulations. Administrative Supervisor
of the Public Transit Authority, Horse and Buggy Department, Bootstraps and Stirrups Division. Nothing Like the
poetic lyricism of English offices: the Chancellor of the Ex-
chequer. The Home Secretary. Viceroy of the Sub-Continent.
The Gentleman Usher of the Black Rod.

"Been on a lecture tour," said Roosevelt, chomping mani-
acally on his cigar. "Boston, Philadelphia, Atlantic seaboard.
Can't stray too far from home now; my younger brother died
two months ago. Alcohol. Dissolute living. Epilepsy. Hallu-
cinations. Confinement in sanitariums. Tried to throw himself out a window. Family's in turmoil. Dreadful. You can't
imagine, Arthur."

Why is he telling me this? wondered Doyle. And why is
he calling me Arthur?

"Terribly sorry," said Doyle. What else could he say?

"Appreciate it. What can you do when someone you love
so fiercely wants no part of living? Nothing. Not a thing.
You have to let them go." With no other sign of emotion, and
without shame, Roosevelt wiped away a tear that dropped
beneath his glasses. "Life goes forward. It's for the living.
Wrestle with it, contend. Don't give in, to your dying breath.
Time will have us all in the ground soon enough."

The man's muscular fortitude struck a sympathetic note. This was what he admired most in Americans, wasn't it? Forthrightness, candor. Expressing strong emotion freely. None of the stiff formality and ritualized chatter that his repressed countrymen hid behind like field mice in a Sussex hedgerow.

Roosevelt took the cigar from his mouth and leaned closer to Doyle.

"My view on such excesses as killed my brother are these: Look around this room and all you see is wealth, refinement, sophistication. Let me tell you that elsewhere there is open warfare on the streets of this city; gangs of toughs and hooligans on the Lower East Side control entire neighborhoods, unmolested. The city's helpless to respond. Here, starkly illustrated, are the two lines along which the human race is evolving: One through the self-improvement and philanthropy of the morally strong, striving to increase their knowledge and broaden their minds; they carry society forward.

"The second is accomplished unknowingly by the morally bankrupt, through drink and immorality; two invisible hands plucking weeds from the garden of life. I predict that by three generations from now the strains of the drunkard, the hedonist, and the criminal, interbreeding as they tend to do, will be extinct or on their way out. Why? Because they weaken the blood line, their bodies give out under their excesses or their crimes kill them before they have a chance to breed. Thus the rotten branch is pruned and over time the average of the race is elevated to a higher standard. Nature has its own devices." He stepped back to assess the impact of his theory.

Doyle stared at him. "Are you running for office, Mr. Roosevelt?"

"I have been a candidate in the past for the office of mayor of this great city, and we do not rule it out in the future," said Roosevelt. The supporters behind Roosevelt came to life and stood a little taller at the mere suggestion. "Do you plan to get out to the West while you're here, Arthur?"

"I'm not certain all the stops on the tour have been

arranged," said Doyle, still reeling from the man's quicksilver transformation from grieving brother to Malthusian geneticist.

"My advice to you, tour be damned: See the West. A hard and dangerous place, the wild parts of it. And a more proper setting for the contemplation of man's puny insignificance you could ever hope to find."

"Do that often, do you?" said Doyle.

"But you'll find that man has gone west for a larger purpose; it's the particular fate of the American to conquer this frontier and the doing of it will shape his character for hundreds of years to come."

"Really? How so?"

Roosevelt slowly rotated his cigar and stared into Doyle's eyes; clearly he was not used to having his pronouncements questioned, but Doyle did not flinch.

"The American will come to believe in his own God-given ability to master nature. Eventually, he will be handed the responsibility of running the civilized world. But he must manage it with respect; indeed, with reverence. And only through exposure to nature will we cultivate the proper attitude for the shouldering of this enormous task. If you visit the West, Arthur, at every turn you will see vistas of such stunning magnificence it will transform the way you think of the world forever. I urge you not to miss it."

"I have always wanted to see some Indians," said Doyle.

Roosevelt's eyes narrowed, focusing his magnetism down to a concentrated beam. "Listen; there's been a lot of warped, sentimental, backward talk in this country about holding up the expansion of our empire to preserve the lives of a few scattered tribes of the plains whose lives are but a few degrees less meaningless, squalid, and ferocious than the wild beasts with whom they held ownership before we came along."

"I have read that, in their own savage way, of course— scalpings and so forth—they're really quite impressive."

"Pay no attention to it. The red man is a relic of the Stone Age and his so-called innate nobility is no match for the march of progress. History never stops turning its wheels out of pity; those unable to move from its path are crushed. This is the fate God has in store for the Indian, and their refusal to adapt to the changing world around them makes them complicit in its execution."

Unexpectedly, Roosevelt reached out and applied another crushing squeeze on Doyle's tender hand.

"Greatly enjoyed your stories," he said. "Holmes. Watson. Splendid stuff. Too bad you had to kill him off. Think of the money you could have made. Bully for you, Arthur. Enjoy your stay in America."

With a compact, commanding gesture to his waiting courtiers, Roosevelt strode off, and the entire group fell into lock-step behind him. Innes stepped into the void left by their wake.

"What was that all about?" asked Innes.

"A shocking example of the species *Homo Americanus*. They could stuff and mount him in the museum."

"Quite a right bunch of toffs, isn't it? Real balmy gaffer over here," said Innes, nodding toward a willowy man in a top hat, swallowtail coat, black cape, and flowing white silk scarf, engaged in conversation but regularly glancing their way. His face was dusky, fine-featured, an East Indian cast to the eyes and an almost feminine delicacy to his lips and nose. A mane of long black hair flowed into a leonine ponytail. He appeared to be in his early thirties and carried himself with the flamboyant confidence of a lionized maestro.

"Started telling me about this concert he plans to give where every instrument in the orchestra's represented by a different smell that he pumps into the auditorium with a machine whenever they start to play. . . ."

"Different *smells*?"

"You heard me correctly; rose for the strings, sandalwood for the brass, jasmine for the flute, and so on. Each scent pouring out of a different nozzle hooked up to and activated by that particular instrument."

"Good Christ."

"Says he already owns a patent. Smell-A-Rama: Symphony of Scents."

"You could knock me over with a feather."

"Only in America."

Innes moved off.

A tall, blond, good-looking man in a dinner jacket emerged from the crowd and walked steadily toward Doyle's back, a hand slipping inside his jacket. Seeing him approach, the elegant, swarthy man in the silk scarf turned and made a direct line to Doyle, took him firmly by the arm, and led him deeper into the crowd.

"Mr. Conan Doyle, the honor is entirely mine, sir," said the swarthy man, in rounded tones of upper-class Oxfordian English. "I have just enjoyed the delightful pleasure of your brother's company and thought perhaps I would seize the liberty of introducing myself to you."

And so you have, thought Doyle. Mr. Smell-A-Rama.

Behind them, the tall, blond gentleman stopped and hung back at the edge of the room.

"My name is Preston Peregrine Raipur but everyone calls me Presto. We are fellow countrymen. I am an Oxford man; Trinity, class of '84," said the dandy; then in a quiet, deadly serious tone with no corresponding change of expression: "Please continue to glance towards the gathering from time to time, if you would, sir, and smile politely as if I had said something of mild amusement to you."

"What?"

"We are being observed. It would be best if our conversation remained brief and appeared to be of an entirely superficial nature," said Presto, the frivolousness entirely gone from his voice, replaced by an earnest, intelligent sincerity.

"What is this about, sir?" said Doyle, smiling, complying with the man's request to mask the discussion's true intent.

"Another time and place is more appropriate for an elaboration. You are in danger. You must leave this place at once," said Presto, grinning and nodding to a passing couple.

Doyle hesitated; a casual glance around revealed no danger.

"And would it be convenient if I were to call at your hotel tomorrow morning, say, at nine o'clock?" asked Presto.

"Not without my first hearing some idea of what this is about."

Raipur waved to someone over Doyle's shoulder and

laughed like a nincompoop; then, under his breath: "Someone is stealing the great holy books of the world, Mr. Conan Doyle; I believe you are already aware of this. Surely such a subject warrants an hour of your time, if only to satisfy your native inquisitiveness."

Doyle took the man's measure; he stood up to the test. "Nine o'clock tomorrow morning at the Waldorf Hotel."

The man bowed slightly. "I shall now create a diversion; take your brother and go immediately," said Presto, producing a calling card for Doyle with a deft sleight of hand. "We shall meet again tomorrow."

Doyle glanced at the card; under the name Preston Peregrine Raipur was printed a title: "Maharaja of Berar." Maharaja?

"Ever so grateful," said Presto, then raising his voice back into the social butterfly register he had earlier employed. "And I can't wait to read more of your fantastic stories, Mr. Conan Doyle: Bravo! Bra-vo! The greatest pleasure to meet you, sir. Best wishes always!"

With that, Preston Peregrine Raipur, the Maharaja of Berar, bowed low and glided off. As Innes made his way back to Doyle, Presto lifted his black gleaming walking stick high in the air:

"*Voilà!*" said Presto.

The stick erupted into a cloud of billowing white smoke and a flashing column of fire. People around him and throughout the room scattered in every direction.

"What the devil . . ." said Innes.

"Follow me," said Doyle, taking Innes by the arm. "Quickly."

The brothers moved through the agitated crowd, losing themselves in a cluster of others heading out the doors. Behind them the smoke cleared, revealing that Presto had disappeared from sight.

The tall, blond man spotted Doyle and Innes just as they left the museum and hurried to follow them.

Outside, Doyle hustled Innes to their waiting coach at the Fifth Avenue curb, glancing behind in time to see the tall, blond man appear at the doors.

"What's going on?" asked Innes.

"I'll explain in a moment," said Doyle.

They hopped into the cab.

"Where to?" asked the driver.

It was Jack.

CHICAGO, ILLINOIS

She climbed off the train at the station, standing on the same platform that had held Jacob Stern a few nights before. Wearing a blue gingham dress that concealed the hard lines of her body and a bonnet over her jet hair, she looked more like a visiting country cousin or a rural school teacher than an Indian woman who had skipped the reservation. She kept her face behind the bonnet and her eyes low, submissive, attracting no attention to herself.

The dream had come again that night on the reserve, as the owl medicine had said it would: She found herself wandering alone through a city of tall buildings and wide, empty streets. Waiting for someone in front of a pale castle with thin, fingery towers. She had seen this place in the medicine dream many times, but it had appeared black before, more threatening, and it always stood surrounded by desert, not in the middle of a modern city. That was as much as this new dream could reveal before the Black Crow Man—she never saw his face, only a twisted humpback and long, scraggly hair—swooped down and washed everything away with fire.

She recognized the city as Chicago; it was the only big city she had ever seen. She did not remember seeing this pale tower during her only previous visit; a school outing twelve years ago, one of a group of reservation high school graduates trotted out to impress white politicians. The city had felt like a place of great anger, confusion, and wild energy that she'd hoped she would never experience again. But now she would stay and search its streets until she found that tower and wait for whoever was coming to her.

As Walks Alone left the station, she caught the eye of a man loitering by the carriage stand. Dante Scruggs shifted the toothpick to the other side of his mouth and narrowed his one good eye; as the dark-haired woman passed by, the evil thoughts that ran through his head more regularly than the nearby trains picked up their frantic roaming. A month had gone by since his last work; it was coming around to the time when the Voices returned, and that same phrase skipped along the surface of his mind like a stone, over and over again.

We got an empty belly and an itch we can't scratch.

He watched her with fanatical concentration; Dante liked the way her haunches rolled when she walked, the way her strong brown hand gripped the handle of the suitcase. He might be half-blind, but he could still spot an Indian a mile away.

When would these women learn they just shouldn't travel alone? Chicago was a rough town; a lady's luck could turn bad any moment, thought Dante, and here she was tempting fate, walking around near the station after dark. As if she ain't asking for trouble, strutting her stuff so shameless, trying to pass for white. Immoral is what it was.

What this squaw needed was to be taught a lesson, and Dante Scruggs was her man. The thought of their future intimacy made him shiver: He would make himself known to every inch of that brown body before they were through. Then he would take her down to the Green River.

But first he waited for a sign; there, the horse by the hitching post. Its tail twitched to the left, then again: twice in a row.

Yes. The Voices wanted this one. . . .

The woman turned a corner and he followed her.

Against the concrete, brick, and cast iron of the new Chicago that had sprung up since the fire in '71, Dante Scruggs's native coloring provided remarkable camouflage. He wasn't handsome, but you wouldn't call him ugly. Average height, blond and boyish, features plump and mild, like his middle-class shopkeeper folks back in Madison, Wisconsin. He looked ten years younger than his thirty-nine and there was no way to pick him out of a crowd. He wasn't big; most of his remarkable strength was in his outsize farmer's hands: He could crack walnuts with 'em. Smart enough to stay one step ahead of the police and two away from jail, Dante showed the world a bland, kindly face. A person would never notice his glass eye unless they were up close and looking right at it; the iris, as blue as a robin's egg, had no pupil painted on it.

Dante was a breed of man the mechanized world had only just begun to produce. He moved through life casting no shadow while inside he was all hooks, darkness, and ripping pain. He had long ago given up resisting the Voices he heard in his head, and he believed with a servant's humility that once he read their signs it was simply his job to obey.

He pictured the city as a jungle and himself a predator at the top of its food chain; that gave a dignity to what he perceived as his life's work. The U.S. Army had thought enough of his appetite for handing out discipline to make him a platoon sergeant. He put fifteen years in before the massacre at Wounded Knee revealed to his superiors the extent of Dante's enthusiasm for expressing his true nature.

Soldiers in his unit who had been near him during the engagement testified that Dante had lost all human restraint after that Dakota arrow took out his eye. But then again, they argued, with his sight so badly damaged, how could he be expected to distinguish women and children? The Army had grudgingly bought that argument, buried his excesses in the cover-up. A quiet discharge with honors soon followed, fully pensioned.

Dante interpreted his misfortune differently; the wound opened up a whole new world. He imagined that his lost eye had simply been turned around to look inside and clarified the Voices. And ever since he'd been so grievously wounded, the Voices granted him permission to exact the sort of retribution he'd only been able to dream about: nine murders in three years that nobody would ever connect him to.

With his pension coming in, he didn't need money so Dante devoted himself to what he had heard gentlemen shooters on the range call "the thrill of the hunt": He'd hired out as a buffalo scout before enlisting in the Army and had nothing but contempt for these rich, idle easterners taking their shots at stationary bulls a hundred yards away. They had it all wrong; the thrill was in the close work, hands on, that's what he discovered. Careful, thorough, calculating. He liked to show his ladies the Green River and then take 'em there, slow and easy, devouring their fear along the way.

And this one was an Indian. That was just gravy on his meat.

This squaw didn't know where she was going, that much was clear, and she didn't know Chicago: looking for street signs, wandering without direction. He didn't care what she was doing here alone; thoughts like that turned them into people and made the magic go away. Her family would be back on the reservation where they belonged; this one was a skipper so Dante felt no impulse to hurry. With prime meat, he liked biding his time. He had followed a woman halfway to Springfield once, hanging back, waiting for the right moment to make his move. That was what made courtship so suspenseful; it might take days or weeks before an opportunity presented itself. But once he'd locked on to one, he never let go until the work was finished.

She took the stairs to a boarding house he knew on Division Street—ladies only, lodging by the week; good, she was planning to stay awhile. Dante had seen this pattern so many times; woman comes into town, finds a low-end job, waitressing, maybe seamstress in a sweatshop. Time passes and the work grinds her down to one of those nameless, faceless bodies no one notices passing by them on the street. Trudging back to her room alone every night. Bone weary, looks wearing out fast. Taking meals with the other thin-faced women in the boarding house; he could see 'em sitting prim and proper through the Irish lace on the dining room windows. Maybe she finds a friend among them and they talk without much hope about meeting a man some day, a fellow who won't treat them too bad, provide some kind of a life. Smoking cigarettes on the back porch, breath steaming in the cool evening air. Washing up in the shared bathroom down the hall, never all her clothes off at the same time. Sleeping with her meager dreams.

Women like empty cups. Drifting through life waiting for

something to happen. Now he was here and the waiting was over. Her life would have meaning.

She would see the Green River.

There she was in a window. Second floor, near the back. That's fine; settling in. The Voices told him it was safe to leave now. He knew where to find her.

But for all his focus on the Indian, Dante Scruggs remained unaware that someone was following and watching him. A dark, quiet man, with a distinctive round tattoo—a circle pierced by lightning—on the inside crook of his left arm. He waited for Dante to pass, then walked slowly after him, blending into the crowd.

YUMA, ARIZONA TERRITORY

Nobody in the hobo camp could remember seeing a Chinaman on the bum before, and in the philosophizing way common to these kings of the road, they viewed it as a true signifier of hard times. Their aversion to capitalism's twin addictions—work and money—did not erase from their minds an abiding curiosity in the larger workings of the world: Their indolence actually gave them more time for sizing up the human condition. Bums kept their ears to the rails of social change; at every stop on their circuit, there were men who made a point of studying discarded newspapers and discussing the evident faults of man like disapproving archaeologists. These hobos were more aware than most good citizens that six hundred banks had failed in the last year, that two hundred railroads had gone bankrupt and over two and a half million people were out of work in America; those kinds of numbers put respectable folk out on the road, crowding up their camps, and made life thornier for the professional vagabonds. Sad-faced men pissing and jabbering about their marital problems or how much they missed their jobs. That line of self-pitying blather turned a real bum's stomach.

The tramps knew, too, that Chinese were family people who took in their own and kept to themselves when things went sour, so when a Chinaman showed up riding the lines, that qualified as news. Slocum Haney said he'd hopped a freight in Sacramento and this chink was already in the boxcar. Never said a word between there and Yuma, not even when spoken to. Never saw him sleep or eat; he just sat in the corner watchful as a cat. Haney didn't even know if he understood English or not. Something crawly about the man, even now, sitting out there alone on the edge of the circle round the bonfire.

"You talk to him, Denver," said Slocum Haney. "You worked with Chinamen before."

Denver Bob Hobbes commanded universal respect from his peers based on his longevity on the bum and a habit of straight talk; in the egalitarian world of the hobos, he held an unofficial post of elder statesman emeritus. He'd been a working stiff once, came west from Ohio pounding rails on the transcontinental back in the sixties, when one day picking potatoes in Pocatello, Idaho, twenty years ago he saw the light and vowed never again to lift his hand in the service of another man's profiteering.

Denver Bob had kept that promise and studied himself into an authority on the economic exploitation of the working man. He'd marched on Washington with Kelly's Industrial Army in '93 to protest the industrial workers' plight—and besides there was nothing like political demonstrations for free food and good company. Bob claimed to have met Walt Whitman once, always carried with him a dog-eared edition of *Leaves of Grass,* and he could talk about the nobility of poverty and life on the open road to a complete stranger until all the oxygen in the neighborhood was depleted. If the presence of this Chinaman was upsetting the harmony of the camp, then Denver Bob saw it as his responsibility to set things right.

"You get cold snaps like this in October here in the desert," said Denver Bob, setting his plump butt down on an empty copper wire spool beside the Chinaman. "Most men start moving toward California around this time of year but it seems to me you've just come from there."

He offered the man a swallow of the homemade raisin

jack they'd brewed the night before. The man shook his head and kept his eyes straight ahead. Denver Bob wasn't used to people turning down his generosity—he was big and round and with his thick, white beard and apple cheeks he looked like Father Christmas—but it didn't set him back. Not much did.

"This camp's been here ten years now, ever since they opened the line from Los Angeles. Hundreds of men pass through these yards every season." The shanty camp occupied the outskirts of the switching yards at Yuma, the major interchange between Los Angeles and the Arizona Territory, on the banks of the Colorado River. "Do you speak English, my friend?"

The man looked directly at him for the first time; Denver Bob felt a chill scamper over his scalp. Not that there was any overt threat in those dull black eyes. There was just . . . nothing. No personality, submission, false good humor. No Chinaman he'd ever known looked or acted anything like this.

"I am looking for work," the man said.

"Work? Well, that feeling comes over a man from time to time," said Denver Bob, bringing his well-oiled geniality to bear. "He don't know whether to shit or wind his watch; it's like a fever, see; best thing is to lie down, have a drink, and wait for it to pass."

"I work with explosives," said the man, immune to Denver's merry creed of sloth.

"Is that a fact?"

"Demolition."

"Yes, I follow you. So you're a working man." Whatever else he might be, this fella was no tramp. Didn't seem much like a railroad hand neither for that matter; too self-possessed, independent. Maybe a miner who just lost his stake. No matter: Everything about the man gave Denver Bob the willies; if there was anything he could say or do to get him out of camp and on his way, it couldn't happen fast enough.

"Where do I find this work?"

"As a matter of fact, brother, I can tell you exactly.

They're still putting in the spur line between Phoenix and Prescott through the Pea Vine; I hear tell there's tunnels to dig and canyons to trestle aplenty, enough to keep a double shift crew working round the clock for another year."

"Where?"

"North-northwest. You can hop a night freight to Phoenix over yonder near the swing bridge, leaves around midnight, have you there by morning."

"The Santa Fe, Prescott and Phoenix Railroad."

"That's the outfit; you'll find their offices right there at the Phoenix rail station. Sure they can set you up nicely—work's scarce most places these days, but a fella with a handy skill like yours is always in demand. Here's wishing you and your ancestors good fortune." Denver Bob raised his tin can of hooch and drank a toast, thinking: You got your marching orders, friend, now remove your spooky ass from my yard.

The man offered no acknowledgment or gratitude and directed his look back to the bonfire. Then something speared the man's attention; he sat up stiff as a bird dog on a scent.

Before Denver Bob could react, the night air around them split with a chorus of piercing whistles; that could only mean one thing, and the cry went up throughout the shanty-town.

"Bulls!"

Railroad cops and Pinkerton men had been running rousts through the hobo camps since the Pullman railroad strike in Chicago that previous May; violent, head-busting rampages, setting fire to the shanties and scattering whatever bums they didn't toss in prison to the winds. Through the summer, the bulls had worked their way down through St. Louis and along the tracks out toward the western camps, preceded by survivors' eye-popping accounts of the indiscriminate and malicious mayhem directed at their brothers. No more free rides, that was the new company policy. Seemed the railroad barons wanted their rails and stations sanitized so as not to offend the refined sensibilities of the middle-classers migrating westward and upon whose traveling dollar the Trust had decided the future fortunes of their railroad depended.

Fifty tramps basking in the numb glow of an alcoholic haze and the bulls burst in from behind a line of boxcars before a single one of them could reach his feet. Twenty headbusters, sneaking in like thieves; an ambush, nightsticks and sawed-off baseball bats in their hands, and they go right to work—most of these bums had endured a brick yard beating or two in their day but this was a whole new game. These boys meant business.

Two cops with torches set fire to the tinderbox shacks; the bulls had made their rush from both flanks, stampeding the hobos into the center of the yard, falling, colliding over each other, trapped as minnows in a net. Most knew enough to go to the ground, shelter their heads and absorb as much trouble as they could with the meat of their backs. Any man who tried to run was cut down around the knees and pummeled viciously. Scalps split open, collarbones cracked, blood flowed into pools.

Denver Bob fell at the first whistle, wrapped himself around the spool he'd been sitting on and waited for the blows to rain down on him. He looked back at the Chinaman, ready to yell and tell him to grab some dirt but the man was gone.

A big yard-bull raised his bat to swing at the tramp standing by the handcar, holding on to his long bundle. The bum gestured as the bat arced down at him and the blow never connected. The bull looked down in surprise; he clutched only the handle of the bat in his hands, sheared off, a clean cut just above his knuckles. As he looked up, the bum swung his arms around again—a chink, fer Christ's sake—and the bull felt something go haywire with his left leg; he tried to take a step and the leg split in two above the knee; his whole leg from foot to mid-thigh tipped away from him and flopped onto the ground; an instant later, the man's balance gave out and he toppled like a felled pine.

This makes no sense, thought the bull. The chink has a sword in his hand. No pain yet but he couldn't breathe. He looked up and saw the sole of the chink's boot screaming toward his face.

Kanazuchi had no time to offer a prayer for the dead

guard as another one charged up quickly behind him, weapon raised high. He dipped, back-kicked, and the out-of-control guard flipped over him and fell heavily; Kanazuchi grabbed the man's wrist and with a single twist removed his shoulder from its socket. A single blow across the bridge of the nose from the stick the guard had wielded drove a splinter of bone into his brain and silenced the man's screams.

Kanazuchi looked around, instantly analyzing the scene: Although they possessed far greater numbers, the men in the camp offered no resistance. None of the other attackers yet taking notice of him or the damage he'd done, preoccupied with the beatings. More of them darting in between the rail cars to his right. Fires flaring dangerously in the burning shacks in front of him. A cold, treacherous river at his back.

Cornered. Capture, overwhelmed by the sheer numbers of these men, carried a high probability.

Kanazuchi settled his breathing, remaining alert, wishing for nothing, escorting the fear from his body with every measured exhale.

There it was—an opening. A narrow gap in the attackers' formation under a water tower led to the rail bridge heading east. He would need to depend on the darkness and the chaos in the camp and keep the Grass Cutter out of sight in order to traverse the fifty yards.

Another guard took a run at him. Kanazuchi flowed to the ground, rose up underneath him and used the man's own momentum to toss him onto the roof of a burning lean-to. Moments later the man emerged screaming, flapping his arms like a bird, wrapped in flame. Distracted guards focused toward the burning figure and now he had his opportunity: Holding Grass Cutter in its sheath along the line of his pant leg, Kanazuchi began to walk across the yard.

Huddled beneath his spool, the guards hadn't found Denver Bob by the time it happened so he was the only man in the camp who saw the entire rush of the Chinaman clearly from start to finish. In the days to come, even with the leeway his eminence among his peers allowed him, it proved a tough tale for anyone to swallow. If the bodies of the seven bulls and the heads of the two Pinkerton men hadn't been left behind for all to see in the morning light, they would have called Denver Bob crazy to his face.

"The Chinaman moved like he was made out of liquid instead of solid flesh," Denver Bob grew fond of saying, but those were just words that did pale justice to a memory; as it was happening before him, he could hardly make sense out of what his eyes reported.

He walked calmly, with a lilting grace, like a man taking a stroll in the park. Every other body in sight making angular, frantic moves; men on either end of a vicious assault. Only by contrast did you even notice the figure moving placidly between them. Guards would catch sight of the man passing a foot away, reach out to swing a stick at him and before they'd taken the club completely back they were already on the ground, limbs snapped like kindling, faces broken. The Chinaman's arms and legs seemed to whirl out away from him in effortless patterns and then circle back; at one point he appeared to hang in the air. By the time he reached the edge of the yard and the two Pinkertons faced him down with their revolvers pulled, news had reached the rest of the bulls that something disastrous was happening in their midst.

That's when in a single smooth gliding motion the Chinaman pulled the sword out of its sheath along his pant leg, swung it around twice in a loop—you could see reflections from the fire glinting off its edges—and the heads of those Pinkerton men dropped like ripe melons.

The Chinaman ran. He was a blur. He was gone.

When they saw the wreckage he'd left behind, the fight gushed out of those bulls like a busted water bag. While they started to tend to their dead, the yard bums who could walk stumbled away into the night, scattering like shrapnel, carrying their bundles and what small fragments of the nightmare they had witnessed. As time went by, Denver Bob did the most talking; thanks primarily to him, in the world of the railroad bums, the story about the man with the sword who had saved the camp at Yuma passed into legend.

By dawn of the following day, a more practical conse-

quence, the manhunt to track down this murdering Chinaman, was already under way.

NEW YORK CITY

Dazzling electric light displays lit up the span of the boule-
vard and revealed a street carnival of humanity crowding
around the theaters and groggeries and dime museums and
particularly outside the town's newest sensation, the five-
cent Kinetoscope parlors lining either side of Broadway.
Roving vendors hawked a warehouse of cheap movable
goods—toys, shoes, scissors, suspenders, pots, and pans.
Knife grinders threw sparks off their whetstones; ragpickers
jangled the bells on their carts. Promenaders dined on baked
apples, hot cross buns, steamed clams for sale out on the
street. Winsome young girls offered cobs of hot corn—an attraction Innes did not fail to pick out of the mix. Some blew
bugles to sound their wares, others wore block-printed sand-
wich boards, most depended on their voices; sharp, repeti-
tive choruses cutting through the din.

Electric streetcar operators leaned on their horns and
carved a path through the dense carriage traffic, edging jittery horses still not accustomed to their presence out of the
way. Double-decked omnibuses trundled tourists looking for
a thrill around the tangled midtown streets; every few yards
of fitful progress brought a fresh sensation into view. Bo-
hemians in berets and garish neckerchiefs. Gamblers and
grifters sniffing out their next big play. Local toughs foot-
padding in striped sweaters and floppy gang hats. Preening
swells in plaid suits, pearl-gray derbies, and matching spats
taking the air with a dolly on each arm. Streetwalkers between jobs stumbling off their gin or hop. Irish cops patrolling a beat, bouncing their sticks off the sidewalk. A
Salvation Army band pounding drums, fishing for re-
cruitable strays. Pimps, rummies, newspaper boys, jugglers,
runaways, Chinese cigar sellers.

"Can you imagine, Arthur?" said Innes. "Ten o'clock at

night and the streets this full of life? By Jove, have you ever seen the like!"

Doyle watched Innes eyeing the parade, feeling a protective swell of affection for his brother's exuberance and untested innocence. Was there a danger he'd corrupt those qualities by leading him further down this path he'd begun to follow? He'd never mentioned a word to Innes about Jack Sparks or what they'd been through together, not even since Jack reappeared on the ship. Was it right to expose Innes to the sort of danger Jack courted as a matter of routine? Given his responsibilities to wife and family and his professional obligations, Doyle questioned whether he had any business putting himself in harm's way, either.

Sparks sat in the driver's perch above them, anonymous, cold. Doyle studied his face as he picked their way through traffic; he had harbored serious reservations about Jack's state of mind ten years ago: his obsessions, dark mood swings, his closeted appetite for drugs. He could only guess at what horrors the man had lived through since; he might have become perfectly deranged by now. Could he be trusted?

"This can't be the most direct way to the hotel, can it, Arthur?" said Innes, not minding at all.

It was not too late to fling open the door, spirit Innes away from Jack Sparks and everything he represented. Doyle saw the image of his wife's hands, folded peacefully in her lap. Irrationally, another woman's face drifted into his mind: the actress, Eileen Temple. The lights of these Broadway theaters must have summoned her up. He knew she had come to this city, leaving him flat at the end of their brief romance, to follow her career and seek her fortune. Her black Irish beauty; their fleeting time together had haunted him ever since. We want most what we can never have, thought Doyle. Could she be out here tonight, nearby, performing on one of the stages they passed, maybe even at this minute walking in this crowd that surrounded them? He scanned the faces, half hoping to find her. After so many years of intimacy with his wife, the thought of seeing Eileen now felt alien, illicit and thrilling. He could hardly remember who he'd been when he'd known her. Would he even recognize her after all this time?

Yes. He would remember her face until the day he died.

Then a third figure materialized. Queen Victoria. Proud. Frumpy. Enormously endearing. The bond of his word to her echoing back to him: He was hers to command whenever, wherever she required. She had never abused the privilege. And he remembered her unshakable faith in Jack Sparks, her most trusted secret agent, the man who had fought so bravely at his side. The man who had been such a friend to him . . .

There, he caught it, the root of his anger: He felt cheated. Jack had come back into his life as Doyle had always hoped he would, but the man that had shown up in his place was a shell, a remnant, depriving Doyle of the satisfaction of a true reunion. Still too early to tell if any trace of the Sparks he had known remained inside the ghostly shade driving their carriage; the evidence so far was anything but encouraging.

But Jack's stepped this far out of the grave against all odds; *perhaps I can help him the rest of the way. Don't I owe him that much? Isn't this man responsible for so much of the good fortune that has come into my life? Yes, my Christ: If there is a chance of his recovering, I have to see this through.*

Jack glanced down at him from the driver's seat. Was there a flicker of feeling in his eyes, that old affinity between them? As if he had picked up Doyle's thoughts and looked down to reassure him:

I'm still here. Have faith. It will take time, not words, to repair this damage.

Or was that nothing more than wishful thinking?

"Arthur?" asked Innes again. "Aren't we going back to the hotel?"

Doyle studied his brother: Innes had enlisted in the Royal Fusiliers at the earliest legal age, a soldier still in his heart, always itching for a fight and eager to serve the interests of the Crown. Hadn't he proved himself beyond a doubt in the action on board the *Elbe*? If he had to take someone into his confidence, who better than his own flesh and blood?

"We have some business to attend to first," said Doyle.

"Business? What sort of business?"

Doyle took a deep breath; yes, he would tell him. "A man I used to know. Name of Jack Sparks. He worked as a secret agent to the Queen."

"Never heard of such a thing," said Innes skeptically.

"That's why it was a secret," said Doyle patiently.

"Hmm. What about this Sparks fellow?"

"We met ten years ago. Innes, you must never speak about this to anyone; I need your solemn word."

"You have it," said Innes, his eyes growing rounder.

"Jack had an older brother: Alexander. When they were boys, Alexander murdered their sister. Six months old. Smothered her in the crib."

"He must have been mad."

"Dyed-in-the-wool. But unable to establish his guilt, they sent him off to school. One night years later, while Jack was at school in Europe, Alexander returned. Their home, an estate in Yorkshire, burned to the ground, killing everyone inside. But not before Alexander defiled and slaughtered his own mother before their father's eyes."

Innes narrowed his eyes in shock. "Terrible." Doyle had never told anyone Jack's story before, but his reaction was no surprise.

"Their father survived long enough to dictate Jack a letter describing Alexander's crimes. From that day forward, Jack dedicated his life to tracking down his brother. Along the way, he made himself into the greatest enemy the criminal element of our country has ever known. Eventually he entered the Queen's service, performing the same duties in service to the Crown.

"Then, ten years ago, Alexander finally revealed himself, mastermind of a foul plot against the throne; six other conspirators, they called themselves the Seven. With some small help from me, Jack thwarted their mad plan and pursued Alexander to the Continent. It ended with them both taking a deadly plunge over Reichenbach Falls in Switzerland."

"But that's, good God, Arthur, that's Holmes," gasped Innes.

"No," said Doyle, pointing at Jack. "That is. And he needs our help."

* * *

"No one has seen my father for nine days," said Lionel Stern. "He has a young assistant, a rabbinical student who comes in once a week to help organize the library—Father forgets to put books back on the shelves when he's finished with them, as you can see. . . ."

Stern swept his arm around the tables, chairs, and stacks of the low-ceiling basement room; every square inch occupied with books. Doyle, a dedicated bibliophile, had never seen such a varied and enviable selection.

"His filing system is to say the least a little archaic, and when he gets lost in following a line of inquiry, well, once he had books piled up so high he couldn't find the door. He had to tap on the window and alert someone passing by to come let him out." Stern pointed to the casement window that looked up and out at a busy street, shaking his head in fond memory. "When Father's assistant came last week and he wasn't here, it didn't alarm him—Father had missed appointments in the past without explanation. But when he came the second time, yesterday, and the room was exactly as he'd seen it the week before, that was quite a different story."

He loves his father very much, in spite of their disagreements, thought Doyle. He's trying to conceal how much his father's absence hurts him.

"Has he gone off like this in the past?" asked Doyle.

"For a day or so, never longer. He took a walk once, trying to sort out some biblical discrepancy—he likes to walk while he thinks; keeps blood moving through the brain, he says—and he solved it all right, but by that time it was dark and he was in the middle of the Bronx Botanical Gardens."

"No friends or relatives he might have gone to visit?"

"I'm his only family. Mother died five years ago. There are other rabbis he knows, scholars, colleagues; most of them live in the neighborhood. I've spoken to them; no one's had any word. Aside from one other occasion, he's never been out of New York City before."

Innes stepped forward to lift up a peculiar leather-bound manuscript embossed with an inscription that appealed to his eye.

"Don't touch it," said Sparks sharply.

Innes jumped back as if he'd burned his hand on a stove.

"Don't touch anything. The answer is somewhere in this room." Sparks moved slowly between the bookshelves, eyes traveling methodically from one detail to another, accumulating information. Doyle carefully watched him work; this much about him seemed unchanged.

"When did you last hear from your father?" asked Doyle.

"He wired me before Rupert and I left London, ten days ago; routine communication, asking about our arrival, business having to do with the acquisition and transportation of the Zohar."

"And you replied?"

"Yes."

"Anything in your answer that might have prompted his leaving?"

"I can't imagine what it might have been; I'd already sent him an identical wire the week before answering all the questions he asked me in his. He probably lost it. Keeping mindful of what he calls the 'bookkeeping' of life is not his strength: you know, comings and goings. Paying his bills. All of that falls to me for the most part."

Sparks pulled a pair of long tweezers from his coat and extracted a sheet of yellow paper protruding a quarter inch out from under a stack of books on the table.

"Here's your first telegram," said Sparks. "Unopened. Unread."

"See what I mean?" said Stern. "If he won the sweepstakes, the check could get lost in here for twenty years."

"It is a most impressive theological library," said Doyle, walking between the stacks. "I've never seen such a concentration of rare volumes in any private collection before; quartos, folios, first editions."

"Must be worth a fortune," said Innes, one of the few statements he'd felt confident enough to utter in Sparks's presence.

"Whatever small amounts of money have passed through his hands over the years ended up in a book, that much I'm sure of," said Stern. "Most of them were gifts, donations from friends, various institutions."

"A fine tribute to your father's standing as a scholar," said Doyle.

"There's really no one else quite like him," said Stern, settling onto a stool. "After Mother died, he began spending more and more of his time down here alone. Most nights he'd sleep on that sofa over there." He pointed to a poor-looking daybed in the corner. "To be honest, I never could understand half of what he was talking about. Maybe if I'd made more of an effort, I could have understood and he—" His voice choked; he hung his head, trying to stave off tears.

"Here, here," said Innes, a hand on his back, the closest to him. "We're sure to find him. Without fail. No quit in this bunch."

Stern nodded, grateful. Sparks turned and walked right up to him, offering no acknowledgment of his emotion.

"Your father's methods of study," said Sparks. "He took notes as he read."

"Yes. Volumes."

"A pen in his left hand. Sitting in this chair." Sparks walked to a chair at the desk.

"How did you know?"

"Worn on the rests; scratches along the left arm; he wore a long coat, with buttons on the sleeves."

"Yes, he almost always wore that coat. He was usually cold down here; poor circulation, the doctor said, but to tell the truth Father was always a bit of a hypochondriac."

Hasn't lost his observation skills, thought Doyle. Sparks sat in Rabbi Stern's chair and stared at the books cluttering the desk directly before him. He peered closer, reached in, and lifted one book off the pile, unveiling a pad of white lined paper underneath. He leaned down and studied the pad.

"Have a look at this," he said.

Doyle and Stern joined him; the paper covered with sketches, doodles, scrawled phrases, snatches of academic doggerel; the quality of the drawings surprisingly expert and detailed.

"Yes, Father often did this sort of thing when he worked," said Stern. "Drew odd bits while thinking something through—he was clever that way. I used to sit with him and watch when I was a boy; he'd sketch street scenes, faces, people passing by."

Two central images on the page: a large tree with drooping, denuded branches, holding ten round, white globes arrayed in a geometric pattern and connected by straight lines.

"That's the Tree of Life," said Stern. "An image I've seen in kabbalistic books. I'm afraid I couldn't begin to tell you the significance of it."

The other image: a black castle, stark and forbidding, a single window illuminated in its highest tower. Sparks's eyes narrowed as he stared at it.

"Looks like something out of, what do you call it, you know," said Innes, snapping his fingers. "The dwarf and the pretty girl . . ."

"Rumpelstiltskin?" said Stern.

"Rapunzel let down your hair and all that," said Innes.

Doyle didn't take his eyes off Sparks; something was rumbling up from deep inside the man.

"What does *this* mean?" said Sparks, pointing to a boldly sketched cuneiform figure on the page below the castle.

"*Schischah*," said Stern. "That's the Hebrew word for six."

"The *number* six?" asked Sparks.

"Yes," said Stern. "It has other meanings, in the kabbalistic sense, but you'd need a scholar to—"

Sparks stood up abruptly and jumped back from the table; chair legs screeched against the floor. He stared over at the bed in the corner, a wild, uncontained look passing through his eyes, as if he'd seen a ghost.

"Jack? You all right?" asked Doyle.

Sparks didn't answer. Tension coming off him permeated the room. A water pipe dripping rhythmically somewhere sounded as loud as gunshots.

"Where is the Gerona Zohar?" asked Sparks.

"The safe in my offices," said Stern. "A few blocks north of here."

"I need to see it. Now."

"I'll take you there."

Sparks and Stern started for the door.

"Bring that pad of paper," said Doyle quietly to Innes. He pried the pad out from under the books without knocking over the stack and they followed Jack out of the tenement.

Gaslight threw weak ripples of light into the damp air. Sparks led the way like a bloodhound straining at its leash; footsteps echoing, streets empty as midnight approached.

In the shadows across the way from Stern's building on St. Mark's Place loitered two young toughs, cigarettes hanging off their lips. As the party went inside, and lights flickered on in the fourth-floor window of the office, one of the toughs ran off down the street; the other stayed to watch.

Lionel Stern dialed the safe's combination, removed the wooden crate, set it down on his desk, and lifted the cover. The Gerona Zohar was large, nearly two feet square and three inches deep, bound in dark antiquated leather. Stern slipped on a pair of frayed white gloves and opened the cover; the binding creaked like an arthritic elbow.

"Backwards, isn't it?" asked Innes.

"Hebrew reads from right to left; this is the front of the book," said Stern.

"I see," said Innes, wishing he could swallow his fist.

Sparks stared at the parchment of the first page, yellow and crusted with age, densely covered with fading handwritten words.

"Let me see that pad," said Sparks.

Innes handed it to him. Doyle watched Jack: What was he on to?

"Is this a drawing of the Zohar, here?" asked Sparks, pointing to a sketch on the pad's margin: an open, leatherbound book, strikingly similar to the one before them. Matching script scribbled inside its front page.

"Could be," said Doyle.

Sparks took out a magnifying glass, leaned over and examined Stern's drawing then scrutinized the first page of the Gerona Zohar.

"Your father has never seen the Gerona Zohar?" asked Sparks.

"No."

"Then how has he in this sketch exactly reproduced its first page?"

Sparks handed the glass to Doyle: The minute writing in Rabbi Stern's sketch was identical to the book. Stern examined the two fragments as well.

"I can't account for it," said Stern.

"What do you make of this?" asked Sparks, pointing to a dark shape on the pad drawn over the corner of the book.

"A shadow," said Doyle, looking closer. "A hand. Reaching for the book."

"Did your father ever talk about his dreams?" asked Sparks.

"Dreams? No, not that I can recall."

"What are you driving at, Jack?" asked Doyle.

Sparks looked at the pad and pointed to the drawing of the castle.

"I have seen this black tower before," he said.

"Seen it? Where?"

Sparks looked up at Doyle, hesitant. "In a dream."

"This same tower?"

"I could have sketched this myself."

"Sure it's not some place you saw once that's drifted up through your subconscious?" said Stern.

"Then how do we explain the drawing?" asked Doyle. "You said your father never left New York City."

"He came here from Russia as a young man," said Stern. "Perhaps something he saw there or along the way."

"Perhaps a picture he came across in a book," said Innes, taking the pad and the glass from Stern.

"What sort of dream, Jack?" asked Doyle, trying to keep him focused.

Sparks stared grimly at the drawing, then spoke softly, as if confessing something to Doyle. "I had the dream first three months ago. Keeps coming back, with greater intensity, always the same. This black tower. A white desert. Something underground. A phrase repeating over and over again in my mind. *We are Six.*"

"Six? You mean—"

"Yes."

"Like the number Stern drew on the pad . . ."

"Yes."

"Who's Brachman?" asked Innes.

"Brachman? Where did you see that?" asked Stern.

"Written here, very small letters, on the edge of this drawing," said Innes, pointing to the pad with the glass.

"Isaac Brachman is a colleague of my father's, a rabbi at a temple in Chicago. . . ."

"And a scholar of the Zohar?"

"One of the most learned. I may have mentioned him to you on the ship, if not by name. We obtained the Tikkunei Zohar, the addendum to the Zohar, for him to study. Rabbi Brachman was a principal organizer of the Parliament of Religions last year at the Columbian Exposition in Chicago."

"Did your father attend that convention?" asked Doyle.

"He did; every major religion in the world was represented. . . ."

"When was the last time you spoke to Rabbi Brachman?"

"I don't recall; weeks ago, certainly before I left for London."

"You must wire him immediately," said Doyle.

"Why?"

"Doyle is suggesting that your father's gone to Chicago to visit Rabbi Brachman," said Sparks, coming out of his fog.

"Yes, of course, that would be possible, wouldn't it?" said Stern, suddenly hopeful.

And preferable to a number of the other alternatives, thought Doyle.

"Do you have the other book I asked for?" asked Sparks.

"Yes, it's right here," said Stern. He lifted a book similar in size and design to the Gerona Zohar from a cabinet and onto the table beside the original. "A copy of the Zohar, nearly indistinguishable, but this is a fairly recent recreation: Only a scholar could tell them apart."

"You might want to have a look at this," said Innes, who had wandered away from the table to the window.

"What is it, Innes?" said Doyle.

"Not sure, but I'd say there's at least twenty of them."

An instant later they were at the window, looking down at the street.

The two toughs outside had multiplied tenfold, and a dozen more were pouring down the block to join them.

"Street gang," said Sparks.

One of the gang looked up, saw the four men outlined in the window, pointed at them and whistled sharply.

At his signal, the gang rushed across the pavement, toward the doors of the tenement.

chapter seven

THE HUNT FOR THE MURDERING CHINAMAN STARTED poorly and went downhill fast. Troops mustered from the Territorial Prison at Yuma told anyone willing to listen that they were a lot handier dealing with criminals who were already behind bars, with their dependable tendency to stay put. What this mob knew about chasing fugitives you could print on the back of a postage stamp. Nor were they exactly at their spit-and-polish best when the call came in to rush down to the rail yard at five in the morning since most of them had been out drinking themselves comatose until two.

The railroad bulls and Pinkerton men who had lived through the Yuma Yards Massacre—as it inevitably came to be known, frontier journalism being what it was—were so consumed with shock, grief, or blinding rage that pulling them into a cohesive militia unit would have been beyond any officer less commanding than Robert E. Lee. That was certainly no description anyone had ever tried to hang on Sheriff Tommy Butterfield.

Sheriff Tommy was the most senior local lawman at the scene that morning. He spent the first ten minutes after he saw the carnage throwing up and the next fifteen wandering around in a daze. Wasn't as if Tommy added to the confusion rampaging through the camp; it's just that at a moment when these men needed a leader to pull them together, Tommy's passivity allowed the vigilante impulse to spin out of control and fracture into a dozen squabbling splinter groups, each with their own ideas about how to find this killer. Tommy had been elected sheriff on a peace platform—the territory was looking toward statehood, working to clean up its image in order to attract some serious money—and this soft-bellied, fat-headed political hack who'd never shot a man, even in anger, was a lot more adept at getting people to like him than he was at telling them what to do.

It didn't help that no two surviving witnesses could agree on a single characteristic of the man responsible, aside from the fact that he carried a sword, and that was hard to swallow even with one leg and two severed heads on the ground. Why would anybody in this day and age carry a sword when with the helpful hand of modern technology you could ventilate a man's lungs from a quarter mile away?

Neither could anyone confirm in which direction the maniac had made his escape, which left them with eight compass points to argue about. The bums could have filled in some blanks for them, particularly Denver Bob Hobbes, but figuring wisely that when the powers that be got around to handing out the blame for this they'd be on top of the list, the hobos were busy making tracks in those same eight directions.

But somebody somewhere heard somebody else say that the killer was a Chinaman, and when that idea raced through camp, it stuck hard and fast: Who else but an unhinged rice monkey would chop suey a bunch of white men with a sword? An Apache, for one, somebody said, and that set off a debate on the relative barbarism of the red and yellow man.

Sheriff Tommy Butterfield couldn't recall later if he was the first person to mention calling in Buckskin Frank—he wasn't—but being the consummate politico, Tommy was more than willing to take credit for the idea: If using Frank worked out, he could plug it right in as the keystone of his next campaign. Tommy knew there'd be a barrel full of details to sort out before they could spring him, but there was one thing the mob in camp could agree on that morning: If any man in the Arizona Territory could track down this homicidal heathen, it was Buckskin Frank McQuethy.

Unlike Sheriff Tommy, Buckskin Frank had shot, stabbed, and strangled a number of individuals on both sides of the law. Frank began his illustrious career as a deputy under Arizona's genius of publicity, Wyatt Earp, during Tombstone's heyday in the early '80s. Long before Wyatt reinvented himself as an all-American folk hero, Frank had worked with the Earps as bouncer and bartender at the Oriental Saloon, one of the grandest whorehouses in the West. Wyatt was a charismatic son of a bitch—Frank couldn't help but admire his verve and relentless ambition—and when the Earps seized economic control of Tombstone, Frank rode their coattails to prosperity and minor celebrity.

But for a man who made his living with a gun, when it came to outright murder Frank had an inconvenient sense of right and wrong, and it led to a falling-out with the Earps when he refused to help slaughter the Clanton clan, a rotten bunch of horse-thieving half-wits who made the fatal mistake of horning in on their operations. With Wyatt busy transforming that nasty, one-sided ambush into the triumph of the O.K. Corral, Frank wandered north and solidified his hard-nosed reputation with a stint as an Army scout in the Geronimo Campaigns. His nickname came from the yellow buckskin jacket he took to wearing; the minute he put it on, the papers started writing that Buckskin Frank could track a man across a hundred miles of hardscrabble and shoot the eyes off a rattlesnake, but then he had learned the art of self-mythologizing from a master.

Except when he was drinking, Frank McQuethy was never anything less than a gentleman. Unfortunately, he had been drinking that night in '89 when he pushed Molly Fanshaw, his favorite girl, off the balcony of Whitely's Emporium in downtown Tombstone. Frank had been so pickled he couldn't even remember what they were fighting about— Molly was a mean drunk and had no doubt provoked him beyond human endurance—but he'd killed the only woman he'd ever loved in front of a crowd, plain and simple, so he pleaded guilty, took his life sentence like a man, and for the last five years had been a model prisoner at the Territorial Prison. And Frank hadn't touched a drop of liquor since Molly went over the rail.

Fellow inmates, the warden, even the guards, were all crazy about Frank; his courtesy, the not too obvious effects of his education, the way he held his head high in spite of his hard time, most of which he spent in the infirmary as chief assistant to the resident sawbones. During the cholera epidemic of '92, at considerable risk of contagion, Frank deprived himself of sleep for weeks to stand by their beds and ease the suffering of the afflicted. Frank's buckskin jacket hanging in a glass case remained the hands-down highlight of the twenty-five-cent tour the prison offered the paying public. Nearly every day, guards at the gate had to turn away some impressionable young dove who'd come to catch a glimpse of Frank exercising in the yard, brokenhearted that law would not allow her to speak with him face-to-face.

But Frank never failed to answer their letters, delicately suggesting that yes, it was likely they were destined never to meet, but perhaps a letter to the governor attesting to his character from such an upstanding woman—or anyone else of weight she might know in the community—could persuade him to reconsider his life sentence and make their meeting a reality. The governor even now had before him a petition to pardon Buckskin. Frank had sown the seeds of his freedom with the diligence of Luther Burbank, but it took the blood of a massacre to fertilize the field.

Sheriff Tommy called in every favor owed him. Warden Gates wired the governor and by breakfast they'd hammered out the deal: On a *conditional furlough,* he was still to be considered a prisoner and never left alone. But it was quietly agreed that if Frank could capture the man responsible for the Yuma Yards murders, clemency would be right around the corner.

At eight that morning, the guards unlocked Frank's cell; one carried his buckskin jacket like a piece of the true cross. By nine, Frank arrived at the shanty camp ready to play the savior and was met by the sorriest excuse for a posse working the sloppiest crime scene he'd ever come across.

Bodies, limbs, and heads of the victims had been jumbled like jigsaw pieces; every key witness was lost, exhausted, or hysterical; the muddy ground had been slogged into a quagmire. Frank's spirits, which had flown high as the warden explained their arrangement, settled around sea level. Five years in prison and he suddenly felt his age: Forty was old out here, and a new breed was taking over the West, stiffs like these, businessmen, desk jockeys. One of the last bona fide shooters, John Wesley Hardin, had been gunned down in El Paso in August, plugged in the back. Buckskin felt a real loss when he heard that news: For all their petty thievery and bullshit, the Earps, John Wesley, and Frank had been birds of a feather. One good look at this bunch and he knew those days were gone for good.

Frank walked the perimeter, followed by this pack of sapheads; he found one faint set of tracks, a man moving at a dead run toward the swing bridge heading east over the Colorado. While the posse waited breathlessly behind him, he rolled a smoke, stood on the bridge, and asked himself: Where would he go if he'd done a crime like this?

Mexico, less than five miles downriver from where he was standing.

Then he had to ask himself a harder one: If one man armed only with a sword could slice his way through a whole gang of seasoned railroad bulls like a stand of green saplings, how could he and this roundup of candy-ass amateurs ever bring him to ground?

Two pleasant thoughts occurred to Frank at once: These knuckle draggers had no idea what their killer looked like except he was a Chinaman, and no white man he'd ever met could tell one of them from the other. Which meant as soon as he had a reasonable suspect in sight, he could drop the son of a bitch with a buffalo gun from a hundred yards and no one would be the wiser. Fuck this sword stuff.

He lit his cigarette.

The other thing was, if it all turned to shit, before this bunch ever caught up with him he could probably make it to Mexico himself.

PHOENIX, ARIZONA

As Frank stood smoking on the bridge, Kanazuchi slipped out of a boxcar in the morning freight arriving at the Phoenix yards. He made his way cautiously along the tracks between trains, alert to dangers resulting from his escape.

The fight was regrettable but capture was not acceptable. Reviewing his behavior in light of the circumstances, no other action had been practical. He willed the matter out of his mind; further examination would cause unnecessary distraction. His brothers had chosen him for this mission because of his fierce dedication to mastery of *budo*.

Sensei's voice came to him: Do not think about winning, losing, taking advantage, impressing, or disregarding your opponent. That is not the Way.

Tired, half-starved, and thousands of miles from home, he reminded himself those perceptions were illusions resulting from an over identification with the concerns of the small self. That was not the Way, either. The future depended on him; if the missing Book was not returned, their monastery would weaken and die like a tree cut from its roots. The Way would fail. Thoughts of failure would only lead to failure.

In the absence of food or water, let that thought sustain me.

The early morning air carried the promise of heat; the ground flat and dusty, alien to him. As Kanazuchi drew within a hundred paces of the terminal, he heard voices approaching; he rolled beneath a car and hung from its undercarriage, tucking himself out of sight like a spider. Footsteps of a dozen men passed within ten feet of his hiding place; loud and purposeful, slamming open doors, examining the cars of the freight he had traveled on. He sent himself into their minds, felt tension and fear turned around into assertive, self-protective violence.

Identify with all things and all people; kill the small self inside and everything in creation can be known.

Word had been sent ahead along the singing wires and they are looking for me, he realized: One of the men had said the word "Chinaman."

After they passed, Kanazuchi lowered himself to the ground, pulled out his knife, and with one stroke sliced off his queue. He buried the hair under a rail tie: time for the "Chinaman" to vanish.

Crawling out, he continued toward the station, inching his way behind a long stack of cotton bales. Kanazuchi observed the bustling terminal; looking past the crowd of passengers, he could see the offices of the Santa Fe, Prescott and Phoenix Railroad, his original objective. But his plan would have to be delayed indefinitely until this pursuit quieted and he could assemble a new identity.

Fifty paces to his right, workers were unloading large canvas-draped cargo from a boxcar onto rolling sleds, which they hauled to a smaller train on a nearby track. A tall, fat man in a feathered hat strutted around, puffed up and busy as a rooster, pointing this way and that, squawking in a loud, empty voice, but the workers weren't even listening to him.

A steamer trunk tumbled off one of the sleds and opened on impact, spilling out its contents: packed layers of men's and women's clothes, heavy brocaded cloaks, clusters of shoes. The man in the feathered hat stood up on his toes and hectored the worker unmercifully; the worker ignored him and casually heaped the garments back into the trunk. The man in the hat pulled them back out and threw them on the ground again, demanding the worker fold the clothes properly before repacking them.

"Hey."

Kanazuchi wheeled to his left; a man had walked in behind him, standing six feet away. He wore a blue uniform and hat and a badge on the breast of his tunic. They stared at one another for a long moment—then Kanazuchi saw a look of fear cross the man's coarse features; before he could react, the man raised a whistle to his lips and blew one shrill, piercing note. He was reaching with his other hand for a gun holstered at his waist when Kanazuchi broke his neck and dragged the body down behind the bales.

Maybe no one has seen this, he thought.

No: Two men wearing the same blue uniform had heard the whistle and were moving out of the station; passengers on the platform pointing in the direction of the bales. Both men blew their own whistles, pulled their guns, and ran toward where Kanazuchi crouched over the dead guard.

A bullet smacked the cotton near his head with a dry splat; to the left Kanazuchi saw a third guard, pistol in hand, sprinting toward him down the tracks.

*   *   *

Throughout the night, between her own bouts of fitful dreaming, Eileen laid her head back and studied Jacob Stern while he slept, his eyes moving rapidly back and forth behind their papery lids, forehead furrowed, lips twitching, small sounds of distress occasionally accompanying his shallow exhales. She didn't wake him, but the incongruity of the sight disturbed her; he seemed much more troubled asleep than awake.

A slant of morning sun touched her face, and coming out of a dream, she realized the rocking of the car had ceased. She opened her eyes and was welcomed by Jacob's warm smile and twinkling eyes watching her benignly.

"Are we here?" she asked.

"Wherever we are, we seem to have arrived," he said.

"Rise and shine! Rise and shine, friends!" Bendigo Rymer strode down the car, rousing the weary Players to groaning protest. "Like the mystical phoenix, whose name graces this fair city, we must arise from the ashes of our deathlike slumber and re-create ourselves in the image of a new day!"

"Piss off," somebody muttered.

Bendigo pretended not to hear their insults but dropped the poetic approach in favor of a more direct line of reasoning. "We've another train to catch, lady and gents, and if you expect to collect your wages this morning, you will remove your rear ends from these seats in short order and carry them along with your luggage to the station!"

Perpetually vulnerable to economic arguments, the Players began to grumble and stir. Peering up from her position on the seat, Eileen saw two enormous pheasant feathers bouncing up and down the aisle: He's wearing that ridiculous Tyrolean cap again, she realized, the one that makes him look like Robin Hood gone to seed. God, what an annoying man!

"Will you be staying in Phoenix long, Jacob?" asked Eileen, as she stumbled out of the car, shielding her eyes against the bright desert sunrise. Her legs felt rusted from sleeping in her seat, and one glance in a hand mirror proved traumatizing; hair tangled as a bramble bush, makeup ruined; mornings were frightful enough ordeals for a woman to begin with and far worse while on the road. Why did he have to see her like this?

"To be perfectly honest, my dear, I haven't the slightest idea," said Jacob good-naturedly, breathing deeply. "This air is marvelous, isn't it? Dry but with a refreshing warmth to it and heavily scented with flowers."

"It's a little early for me, Jacob," she said, thinking he could make a trip to the dentist sound like a country picnic.

"But can't you smell it? It's almost sweet to the taste."

"Life on the road, love; for we jaded sophisticates, one stop is pretty much the same as another."

"What a pity; think how much you must miss."

"This from a man who hasn't left his library in fifteen years."

"And realizing the error of his ways, I assure you. But how fantastic to travel so much; you must have seen the entire country by now. Where are you off to next?"

"Our head thespian has booked us a week in some god-forsaken whistlestop somewhere out west of here. . . ."

"Where is that?"

"Don't know; some sort of religious settlement—what's it called again, Bendigo?" she asked Rymer as he hurled by them. "This oasis you're taking us to."

"The New City; capital T on the 'The,' " said Rymer, racing to oversee the transfer of sets and costumes to their connecting train. "A joy to meet you, Rabbi. May God always shield you from the storm."

"And you, sir."

"Lord, he makes my teeth hurt sometimes," said Eileen.

When they reached the planked platform of the terminal, Eileen set down her makeup case, looked at Jacob frankly, and smiled, a winsome blend of affection and regret. "I'm sorry to say we're moving on within the hour actually."

Jacob swallowed hard and looked down at his feet, shuffling them on the knotted wood. *What's the matter with you, Jacob? She's a beautiful woman less than half your age that you've known for twelve hours whom you're never going to see again and you're behaving like a heartsick schoolboy.*

He groped through his thoughts, desperate for a conversation starter.

"What sort of religious settlement is this place you're going?"

"Like the Mormons, I guess. Bendigo's been as evasive as usual," she said, hearing the man's raised voice and turning to see him in the distance screaming bloody murder at some poor railroad hand transferring their sets between trains: Rymer had a gift for terrorizing menials.

"Like the Mormons in what way?"

"He didn't say. They probably all keep twenty-five wives apiece; a regular Sodom."

Jacob blushed and Eileen instantly regretted her off-color tone, unused to censoring herself and feeling unladylike, realizing how long it had been since she'd kept company with a man who made her feel any other way.

"Actually all he's told us is it's in the middle of the desert and they've built themselves an opera house and they're very keen to have some first-rate entertainment come through. So why they hired us is anyone's guess."

"I hope this place is not too dangerous."

"Compared to some of the dumps we've been, how bad could it be? Looking forward to it, actually; he said they're building a great big black castle out there that's really something to see."

Ice water would not have been more effective: Jacob snapped instantly to his senses. "What sort of castle?"

Before she could answer, a sharp whistle cut through the clatter of the station; her eye was drawn toward Rymer and the trains: fifty yards off, halfway between them, some kind of commotion behind a stack of cotton bales. She could see people moving toward the disturbance: a struggle?

Two guards rushed out of the station behind them; Eileen and some other passengers on the platform pointed them toward the cotton bales. The guards blew their own whistles and pulled their pistols as they ran.

Somewhere a shot was fired.

"What's going on?" she asked.

"I don't know," said Jacob.

*   *   *

"Which way to the roof?" asked Jack.

"I'll show you," said Stern. "What about the books?"

"Bring them both," said Doyle.

"I thought we wanted them to take the copy," said Stern.

"We do but we don't want it to seem too easy," said Jack.

"We don't even know if these are the same men," said Doyle.

Footsteps crashing up the stairs. Stern slipped the original Zohar into a well-worn leather pouch while Jack picked up the copy.

"And we don't care to wait and find out. Which way?" asked Jack.

"Follow me," said Stern. He stuffed the Gerona Zohar under his arm like a football and led them out the nearest door, through a warren of cramped rooms connected by tiny L-shaped corridors, and up a seldom-used set of back stairs.

"They" were the Houston Dusters, a street gang with a talent for prolific, unparalleled violence. The Dusters had ruled the Lower East Side from Houston Street to East Broadway for a generation, but new gangs were always stepping up to challenge their borders, in addition to their traditional antagonisms with more established outfits like the Gophers, the Five Pointers, the Fashion Plates, and the rising tongs of Chinatown.

Economic hardship, collapse of the immigrant family structure—nearly all the Dusters were first- or second-generation Irish—and society's failure to provide a legitimate toehold for its disadvantaged undoubtedly contributed to the flourishing of gang culture, but when you came right down to the heart of the matter, the matter, the Dusters were a bunch of wrong guys, a character flaw that had never proved a detriment to getting ahead in New York. These ruffians absorbed the lesson early in life that a career in crime might be a disreputable path to prosperity and the American dream, but it was a crowded shortcut.

Unmistakable, intimidating figures in their neighborhood, well over two hundred in number, the Dusters communicated with a vocabulary of savage war whoops inspired by the Indians their leader once saw in Buffalo Bill Cody's Wild West Extravaganza at Madison Square Garden. The nattiest of East Side gangs, they sported round, heavily padded leather caps that pulled down over the ears and doubled as protective helmets, steel-toed hobnail boots—the better to stomp you with—and pants with a loud red stripe running down the leg, symbolizing their fleetness of foot. Blades, concrete-filled lead pipes, and home-crafted blackjacks were their weapons of choice. The gang's code of honor considered shooting your enemy at a distance a coward's way to settle disputes. Blood on your hands, that was the Duster motto.

For the last nine years, the Dusters had been commanded by a ruthless evil-eyed weasel named Ding-Dong Dunham, an unusually robust term of office in the gang racket. Ding-Dong had clawed his way up through the ranks, equipped with the sociopath's advantage of caring not a penny for the value of human life: His nickname derived from the greeting Dunham used to gleefully scream in the ears of robbery victims after his spiked cudgel connected with their hats. He also had a penchant for writing epic poems about the more fanciful acts of mayhem he and his cohorts committed; Ding-Dong regularly forced the Dusters to endure recitals of his work, an act of debatably greater cruelty than the crimes he was immortalizing.

Earlier that day, Ding-Dong had accepted a commission from a goodlooking German man—Dunham ascertaining that by the man's Teutonic accent, clever lad that he was—who said he was fresh off the boat, had no associates he could rely on in New York, and needed someone to keep an eye peeled on a particular fourth-floor office in a building on St. Mark's Place, just north of the heart of Duster territory. If anyone showed up in that office, Ding-Dong's boys were to take them into custody and escort them to headquarters so this kraut could question them personally.

No mention had been made by this tall, blond fellow to Dunham about an old holy book or whose offices they were watching, but the man paid half his generous fee for the work up front in solid gold ingots, which went a long way toward discouraging Ding-Dong's idle curiosity about what this pretzel twister was up to.

But the subtlety of detaining somebody and hauling them back for questioning was wasted on the thirty Dusters rushing up the front stairs of the tenement, most of them flying on cocaine—or "dust"—and cheap dago red. With their clubs and knives and saps at the ready, these psychotic brutes had no intention of deviating from their standard operating procedure: Beat the holy hell out of whoever got in the way and if they lived through it, drag the pieces back to Ding-Dong for him to sort out.

As Stern led the others onto the roof above the sixth floor, the men could hear Dusters breaking into the offices below, sacking the place, smashing windows, destroying everything in their path like berserk Visigoths. Stern locked the door behind them, an act that might buy them two seconds of time, and directed them across the rooftop to the north.

Jack handed the fake Zohar off to Doyle, waved them on ahead, and hung back, pulling something from a nest of pockets inside his coat as he knelt beside the locked door. He caught up with them as they climbed down a short ladder to the next roof, just as the first Dusters busted through the door behind them.

The report from the explosion they triggered wasn't booming, it generated more of a loud theatrical hiss, but the flames were white-hot and the smoke laced with pepper and saltpeter. The first two Dusters went down, scorched and dazed by the detonation; a third, engulfed in fire, and "dusted" beyond the reach of rational thought, jumped off the roof. The second threesome through caught the full effect of the gas and fell to their knees, gagging, blinded, screaming bloody murder. The next ten Dusters that followed got wise, pulled their kerchiefs up over their faces, held their breath, and sprinted to the far side of the smoke, barking orders back down the stairs: Send the rest of the boys to the street; they're taking the roof!

Jack jumped from the ladder and joined the Doyles as Stern took off ahead of them, picking his way through a tangle of clotheslines, box gardens, pigeon coops, and exhaust pipes on the tar paper roof; about thirty seconds behind them, ten Dusters reached the ladder and leaped down after them. The roof of the next tenement required a climb up twelve rungs; Jack brought up the rear and stopped at the apex, sacrificing half of their lead to pack something from a vial in tight against the bricks. By the time he planted a short fuse in the claylike substance and lit a match, the Dusters had reached the bottom rungs. Jack dodged a thrown knife, as Doyle and Innes drove the hoodlums momentarily back to the cover of a chimney with a barrage of bricks ripped from a retaining wall. Jack lit the fuse and they ran on again; the Dusters were halfway up the ladder when Jack's charge went off, ripping the bolts from the wall and sending the ladder and two lead Dusters crashing backward to the roof.

Doyle diverted his path to the street side edge of the rooftop and glanced uneasily down through the soupy night air; the main pack of Dusters was keeping pace with them below, others sprinting ahead trying to anticipate where they could enter a building, climb up, and cut off their line of retreat. Doyle thought the Dusters, shouting taunts and whooping battle cries up at their quarry on the roof, looked and sounded like Stone Age savages on a hunt, which in many ways was exactly what they were.

"Handy fellow to have along, your Jack," said Innes, joining him at the edge.

"Quite," said Doyle.

"Wish I had my Enfield," said Innes, squeezing off an imaginary shot at the Dusters in the street: anger in his eyes. In his element, Doyle noted with pride.

"This way," said Stern.

The roof of the next tenement turned out to be the last on the block; the top of the building on the street running to their left stood across a ten-foot gap with a drop of fifty disappearing below into darkness. They stopped and looked two roofs back where the pursuing Dusters, with their profound native ingenuity, had formed a human pyramid; half their platoon, already elevated up the ladderless wall, were pulling the others up behind them.

"We'll have to jump," said Jack.

"Is that really necessary?" said Doyle.

"Unless you have any other suggestions," said Jack, laying a loose board on the bricks edging the roof, creating a small ramp.

"What about the books?" asked Stern, who had done nothing to tarnish the sturdy impression of his mettle Doyle had formed on the *Elbe*.

"I'll manage it," said Jack.

Jack took both books from the men, stepped back, made a measured run up the ramp, and spanned the gap easily, landing nimbly on his feet.

"You go next," said Doyle.

"Don't fancy heights much, do you, Arthur?" said Innes, making his run. "You'll be fine."

Stern followed: Jack and Innes caught him as he fell slightly short and hauled him over the lip.

Doyle stepped back as far as he could for his try at the jump, steeled himself, wished he wasn't wearing his smooth-soled brogans, took a dead run, and closed his eyes as he went airborne. His crash landing put a dent in the roof and knocked out his wind.

"All right then, Arthur?" asked Innes, as they lifted him to his feet.

Doyle nodded, gasping for air.

They caught up to Stern, standing at the edge of the next roof, staring apprehensively at the building a few steps below them.

"What's wrong?" asked Innes.

"The Gates of Hell," said Stern.

"Here? In New York?" said Innes. "I thought they were in Wapping."

"What do you mean?" asked Jack.

"That's what this building is called. It's the most notorious slum in the city; over a thousand people live in there."

Even viewed from above, amid the squalor of its neighbor tenements, this one stood out. Tents and shabby huts congested the rooftop, and a solid column of stench that was nearly unendurable rose from the borders of the place; filth, ordure, disease, decaying meat.

Whooping cries from the gap behind them, answered from the ground below, heralded the imminent arrival of the Dusters; there was nowhere to go but forward.

As they ran across the roof, faces peered out at them from the huts; bone-white, starving, dispossessed. Inside the flimsy structures, they saw shadowy figures huddled around small ash can fires, waiting passively for more misfortune. As they neared the far side of the roof, the cries of the trailing Dusters were echoed by identical voices directly ahead; the vanguard of the pack on the street had outflanked them and climbed to the next roof, pinching them in. Following Stern's lead, the men doubled back and found a door leading down into the Gates of Hell.

As dreadful as the smell had been on the roof, what they encountered inside was disabling: an abattoir, a battlefield left to rot in the sun. Each man was forced to cover his mouth and nose and fight a constant struggle to keep his gorge from rising. Stern moaned involuntarily. Jack distributed small capsules of ammonia, which they snapped into their handkerchiefs, burning their eyes but partially neutralizing the stink. Now it was a question of finding their way out through the nightmarish tomb; light from the noxious open gas jets was scarce, almost apologetic in the close halls choked with fumes from lamps and kerosene stoves.

They could find no coherence to the nesting of the tenement's corridors and stairways, each floor a jumble of demolition and shoddy reconstruction; as they stumbled from room to room, none of its denizens offered any protest at their presence: Accustomed to invasion, they owned no sense of borders worth defending. No furniture aside from huge rough beds where multiple sets of dull eyes stared at them fearfully out of the darkness. Bodies slunk away from them like swollen insects. Aggressive rats the size of terriers stopped to regard them with less alarm than the humans. Opening one door that threw baleful light into a murky room, they were shocked by the sight of the far wall melting away, until they realized what they saw moving was a solid blanket of cockroaches.

In one cavernous space, Doyle lost count after estimating

at least sixty people lived there, most seeking solace in a sleep indistinguishable from death. The smells thickened the farther they descended, and everywhere they ventured lay a dread and dreary silence. They found a family of six huddled around a candle in the crawl space under a flight of stairs, all stamped with the same hollow-eyed expression, their poor possessions scattered around them. Doyle had read Dickens's devastating accounts of poverty in midcentury London, but nothing he'd ever witnessed could match this intolerable misery. The violence of this cold hell was first and foremost spiritual. With what high hopes had these damned souls journeyed to the New World? wondered Doyle, his feelings a hot whirl of pity, sympathy, and horror.

They picked their way down three floors before realizing they had heard no sounds of the gang following behind them: There were apparently some places even the Houston Dusters wouldn't go. Easy enough to stake out the rooftop while the rest of their war party waited on the street below, and, yes, when the four men looked out a filthy staircase landing window, there they stood, fifteen strong, outside the front doors.

"What do we do?" asked Stern.

Jack did not answer, took a reading on their location to set his internal compass, then led them to the western extreme of the tenement, into a room lined with six dark masses huddled on wooden pallets; entire families, they discovered, staring at them like wounded herd animals waiting for predators to finish the job. Doyle noticed one group sheltering the frail shrouded body of a dead child. Jack threw open the room's single window and measured the distance to the next building; eight feet away across an open air shaft. As the cowed inhabitants scurried away, Jack pulled a short iron bar from his jacket and pried loose a sturdy length of planking from the floor. He worked tenaciously, his expression never changing, the only one of them outwardly unaffected by their journey down through the tenement; his actions under fire, which had once seemed to Doyle the model of dash and heroic vigor, were now ruled by a brutal efficiency.

They laid the plank from one ledge to another across the

air shaft and Jack went across first, testing his weight; the plank bowed slightly as he reached the middle but held firm. He smashed the window of the far tenement and hissed ferociously at the darkness inside, discouraging its residents, if there were any, from defending their territory. Stern followed, clutching the Zohar to his chest, then Innes, in three vaulting steps, and finally Doyle, whose bulk strained the plank to its limit. He could not sensibly close his eyes, but neither could he bear to look down; when the plank cracked, he was exactly halfway across and his response was to shout once in alarm, stand perfectly still until the board stopped bouncing, and then to stand still some more.

In spite of the others' frantic prompting, Doyle seemed completely unable to manufacture another step forward; a massive short circuit between his brain and feet. When the cries and war whoops from the ground below indicated that his shout had drawn the Dusters around the side of the building to them, he was still unable to move. Even when rocks and debris began flying around him, he could not convince his legs that one more step on this plank wouldn't splinter it and send him crashing to his doom, but as he waited the rift in the wood spread through it like a spider web.

"Come on, Arthur . . ."

"Two steps, old man."

The plank seemed to shrink down to the width of a toothpick; a single move in any direction will spell your end, Doyle's brain screamed at him. The three men in the window flapped their lips and waved their arms at him but he seemed to neither hear nor recognize them, resigned to spend the rest of eternity locked in this moment. A rock thumped into his shoulder, setting him swaying; the stinging bite of the blow had the salutary effect of unscrambling his mind and returning to him control of his limbs.

"Good Christ!" he shouted, realizing his predicament.

He took one long stride forward on the board and it caved in toward the middle, forming a momentary V before collapsing altogether; his hands desperately groped forward and found something to grab as the plank fell away beneath him. He looked up into Jack's face, framed in the window, felt something cold in his hands, and realized he held the hooked end of the crowbar that Jack was grasping. Jack and Innes pulled him up through the window and over the sill like an exhausted trout.

"I'd forgotten about your fondness for heights," said Jack.

"Like riding a bicycle," said Doyle. "You never forget it."

Bricks and bottles smashed against the walls, spraying shards of glass around them, and a second barrage angled down through the window from above; the Dusters on the roof of the Gates of Hell had discovered their position as well.

"We're not out of it yet," said Jack.

Doyle nodded gamely and climbed to his feet, the knees of his worsted trousers shredded, the toes of his shoes scrubbed raw. They moved into the hallway of the new building, ran down the first flight of stairs they came to, and immediately heard the Dusters breaking through the doors two floors below. Thumps and war cries from above told them that the rooftop contingent had bridged the gap as well: both feet in the jaws of a trap with nowhere to run.

Another sound took over: a low rumbling that increased with shocking suddenness, bearing down on them from every direction at once. The walls shook, plaster clogged the air, banisters and light fixtures rattled, and the intensity of the turbulence grew to a deafening roar. Jack threw a shoulder to the door directly before them; they rushed through an unoccupied apartment and were astonished to see the lurching, illuminated interiors of a train whipping by a few feet outside the window.

"The elevated train," said Stern. "Thank God; that's Second Avenue, I'd nearly forgotten where we were."

After the train passed, they leaped from the window to the train platform, resting a floor above the empty shop-lined street, running north and south as far as the eye could see. No sight or sound of the Dusters.

"Two questions," said Jack, staring down the narrow tracks. "Where's the next station and when's the next train?"

"The next station is north, Fourteenth Street, that way about nine blocks," said Stern, pointing ahead. "The trains run every few minutes."

Jack took off running to the north, stepping nimbly between the rails and ties, and the others tried to match his pace. Doyle could not accommodate his longer stride to the awkward width of the gaps, misstepped frequently, and was soon lagging behind, so he was the first to hear the yelps of the Dusters as they discovered the path they'd taken to the platform. Glancing over his shoulder, Doyle saw hoodlums pouring out of the window onto the elevated tracks two blocks behind; they ran after him right along the top of rails, their unnerving whoops and hollers echoing through the artificial canyon of the street.

"Come on, Arthur; don't look back," said Innes, slowing to run alongside him.

Doyle nodded. Lungs on fire, speech beyond their capacity now, the brothers devoted every last effort to following Jack's lead, but the relentless hunters held the edge of local knowledge: As they moved north, the gap slowly and steadily closed. Runners following on the street below actually began to pull ahead. On the parallel south-running tracks across the street, a train lumbered by, momentarily obliterating the scuffling of their footsteps in the cinder bed, the rasp of their breathing. Rocks and bottles began to crash around them as the Dusters pulled within range. Doyle caught a glimpse of a gingerbread Swiss chalet built onto the margins of the platform and wondered if he was hallucinating. A street sign popped into his field of vision: still three blocks to go.

Jack stopped abruptly ahead of them and tossed back a cannister into the narrowing span between the Doyles and the Dusters: White pepper smoke billowed, but the Dusters had learned from their earlier engagement and either sprinted quickly through or waited for the cloud to dissipate: a net gain of only seconds.

Now the station came into sight ahead, but the gap between groups was less than fifty yards and closing fast—on the verge of collapse, Doyle's muscles seizing up, Jack apparently out of tricks—when the platform began to rumble and hum. A hot white beam of light sharply outlined the churning Houston Dusters as the train bore quickly down on them. A hundred yards to the platform: Innes grabbed Doyle's arm and urged him to the finish like an Irish jockey.

The booming sonic horn of the speeding engine blasted the Dusters off either side of the elevation, some dropped to the street, others clung to the outside shell of the scaffolding as the train thundered by. Doyle tripped and fell hard, cinders embedding his palms as he skidded on the railbed. Drawing on some untapped superhuman reserve, Jack appeared beside them and, with Innes's help, lifted and threw Doyle up onto the platform just as the braking train glided by them into the station.

The doors opened. Stern carried the Zohar; Innes dragged Doyle into the last empty car, and they collapsed in the final row of seats. As the train pulled away, Jack dropped the false copy of the Zohar on the tracks and they watched the reassembled Dusters' final rush toward the back of the car fall short by inches.

chapter eight

WHEN THE RINGING AT HIS DOOR WOKE HIM FROM A DEAD sleep in President Cleveland's bed the next morning, Doyle had completely forgotten his appointment with Peregrine "Presto" Raipur, the alleged Maharaja of Berar. Elaborate apologies from both men as Doyle rang down for breakfast. Jack, who had spent what remained of the night in one of the suite's vast parlors, materialized like a wraith as Innes and Stern—wonderful, capable, reliable Innes—arrived with a timely pot of coffee. Doyle on his feet, trying to work the persistent kinks out of his joints, mildly concerned about the scene he'd caused in the lobby last night, arriving after midnight covered with grime, bloody knees poking out of the rips in his trousers; another tourist finding fun and adventure in Old New York.

Jack and Presto sized each other up like opposing chess players, Jack finally outlasting the stranger, but Presto did not rattle easily. Although he was still dressed for the part— riding jacket, jodhpurs, high boots, a red velvet vest—the foppish persona he had projected at the party was clearly an invention. His gaze level, steady, and assured, his voice a pleasing baritone; instead of fluttering like startled pigeons, his hands moved in silky, confident gestures that underscored his story about another missing book.

A rare manuscript edition of the Upanishads, centerpiece of the Rig Vedas, the constellation of books that formed the foundation of the Hindu religion: stolen six months ago from a holy temple in the city of Golcanda, in the princely state of Hyderabad, India. The theft had been kept a state secret by order of the sixth Nizam of Hyderabad, the ruling maharaja, estimated by many to be the richest man in the world. When he tapped someone to investigate the crime, the Nizam called on his distant cousin and contemporary, high-born, English-educated Presto Raipur, one of the few members of his privileged generation who had devoted his life to anything other than the pursuit of self-indulgent pleasures.

"Does that mean you're actually a prince?" asked Innes.

"In a word, and I say it with some embarrassment, yes: I am, technically speaking, the Maharaja of Berar, which I assure you sounds more impressive than it actually signifies." As he spoke, Presto effortlessly rotated a silver coin back and forth between his long, tapered fingers.

"Why so?"

"Forty years ago, in a spasm of misguided loyalty, my grandfather deeded our ancestral lands to the Nizam, ruler of the neighboring province of Hyderabad; the Nizam promptly turned over control of our holdings to the British as settlement of a long-standing debt. My outraged father, denied his title and left virtually penniless, further scandalized the family name by marrying an Englishwoman, taking a job as a banker, and living in London, where I was born and raised."

Presto paused, made the coin disappear, and with formidable self-possession took careful stock of their reactions.

"My interest in magic began as a child, attending the English music hall. I've grown accomplished enough to perform the occasional benefit myself: Presto, the Prestidigitating Barrister!"

He gestured; the coin reappeared in his hand. Doyle stopped pacing, gulped down his coffee, and for the moment forgot about the pain in his knees. Stern and Innes leaned anxiously forward. Only Jack's expression did not change, his eyes frigid, analytical.

"I see that I have your attention," said Presto.

"Please go on," said Doyle.

"I spent each summer as a boy visiting my grandfather, who still lives as a retainer in the Nizam's court at Chow Mahalla; the Nizam's son, the current Nizam, and I were playmates together. My friend the Nizam ascended to the throne of Hyderabad eleven years ago, at the age of eighteen; I had seen him only briefly in the intervening years while starting my career as a barrister—one of the first men of mixed racial heritage to practice before the English bar, a matter of some pride to me—when I received an urgent summons to visit the Nizam in Madras six months ago; I thought surely my grandfather's health must be failing so I undertook the journey. Instead I discovered my grandfather to be, as they say, in the pink, and living with a most extraordinarily nubile fifteen-year-old dancing girl—"

"Really?" blurted Innes. "How old is he?"

"Eighty-five and still a dedicated libertine. I should explain that their culture does not share our Christian conviction that earthly delights have a corrosive effect on the soul: Quite the contrary, some of the most devout Hindus believe the road to heaven is paved with sensual gratification."

Doyle cleared his throat theatrically, and Innes retrieved his jaw from the floor.

"As happy as I was to find Grandfather in such high spirits—this nymph was truly quite delectable—my purpose in being there remained obscure for three more days until the Nizam returned from a tiger hunt. That night we shared a dinner in his private quarters—my friend has spent the last decade decorating his palace to compete with the excesses of Louis Quatorze: a solid-gold water closet for starters; appallingly tasteless but nonetheless impressive for it—and then he told me of the missing Upanishads. The crime had been committed in the dead of night; there were no clues and no offers had been received to return the book for ransom, which the Nizam would have been only too willing to pay.

"With my background in English law, the Nizam had assumed, however illogically, that of all the men he knew in the world I would be the one most able to shed light on this mystery. When I attempted to graciously decline, citing the fine but crucial distinction between a barrister and a policeman, the Nizam expressed sympathy for my position then casually intimated that it would be a shame if he were unable to retain Grandfather in the manner to which he had throughout his life been so thoroughly accustomed."

"Why, that's just plain extortion," said Innes.

"And spoken with a smile; my friend the Nizam has the

personality of a cobra. As you can imagine, any thought of bringing the old man to London after eighty-five years of princely extravagance was unsupportable—and an absolute disaster to my social life—so I agreed to lend a hand as best I could. For my troubles, I received what is by any man's standard a staggering amount of money from the Nizam to cover my expenses, not thinking for one moment that accepting this assignment would lead me to the highest levels of English government and then to America."

Presto paused dramatically to take another sip of coffee.

"Don't you find this to be the most peculiar country?" he asked pleasantly.

"Absolutely," said Doyle.

"Fantastic," said Innes.

There's the pots calling the kettle black, thought Stern, the only American in the room, glancing around at these odd English ducks.

"What involvement with English government?" asked Jack.

"When I returned to London and began making inquiries about stolen holy books of my acquaintances in the Foreign Office, I was greeted with an increasing chorus of astonishment, steadily ushered up a ladder of ever more eminent representatives of state—each of whom made the mistaken assumption that I appeared in some official diplomatic capacity, which I'm afraid I did nothing to disabuse them of—finally landing in no less than the office of the Prime Minister."

"Gladstone?" asked Doyle.

"Lord Gladstone himself. We chatted briefly about some mutual friends, and he then explained that a book of equal importance to the Anglican Church had similarly gone missing and that the trail as far as they could tell led to New York, with grounds for suspicion that a wealthy American collector of books might be responsible."

Doyle glanced at Jack for his reaction; there was none.

"I arrived here two weeks ago and have been making the rounds of society in the ridiculous guise with which I greeted you last night, Mr. Conan Doyle: This is regrettably what people seem to expect from a maharaja, and I have succeeded in making a perfect ass of myself, if I do say so. . . ."

"Smell-A-Rama?" said Innes.

"The most outrageous attention getter I could think of; you'd be amazed at the offers I've received from potential investors. . . ."

"How stupefying," said Doyle.

"Americans seem able to sniff out a potential for profit the way sharks find blood in the sea. And all the while, I've been busy dropping hints about my interest in the illicit traffic of rare religious books. . . ."

"Why did you approach Doyle?" asked Jack, still holding his approval in reserve.

"Fair question: I received a wire direct from the prime minister's office day before yesterday that upon Mr. Doyle's arrival I should attempt to contact him and enlist his assistance; here, I've brought the wire along."

Jack snatched the telegram from Presto's hand and studied it, finding no fault with its credentials. Then he stared at Presto with an unnerving intensity, as if realizing some secret about him.

"What were you trying to warn me about last night?" asked Doyle.

"I saw a man watching you from the corner of the room: a tall, blond man with a look of unmistakable bad intent. When he began to approach you from behind, reaching into his jacket for what I imagined might be a weapon, I simply acted on instinct."

"A tall, blond man?" said Doyle, remembering the man who had replaced the young lieutenant on the bridge of the *Elbe*. Before Presto could elaborate, Jack pulled the paper with Rabbi Stern's sketch from his pocket and held it out to him.

"Does this mean anything to you?" asked Jack, pointing to the drawing of the tower.

Presto's dark-rimmed black eyes widened, and he blinked repeatedly. "Good God; you'll think I'm absolutely mad."

"Why is that?"

"I have been dreaming about this place."

* * *

Later that same day, in a rat-infested alley outside his head-quarters, two patrolling policemen found the body of Ding-Dong Dunham, notorious leader of the Houston Dusters. No tears were shed at the precinct over this discovery, but even the most hardened cops expressed shock at the loathsome brutality of the murder: Whatever Ding-Dong had done to inspire this mutilation must have been off the scale they used to calculate his previously established low standards of behavior.

Only one witness came forward, one of the Dusters, a mental defective named Mouse Malloy, who, no longer able to function productively as a street criminal after being kicked in the head by a horse while trying to knock over a beer wagon, had since served as their clubhouse mascot and errand boy. Shaken and terrified, he claimed to have watched from a room in the back as a tall, blond German man came into headquarters earlier that day with a suitcase full of gold coins. When Ding-Dong refused to hand over to the German an old leather-bound book, demanding to know why he wanted it, the man smiled, pulled a knife, and went to work on Ding-Dong like a priest carving a Christmas turkey.

Like most of the rest of what Mouse told the cops—he had a reputation for running his mouth, and his stories tended to veer toward the fanciful ever since the horse had made such a strong impression on him—they paid no mind to his unlikely account, figuring Ding-Dong had simply met up with the sordid, inevitable end that awaited every gang-land leader, and from their point of view the sooner the better. Case closed.

The only difference being that this time Mouse Malloy was telling the God's truth.

PHOENIX, ARIZONA

In spite of Bendigo Rymer's histrionics, or maybe because of them, the authorities at the Phoenix station would not allow the mail train to leave for Wickenburg until the cars were searched upside and down and every last member of the Penultimate Players had been questioned. And no, as it turned out, none of them had seen a Chinaman running around the train station waving a sword—which was what Rymer had ordered them to say even if they had. The delays incurred by having members of his troupe held over as witnesses at a murder trial could puncture the solvency of their tour as quick as a spike through a pneumatic tire.

Bendigo himself was actually the only Player who had caught sight of Kanazuchi; from a distance he hadn't clearly seen his face, but he did look Chinese, and as he ran off from behind the cotton bales, the man had been brandishing something that looked to Rymer's well-trained eye for steel-edged weapons suspiciously like a scabbard.

Railroad cops found the dead guard stashed behind the bales, uniform missing, his neck badly broken, but they couldn't find his assailant. Rumors had started to circulate about a series of gruesome murders committed at a railway yard in Yuma. Atrocities, crimes against nature: men with heads chopped off and mounted on spikes, women raped, children devoured; the usual human embroideries. And word was spreading fast that this smorgasbord of crimes had been committed by a crazed Chinaman.

If their delayed departure wasn't irritating enough, this annoying old rabbi had now decided to travel with the Penultimates at least as far as Wickenburg and perhaps beyond. He wasn't prepared to say why, but what reason could he possibly have except a ridiculous infatuation with Rymer's leading lady? And her doing everything this side of decency to encourage him: The woman knew no shame! Bendigo kicked himself as he watched the two of them billing and cooing in their seats three rows in front of him: Trouble usually showed up wearing a skirt and this English strumpet was just the latest in a long line the enemy camp had sent to torment him. He should have obeyed his instincts and booted her unceremoniously out after that first night in Cincinnati when she either seduced him or refused to sleep with him; the memory was a little hazy.

His heart beat like a caged bird. How could he go on? The strain of holding the Players together in order to faithfully interpret the eternal works of the Masters simply shredded a man's soul. Bendigo threw back his head and laid his hand against his forehead—his fondness for melodramatic gestures was so ingrained he used them even when no one was around to watch. He glanced around the train car at his company—no one *had* noticed him suffering, damn their miserable hides—and his upper lip curled in disgust: These blocks, these stones, these worse than senseless things; wild donkeys have more appreciation for genius. And did they ever bother to thank him for providing them a life and a livelihood? No; instead it was always "Bendigo my room's too small," "Mr. Rymer, there's no hot water," and inevitably, "What about my money?"

Look at me, Bendigo wanted to rail at the heavens, I'm running a provincial tour in the middle of a desert! There has been a terrible mistake; I was supposed to be one of the great men of the stage! If Booth hadn't ruined my career, they'd been naming theaters after me on Broadway!

"Actors," muttered Rymer bitterly.

Staring this cruel fate in the eye was enough to reduce a strong man to tears, and he was no Hercules; a couple of big, wet ones rolled forlornly down his cheeks—Bendigo had always prided himself on his ability to cry on cue, but it never hurt to practice.

A shimmering mirage swam before his eyes, and he sought refuge in it: the twenty-five thousand dollars he'd cleared from past tours. He visualized his fortune as great chunks of gold bullion, resting in the impregnable vault of his Philadelphia bank. Add the six grand he'd pocketed from the current tour, plus the four he had signed to receive from this religious outpost they were on their way to play, and he was ready to mount his triumphant return to New York—lose a little weight first, cut back on the drinking—producer, director, and star of Bendigo Rymer's once-in-a-lifetime production of the Bard's immortal *Hamlet*!

Bendigo had spent every spare moment of his twenty years in theatrical exile restructuring and simplifying *Ham-*

let's convoluted text to play to his strengths—more sword-play, a sunnier relationship with Ophelia, less morbid intro-spection—and finally his apotheosis was within reach. How many hundreds of times had he rehearsed the scene in his mind: opening night; Booth seated front row center, reduced to a sobbing puddle by the magnificent soaring humanity of his performance, falling to his knees and begging Bendigo's forgiveness for his rank, vicious stupidity, right in front of a crowd that always included all the important critics. . . .

His reverie was broken by the sound of Eileen's happy laughter: the old man laughing, too.

What could those two possibly have to laugh about? Bendigo fumed and snuck a healthy pull from his flask. Something humiliating about her interest in the old man. It was enough to make him want to sleep with Eileen, if it had ever actually happened, all over again.

When Buckskin Frank and his posse arrived in Phoenix by special train that afternoon, he was pleasantly surprised to find this crime scene had been roped off and left largely in-tact: The guard's neck was broken—snapped like a twig; worse than a hanging—and a set of footprints he found be-hind the bales matched the tracks he'd spotted leaving the Yuma yards: a flat print, no heel, like the slippers he'd seen coolies wear. Furthermore, a guard who'd fired the shot at the killer had managed a clear look at him and yes, the man was indisputably a Chinaman, which was as specific as the guard could get. That qualified as good news.

The bad news was that Frank wouldn't be able to trail whoever the hell they were after down into Sonora, shake this bunch of greenhorns, carve out a little grubstake for himself, and settle into a slow decline of pan mining and tequila sipping while leisurely shopping around for the best bordello south of the border: That defined the honest limit of Frank McQuethy's remaining life ambitions.

Frank lit a cigarette, stood tall, and strolled down the tracks away from the swarm of lawmen and volunteers: Whenever he tried to look like he was thinking hard, they cut him a wide berth. With his high hat and boots, he tow-

ered above the crowd; that yellow buckskin gleamed in the
sunlight; his handlebar moustache advertised brawny, un-
selfish heroism. He was dimly aware of a gaggle of women
watching from the passenger platform, giggling and chattering like barnyard hens; apparently they'd recognized his
jacket: A story had already appeared in the local paper about
Frank's newsworthy release and involvement in the manhunt.

Women: There was the bedrock of his mountain in life.
Try as he might, Frank had never completely grasped the nature of his indestructible appeal to the fairer sex: What did
they see when they looked at him? He didn't have a clue
what it was, but he knew it wasn't him. Did it have something to do with his having killed a woman in front of a
crowd—poor Molly; the best of him had died right along
with her—and getting his name in the papers that made the
rest of them swarm around like flies?

Most of the women who tried to visit him in prison
couldn't hear enough about the who, how, and why of every
human life he'd ended; some sort of sick electric thrill ran
through them. He failed to find any sense in that and none in
them: Like any man of principle, all he wanted to do was
forget about the people he'd killed. Maybe their interest was
another side effect of all those dime novels over the years
with his stupid picture on the cover that in hindsight he
hadn't done enough to discourage. Hell, he'd even tried
writing a few himself; the guards had a pile of 'em back at
the prison they used to hawk to the tourists. *Buckskin Frank:
Geronimo's Nightmare. I Rode with Wyatt: Tombstone's Invisible Man.* Half a dozen others. Big sellers, every one.

He had to face facts; through some fault of his own, fame
had destroyed his privacy and it made Frank's brain ache
like a rotten tooth. Five years in prison had brought him a
peace uninterrupted by a woman's ceaseless demands that
he behave like some crazy idea she had in her head—obedient, mild-mannered, devoted to her every mood: in other
words one hundred percent back-asswards from his actual
personality. This tranquil stretch had led Frank to conclude
that the main reason a woman wanted a man around in the

first place was so she could bombard him with the arsenal of dumb questions ricocheting around in her head:

Did he like this dress? Didn't she look too fat in it? What about this new shade of rouge? Did he like his steak red or pink? Could he believe how much they wanted for a yard of calico at the dry goods store? Did he want to hold hands and sit swinging on a glider in the moonlight? Well, no. He liked a poke in the hay well enough, but beyond that he couldn't figure out why they expected so much from him. He didn't know any of the answers to their questions: As far as he was concerned, all these choices having to do with daily existence were equally weighted and to fuss and bother like it was life-or-death about what to eat for breakfast or wear to the square dance squeezed the juice right out of living. Molly was the only woman who'd ever figured that out about him, and look what happened to her.

Husbands were men who brought home the bacon, never drank before dark, and always woke up in the same bed they started the night in. Before they got down to doing the deed for the first time, he had always meant to stop and ask one of these hungry gals flat out: Did he honestly look like husband material to them? And if the answer was yes, he would reach for his hat because that was a conclusion that could only be made by a lunatic. What Frank wanted, what he thought any man who'd lived life as he had wanted—more than fame, more than fortune—was to be left alone.

Frank felt pathetic: Here he stood scarcely twenty-four hours out of the calaboose and already feeling sentimental about it. The trustees used to smuggle in a whore for him once a month or so—there'd been no shortage of soiled doves lining up for the assignment. To his astonishment, he had discovered that, with Molly gone, this turned out to be all the feminine companionship he required.

Wait, thought Frank, and the clouds parted: Who was to say he couldn't work out the same arrangement now that he was nearly free again? Was he doomed to keep hitching his fate to some sage hen's apron strings the minute she salted her tail for him? No. He felt joy bubble up inside him like springwater. That was it: He would blaze a new trail for himself. No more box canyons. No more cow bunnies putting their brand on him.

As he ground out his cigarette, the tubby stationmaster came running up with the schedule of trains that had left Phoenix that morning: two freights, two passenger, one local mail run. Why they had let any train out of the yard under these circumstances was beyond Frank, but he'd long ago given up any hope he'd be put in charge of running the world. A small crowd of anxious volunteers gathered around him waiting for his response.

"You wire ahead to the next stop on all of these trains?" asked Frank.

The stationmaster screwed his face into a ball; he'd read a couple of *Buckskin Frank* books and felt plainly intimidated. "You think we should?"

"Well. Yes."

"But, but we searched through all the trains before we let them go."

"So?"

The station master grinned like he had a painfully full bladder, took the schedule back from Frank, and headed back to the terminal.

I'll give him ten before he breaks into a trot, thought Frank, watching the man go. It took eight.

Frank sighed heavily and scanned the crowd; nearly a month had passed since his last conjugal visit at the hoosegow. He wondered idly how complicated it would be to get his wick dipped before the manhunt moved on. He rolled another cigarette and walked away from the gawkers like he was searching for clues and they left him alone again.

Thirty paces later he found a puddle of blood in the dirt. He dipped in his finger: dry. At least two hours old. A trail of gouts led away and ended at an empty set of tracks; the stationmaster would know which train had been sitting on these rails.

"Mr. McQuethy?"

He turned: a group of five women, the ones he'd seen watching him from the platform, standing ten yards away. He tipped his hat.

"Ladies."

The one who'd spoken stepped forward; a big-boned strawberry blonde. Best looking one in the bunch, which said less than he might have hoped for. "If you'll forgive the intrusion: We read about your release in the paper this morning."

"Uh-huh."

The woman blushed. "And we, well, I guess we're just about your biggest fans here in Phoenix; we've read all your books and followed your career with a great deal of interest."

"Uh-huh."

"I think you knew a cousin of mine down in Tombstone a few years back, Sally Ann Reynolds? She was a waitress there at the Silver Dollar Saloon?" The blonde blushed red as an apple when Frank didn't immediately respond. "Anyway . . ."

"How is Sally Ann?" he said with a smile, and not the slightest idea who she was talking about.

"Fine; she's married now, living in Tucson, has a couple of kids."

"You must be sure and give her my regards."

"I can't tell you how excited she'll be to know we've spoken."

There was that look in her eye: the flash of light in a cheap diamond. Frank felt simultaneously cornered and stimulated. Story of his life.

"We know you have a terribly busy time ahead of you, but we were wondering if it would be possible to invite you to lunch sometime while you're here in town."

Frank smiled again and, as was perpetually the case, every memory of every unhappiness ever visited on him by a woman vanished like tax money.

CHICAGO, ILLINOIS

Her name was Mary Williams: Dante Scruggs found that out from two old biddies at the boarding house. She'd told them that she came from a small town in rural Minnesota, where she'd been a schoolteacher, and that she was hoping to find the same work in Chicago. They took her at her word. Dante told them he was from the school board and wanted to check her references: Better if you don't tell Miss Williams I stopped by, he said with a smile. What a charmer, the old ladies thought.

Mary was of Greek heritage, they had decided; that accounted for her dark exoticism without violating any squeamish racial borders. The fools had no idea she was an Indian.

She left the house each morning at eight o'clock sharp. The first day she bought a map of Chicago; following the map, she methodically walked each block of the downtown area, looking for something. Dante followed her around that way for three days. Always stayed far back in the crowd, never moving too close. Once she turned sharply around as if she had forgotten something and marched straight at him; he turned his back and stared into a shop window. He was sure she didn't see him, but she kept to the busiest streets and always returned to the boarding house before dark.

On the third afternoon, she seemed to find what she was looking for: They called it the Water Tower, on Chicago Avenue. One of the few buildings that had survived the Great Fire; spires of sandstone arrayed around a pale central tower like something from a fairy tale dropped into this hub of modern commerce.

She wandered up and down the street for over an hour, examining the Water Tower from every angle, but never went inside: What was the woman doing here? Dante wondered.

He asked himself that question a hundred times that day: She stayed on that street corner in front of the Tower until twilight. Never said a word to anyone, just watched people coming and going. Like she was waiting for somebody. An odd one, Dante decided, watching from a soda fountain across the street, sipping a root beer float. He followed her back to the boarding house just as the lamplighters started to make their rounds.

The man who had spent the last few months watching

Dante Scruggs, the dark-eyed man with the tattoo on his left arm, trailed quietly behind. He would watch Dante enter his apartment and then return to their local office to finish up his report; the man's superior was arriving the next day by train from New York—he had the book with him—and then they would take action in the matter of Mr. Dante Scruggs.

NEW YORK CITY

As the Toast of Manhattan, Doyle drifted through his responsibilities, dutifully playing the part of the Famous Author but feeling as if his real self lagged one step behind this frantic routine; the cloud of intrigue swirling around Jack and the missing books was far more compelling than endlessly answering the same set of questions about his dead fictional character, a level of journalism on par with the now almost fondly remembered Ira Pinkus. But pressing the flesh in bookstores, feeling the honest enthusiasm of his readers firsthand, restored him; occasionally some dear soul who had even read his historical novels materialized with a rare copy for signature.

His dramatic reading at the Fifty-seventh Street Calvary Baptist Church that night was a smash; Doyle had decided to give his audience, packed to the rafters with the faithful, exactly what they had come to hear: Holmes, Holmes, and more Holmes. Applause deafened the hall. Celebrities crowded the reception afterward—the same faces showing up at these things with depressing regularity—elbowing each other out of the way to grab Doyle's hand and pump his arm in that peculiar American way, as if they expected oil to gush from his mouth.

A distressing percentage of them came equipped with business investments to propose; from a line of Holmes-inspired apparel to an English-style pub called Sherlock's Home, complete with waiters wearing deerstalker hats and cloaks. I ought to introduce these two, thought Doyle; it's a match made in heaven.

An intense, muscular young man named Houdini made an indelible impression: He eagerly offered to demonstrate for Doyle how he could escape, while wearing a chained strait-jacket, from inside a locked safe deposited at the bottom of a river.

I'd be far more interested if you could show me how to escape from this party, confided Doyle.

The young man laughed; at least he had a sense of humor.

Major Pepperman glowed like a signal fire as they totaled the box-office receipts; his ship may not have come in yet, but if this was any indication of how the tour would go, his fleet was drawing within sight of the harbor. After wrestling his way through a crowd to his carriage, Doyle again declined Pepperman's invitation to dine—hate to disappoint, responsibility to this taxing schedule, etc., etc., leaving Pepperman no reasonable objection—and he and Innes returned to the more abiding concerns awaiting them in his Waldorf suite; Jack, Presto, and Lionel Stern, already convened for a briefing of their day's activities.

After attending Rupert Selig's funeral in Brooklyn, Stern had found waiting for him a detailed wire from Rabbi Isaac Brachman in Chicago: Jacob Stern had been with him there as recently as four days ago. When he left, Brachman assumed Jacob had traveled back to New York and was shocked to hear he hadn't arrived; no other destination had been discussed, and regrettably he had no idea where Lionel's father might have gone.

Rabbi Brachman's telegram brought another serious matter to light: The Tikkunei Zohar, the book Lionel had obtained last year for Brachman to study, had disappeared five weeks before from the archives of his temple. Brachman did not elaborate beyond a tantalizing hint that he suspected the theft held some connection to the Parliament of Religions, part of the 1893 World Columbian Exposition in Chicago, an event Jacob Stern had attended as a representative of American Orthodox Judaism.

Presto gave his report: He spent the day returning to rare book shops he had visited upon arriving in New York, and one Lower East Side shop owner reported an intriguing encounter.

"A well-spoken German gentleman—good-looking, tall, athletic build—came into this man's store just yesterday, representing himself as the agent for a wealthy private collector interested in purchasing rare religious manuscripts. He understood that such documents were exceedingly difficult to come by and usually resided in the hands of established scholars or institutions. He expressed particular interest in the Gerona Zohar and wondered if the man had heard about the book recently coming into this country. This bookstore"—Presto paused for effect; melodrama an inescapable part of his nature—"is less than two blocks away from the offices of Mr. Stern."

"The German bloke again," said Innes.

"He told the shopkeeper that he had recently returned from Europe," said Presto.

"And he's undoubtedly by now in possession of the false Zohar we left on the railroad tracks," said Doyle. "Any idea who he claimed to be?"

With his flashing smile and a flourish worthy of a magician, Presto produced a business card out of thin air: "Mr. Frederick Schwarzkirk: Collector. No other title. Offices in Chicago."

"Schwarzkirk? Odd name."

"That means 'Black Church,'" said Jack.

Doyle and Jack looked at each other: the dream about the tower. This was no coincidence. Silence in the room.

"Is your tour scheduled to take you to Chicago?" asked Jack.

"As a matter of fact, it is," said Doyle.

"We travel tomorrow," said Innes.

"We're going with you," said Jack.

"Capital," said Doyle. Jack continued to stare at him. "What is it?"

"Someone I want you to meet tonight."

"Late in the day for a social call."

"My friend doesn't keep regular hours," said Jack. "Up to it?"

Doyle looked to Innes, who was nearly bursting with eagerness.

"Lead the way," said Doyle.

The wind blew colder as they rode uptown, the streets empty, leaves beginning to turn. Even this deserted, you could feel the immense restless dynamism of the city, thought Doyle, coursing up through the ground like the hum of a massive turbine engine.

As they trotted past the terraced palazzos and mansions on Fifth Avenue, he felt a twinge of self-reproach, realizing that a part of him still yearned after a style of living scaled to these grandiose dimensions. The homes of the ruling class sat silent as medieval fortresses, eye-popping shrines to vanity and greed, and yes, he still wanted one. In England, the rich handled fortunes discreetly, tastefully tucked away in the country behind the tall hedges—Doyle had a country house himself now, albeit a modest one. In America the robber barons erected these self-celebrating monuments along the busiest street in the world: By God, look at me, I've done it! Cracked the bank! Beaten the gods at their own game!

Telephone wires clogged the air between the mansions and the street, connecting the rich to each other by means of this latest craze; they hardly had anything to say to each other when they were face-to-face, thought Doyle, why did they need so many telephones?

What an exhausting interior life the wealthy must lead, driven to these superhuman accomplishments by fitful longings for immortality; the thought of all that misguided passion filled Doyle with melancholy before he corrected himself: Who was he to say these titans of enterprise had it wrong? Two thousand years from now, with this great city fallen into dust, there might be little else left standing besides these sturdy secular temples for archaeologists to sift through, weaving together from their artifacts the life of a dead and distant culture. A hairbrush, an urn, a privately commissioned bust, these intensely personal possessions might one day find themselves behind museum glass, transformed into relics of worship. What if some fragment of a dream or, to put it more plainly, a few resilient molecules of its owner survived embedded in the matter of the object? That seemed to Doyle to be as close to immortality as any human could hope for; the body would fail, memories would fade, but we might live on for centuries in the form of a toothbrush or a hatpin.

After they turned west and reached the Hudson River, a ferry conveyed their coach-and-four to the palisades of New Jersey. The four men inside settled into the rhythms of a long carriage ride through the dead of night. No one but Jack knew where they were going, and he sat above them in the driver's seat, holding the reins lightly in his mangled fingers. As they rode, Presto entertained them with tales about the princes and maharanis of Gwalior and Rajputana; cursed jewels, palaces of ivory and gold, man-eating tigers, marauding elephants, and, of the most interest to Innes, the illicit mysteries of the harem: Did these girls really paint certain essential parts of themselves crimson? Indeed they did, confirmed Presto: Oiled, polished, and sheened, the houris lived a life devoted to the giving, and receiving, of pleasure. In each other's arms, as well as those of their master. Innes's mind spun like a pinwheel in a stiff breeze: Had Presto actually visited any of these perfumed seraglios?

"But how different are these women, finally, from the well-kept wives of our Western high society?" said Doyle, sparing Presto the indignity of confessing the obvious. "I don't mean all of them, but those who spend their lives maintaining their physical charms—facial massages, six-gallon shampoos—transforming themselves into a prize or accessory to decorate their wealthy husbands' arms."

"You can't keep up to fifty of 'em at a time, for starters," argued Innes.

"You'd be surprised," said Presto, with a salacious grin. "Provided money was no object."

"Putting the issue of multiples aside," said Doyle.

"I can think of one important distinction," said Stern. "In the West the sort of wife you're describing can leave the house if she wants to."

"Right, she's not a slave per se," said Doyle. "But what

I'm getting at is, aren't they in a similar way slaves of the spirit? The wife here may leave the house as you suggest, but can she leave the situation? Fed up with her lot, can she run off and make a life of her own?"

"Why would she want to?" asked Innes.

"Theoretically speaking, old boy."

"She should be able to," said Presto. "And she certainly has legal recourse under Western law."

"But the reality is quite different: Western society is rigged to support free action on the part of the male and defended against the same rights being accorded the female. I believe it's something to do with unconscious protection of the reproductive function; the species must survive, at any cost; the woman must be shielded from harm, even if we aren't aware of it."

"I've always been too busy to take a wife," said Stern sifting through his regrets.

"Harem life doesn't sound so bad to me," said Innes. "Not much work. Lots of free time."

"You're lost in a dream about the harem's compliance and round-the-clock availability; do you have any idea what can happen to one of these girls if she runs afoul of the ruling male?" Doyle turned to Presto.

"Torture, disfigurement. Beheading," said Presto.

"Really? That's dreadful."

"But how would you feel if these women were granted the same equality of sexual freedom you enjoy? If they could choose to make love with whomever they wanted, whenever they wanted?"

"What an appalling thought," said Innes. "I mean the whole point of the thing is lost then, isn't it?"

"My argument is that while men have made the civilized world as it is, they have done so at the expense of these partners our Creator had the good sense to grace us with; they are the invisible oppressed among us."

"Are you in favor then of giving women the vote, Mr. Doyle?" asked Presto.

"Oh good God, no," said Doyle. "You have to go about these things sensibly. We should educate them first; they need to know what they're being asked to vote on. Rome wasn't built in a day."

"Maybe it wouldn't be so bad," said Innes, summoning up a rosy world of sexual equality. "Be a lot less expensive getting a bird in the bed; no flowers, no fancy dinners for two in some pricey bistro."

"I'm afraid the prospect fills me with despair," said Presto. "To abandon the ritual of the hunt, the thrill of conquest, and have everything I desired about a woman handed to me from the first moment without resistance or some modest reticence would ruin the entire experience."

"So you didn't actually enjoy your visits to the harem, then?" said Innes, like a dog digging up his favorite bone.

The discussion continued, lively and spirited, nothing laid to rest, as if in this delicate and fertile area anything could ever be settled. Doyle looked up at Jack driving the carriage, missing his participation in exactly the sort of philosophical free-for-all in which he used to take particular delight. Certainly, Jack could hear what they were saying from up on that lonely perch, but he never glanced their way, remote and purposeful as a lighthouse keeper watching a storm out at sea. How far had Jack journeyed beyond the reach of these essential animal concerns; and if they were lost to him forever, could he still in the same way be thought of as a man?

It was nearly one in the morning when their destination appeared, in a valley spreading below them illuminated by an impossible volume of light: a quadrangle of long brick buildings ringed with electric lamps and a high white picket fence. No identifying signs. After a whispered conversation with a guard stationed at the gate, their carriage was admitted; Jack drove them to the tallest structure in the center of the square and parked outside; through its large windows, they could see vast rooms crowded with machinery, laboratory apparatus, and scientific supplies.

They followed Jack through a steel door, down a corridor, and into a great hall sporting a thirty-foot ceiling; second-floor galleries flanked either side of bookshelves climbing the far wall—at least ten thousand books, estimated Doyle. Immense glass cases displayed stores of minerals, compounds, and prototypes of various inventions. Greek statues filled corners; photographs and paintings packed every available inch of wall. The room felt both cluttered and spacious; objectively grand and intensely personal.

At a simple rolltop desk in the middle of the room, a rumpled middle-aged man slumped in a tilt-back chair, angled away from them, his worn boots resting on the edge of an open drawer. He appeared to be asleep; a steel bowl sat in his lap below his folded hands. Touseled, graying hair lay every which way on his large, noble head. Jack signaled the others for silence, and he crept closer to the man in the chair. Lionel Stern suddenly gasped.

"Do you know who that is?" whispered Stern.

Two steel balls fell from the man's hand and clanged in the steel bowl. The sound woke him; instantly alert, looking up to face them; broad brow furrowed to a deep cleft between bushy white eyebrows, a wide frowning mouth, and the keenest intelligence in his eyes. He spotted Jack first and beckoned him to the desk, shaking his hand, exchanging quiet pleasantries.

"That's Thomas Edison," said Stern.

Jack waved them over and made the introductions: Edison lit up like his famous incandescent bulb when he met Doyle.

"The Holmes generator, in the flesh," said Edison with a laugh; to their puzzled silence he explained that the "Holmes generator" was well known in scientific circles as a precursor to the electromagnetic engine.

"Oh," said Doyle.

Edison seemed unable to express strongly enough his enthusiasm for Sherlock Holmes: Most novels teemed with creatures of such uninspired and feeble dimwittedness it was a wonder any author could be bothered to write about them; but what a joy to encounter such unapologetic brilliance in a fictional character! Doyle was flattered into utter befuddlement.

Edison leaped to his feet with the spring of a teenager, shimmied up the rolling ladder bolted to his library stacks, pulled down a leather-bound volume of Holmes, and insisted Doyle sign the title page for him.

"Any more Holmes stories in the works?" Edison eagerly wanted to know. "Surely our man's sharp enough to have found a way to survive that little problem at the waterfall."

"There's been some talk about it," said Doyle, hating to disappoint the great man. Innes stared at him as if he'd just spoken in tongues.

They chatted about Doyle's work habits, Edison keen on facts: How many hours a day did he write? (Six.) How many words did he produce a day? (Eight hundred to a thousand.) Did he write by hand or with one of the new mechanical typewriters? (Fountain pen.) How many drafts of each book? (Three.) Then the conversation shifted to the mysterious origins of creativity in the mind. They agreed that the brain's relentless appetite for order resulted in the spontaneous development of organized ideas attempting to simplify the problems of daily living, be it a story that shed light on some troublesome aspect of human behavior or a machine that reduced the difficulty of essential physical labor.

"We're all detectives," said Edison, "wrestling with that question mark at the end of our existence. A large part of the universal appeal of your Mr. Holmes, I think."

"But he's just a machine, really," said Doyle modestly.

"Oh, but I disagree; with all apologies to Sherlock, and the prevailing medical wisdom, our brain is not a machine. When induced into the appropriate state of readiness, the brain, I believe, enters into contact with a field of pure ideas; not a physical place as we understand it, but not a purely theoretical one, either. A dimension of abstract thought that parallels our own, overlaying and informing our world in ways hard to imagine. We experience it directly only through the auspices of a properly prepared human mind. And drawing down the visions that we find while visiting this 'other place' is the source of all great human inspiration."

"May I ask, sir, what you were doing with those balls and the steel bowl when we arrived?" said Doyle.

"I can see where our Mr. Holmes comes by his observational acuity," said Edison with a smile. "I discovered early in my life that the best ideas took shape in my mind when I passed through the dreamy borderland we cross on our way either into or falling out of sleep; I've come to believe this brief passage is when the brain reaches its optimum state of receptivity for making contact with this realm of pure reason. The difficulty comes in trying to maintain ourselves in that dreamy middle ground: We quickly fall either deeper into sleep or back toward wakefulness. So . . ."

Edison picked up the bowl and the balls and sat down in his chair to demonstrate.

"Whenever I feel drowsy, I sit just so with my hand holding these over the bowl and let myself drift into that in-between territory. If I fall asleep, the balls drop from my hand and the clanging brings me back—I'm somewhat deaf, I need a good racket to do the job; I quickly pick the balls up and float away again. The more I practice, the longer I'm able to stay there. The thoughts come. Good things result. Any man can train himself to learn this technique, and I have found that with an hour or two spent in this productive state, I feel more rested than after a full eight hours in bed."

"Why, this is very much like the meditative states attained by the yogis in the Far East," said Presto.

"Is that a fact?" said Edison, who had not paid much attention to the other men beyond an occasional friendly glance. "I'm very interested to know this; are you a Hindu yourself?"

"I am the Episcopalian son of an Irish-Catholic mother and a Muslim father who fled a Hindu culture to live in England," said Presto with a bow.

"Well, America certainly sounds like the right place for you."

With a glance at his pocket watch, Jack suggested they not take up too much of Mr. Edison's valuable time but should proceed with their reason for the visit. Edison, who seemed more grateful for the interruption than annoyed, marched them through the massive laboratories they'd glimpsed through the windows. Sixty full-time employees did the lab work, as teams assigned to various projects. Most of Edison's time was now taken up with administrative details, he explained grumpily; his investors insisted on it.

Money drove everything now, not like the good old days in Menlo Park when energy was boundless and trust of one's fellows came unquestioned.

They left the main building, walked to a far corner of the quad, and entered a low oblong wooden shack fifty feet long, topped by a strange sloping hinged roof. Black tar paper covered the interior walls; black curtains draped a small raised platform at the far end. Doyle decided the hinging at the tops of the wall allowed the roof to slide open, for what reason he could not imagine. The men took seats on folding chairs before a square white screen hanging straight down from the ceiling, while Edison disappeared behind a black box of curtains at the back.

The room went dark and Doyle took advantage of the pause to lean over to Jack and ask, "How did you come to know him?"

"Came to his door unannounced. Three years ago when I reenlisted," said Jack. "Identified myself, showed my credentials: agent to the Crown."

"Why?"

"Mysteries I'd come across. Ideas. Questions I wanted to ask. He was surprisingly cooperative; he found me quite exotic. I lived on the grounds for two months. He told his people I was a visiting engineer. We shared a few ideas for applications of his new technologies. . . ."

A rhythmic humming issuing from behind the curtain cut him off; moments later a narrow beam of light shot out of a peephole cut in its center, flooding the screen with a square of brightness painful to the eye.

Edison reappeared and stood beside them. Writhing black squiggles danced across the screen.

"Dust on the lens," he explained. "There is some extraneous footage attached to the front of the reel, Jack, but be patient; this does lead to the material you asked me to show you."

The screen went dark again, and then suddenly two prizefighters appeared before them, circling around a roped-off ring, slapping punches at each other; there was no sound, the image leeched of color to a flat black and white and the figures moved with an almost comical jumpiness, but the spooky, larger-than-life spectacle appearing out of thin air astonished them.

"That's Gentleman Jim Corbett, world heavyweight champion," said Edison, pointing to the larger of the men. "Filmed in this same room a few months ago. His opponent's a local fellow we recruited from an obscurity—"

On the screen, Corbett floored the man with a single punch.

"—to which he quickly returned."

The image changed to an exterior landscape; a train tunnel cut in the side of a mountain, tracks running from it directly at the screen. Moments later, a steaming locomotive charged out of the tunnel and hurtled toward them; the men yelled involuntarily. Innes dove out of his seat.

Edison guffawed and slapped his thigh. "No matter how many times I see people react to that it still gives me a chuckle."

The screen changed again to an intimate boudoir draped with tasseled gauzes and silks, lush pillows crowding a leopard-skin rug. A shapely arm encircled with silver bracelets slithered out from behind the curtains, followed by a barefooted leg; then their owner revealed herself, a sinuous, dark-haired dancing girl in diaphanous harem pants and a filmy halter; flowers adorned her hair, pearls ringed her neck, a hefty dew-drop jewel ornamented her navel. She flirted with them from the screen, flashing her kohl-rimmed eyes, and began to shake and shimmy in a way that could only be described as extraordinarily professional.

"Good night!" said Innes. "Who is *that*?"

"Her name is Little Egypt," said Edison. "Actually her name is Mildred Hockingheimer from Brooklyn. Our nation's foremost practitioner of the hootchy-kootchy. And she is going to be very, very famous."

They watched her for a while and could find no basis for disagreement.

"Very talented girl," said Stern.

"From Brooklyn?" said Presto. "It hardly seems possible."

"She found the inspiration for her act in a Syrian

woman—not so coincidentally also named Little Egypt—
who scandalized last year's World's Fair: There are currently
twenty-five Little Egypts plying their trade around the country. We've got the jump on them, though: *Our* Little Egypt
is already the biggest attraction in every Kinetoscope parlor
we've put her into; we could charge a quarter a peep and
men would still be standing in line."

"Worth every penny," said Innes.

"And all a trick, her sense of motion, that is. Retention of
vision; a trick the eye plays on us. Separate still photographs
shown so quickly in succession the mind perceives the
movements as continuous."

"The possibilities," said Doyle, thinking well beyond the
scope of her current performance, "are limitless."

"Do you think so? I'm afraid it may not have much appli-
cation beyond the prurient or purely sensational. Eye-
catching, of course, but something kind of shameful about it
finally, isn't there?"

"For two hundred years, the most popular attractions in
England were public executions, followed closely by bear-
baiting and cockfights," said Presto. "If your marvelous invention moves the masses toward voyeurism, they shan't
have much distance to travel."

"Hope you're right. People are usually suspicious of new
inventions," said Edison. "For the longest time, they were
afraid diseases could be transmitted over the telephone. But
not moving pictures; I've never seen anything like it; people
take to it like camels to water."

"How ever did you find her?" asked Innes, untroubled by
Edison's concerns, his mind doing handsprings around some
pretext—a convention; a class reunion of sorts—that would
unite all twenty-five of the Little Egypts.

"Dancing at Coney Island, although this performance was
recorded right here in our Black Maria. Quite a gal, Mildred;
she likes to tell you her dance is patterned after the secret
ceremonies of the ancient Egyptian temple. How they happened to fall into her hands in the middle of Flatbush remains a mystery she will carry to her rest."

Little Egypt vanished without revealing any of the secrets

she seemed to have been leading up to: A stunning vista of white Grecian and Italianate pavilions took her place on the screen, immense crowds scurrying in and out of the buildings like insects.

"This is the World's Fair now," said Edison. "Ran for six months last year—any of you gentlemen have the good fortune to attend?"

No, none of them had, they said.

"Sorry to say you missed one of the great spectacles in creation. Originally the town fathers wanted to show the world how Chicago had recovered from the great fire in '71, but it quickly became clear that the unseen forces which occasionally conspire to push forward the progress of man had something more significant in mind. In the middle of our worst economic crisis in forty years, the Fair was visited by twenty-seven million people; nearly half our country's population. And between my company's efforts and those of our competitors, it was the most widely photographed event in human history."

A dazzling flood of images cascaded over the screen: exhibition halls filled with gargantuan manufacturing displays; dynamos, hydroelectric power, models of machines from the new Golden Age of Science. An entire building full of turbines and generators, seemingly the work of a race of giants. Steam-powered fire engines. Horseless carriages. The latest advances in luxurious rail travel; gloriously appointed sleeping cars with silk curtains and silver washbasins. In its central chamber, a tower of electricity reached to the roof of the vast steel hall, the words "Edison Light" flashing around its pinnacle—as he stood beside them, Doyle watched the flickering shadows play off Edison's face, marveling at the riches of inspiration that must animate his mind; godfather to the march of progress they were witnessing.

A separate pavilion displayed Edison's Inventions of Tomorrow, machines predicted to better the lives of every man, woman, and child; vacuum cleaners, laundry machines, refrigerated ice boxes. And most astonishing: the Telectroscope, a viewing tube, like a telescope, that when perfected would allow a man in New York to see the face of a friend in Chicago as if they were standing side by side.

Rising from an amusement area called the Midway, a gigantic wheel of light carried passengers in swinging baskets, up, down, and around in a fiery circle—invented by a local man named George Washington Ferris, Edison told them—as if a wonder from Mount Olympus had fallen among the mortals. One dizzying shot demonstrated the point of view of someone sitting in the revolving chairs; from its apex the fairgrounds spread out beneath the wheel like the dawning of a new civilization.

"Two hundred and fifty feet in the air: Our cameraman nearly fainted and fell to his death," said Edison.

Now pictures documented groups of men and women gathered on stairs in front of various Fair pavilions; in wide-angle shots, a banner in their center announced the group's identity—Pan American Association of Horse Breeders; the Chicago Club; United Women's Congress—followed in each instance by closer shots of the camera slowly panning across each stationary membership, most of them, used to posing for still photographers, standing as rigidly as statues with unwavering smiles on their faces.

This is all very interesting, thought Doyle, on the verge of asking: What was the point?

Then came the Parliament of International Religions: one of the largest groupings, a swell of clergy populating the steps around their banner and a second sign that read: Not Men, but Ideas. Not Matter, but Mind.

Lionel Stern leaned forward in his seat. The closer examining shots began: bishops, cardinals, deacons, vicars, Protestant and Catholic in their clerical collars standing shoulder to shoulder with rabbis, both Orthodox and the more contemporarily outfitted Reform. . . .

"There, there he is, there's my father," said Lionel Stern, leaping forward to the screen and pointing at a briefly glimpsed angular figure in the center of the group. "Is there any way to stop the picture?"

"I'm afraid not," said Edison.

The camera continued to slip to the right across the congregation; Lionel watched anxiously as Jacob's grainy image drifted to the edge of the screen and disappeared. Now the many races and religions of the East made their appearance, eyeing the camera with more variety of expression—from quiet humor to outright suspicion—all wearing their distinctive traditional vestments: clusters of draped and turbaned Muslims and Hindus, Buddhists in dark saffron robes, ascetic Confucianists, Coptic Christians, Tibetans, elegant Shinto priests, forbidding Eastern Orthodox patriarchs.

As the camera reached the far margin of the group, it stopped moving and held the frame. A lone figure in the back row captured their eye: a tall, arresting man, thin as a scarecrow, wearing a high stovepipe hat and a severe black frock coat, cut like an undertaker's. Long, scraggly hair flowed to his shoulders; out of his back on the left side rose a spiny deformed hump. The features of the face remained blurry; alone among the entire membership, this man was moving his head from side to side. . . .

Jack stood straight up, jolted from his seat. He moved quickly to the screen and studied the faint image; moments later the film ended, the screen trailed off in a congestion of lines, sprockets, motes of dust. Edison turned off the projector and the room went silent. Jack turned to Doyle, eyes wide with alarm, caught for a moment in the stark white light on the screen.

"I must see it again," said Jack.

"I'll have to rewind the reel first," said Edison.

"No; let me see the film plain, in my hands, one picture at a time."

"Of course," said Edison.

"What is it, Jack?" said Doyle, watching him closely.

Jack didn't reply.

Minutes later, in Edison's lab, the length of film spread out across a glass panel lit from below, Jack pored over its individual frames with a magnifying glass as the others stood quietly by.

In one of the frames, between his constant movements, Jack found an image of the humpbacked preacher that caught the outline of the man's features nearly distinct.

Jack went instantly pale: Doyle noticed his hands shaking.

"We know this man, Arthur," said Jack gravely.

"Do we?"

"We know him all too well," he said, handing the glass to Doyle.

book three

CHICAGO

chapter nine

EILEEN TRIED TO STEAL A GLIMPSE OF THE SKETCH PAD IN Jacob's hand, but he shooed her away with mock annoyance. She sighed and continued to stare wistfully out the window as he instructed, only too accustomed to following a man's directions, watching his pencil working furiously out of the corner of her eye but unable to see the results. Oppressive heat shimmered the horizon line as the train pulled its way through a winding arroyo and began to climb from the flat, sandy landscape into broken promontories of rock.

What went haywire inside a man's head when exposed to a woman's physical charms? Eileen had been bedeviled by the question for years: Put an otherwise sensible man in the company of an uncommonly attractive female—she had enough perspective untainted by wishful vanity to include herself in that category—and the poor fellow was either rendered speechless or consumed by an impulse to possess and dominate her.

She rolled the issue around in her mind: Is this madness a reaction to something I'm doing or the work of invisible biological mechanisms? Either way, short of entering a convent there didn't seem to be a thing she could do about it; nature did not yield to logic. Sex itself wasn't the problem, anyway; it was these damn mating rituals. Better to be born a cat or dog and confine all the torment over who sleeps with whom to quick seasonal frenzies. Part of her sentiments looked forward to getting past the breeding years so she could be treated like any other human being.

On the other hand, old girl, she corrected herself—remembering her worn face in the mirror that morning and how welcome were the full thrusts of a man's attentions when she felt receptive—let's not be too hasty.

"Let me see if I understood you," she said, resurrecting a

recent conversation. "You're a certified member of your clergy, doesn't that give you the authority to communicate directly with God?"

"Oh, thank heavens, no; only Moses and a few other Old Testament Jews were saddled with that responsibility, and even their conversations were usually filtered through some sort of intermediary; an angel or a burning bush," said Jacob, bent over his drawing.

"But there must be hundreds of Christian ministers in this country who believe they receive the word of God straight from the horse's mouth."

"Yes," said Jacob, with a sad smile, "I know."

"But if you have no contact with whoever He is, how can you claim to perform God's will?"

"A rabbi makes no such claim, my dear; that is far too important a job to be entrusted to professionals. If God speaks to anyone it is only through the voice of the human heart and everyone you meet has one of those."

"Theatrical producers aside."

"Not to mention certain neighborhoods in New York," said Jacob. "My people have a belief that the existence of the world is sustained by the righteousness of a small number of perfectly ordinary people who attract no attention to themselves and very quietly go about their business."

"Like saints, then."

"Hidden saints, you might call them, seeking no reward or recognition for what they do. Pass them in the street, you'd hardly notice them; not even *they* have the slightest idea they are performing such essential service. But they carry the weight of the world on their shoulders."

"Sounds more like a job for the Messiah," she said.

"This whole Messiah business is so terribly overemphasized. . . ."

"You don't believe in the Messiah?"

"There is a tradition in Judaism that if someone tells you the Messiah has come and you are planting a tree, first finish planting the tree and then go see about this Messiah."

"Hmm. I guess if a fellow actually was the Messiah, the last thing he'd do is run around announcing it to people."

"Not if he wants to live until suppertime. If you look at the subject historically, this idea began because the Jews in Israel wanted a man with supernatural powers to fly down from heaven and rescue them; quite a natural response to a thousand years of slavery, wouldn't you agree?"

"I'd wish for a squadron of them."

"Then Jesus came along and, regardless of who you believe he was, the rest is history. But ever since in Western culture when we approach the end of a century, as we are now, a terror that the Judgment Day is at hand awakens in us this hunger for a savior to appear and set things right. And with it the strange notion that there can only be one of these persons."

"More than one Messiah?" asked Eileen. "But he's one of a kind, isn't he, by definition?"

"In Kabbalah there is an alternative idea that has always struck me as infinitely more reasonable: Within each generation that passes through this life there are a few people alive at all times—without any self-awareness that they possess such a quality—who, if events called upon them to do so, could assume the role of the Messiah."

"The 'role' of the Messiah?"

"In the same way we are all playing a part in our own lives: strutting and fretting our hour upon the stage, full of sound and fury, signifying God knows what. If you look at it from this perspective, in the great pageant of life the Messiah is simply one of the more interesting characters."

"So what sort of events might bring these Messiahs forward?"

"I suppose the usual calamities: cataclysm, pestilence, apocalypse. Our hero needs a good entrance. Although according to this theory, He would have been standing in front of us the entire time without anyone noticing."

"What happens to these people when they don't become the Chosen One?" she asked.

"They live out their days and die in peace, the lucky creatures."

"Never knowing about the part they might otherwise have played."

"For their sake let's hope so. Messiah; what a dreadful job. Everyone throwing themselves at your feet, asking you to cure their rheumatism. Pearls of wisdom expected to fall with every utterance. All pain and suffering and never a kind word in the end."

"Speaking of being nailed to a cross, would you mind if I moved? I'm on the verge of a crippled neck."

"Not at all. Nearly finished," he said, the tip of his tongue tickling his lip in concentration.

Eileen relaxed and turned to face the other direction, looking past Jacob out the far window. "Tell me: I've always been unclear on exactly what the Messiah is supposed to do for us if He does come back."

"There is a remarkable division of opinion on this subject. One school of thought has Him riding down from the sky in the nick of time to save the world from eternal darkness. Another believes He will appear wielding a vengeful sword to judge the wicked and reward the faithful, of which there are only about twelve. A third version says if enough human beings straighten themselves out and follow the path of goodness, He would show up at once and lead us all through the pearly gates."

"I guess it depends on who you talk to."

"Not to mention the two thirds of the world who don't believe in the idea at all."

"What do you believe, Jacob?"

"Since I have come to the conclusion this is an area about which I can only confess my staggering ignorance, I've decided it's far too important a question to be answered with any degree of certainty."

"Leave certainty for the fanatics, you mean."

"Exactly. I take a wait and see approach. I'll either find out when I die or I won't." He laughed heartily, turned his sketch pad around, and showed her the finished portrait. His hand was sure and his eye discerning: Her features accurately rendered, the high cheekbones, the dramatic arch in her dark brow, but the resemblance ran deeper than appearances.

He's captured my character, she thought with a jolt: the

pride, willfulness, and deep-seated vulnerability. Penetrating the layers of accumulated toughness, Jacob had seen the romantic idealist submerged below. An actress spent unnatural amounts of time before the mirror contemplating the state of her face—constantly on alert, shoring up the battlements, fighting to stave off every line and slippage—but she had not seen this forgotten gentle quality in herself for so long, the sight brought tears brimming to her eyes.

Was that naive, fresh-faced girl from Manchester still inside her? She felt a fool, weeping over such long-lost territory, but that youthful part of her nature had been good and true and Jacob had seen it clearly. She looked at the kind, frank tenderness in his azure eyes and for once didn't worry about whether her hair was in a tangle or her makeup ruined.

What does this man want from me? she wondered. Maybe nothing. What a shocking idea.

She tried to hand back the portrait, but he insisted that she keep it. She looked away, dried her eyes, blew her nose—it sounded like a trumpet to her; how attractive—and swallowed a fractured thank-you.

"If you'll excuse me for a moment," said Jacob, rising from his seat. She nodded, grateful for a moment alone, and watched him walk away.

He needed a breath of air; that queasy throbbing in his chest again; the third time since leaving Chicago. She hadn't noticed, he was sure of that, but he'd felt the blood drain from his face like water from a bath. A desperate light-headedness came over him, his vision tightening down to woozy tunnels. He gripped the handle of the car door and pulled with what little strength he could spare. Standing on the platform between the cars, now that she couldn't see him, he dedicated all his energy to recovering. . . .

Breathe, you old fool: worse, much worse.

He doubled over, swallowing great gulps of hot desert air, feeling it sweep ineffectively through the dry bellows of his lungs; heart throbbing with effort, missing a beat, losing its rhythm—

Come on, Jacob, enough of this nonsense, you have work to do.

—tingling in his limbs, fingers going numb, knees on the verge of collapse, he held on to the chains that ringed the platform, looked down at the bright ribbon of steel rushing by beneath the train; sweat ran down off his forehead, soaked through his shirt—

This is worse than before; this is worse than it's ever been.

—his balance grew precarious, his mind shutting down to a single thought: Hold on to this chain. If he lost his grip he would pitch right over the side. Darkness grew around him, eyes barely able to see, heart skipping like a stone, hearing nothing but the tidal roar of his turbulent pulse. . . .

One more step; so close, death hovered above him as light as a feather.

Then like flood waters cresting, the crisis began to recede; his vision cleared, widened, black spots swirling away, his lungs pulled in a satisfying breath, desperation eased, feeling returned to his fingertips. He slumped against the wall, legs quivering, but he felt the pressure loosen inside his chest. Muscles cracked like straw as he regained his footing. Terrible weakness. Blasts of hot air dried the sweat on his forehead; he stepped tentatively across the platform and coaxed open the door to the next car.

Cool and dark inside; welcoming. He smiled weakly; not so bad, was it, Jacob? He had ventured closer to the brink than ever before. If that was death's hand on his shoulder, all he had to do was turn and face it. He'd always been averse to pain, but if this was all it took to leave, it seemed effortless. A matter of surrender not struggle: Let go and quietly slip away.

Jittery light angled in through a slatted window. Jacob settled onto a bench; his eyes adjusted, his surroundings came into focus. What are all these strange shrouded shapes? Where am I, in some purgatorial waiting room?

Then he remembered seeing the cargo being loaded at the station; a protruding sleeve of red velvet curtain, a bucket of spearheads pointing toward the ceiling confirmed it. Theatrical props and sets. Trunks, wardrobes; tools in the workshop of creation.

"What an appropriate place to die," he whispered.

He heard something moving in the corner, a rasping sound, metal on stone. Arhythmic, purposeful, owing nothing to the rocking of the train. Jacob listened a minute, rallying his strength, before curiosity overtook him. He stood and moved quietly toward the sound through a narrow passage between backdrops. To either side of him: glimpses of painted mountain tops, palace walls, an impossibly lush sunset.

The sound ended. Jacob stopped. Something rattled behind him. He turned slowly. The tip of a long knife lightly touched his throat; holding the weapon a man dressed in the blue uniform of a railroad guard. A whetstone in his free hand; the sound Jacob had heard, sharpening the blade.

The man's face: Asian. Chinese? Pale and strained as Jacob imagined his own must be. His tunic loosely buttoned; bloodstains below the shoulder turning the blue a rusty violet.

This is the one they were talking about at the station, Jacob realized. The manhunt, the killer with the sword. It looks as if I'm going to die in this place after all. . . .

If that is the case, why do I feel so calm?

His heart had not increased a beat.

Solemn concentration on the man's face gave way to an interest equaling Jacob's; clearly he perceived no threat from the old man. Slowly the blade came down and they regarded each other with increasing fascination.

"Forgive my intrusion," said Jacob. "I was looking for a place to die."

The man studied him. Jacob had never seen eyes that betrayed so little; flat and black, pure neutrality.

"One place is the same as another," the man said, fingers expertly finding and guiding the long knife into an ornate scabbard.

What is it about this man that feels familiar? Jacob asked himself. Obviously I've never seen him before—the thought was ridiculous—but he experienced a deep, quiet sensation of affinity.

"How curious," said Jacob quietly.

The man sat on a stool between the backdrops; out of necessity, Jacob realized, seeing the blood that had already spilled onto the floor. He had dressed the wound with a band of white cotton wrapped around his chest; left side, under the arm.

A second, longer scabbard lay at his feet, identical in design to the smaller one; black lacquer highlights shining along its edges, the worn silver hilt of a sword extending from its mouth. The man carefully laid the knife scabbard alongside the sword, adjusting them to mirror the same angle.

"*Dai-sho*" said the man. "Large and small."

"Large and small?"

"*Katana, wakizashi,*" he said, pointing to the sword, then the knife.

"I see."

"It is called Kusanagi." The man gingerly leaned over and picked up the sword. "The Grass Cutter."

"Why is that?"

"Legend says it belonged to Susanoo, god of thunder; he carved the sword with lightning from a mountaintop. One day Susanoo went out to hunt and left it behind; the sword became angry and cut down every tree and blade of grass on the island. Why there are so few trees in Japan. . . ." He stopped, closed his eyes, went pale as a shiver of pain ran through him.

"It's self-propelled, this sword?" asked Jacob.

The spasm passed; the man nodded.

"That's quite a sword."

"*Honoki,*" the man said, running his hand along the gleaming scabbard. "Hard wood: cut from the last tree the sword chopped down. *Same:* fish skin; from a whale Susanoo killed. *Habuki:* the collar; keeps blade from wearing against the sleeve. This peg fastens blade to hilt, bamboo: *mekugi.* Metal pins cover the peg: *menuki.*"

Sweat dripped freely off the man's forehead; his fingers trembled. He's reciting this inventory as a meditation, Jacob decided; to stay awake, alert. Maybe to stay alive.

"What is this?" asked Jacob gently, pointing to the pommel grip.

"*Kashira.*"

"And this?" he asked, pointing to a plate resting against the scabbard.

"*Tsuba.* Separates blade from handle."

The man pulled out the sword a few inches to show Jacob the *tsuba;* an elliptical stack of fused metal plates half an inch thick with an oxidized red patina, its exposed surface exquisitely engraved with the double image of a fiery bird, each gripping in its beak the other's flowing tail feathers: one rising from and the other falling into stylized tongues of flame.

"This is the phoenix," said Jacob, amazed to find such delicate artistry as part of a deadly weapon.

"Phoenix," said the man. "Name of city." He tilted his head toward where they had come from.

Not without irony, realized Jacob; there's more going on inside this man than meets the eye.

"To fall and rise again," said Jacob. "From the ashes."

"Long way to go." The man shrugged, referencing his own reduced condition. He laid the sword down again beside its mate, took a shallow, painful breath.

"How badly are you hurt, my friend?"

"Gunshot. Hit in back, under left shoulder."

"Would you like me to look at it?"

"You are a doctor?"

"The next best thing," said Jacob. "I'm a priest."

The man's eyes brightened as his forehead furrowed in doubt. "You? Priest?"

"What, such a look I'm getting."

"You don't look like a priest."

"Priest, rabbi, what's the difference?" said Jacob, helping ease the tunic off his shoulders. "Where did you learn to speak English like this?"

"From a priest; he was Catholic."

"Ah, well; you see, there are priests and then there are priests."

Dried matter saturated the rough bandaging around his back; fresh dark blood still oozed from its center.

"I am priest, too," said the man.

"Are you a Buddhist?"

"*Shinto.*"

"So you are Japanese, then."

"You have heard of *shinto?*"

"I have read about it and I met *shinto* priests from your country last year, in Chicago. Which island are you from?"

"Hokkaido."

"These men were from Honshu."

"*Hai.* Big city men."

"*Shinto* means 'the way of the gods,' doesn't it?"

Jacob peeled the bandage away from the wound; the man flinched slightly as the last layer of muslin pulled a ridge of crusted blood off the injury; a small, round hole just below the shoulder blade. Bruising around the trauma; no redness or infection yet.

"Yes. *Kami-no-michi,*" said the man, his voice betraying no discomfort at Jacob's probing. "*Kami* means 'superior'; the gods above."

The bullet had entered his back in the meat of a muscle, glanced off a rib, tumbled, and exited the side of the chest; another larger hole there, two inches below. The man's breathing unaffected, the lung must be all right, Jacob thought, feeling a bit ridiculous; what am I now, suddenly a surgeon?

"You can thank the gods above you're not walking among them now," said Jacob, his own frailties forgotten for the moment. "We need something to clean this wound."

"Alcohol."

"You're in luck; there's a whole car full of actors up ahead. Where did you find this bandage?"

The man pointed to a bolt of cotton gauze sitting in a trunk nearby.

"A regular infirmary back here." Jacob retrieved the cotton from the trunk and began folding a bandage from the bolt. "Tell me about this priest, the one who taught you English. . . ."

"He lived at our temple. American missionary."

"Came to convert you, did he?"

"In the end we converted him; he is there still."

"One good turn deserves another. I'd better go get that alcohol."

Jacob didn't move for an awkward moment. Would the man trust him enough to let him leave? Apparently so: He didn't even turn around.

"Where did you read about *shinto?*" the man asked.

"A book in my library at home, translated into English, of course. I don't recall the title. . . ."

"The Kojiki?"

"Yes, I think that was it."

"Where did you see this book?"

"One of the *shinto* priests gave it to me last year in Chicago during the Parliament; he said it was the first translation anyone had made."

"Have you seen any other copy?" the man asked, turning to face him with violent intensity. "In Japanese?"

"No," said Jacob, but the question made an odd sense to him; something coming together in the back of his mind that he couldn't quite define. "Why?"

The man stared at him with his strange matted eyes. "The Kojiki, the first book, was stolen from our temple."

"That's what I thought you were going to say," said Jacob.

SEPTEMBER 26, 1894

Our train left the Grand Central Depot at eleven o'clock sharp this morning—Americans are nothing if not obsessively punctual. We're traveling on The Exposition Flyer, *an express introduced last year to accommodate traffic back and forth from the World's Fair. We will cover the eight hundred miles to Chicago in under twenty hours; extraordinary, as are the train's lush appointments. Luxury of the first order. Competition for the customer's dollar drives everything here; bigger, faster, stronger; there's no end to this fetish for improvement, but in a country without much his-*

tory their thoughts run inevitably, sometimes exhaustingly, to the future. But before they can consider themselves truly civilized, something must be done about their incessant public use of the spittoon.

The broad reaches of the Hudson River accompany us as we make our way north; the train has just passed the farthest outskirt of the City and what greets us is a riot of autumnal colors the brilliance and variety of which I have never conceived. If the Creator of our universe is an artist, He has emptied his paint box in these woods; reds, rusts, vermillions, violets, ambers and golds, all made sparkling and radiant by a brilliant warming sun. Hawthorne called this region home; Irving, Melville, and Fenimore Cooper as well; it is nothing if not inspirational. Major Pepperman, our indefatigable host, has termed this glorious weather an "Indian Summer." Not hard to imagine Indians living in these sheltering forests, doing whatever it is Indians do, paddling their canoes, shooting off arrows, scaling the craggy palisades that line the western shore.

I have just completed the morning's correspondence— letters to Louise; notes and gifts for the children; Martha Washington dolls for Mary, a splendid tin soldier set for Kingsley; now he can restage the American Revolution and continue to rewrite history. A wire from Louise yesterday makes no mention of her health; this of course, entirely without foundation, leads me to suspect only the worst.

New York City has left me knackered; another few days might have finished me off. What a pace! Amazing its residents don't drop every night and sleep where they fall. I have never visited a city whose residents were so confident, one might say arrogant, about their own significance. The city may well be preparing for greatness but they never let you forget it.

Two observations: Every man you meet on the street seems utterly consumed with baseball, a local game, apparently derived from cricket, whose elusive appeal they are equally incapable of conveying by any means of common speech. Their professional "season" has just concluded or I would certainly by now have taken in one of these contests,

*if only to sort out the dizzying and contradictory welter of rules
and regulations its enthusiasts are only too eager to inflict
upon the innocent. The second: In the heart of a neighborhood
they call Greenwich Village, one of the earliest settled areas of
the city, stands Washington Square; entrance framed by a
graceful monument to their founding father, it is as charming and picturesque a green, and a virtual oasis of peace
and quiet, as any city this size could hope to provide. If
Holmes had ever found himself in America, I believe Washington Square is where he would have hung his hat.*

*We're quite the odd entourage; Lionel Stern sharing a
sleeper compartment with Presto, the Maharaja of Berar—
stranger bedfellows would be hard to invent—Innes and myself bunking in the next; Jack, alone, lugging around that
compact suitcase Edison gave him as we left his compound:
He has yet to reveal its contents to the rest of us. And poor
hangdog Pepperman, clutching his wires and newspaper notices, believing he travels with the brothers Doyle alone,
ready to retreat into wounded, sheepish solemnity—so incongruous in such a gigantic human being—whenever I invoke
the desire for privacy, which on this trip will be often. Heaven
forbid the Major catches wind of our actual mission; the anx-
iety might cause him to spontaneously combust.*

ON BOARD *THE EXPOSITION FLYER*

Before reaching Albany, the train parted company with the
Hudson and muscled west, taking on in its place the unwavering companionship of the Erie Canal. Buffalo, New York,
came and went shortly after dinner: bloody steaks and great
piles of mashed potatoes at Pepperman's table. He made a
vain attempt to evoke the great spirit of adventure about
their journey—"Look, Lake Ontario, one of our five Great
Lakes; bet you've never seen a lake that big before!" and so
on—but the man was once again left puzzled and slightly
deflated by the Doyles' polite, lukewarm responses.

Occasional glances passed among Doyle and his companions dining at nearby tables—Stern and Presto together,

Jack alone. The Major took no notice and consoled himself with an extra serving of strawberry shortcake, a dish new to the Doyles that prompted their most enthusiastic outburst of the trip, elevating Pepperman's hopes for an improved camaraderie only to have them immediately dashed when the brothers declined an invitation to repair to his berth for a few hands of whist.

Doyle had determined he must take advantage of their confinement on the train to lay siege to the wall of silence surrounding the lost ten years of Jack Sparks's life. Before venturing any further into danger, Doyle felt a compelling responsibility to crack the mystery of the man who was taking them there. Earlier attempts based on sincere, straightforward concern had failed; time to give subterfuge a try.

Doyle nicked a bottle of brandy from the bar and found Jack alone in his sleeper, reading by the light of a sputtering gas jet. Jack immediately concealed the cover of the book—a perfectly innocuous scientific treatise on the principles of conductive electricity—but secrecy was by now so second nature to him, under the seat it went, on top of Edison's mysterious suitcase.

Doyle ceremoniously settled himself across from Sparks; Jack refused both the brandy and an offered cigar, reached up and nozzled down the gas, bathing his half of the berth in a flickering half-light from which he watched Doyle with sharp, hooded eyes. Doyle said nothing and took no apparent notice of Jack's scrutiny, lit his Havana, savored his brandy, and feigned a high level of self-absorbed contentment.

Jack stared holes in him.

Fine; if all else fails I'll outwait you, Doyle thought; I made it through five years of medical lectures, I can sit here until one of us rots.

Jack grew uncomfortable under Doyle's mild, disinterested gaze; a single fidget, a restless finger of his mangled hand tapping on his knee. Minutes passed. Doyle blew smoke, smiled absently, peering thoughtfully behind the shade at the darkness outside.

"Hmm," he said, before closing the blind.

He glanced back at Jack and smiled again. Jack shifted in his seat.

Doyle ran a hand over the mohair seat, leaned over to inspect the seams.

"Hmm," he said.

Jack folded his arms across his chest.

Now I've got him on the ropes.

Doyle held up a foot and inspected the laces on his boot.

Jack exhaled heavily.

Time to apply the coup de grâce.

Doyle began to hum. Aimlessly, tunelessly. A bit of this, a snatch of that; nothing at all. Spikes driven under one's fingernails could scarcely have been more effective. Three minutes of this before . . .

"I mean, really," said Jack.

"What's that?"

"Must you?"

"Must I what?"

"Are you deliberately trying to aggravate me?"

"Why, that's not my intent at all, Jack—"

"Good God, man."

"—whatever do you mean?"

"Barging in here. Brandy and a cigar. That appalling noise. This isn't the reading room of the Garrick Club."

"Oh, am I disturbing you? Terribly sorry, old man."

Another patient smile. Not the slightest twitch of intention to vacate. Jack looks away. Another minute elapses. Then. Begins moving his head slightly from side to side— silent humming—while he conducts the imagined music with small waves of his cigar.

"What?" said Jack, exasperated.

"What?"

"What do you *want?*"

"Not a thing; perfectly content, old chap; thanks, ever so—"

"Monstrous; rude; invasion of privacy. Not like you at all."

Then, as if a subject he'd been meaning to bring up had come rushing back into his mind, Doyle fixed Sparks with a benign physician's eye and paused dramatically before asking, "How have you *been,* Jack?"

"What sort of a deeply moronic question is that?"

"I can't honestly say I don't have my concerns about you. . . ."

"Now you are really making me angry—"

"Perhaps if I express it this way, Jack: There are certain . . . behaviors you exhibit that, as a *doctor,* one can't help but take notice of."

"What?"

"Certain symptomatic tendencies—"

"Stop mincing around and come out with it: What do you mean to say?"

Doyle regarded him with a thoughtful series of nods. "It occurs to me that in the years between our periods of acquaintanceship, you may have become mentally deranged."

Even in the shadowy haze, Doyle could see blood rush to his face like mercury up a raging thermometer; it seemed to require a supreme act of will for Jack to contain the violence that fireballed inside him. For a tense moment, Doyle feared his strategy had backfired and he might have to physically defend himself; he knew how to box but Jack knew how to kill. But instead of attack came the rigid pointing of a scarred and crooked index finger and a voice strangled with fury.

"You . . . don't know . . . a bloody thing . . . about anything." Corners of Jack's mouth flecked with white. Snorting like an agitated bull.

"I don't know the facts, of course," said Doyle, somehow keeping his pitch at the same infuriating even keel. "All I have are my observations. What else have you given me to go on?"

"Would you like to hear that there were times when I begged whatever passes for intelligence in the Creator of this world to let me die? That I got down on my bloody knees and prayed like some simple-minded vicar to a God I don't even believe in? Is that what you want, Doyle? Because that would be true. And I am pleased to report that there *is* no God of the kind they try to sell us, because nothing bearing a resemblance to such a being would have left one of its creatures alive in such a state."

Right, thought Doyle, *now we've primed the pump.*

"So instead He . . . left you alive to suffer, is that it?"

"What a stupid, common presumption: Didn't you hear a word I just told you? Regarding *our fate* no decision is made; no one presides, no being, no *thing* even bears witness. Can you begin to understand me?"

Doyle stared at him mutely: *Let him talk.*

"No great or lesser intelligence takes any notice of our existence whatsoever because we are alone, Doyle, every one of us, left adrift in cold and empty space. That's the dirty joke on the washroom wall: It's all a mistake; cruel, random, and senseless as a railway accident. . . ."

"Human life?"

"I mean *creation.*"

Jack leaned forward; the piercing lightness of his eyes like diamonds in the dark of the carriage. His voice fell to a whispery rasp. "Every stone, every blade of grass, every butterfly. Man most assuredly of all: no design, no underlying purpose; it's a folly, our so-called mind, a japery; if there's poetry in our nature, it bleats out of us with no more conscious intention than the babblings of an ape. But the world of man—*society*—conspires to keep this secret from us. Don't you find it curious? With all your scientific training?"

"What's that?"

"Animals are born with instinctual drives for survival and develop techniques to ensure it. Man is the only creature that needs to delude himself into believing there's a more elaborate reason he's alive; we flood our minds with lies and fantasies about love and family and a benign God in the heavens watching over us.

"But it's only a survival instinct, drilled into each of us from our first breath; it's vital to a society's survival that its members be prevented from discovering how squalid and meaningless their existence truly is. Otherwise we might lay down our tools, leave all this soul-destroying work behind, and where would your precious *society* be then?"

The silence lay deep between them, broken by the distant,

rhythmic clacking of the rails. Jack never blinked, never moved his eyes from Doyle's: Doyle looked through them to darkness, thick and churning.

"Picture another possibility: What if the origin of our world is worse even than this? What if there is a Creator who worked to give our earth design, forethought, shape and contour? And what if this creature is completely and utterly insane?"

"Is that what you believe, Jack?"

"Do you know what you find, down here"—he stabbed a fist sharply into his gut—"when every article of civility, every habit, cherished memory, every manufactured shred of this puppet we assume ourselves to be is stripped off us like the skin of an animal?"

Doyle swallowed hard. "Tell me."

"Nothing," said Jack, his voice barely a whisper. "A void. No sight, no sound, no thought; not a ripple or the faintest echo. That's the secret at the base of the stairs no one is supposed to find. They warn you when we're young: Don't look down there, children; stay here by the fire and we'll tell you the lies our parents beat into us about the greater glory of man. Because they know coming face-to-face with that emptiness would obliterate every trace of who you thought you were like a beetle crushed under a jackboot."

Jack held up his ruined hands. "And this is the glorious mistake you see before you: I entered into the emptiness. I'm there still. And I'm still alive. And it means . . . nothing."

Sparks smiled, a death's-head grin, eyes shining with a diseased and twisted triumph. The train shot into a tunnel, plunging them into darkness. Doyle clenched his fists, not knowing if he was about to live or die, but he would have welcomed a physical fight, pain, anything palpable and real in place of Jack's spiraling fall.

"So with this cheery whisper in my ear, I greet each new dawn," Jack continued quietly, his voice worming sinuously out of the dark. "It never leaves, I have no relief, and in this way I go on living. Mentally disturbed? Don't waste your pathetic shopworn judgments on me, *Doctor*. Posing at enlightenment. No better than the rest of them; you put a name to what you can't begin to comprehend to push the darkness away. That's the first refuge of a coward. There was a time when I could expect more from you than the parroting of empty screed. Or has success seduced the better part of your mind as well as your pockets? Maybe that's it. They haven't cut you down yet; you're still a fresh face, drunk on the adulation of the masses. Prepare yourself, Doyle; a reckoning is due. They won't tolerate any success from one of their own for long. They cut down all the tall poppies."

The train left the tunnel; lights flickered back on. Jack sat only inches away; his eyes trained on Doyle, who didn't know how to keep the fear and disgust off his face. Doubt crowded in on him: This man's sickness was not only of the mind but of the soul, and its profundity crippled his ability to respond. Where had it come from? What had caused it? He had to press forward with his questions: "If you had come to such a pass, why didn't you take your own life?"

Jack leaned back, shrugged, and casually picked a piece of lint off his sleeve.

"This . . . place . . . is hellish but not without interest. Picture happening upon a street fight: You come around a corner and find two strangers trying to kill each other with every reserve of viciousness in their bodies. The outcome means nothing to you, but the flow of blood, the raw naked spectacle, rivets you; you can't tear your eyes away. Embrace the emptiness and it exerts the same mesmerizing hold on the imagination: How perfectly and regularly human beings embody a vast, horrific meaninglessness. It would almost qualify as tragic if it weren't so deeply hilarious; all the pomp, the effort, the strained, puffed-up self-importance of people, handing out awards to ourselves, parading around; achievement. Working, striving, worshiping, loving. *As if it mattered.*

"Why didn't I kill myself?" Jack laughed, a harsh, brutal rasp. "You might well ask. Because life is so cruel that it makes me laugh, and that's the only reason to go on living."

Doyle struggled to keep any judgment or emotion from his voice; any appeal to the man's fellow feeling offered no avenue to reach him now, if he could still be reached at all. "How did you come to . . . this place?"

"Oh, I suppose you want the facts, don't you? Always the facts with you; fine, why shouldn't you have them? I won't spare you a detail. You can use them like bricks and build a wall to hide behind or put them into one of your little stories. I haven't read them, by the way; I gather you've used me as a model of sorts for your dear detective."

"I suppose that's true, in a way," said Doyle, feeling a rash of anger.

Jack leaned forward with an almost friendly smile and lowered his voice. "Then my advice to you is this, old boy: Don't incorporate a breath of what I tell you into your characters. People won't like to hear a word of it; not sentimental enough, no warm and happy turn. You know how to give them what they want: lies, gilded and framed like a hall of mirrors. Beware of telling them the truth: You'll kill the goose that lays the golden eggs."

Jack laughed again bitterly. Doyle felt himself go cold inside: to bear this much and now an assault on his dignity. Why should he subject himself to another word of this bullying? What lost quality in the man made him certain he was worth the trouble? The Jack he had so admired was nowhere in evidence; this one sounded like an utter stranger and like no one else now so much as Doyle's memory of his mad brother—and if Edison's moving pictures were to be believed, Alexander Sparks had somehow survived the fight at the waterfall as well. Twin ruptured souls, damned and irredeemable; blood ties run deep. This was not his business: easy enough to walk away and leave them both to burn in their private hell.

But a deeper responsibility rose up in him; if either man posed a danger to other people, to simple common decency, then Doyle knew his obligation to proceed along the path he'd chosen outweighed any wounding to his pride. He possessed reserves of faith and strength they knew nothing about and until proven otherwise he would continue to assume they were a match for the darkness that had flowered inside Jack Sparks. Doyle called on those reserves: If that flower could still be cut, Jack might be redeemed. He needed more information.

"Obviously you both survived the Falls," said Doyle matter-of-factly, giving him nothing to scorn. "Why don't you start there?"

Jack smiled as if the memory were fond. "And what a fall it was; endless, like flight or close to it, a dream of flight. Clutching each other, rocky cliffs whistling by as we dropped. Pure hatred in my heart; the desire to kill him stronger than any emotion I had ever known.

"I didn't lose hold of him until we hit the river, two hundred feet, that's how far we fell together. Death seemed a certainty, but over thousands of years the Falls had carved a natural pool in the riverbed at its base. I went down into the depth; the concussion of the landing knocked me senseless. I felt a swift current near the bottom take hold and off I went, a leaf bobbing down towards the sea."

"And your brother?"

"I never saw him again. I came to nestled in a bed of rocks; black night around me. Who knows how much time had gone by? A day might have passed, maybe two. My eyes could make only the slightest adjustment; rock walls around and above me; no sky; in a cave, fed by this underground stream, the mountains there honeycombed with these pockets, as I discovered. I lay on the rocks for the longest time, unable to move, in a twilight state.

"A dullness crept over me, my entire body bruised, battered, but no single outstanding pain to speak of. Plenty of water beside me to drink as I needed. I crawled, then walked, defined the boundaries of my confinement—a space ten feet by twenty; I could barely stand and only in the center. My world reduced to that cramped chamber. Comforting really. Not much difference between a womb and a tomb.

"So at a moment when panic should have taken root I felt increasingly peaceful; when you live in darkness—sleep and move and wake in it—you come close to your own true nature. No distractions with that face in the mirror; dirt under your fingernails, the backs of your hands. Alone with yourself, whatever that is. That ruling voice inside: Who am I? What am I? The first few days my journey began with those questions. Eventually I came to question everything. All the basic assumptions lose their potency, until you realize that all you have, all you are, is what is in your mind.

"I would have stayed there but I had no food, and as I explored my cave I realized there was no other way out; I would have to go back into the river. I waited, building my strength, and then took the plunge. The currents were more negotiable in these subterranean channels and I could swim for some distance in a number of directions, but in the pitch dark and not certain of a place to surface I had to constantly return to my cave. I've no idea how many days passed—how dependent on the cycle of light and dark is our perception of time—but my strength had reached as high a peak as it could without sustenance and would soon begin to dissipate. I staked everything on one last attempt.

"I dropped into the river, swam down into the deep, and passed the point of safe return. Living in the dark had raised my other senses to exquisite levels; I could detect the slightest variation of flow in the river so I let the water guide me: nothing to be gained by struggling. Minutes elapsed. Breath used up, I came very near surrender, how tempting to let everything go . . . at that moment I saw a light in the water and I called on the finishing kick I had held back. I lost consciousness as I broke the surface and drifted to shore. That's where I awoke, in a bed of bulrushes, like some antiquated Moses. Middle of the night, a secluded bend in the river.

"As my mind came back, I realized the most curious thing had occurred: Every concern, every burden that had brought me to this moment had vanished. I remembered each circumstance of how I had fallen and why, but I no longer cared. In its place, a lightness, a freeing up, a release from gravity. My family, my brother, my private torments. I hear your thoughts, Doyle: *He suffered oxygen deprivation. Damage to the brain.* Believe what you like; what I had undergone in that cave was nothing less than a second birth. A chance to create a new life. The dead weight of Jack Sparks slipped off me like the skin of a snake: If everyone thought the man was dead—and why wouldn't they? the terrible fall, credible witnesses—I could quite easily oblige them.

"I saw stars above me in the night sky for the first time

uncluttered by my private despair: An interior objectivity I had never suspected was possible—rock, water, tree, meadow, moon; each thing I saw just the thing itself and not some shadow colored by my inner demons—a release from every earthly obligation, every lingering nightmare. A voice spoke inside my head that I had never heard before: *This way,* it said; *follow me.* Clear and calming. Promising a peace I'd never known. I listened.

"I walked all night, through an alpine valley following the river. No concern about where I was going; my path assured, every footstep. Sure enough, I happened upon a deserted cabin; a shepherd's roost, stocked with supplies. Stayed there until the food was gone. My strength renewed, with the voice guiding me I walked two hundred miles south, down through the Dolomites, to Padua, then finally to Ravenna on the Adriatic Sea. Spring stirring in the air. I found work on the docks as a laborer and took a room near the canal. Ate at the same café every evening; black olives, thick dark bread, red wine. Lots of red wine.

"I'd spent my entire life hunting my brother: I had no idea this was the way most people live. They work, eat, sleep, make love. Never concern themselves with aspects of living they can't control—meaning, purpose; they're never questioned, easier to leave all that in the hands of an employer, the Church, the tax collector. Existing from one day to the next; part of the landscape, never straying far from the ground that produced them. So self-evident but for me an entirely new conception. Living among them gave me an experience of true grace. Days ran into months, spring into summer and fall. I worked my body to exhaustion every day, slept with as many women as I could manage, and worried about exactly nothing.

"Casting off all ties to who I had been allowed me to become anyone I wanted: What are we except what we imagine ourselves to be? One morning I woke with an impulse to move on: I made myself a sailor from the Isle of Man—forged the documents I needed—and signed on a merchant steamer, bound for Portugal. A restlessness wormed its way into my blood: Out of Lisbon, I joined a freighter shipping to Brazil, where I wandered the coast, working smaller ships until I finally found a world to lose myself in.

"Four years in the city of Belem, near the mouth of the Amazon River: an international port, dozens of cultures colliding in a thousand intrigues; equatorial heat, thievery and bad intent. Surrounded by jungle, and its influence seeped into the bloodstream of every human behavior: ruthless, predatory, vampirish. Who would have guessed you could find such authenticity in a city populated exclusively by liars? Not a single soul in the place paid the slightest allegiance to the truth. I felt immediately at home.

"I made myself an Irishman, a relative exotic in that hothouse: I used the name Doyle, an *homage* to you. My first job; a steamboat traveling up and down the river, transport to a rubber plantation in the Amazon basin beyond Manaus, deep in the interior near the Rio Negro. A local tribe worked the fields there for the Portuguese bosses; the En-aguas, the 'good men.' Fitting name for these people. I thought I had experienced a simple life in Ravenna; the En-aguas embodied simplicity. They live in thatch huts, raised ten feet off the jungle floor as protection from the floods. In spite of their long contact with the whites, they remain uncorrupted: almost no trade; everything they need is taken from the jungle.

"I spent all my spare time with the En-aguas, slowly ingratiating myself with the headman. They had information I wanted about local pharmacology; the breadth of their knowledge about extracted medicines and the properties of herbs astonished me. The tribal shaman, their priest, used a tonic brewed from a root, *ayaheusco,* in ritual ceremony. After gaining their trust, I eventually took part in one; this substance severs the mind from its natural moorings; as it takes effect, they say, your spirit leaves your body and the priest guides you to enter into the consciousness of an animal, a boa, a jaguar, whichever one you own a true affinity for: your spirit guide. I became an eagle, Doyle, flew above the jungle, felt wings beating at my sides, looked down at the treetops with the same keen vision, felt the sharpness of its hunger; I lived and moved in the body of this bird, every bit as tactile and vivid as any physical experience in my life."

Sparks's eyes glowed with zealotry: Now that Doyle had persuaded Jack to start talking, how painfully eager he seemed to share these experiences. How many years had passed since Jack had spoken a word of this to anyone? How many years since he'd been in the company of anyone he could trust? Doyle felt a sharp twist, realizing the depths of Jack's isolation and loneliness, how far afield he'd wandered from any sense of community. Could any man long survive so cut off and alone—Doyle knew he couldn't—even one as resilient as Jack?

"This experience confirmed the discovery I had been pursuing from my first moment in the darkness of that cave: that this consciousness which moves us is inside every aspect of creation, fluid and malleable, and our experience of it is transferable from any manifestation of life to another. Can you grasp the implications? If everything in man and nature is wrought from the same stuff, whatever you call it—Holy Ghost, the spark of life—if every molecule is informed by the same defining spirit, that means individuals are free to act according to our own private beliefs; there is no universal morality or supernatural authority that governs our behavior, and regardless of our actions we will experience no retribution from anywhere outside the physical realm. Shipwrecked on this earth like Robinson Crusoe.

"For anyone with the courage to liberate their conscious mind from the conforming pressure of society and remove all that conditioned rubbish, all that's left is free will. From that moment, you have the power to define what is good and what is evil. This is purity. A higher moral rigor that answers only to itself. What I needed now was a structure on which to exercise my philosophy."

"How, exactly?"

Jack nodded. "I had acquired a reputation, someone who could get things done. I was asked to work for a man I had heard about in Belem, a local thug, a boss in the underground. A perfect test for my theory; I took the job, admitting me into the secret heart of the city. Within a month, I was supervising the man's smuggling operations: goods lifted from every ship that docked; guns and ammunition stolen from the military. Money flowed but I lived simply, in a shack on the beach. Drugs, drink, every imaginable earthly pleasure available; crime stimulates these low hungers in our nature and depresses the moral impulse. Indulgences. Excesses. Flesh. A cycle that perpetuates criminal behavior. I watched; I did not partake.

"I kept a girl at my little shack, an extraordinarily beautiful girl I found on the beach one day. Her name was Rina; mixed blood, Indian and Portuguese. Sixteen years old. Her mother was a whore; she'd never known her father and she'd never spent a day in school. I had never met anyone like her. Sweet, simple, unquestioning. She had an uncanny ability to make me laugh. Rina intrigued me in a curious way; how any human being could be so utterly and complacently earthbound I found appalling and fascinating. Like her physical beauty, her ignorance had a round, sullen perfection to it that felt obscurely instructive.

"I made love to her every night for six months and began to feel really animalistically connected to the girl. It was then I realized I had never in my life been close to anyone before, certainly not a woman. One morning not too long afterwards I woke, saw the light striking her face a certain way, and decided never to see her again. That feeling of intimacy was claustrophobic, intolerable. I gathered my few belongings and left Rina asleep in my bed. That same night, I killed a man who tried to rob me in an alley; broke his neck and left him lying there like a weed. And these two events—leaving Rina, killing this man—linked together in my mind: free will, you see. I hadn't killed anyone in years. I began to think about murder a great deal. How easy it was, how often I'd done it in the past, how little it had ever troubled me. An idea developed that I should commit one murder in particular, with intention, of someone I knew, as an experiment. To see what I would feel."

Doyle took a slow, deep breath, hoping Jack would notice no change in his responses. He had been in the presence of such a fevered and alien personality only once before: Jack had drifted into territory that had entirely deranged his brother. Had their genetic similarities led them to the same divide? Had this kind of evil been inevitable in Jack from the beginning?

"I decided to kill the man who had hired me as his underling: Diego Montes. They called him Ah Aranha, the Spider. Montes had grown to depend on my cunning; he lived like an ignorant beast, little more than a bloodsucking insect, thoroughly corrupted, a despoiler, stealing life from everything he touched; a whoremaster, running strings of girls kidnapped from Indian villages in the interior, selling them until their looks collapsed, then casting them into the street like garbage. His face, the rattle of his septum as he breathed through his mouth, the drugs and liquor he ingested massively, even the stuporous way he ate, disgusted me. Carrying out his death sentence came to represent the supreme expression of my free will.

"I crept into his villa one night and cut his throat with a razor while he slept. It required little effort; I severed the vocal cords first so he couldn't cry out. When he woke, I pinned his body to the bed and watched the life drain out of it."

Lost in cool reflection, Jack looked as if he might be recounting a story about a book he'd read once. Doyle couldn't move.

"I felt calm. Empty. As pitiless as that eagle with a rat clutched in its talons. I sensed the presence of no sacred spirit or a soul leaving the body; no angels watched us from on high. And no remorse. All I felt was the harsh indifference of the jungle. I had the confirmation I was looking for. My experiment was a success.

"With one complication: a witness, a woman who had gone to wash up in the next room. I heard her move as I was about to leave. It was Rina."

Doyle must have looked startled.

"That's right, the same beautiful, ridiculous girl I'd been living with. Terrified by the crime she had seen me do. She was a whore now; Montes had recruited her. She cried and told me how she had fallen into that life in despair when I abandoned her. I should have killed her, too, right then, but her presence seemed so fortuitous, I reasoned it could not be coincidence, it must have a meaning that would eventually reveal itself. I suppose what actually influenced my decision most was a kind of tenderness. So I let her live. Helped her escape the house. Even made plans to take her with me when I left the country, which I intended to do immediately.

"And I was right. My finding her did have meaning. Two days later, twenty men who worked for Diego Montes captured me as I was waiting to board a ship to Belize. Rina was supposed to meet me at the docks; I had left her alone for half an hour to buy a hat and she had betrayed me. She cared nothing for me. But this was her free will at work, you see. Available to us all; no inconsistency.

"They clapped chains on me and threw me into a cage, a pit dug into the clay in the yard of the local prison, its mouth covered with steel plates. Darkness was not exactly the hardship to me that they anticipated. But this time without water, and the temperature during the day reached one hundred and twenty degrees. The guards used it as a latrine. Three days passed before they spoke to me. They wanted a confession; Rina had already identified me as the killer, but they were determined to hear it from my lips.

"When they thought the pit had sufficiently softened me up, they brought me into a room, empty, save for a square block of white marble in its center. Stained red. Arm and leg irons at its base. They secured me kneeling before this stone and laid my hands out across its surface. The guards took turns, stepped up onto the block and walked on my hands. Stomped on them. Some danced. Dropped heavy stones. I could hear the sinews snap, bones cracking, watched one finger as they crushed it beyond recognition, all pulp and matted fiber. This went on for hours. They enjoyed their work; skilled and honest craftsmen. I realized they did not intend to kill me until I had confessed; an odd outburst of fastidiousness.

"But I would not cooperate. The pain somehow remained manageable, and I had grown to fancy this free life of mine; I was in no mood to give it up so easily, so I continued to protest my innocence. Hands are extremely personal parts of our bodies, aren't they? Their abuse made me very, very angry. Finally, when I feigned an unconsciousness from which I couldn't be revived, they slipped the irons off and dragged me from the room.

"I kicked the first one, here, the bridge of the nose. A kill. A second tried to pull his gun; I sent him crashing out a window and followed him out before the others could fire a single shot. His body cushioned my fall. As alarms sounded and shots missed me, I ran to a corner of the yard where they stacked provisions. A stairway of barrels took me to the top of the wall and over.

"The prison was set on a peninsula, ocean on three sides. I made it to the jungle before they cut off the road. They were reluctant to follow me at night; their pursuit fell away the deeper I went. Undergrowth became too thick; I took to the river, upstream with the incoming tide. When dawn broke, I was miles inland; they would never find me. Now the pain began; I gathered medicinal herbs—roots, some bark; using my teeth, primarily—to treat my hands, numb the pain. Infection set in quickly in that dank, humid air. I couldn't chance a return to the city for a doctor; my friends, the En-aguas, the native people upriver, had knowledge of these things. Six days to reach them. By then I was half-dead. Spiking fever. Delirious."

Jack laid his hands out on his knees, fanned the remaining fingers, looked down at them dispassionately.

"Their medicine man cut off the two most damaged fingers. Saved the others; I have no memory of it. When I woke two days had passed. My hands were covered with salve bound with a compress of leaves. They asked no questions, I told them nothing; brutality was routine in their view of the outside world. Two months passed before I was strong enough to travel. Three of them paddled me downriver by canoe, disguised as a priest; the birth of Father Devine. They would take me north to Porto Santana, where I would take a tramp steamer to the Indies. But first I had business in Belem.

"With my friends' help, we filled the bottom of a wagon with black powder stolen from the military depot. Then I tracked down Rina in Belem. Working in a brothel. Drugs, looks decaying, her little life already failing towards a sad

predictable finish. I took her out of there, tied her to the seat
of the wagon, a gag in her mouth. Never said a word to her:
What was there to say? There were no words. I looked into
her eyes for a long time. She understood perfectly.

"At dark we sent two mules trotting towards the prison
with the wagon behind; guards saw Rina on board and took
the wagon inside their gates. They didn't see the burning
fuse concealed beneath the floorboards and with her screaming no one heard it hiss. But you could hear the explosion
for fifty miles."

Sparks paused, swallowed a deep breath. Circles under
his eyes, black as paint. Was there regret behind his words?
Doyle couldn't hear it, only the throbbing of his own heart.

"I was on board that ship the next morning, carrying papers taken from a man who had died upriver: a Dutch businessman, Jan de Voort. My story: traveling home after an
accident ruined my hands. Another white European consumed by the jungle. Shall I go on?"

Doyle nodded: Who knew if Sparks would ever expose
this wound again? Hold your tongue, he told himself. Remember how a patient left to ramble so often unwittingly reveals the secret of his ailment. He refilled his glass, hoping
Jack would not notice how severely his hands trembled.

"I took my time moving north through the islands: Cu-
raçao Antigua. Hispaniola. No destination in mind. Soaking
up sun. Rebuilding my hands, thrusting them again and
again into hot sand. Drinking a great deal of rum. A new
woman in each place, making conquests. Leaving when I
tired of them, which never took long; they all want to heal a
man in such a state. So predictable and tiresome. I couldn't
bear that first bloom of disappointment on their faces when
they realized no part of me was theirs.

"One day I landed in New York. What I'd intended as a
brief stay turned into three more years of wandering, one
identity folding neatly into the next; people don't ask many
questions here. Take a man at his word if he can back it up
with work.

"I committed no crimes. Ordinary man again. Six months
as a surveyor in the Alleghenies; a groom in a Philadelphia

stable. Drove a stage in the Ohio Valley for a year, through this same route we're traveling now. Stevedore on a paddle-wheeler down the Mississippi. One day I was unable to get out of bed. Looked in a mirror, didn't know who I was. An exhaustion of the soul had crept over me so steadily I couldn't put a name to it; every cell in my body depleted, used up. My hands ached constantly, the pain deep, rock hard; haunted by wholeness. I slowly made my way to New York. Enough money saved to last years in the way I'd been subsisting.

"With my brother dead, my only reason for living had been lost. I'd never known another; no compelling purpose for going on had come to me. It didn't occur to me that he might have survived. I no longer had the slightest idea why I'd been left alive. And I didn't care. I touched the bottom of the pit I had dug for myself.

"I went out walking one day, near where we were the other day, Lower East Side. March, this was, clear and blustery. I saw a Chinese man standing on the street. Tall, emaciated; he caught my eye as I walked towards him. Maybe he saw something in me, some obvious or subtle longing. He held up his hand as I approached; his fingers were strange, malformed, bulbous at the tips, like inverted bowling pins.

"Between his fingers nested a small packet of foil, the size of a silver coin. He didn't look at me; he didn't speak. He didn't turn when I stopped and looked back at him. He lowered his hand and went inside a door. I followed him; down an alley, a narrow flight of stairs. A cheap red paper lantern bouncing in the wind outside a door. Inside: wet brick walls, stale mattresses on the floor, bodies laid out, dozens of them, languid, moving like seaweed. The Chinese man unwrapped the foil and stuffed a dark plug inside into a long black wooden pipe. He asked me for money. I gave him some. He never looked at my face. Showed me to a mattress. Held the pipe for me and lit it with his malformed hands."

"Opium."

Jack nodded; he couldn't meet Doyle's eyes. "I quit the needle after I fell; that was part of my rebirth, part of the hell

I faced in that cave as my body gave up the hunger. I'd quit and never gone back. Not even in Belem where it was all around and I had every opportunity. Not *once*."

Doyle offered no response: After all the rest, why does he so badly want me to think he's telling the truth about this?

"The pipe took away the pain in my hands. It filled the emptiness that had eaten away at me; a warmth, some feeling, anything—"

"You don't need to explain."

"—the pipe became my world; my world became that room. Three years. The most exquisite feeling when the hunger comes on and all you need is to strike a match. The ease of it. Never out of reach. If I'd found darkness before, now I dropped into the center of the earth. The man kept jade figurines by the beds; statues of gods, demons. You hold one in your hands after the pipe and stare at it, let the cool sheen of its surface come into you; patterns, crystalline swirls that solve the deepest mysteries. Peace you can't reach even in dreams. Time erased; only the now, that moment. I felt more love from that pipe than any human being ever gave me. The happiest moments of my life."

"But it was false, a false happiness. It wasn't real," said Doyle, unable to contain the greatest agitation he'd felt since their conversation began.

"Who's to say? It's only our perceptions anyway. . . ."

"Rubbish; it's drug-induced, not a natural state. Surely you haven't gone that far adrift from common sense."

"Bless you, Doyle; consistent to the end. Let's have that feet-planted-firmly-in-the-garden-of-man's-innate-goodness nonsense from you now; I could always depend on you for that. . . ."

Doyle could no longer restrain himself. "Why would you speak to me that way? What harm did I ever do you? You've done it all to yourself."

Sparks turned away: Was that the hint of a smirk or a grimace?

"So you added opium addiction to your curriculum vitae; bravo Jack, I was afraid you might leave it out entirely. What's next on your agenda, rape? Pedophilia? Or did you cover both of those with that Brazilian girl? Heartless murder's already on the list; shame to let a little free will go to waste. Since that's your *modus operandi* now, why deny yourself anything? It's all defensible the way you've defined the game."

"What is it that offends you: My crimes or their so-called immorality?"

"As if they could be so easily divided. I'll tell you: It's the casual contempt with which you dismiss the efforts of what you call ordinary people to live a life that adheres to a semblance of decency; that you 'discovered' the way human beings live, as if you were observing a colony of ants. What gives you the right to pass such judgments? Where's the virtue that elevates you to such a godlike plane? You think your suffering entitles you to an exclusion from justice? Let me tell you: Everyone suffers and it relieves no one of his responsibility to obey the law. Do you honestly believe you're above the reach of consequences for what you've done?"

"Far from it . . ."

"I'll tell you to your face, you sound like a lunatic, Jack Sparks, and a menace to any person you might meet, myself included. The truth is you've fallen onto the same road that led your brother to that disastrous ruin of a human life. Or has that been your ambition all along?"

Jack couldn't face him now. "No . . ."

"I dispute you. I've built a life for myself these last ten years. I did it with determination and hard work and, yes, through obedience to standards of social order. Without that contract binding us, every man dedicated to his own pleasure according to an unfixed code of moral conduct, all you have left is unmitigated savagery and a civilization no better off, no more advanced, than the sort lived by jackals. I thought you were a good man once; no, a great man. I wanted nothing more in my life than to be like you. I am shocked. Shocked and I am bitterly disappointed. If you're the result of a life lived to the contrary, then I say thank God for society and thank God for the laws of man. You've left them behind; you're beyond the pale."

Jack turned slowly back in his seat and looked at Doyle:

his pale face stark white, the scar lining his jaw livid, radiating tension and despair. His mouth hung open; his eyes sank deep into their sockets.

"I never claimed there were no consequences," he whispered harshly. "Consequences are all I've been describing."

"Then let's be clear about it: Are you telling me all this to ask for my sympathy or approval?"

"No . . ."

"Because if what you want is absolution, I can tell you I haven't the authority or inclination to give it."

"No, no. I thought . . . all I had hoped for . . . something closer to"—Jack's chest heaved with sudden uncontainable emotion; his breath quivered violently, face contorted in pain—"to understanding. You, of all people. I thought you might . . . understand."

Jack inhaled sharply, then he sobbed. "I don't know . . . who I am. I don't know how . . . I don't know how to live. . . ."

Doyle watched in shock as the man before him came disastrously undone. His crippled hands clenched spasmodically at the fabric of the seats, tears splashed from his scarlet eyes; he sat upright for a long moment, rigid as a post, then sagged over as if his spine had collapsed.

"I'm so . . . ashamed, the things I've done . . . what I've turned into. Like *him*. You're right: *Like him*." Jack's self-hatred so much deeper than any other could have felt for him: Doyle stunned. "Should have died before I let that happen, should have found courage to kill myself but I couldn't . . . I couldn't. . . ."

Words tumbling out in a rush, fractured by his sobs. "Put a razor to my wrist . . . gun in my mouth . . . too afraid to finish. Couldn't, so afraid to die, any emptiness greater than what . . . I'd been living. That fear . . . all that kept me alive. Worse than a coward. Worse than an animal . . . God . . . God help me, please, God, help me. . . ."

Jack doubled over, sobbing until it seemed his heart would shatter with the strain. Wounded bellows crashed out of him like the roll of immense waves, washing Doyle's anger away; pity rose up in him, and remembrance of the good in this man. He reached out to Jack, who seemed now so far beyond human reassurance.

"Jack, no. No, Jack."

As Doyle's hand sought out his and took hold, Jack stiffened, unable to accept any comfort, his shame even stronger than the pain. His sobs fell away like a retreating tide. He slid his hand from Doyle's grasp, stood up, turned to the wall, and covered his face with both hands. Shudders rippled his back as he struggled to control himself.

"Forgive me," he whispered. "Please forgive me."

"It's all right."

Jack shook his head once, sharply, and fled from the room, never showing his face, never looking back. Doyle went immediately after him into the hall, but Sparks had already disappeared from sight.

chapter ten

APPARENTLY THE RABBI HAD TAKEN ILL SOMEWHERE BE-
tween Phoenix and Wickenburg; a porter had come into the
car about half an hour after the old man had gone off to
stretch his legs and quietly asked Eileen to accompany him.
She returned a few minutes later asking for a flask of
liquor—Bendigo wasn't about to give his up—then exited
the car again with one borrowed from a stagehand and her
makeup case; God forbid a woman should ever leave *that*
behind.

When they left the train at the Wickenburg Station, Eileen
insisted on tending personally to Rabbi Stern, warning off
other members of the company by telling them that whatever he'd come down with might carry dire threat of contagion; more than enough warning to keep a bunch of
superstitious actors at a healthy distance. Bendigo watched
Eileen and a tall, thin man in an ill-fitting formal black suit
help Rabbi Stern down the steps of the cargo car, where he'd
been resting since his "episode."

Stern walked slowly, stiff-legged, doubled-over, leaning
on their arms for support, still wearing his hat and half-
covered with a blanket even in the brutal noonday heat; his
long white beard poked over the blanket, but not much else
of him was visible. Eileen and the tall volunteer passenger—
he was a doctor who happened to be on board the train, according to Eileen, although if he was a doctor, where was his
bag?—guided the rabbi inside the station where he rested in
seclusion on a cot in the ticket office. Something about the
doctor and the suit he was wearing felt familiar, but
Bendigo's mind moved on to administrative concerns before
anything could surface.

Sets and costumes were loaded off the train and onto the
prairie schooners Rymer had hired from a local livery for the

last leg of their journey—some sixty miles of rough road; they were scheduled to spend a night on the way at a charming little way station by the name of Skull Canyon. Eileen handily won the argument with Bendigo for allowing Rabbi Stern to continue on with them: Yes, Jacob was fit enough to travel and no, if Bendigo refused to let him go, then she'd be staying behind in Wickenburg as well and if that meant she missed their performances in the New Village or the Happy Hamlet or whatever this place was called, then that was the price Rymer should be prepared to pay. Her understudy was a dim-witted ninny who would never make it through an entire show without a nervous fit, and as near as they were to the end of the tour Rymer wouldn't dream of laying out the cash required to replace his leading lady.

Actresses! Everything a melodrama! A bizarre infatuation striking as relentlessly as yellow fever or desert disaster, or whatever mysterious disease this rabbi suffered from. Never again, vowed Rymer, would he place himself at the mercy of the female disposition. Certainly not after he had returned and conquered Broadway. . . . Wait: a brainstorm!

Why shouldn't he find some ravishing young boy to play Ophelia; yes! It's not as if Shakespeare hadn't done it in his day; all the great female roles were originally *written* for boys to play. That was it; a revival of the grand tradition! And why stop there? Why couldn't a man play Gertrude as well, and every other female part? Why not do away with these bothersome strumpets once and for all? Nothing but trouble anyway, and the critics would surely stand and applaud his reverence for the classics!

Brilliant idea, Bendigo: You see? Even *this* cloud hides a silver lining.

But Eileen went on to impose one more intolerable condition: a private wagon to transport Rabbi Stern. He had to be quarantined, she argued logically: No other symptoms had appeared among the Players yet, thank God, but did Bendigo want to take the chance of infecting his entire troupe? Fine, Rymer agreed to the wagon, thinking: I'll be rid of you soon enough, you meddlesome harlot.

So, following at an agreeable distance, the hospital

schooner brought up the rear of their five-wagon mule train as it rolled out of Wickenburg; the Rabbi and Eileen in back, doing her best Florence Nightingale. Once they were out of town, the tall, thin doctor—who happened to be headed for The New City as well; who was in fact *driving* their wagon—peeked through the ratted burlap curtain at the nurse and her patient.

"Sorry about the bumps," he said, "but I don't think you can attribute it to my driving, however incompetent it might be. A little asphalt they could use in Arizona."

"You're doing fine, Jacob," said Eileen.

"What about my suit? Did any of your colleagues recognize it?"

"I took pieces from three different costumes we aren't even using in this production; if anyone noticed, they would have mentioned it by now."

"I hope nobody else comes down with anything," said Jacob. "If I'm supposed to be a doctor, I'm afraid they'll find my knowledge of medicine to be slightly deficient."

"If anyone asks, we'll tell them I misunderstood; you're actually a horse doctor."

"Good; at least the horses can't contradict me. But please God don't let any of *them* get sick: I won't even know which end to look into."

She moved back in the wagon, removed Jacob's round hat from the ailing man's head, and wiped his forehead with a damp cloth; he looked up at her with his dull strange eyes.

"Thank you," said Kanazuchi.

"That beard doesn't chafe too much, does it?" she asked. "Afraid I used a bit too much spirit glue to fix it on but we couldn't have it melting in the heat and have any hope of carrying the whole thing off, could we?"

Kanazuchi shook his head. His hand found Grass Cutter lying under the long black coat at his side and he closed his eyes, letting the bumps and jolts of the wagon carry him toward meditation. He needed sleep now; the wound cleaned and freshly dressed, no sign of infection. The dry desert heat felt comforting. He trusted the wisdom of the body to take care of the rest.

Eileen watched the Japanese until he drifted into sleep, still trying to digest everything he and Jacob had told her: stolen books, haunting dreams about a tower in the desert, disturbingly similar to the one that rumors said was being built in the town they were headed for. As he slept, she moved across the wagon, settling just behind Jacob on the driver's seat.

He rattled the reins and called out to his charges, "You are the most excellent mules, you're driving very straight now in a very satisfactory way. I can't tell you how pleased I am with you."

"How are you getting along?" she asked.

"Splendidly! Driving is a very simple procedure; you pull the reins to the left, they go to the left; pull to the right, they go right," said Jacob; then he leaned back toward her. "You're the first person I've ever confessed it to, but I have always had a secret desire to be a cowboy."

"Your secret's safe with me," she said.

Jacob ran a hand over his smoothly shaven face, looking fifteen years younger shorn of the Old Testament whiskers Eileen had then diligently pasted onto Kanazuchi. "I haven't been without a beard since I was a boy. Sixteen years old; part of my religious requirements, you know. We're not supposed to touch a razor to our skin; they say it's too reminiscent of pagan bloodletting rituals."

"Thank heaven you didn't cut yourself shaving."

"Thank heaven I didn't try shaving while bumping around in these *feckukteh* wagons; I'd look like one of those revolving poles outside a barber shop."

"You look very handsome, Jacob. You'll probably have women chasing you all over the desert."

"Really?" he said, stopping to consider the idea. "What a strange experience that would be. Tell me, how is our patient?"

"Resting comfortably."

"Good. What a marvelous sensation: to feel the air on my skin again. I feel as naked as a newborn baby. To be honest, if I were to look in a mirror I would hardly know whose face this is."

Yours, she thought. Only yours, you dear sweet man.

The mules slackened their pace, looking for guidance from the reins.

"Oy there, giddyup, I think that's the appropriate expression, isn't it? Giddyup, *meine schene kleine chamers.* Oy there!"

The special express train carrying Buckskin Frank and his volunteer avengers did not reach Wickenburg until just after sunset. Procedural details of commandeering a train after Frank found blood on the tracks had delayed them in Phoenix for four precious hours. Drawn by the announcement of a five-thousand-dollar reward, the posse had snowballed to include nearly forty men by now, picking up self-righteous crusaders like dog hair on a dust mop as they rolled through Arizona, and a plague of journalists had attached themselves as well. The result: A simple task like questioning the Wickenburg Station personnel turned into a Tower of Babel; every volunteer and reporter taking it upon himself to conduct his own investigation until Frank had to fire his Henry semiautomatic carbine into the air to shut them up.

As it turned out, no one at the station had seen a Chinaman get off the noon mail run with the Penultimate Players, but the train was still standing in the yard and, even though somebody had tried to clean up the traces, Frank found a fair amount of blood had spilled out onto the floor of the cargo car. Enough evidence to move on; and more than enough to fire up this pack of amateur headhunters into wanting to make a night ride to Skull Canyon, where the troupe of actors was scheduled to bunk in.

Following Frank's advice, the posse did not wire ahead to the Skull Canyon telegraph office for fear of tipping anyone off: Easy enough to convince his fellow pursuers that was the prudent move; if Chop-Chop—a Phoenix newspaper had hung that headline-grabbing nickname on the marauding Chinaman and it was catching on fast—was this close at hand, the posse naturally wanted the glory of his capture to rain down only on themselves. After posing for a flurry of self-aggrandizing photographs, weighed down with so many weapons and bandoliers they might be mistaken for Pancho

Villa's army, the posse repaired to Wickenburg's only saloon for some serious drinking.

Figured these *actors* would be the ones to harbor a murdering fugitive, the talk in McKinney's Cantina soon developed. Two peas in a pod. Can't trust theatrical people—that much was common knowledge, if not sense—ever since John Wilkes Booth shot the President, an event nearly every one of these armchair lawmen was old enough to remember. Actors were liars by profession, 'specially the traveling kind: whorin', thievin' rascals. Lock up your daughters and hide the silverware. Ought to be a law, and so on.

In plenty of places out west there *were* such laws, Sheriff Tommy Butterfield pointed out in his bland, pedantic, meandering way; upon their arrival, actors are required to notify local law enforcement of their comings and goings. Not in Arizona, mind you, but plenty of other places.

Well what in damnation are we paying our elected representatives for if not to protect us from the likes of these roving bands of actor-desperadoes, some paragon of well-heeled civic virtue piped in, and furious debate was joined pitting leading citizen against elected official. The whiskey that had started to trickle on the train flowed like the Colorado and any hope of the posse riding on that night faded faster than the dying twilight.

Buckskin Frank, who was not in a drinking mood by choice and never in an arguing one by nature, realized a squall had started inside that could take hours to blow over; so as the storm raged, he slipped quietly out the door.

A night ride with this bunch of knuckleheads was a dumb idea anyway, realized Frank: They'd probably trot themselves right off the top of a mesa in parade formation. Nor was Frank looking forward to making the trek with them during the day, when this high country turned hot as the hinges of hell. The only activity these big bellies had ever shown any talent for was sucking the money out of poor folks' pockets. Hunting down criminals in the wilderness didn't even qualify as a hobby.

Frank lit a smoke, looked around, and realized with a jolt he was alone for the first time since they had unlocked the door of his cell. Empty streets; the whole town busy jawing in the saloon. The posse had carried their horses up from Phoenix on the train; his roan was morning fresh and saddled up in a stable less than fifty yards from where he was standing. A wild thrill ran through him: Maybe he should light out for Mexico right now.

Molly's voice came into his head: Get a grip on your bishop, Frankie boy; there's a hundred angles could go haywire between here and the border. That's exactly the bullbrained sort of shortsighted scheming that has plagued you all your life. If these bumblers come after you with all that firepower, you'll have more holes than a harmonica. Ask yourself, darlin': What's the smart card to play?

Frank knew his only sure ticket to stay on this side of a prison wall was a dead Chinaman, and if that Chinaman was in Skull Canyon and already winged and dangerous he stood a hundred percent better chance of taking the man out by going in after him alone than as part of this traveling freak show. One clean shot was all he'd need. And if he turned out to be the wrong Chinaman, there'd be a lot fewer questions asked if he came back with a body instead of a suspect. Nobody'd be the wiser.

Once Frank made up his mind about something, he wasn't one for square dancing around. He could make that ride tonight in his sleep. Sky was clear, there'd be a moon later; he might even reach their camp before those actors cleared out of Skull Canyon in the morning.

Before riding off, he nailed a note to the stable wall:

GONE AHEAD TO SCOUT. MEET ME AT SKULL CANYON TO-MORROW. WILL WIRE ANY CHANGE IN PLAN.

> YOURS TRULY,
> BUCKSKIN FRANK

CHICAGO, ILLINOIS

Major Pepperman insisted on driving Doyle and Innes all over Chicago after they disembarked at Union Station. The

Major had been born and raised in the city; he swelled up with a native son's pride as soon he set foot in his hometown, and by God if he couldn't get a rise out of these diffident tea bags by showing off the highlights of his metropolis, then he had lost his touch as one of America's preeminent impresarios.

His emphasis, once again, tended to dwell predominantly on size. There was Marshall Field's Department Store: *thirteen acres of floor space!* The Reliance Building: *fifteen skyscraping stories of shimmering glass!* Wrigley's gum factory: *most popular gum in the world!* ("Here, have a stick of Juicy Fruit! The hit of the World's Fair!") By the time they reached their hotel ("The Palmer House: biggest hotel between New York and San Francisco!"), the Major's well-intentioned but increasingly desperate enthusiasm had numbed the brothers' minds to a frazzle.

As they had arranged on the train, Sparks, Stern, and Presto took rooms at a smaller hotel around the corner from Doyle's and secured the Gerona Zohar in the hotel safe. In the moments they spent alone before parting at the station, no reference was made by either Sparks or Doyle to their conversation the night before; Doyle experienced gnawing discomfort about both the damning content of Jack's confession and what he felt to be the inadequacy of his own cold-hearted response. What could he do to break this impasse? Sparks, still shamed, barely met his eye.

During the day, while the Doyles executed the responsibilities of Arthur's tour, the other three men paid a visit to the temple of Rabbi Isaac Abraham Brachman, the results of which they relayed to the brothers that evening in front of the fire in Arthur's suite at the Palmer House. Lionel and Presto did the talking; Jack sat apart, silent, unresponsive.

Rabbi Brachman had received no further word from Jacob Stern. Nor could he draw any clues from Jacob's behavior during his visit that threw light on his subsequent whereabouts. He had seemed very much himself: cheerful, a trifle distracted, more attuned to the abstract than the physical. Terribly concerned, as all the scholars were, over the theft of the Tikkunei Zohar, about which Brachman could offer no en-

couraging news, either. The matter had been referred to the
police, who were at best dutiful, if not indifferent, to the loss
of such a rarefied item: If it had been a draft horse or a vintage cuckoo clock, it might have stirred them to action, but the
value of an obscure religious manuscript, and a non-Christian
one at that, seemed to elude their grasp.

Facts were spare: The Tikkunei Zohar had simply disappeared; there one night, studied by Brachman, locked in a
cabinet in the temple library; the next morning gone. No
physical clues; no breaking and entering; the lock picked
cleanly. Thoroughly professional job. They chose not to burden Rabbi Brachman, a frail, wispy man of seventy-five,
with any information about the possible involvement of the
Hanseatic League or the other missing holy books. And
Brachman took great comfort in hearing that the Gerona
Zohar still rested safely in their possession.

More disappointment: The Rabbi could not recall a tall,
raggedy evangelist preacher who had attended the Parliament of Religions. Over four hundred clergy from around
the world had taken part and a year had passed; nearly impossible for a man of his age and failing memory to pick one
face out of the crowd. He would be more than willing to
comb through his records to see what he could find; that
would take a day or so.

Not until Presto asked Brachman if he had received any
unusual visitors in the days leading up to the robbery did
any startling information emerge. No one before the robbery, he told them, but strange you should mention it: A
collector of rare religious manuscripts had been to see him
that very morning. A German businessman, Gentile, blond,
tall, good-looking: come to express his sympathy about the
theft of the Tikkunei Zohar. After some related idle conversation, the man mentioned he had recently purchased a
rare religious book in New York; if he brought it to him,
would the Rabbi be able to authenticate that the manuscript
was indeed genuine?

Although the man seemed the soul of unobtrusive friendliness, solid instinct advised Rabbi Brachman to hold his
tongue. How had this fellow heard about the theft of the

Tikkunei Zohar? Only a few people outside of their temple had been told; it had not even been publicized.

No, he was sorry but his eyesight was failing, said Brachman. To be of any help in a matter requiring such rigorous examination would be quite impossible. He had a friend who might be of assistance but the man was away on a trip at the moment. They spoke awhile longer, quite innocently, before the man departed, leaving his card with Brachman; if the friend returned soon, would the Rabbi be good enough to let him know?

Presto magically produced an identical copy of the business card he had shown to them in New York: Frederick Schwarzkirk, the same Chicago-based collector whose path had crossed Presto's before.

The Zohar ruse had worked, said Doyle; the man had the false book, but he also had his suspicions. If the information on his card was correct, Mr. Schwarzkirk's office lay within walking distance of the Palmer House. That would be their next stop, one consequence of which did not occur to them, as it seemed to offer no significance at the time:

Traveling there by the more direct route would take them directly past the Water Tower on Chicago Avenue.

All day the Voices in his head told Dante Scruggs this would be the night his luck would turn. The Indian bitch had spent nearly a week staked out in front of the damn Water Tower, dawn to dusk, hightailing it back to her boarding house before dark. Hadn't looked for any work; hadn't even stopped in a single store, and that just wasn't natural in a woman. All she did at the Tower was stand and stare at people as they walked past, drifting every hour from one side of the building to the other, always staying with the crowds, never leaving him a single opening to make his move. There were times when Dante began to wonder if she sensed that he was tracking her: Indians were crafty that way, like animals.

Frustration began to boil up inside him like steam in a locomotive; had he picked himself out some sort of wrongheaded freak? If the bitch was crazy, that cut the edge off his interest; she wasn't prime. Maybe the time had come to reconsider his original investment. But the Voices that morning sounded so confident; something was in the wind and he couldn't ever remember a time when the Voices steered him wrong.

Sure enough: Night came on and when the lamplighters made their rounds, she stayed put in front of the Tower. He had no way of knowing the Indian heard voices she depended on, too—voices of her ancestors—and tonight they had advised her to wait this one time until after dark. As the streets and sidewalks emptied, she planted herself under a gaslight near the Tower entrance. Seven-thirty came and went, then eight. Getting on toward Green River Time: Dante Scruggs watched from across the street, out of her sight, his anticipation and excitement slowly mounting, hands deep in the pockets of his pants; one on his Johnson, the other on his knife.

And once again, intent as he was on his prey, Dante remained unaware that he in turn was being observed: a tall, blond man this time, wearing an expensive suit, sat in a carriage on the far side of the street, eyes trained on Dante Scruggs.

Nine o'clock rang out on the city's choir of church bells. As the last peal faded, the woman seemed to have reached some kind of limit; her shoulders drooped with disappointment and she started slowly walking away. Dante perked up: This might be it. Just one more sign . . .

A man walking across the street dropped a newspaper. There it was; the Voices had spoken.

Dante unscrewed the cap on the bottle of chloroform in his pocket and shook some out into his handkerchief, put the cap back on the bottle, shoved the handkerchief and his hand down into the outside pocket of his coat, and stepped out to cross the street. If she followed her usual path back to the boarding house, the first left turn would take her down an empty side street lined with warehouses where the gaslights were few and far between, and one of them hadn't worked in the three days since Dante pinched off its supply line. The mouth of a dark alley intersected the street a few steps away. That was the spot he'd picked out to take her: under the dead lamp.

Yes; she made the turn. He picked up speed, twenty yards back, his soft-soled shoes making no sound, closing slowly at a pace that would put him on her at the exact moment she entered the dark circle; no last-second rush to warn her off. Her head down, feet scuffling along, paying no mind. Perfect. Electricity zinged through the bones and wires of Dante's hands, fists clenching in his pockets, warming to the task. Ten yards now. These were the moments he lived for, sometimes better than the work itself. How could any man ever feel more alive than he did right now?

The squaw did not turn and never heard him coming. As she took that step into the dark, he lifted the handkerchief from his pocket, and as he reached her he brought the hand up around her mouth, his left locked onto the back of her head, grabbing the hair, clamping the handkerchief down so her first big surprised breath brought in the full impact of the fumes.

Instant, violent reaction: Her elbow shot back into his mid-section, a foot stomped down, raking his shin, smashing his instep. He was used to the meat struggling at first, but Jesus, this one thrashed like a wildcat. A handful of sharp nails ripped across his face, just missing his eye; a knee that he barely sidestepped shot out at his balls. Dante paid no attention to his own pain, but the bitches never fought like this; some of them so paralyzed with fright when he jumped, they melted into his hands. That first shot of fear running through them was practically his favorite feature of the work; he could smell it through their skin, drink it right out of their eyes. Shit; this one didn't even look scared. One thing in her eyes: hate. The bitch was ruining everything.

Somehow as they wrestled he managed to keep the handkerchief in place, clamped over her nose and mouth while he held her away at arm's length, waiting for the drug to bite through her resistance. Her teeth snapped at him, boots barked at his ankles; no weakening but she couldn't hold her breath much longer. She was trying to reach down to her leg.

Then her hands shot down onto his forearms; nails scooping in like knives, drawing blood. Dante bit his tongue to keep from howling; that pain registered. She tried to lift his hands off her head; Christ, he'd never known any woman to be this strong, nearly his match, maybe more. Actually prying his hands loose; Where in bejesus was the drug? He couldn't chance letting go to reach for his knife; she was too dangerous. Hot liquid ran into his good eye, blurring his vision: Shit, his own blood; she'd cut his face. Damn this troublesome bitch; once he finished ringing up the bill for this, there was gonna be hell to pay.

There: her hands beginning to lose their grip. Her eyes blinked rapidly, then rolled back up under the lids. Operating on stubborn instinct, she still resisted, kicking and scratching, but the strength flowed out of her fast until her body wilted; he caught her around the waist with one hand but kept the handkerchief tight to her face as a precaution as he lowered her gently to the ground. Her fists relaxed as she went completely limp, and he finally felt safe enough to take the handkerchief away. She sprawled at his feet, his now, still and ready. He knelt down beside the Indian and ran his hands over her, probing what she had. Hard around the belly. Thumbed her nipples. Ran his fingers over her breasts, her firm hips, between her legs. The meat was a little thin for his taste but would do just fine. . . .

Jesus, she had a knife strapped to the inside of her thigh: That's what she'd been reaching for; probably knew how to use it, too.

All right, that tore it; the courtship was officially over: Dante slapped her hard and had to restrain himself from kicking in the side of her skull as she lay there, his injuries minor but the Voices stinging with outrage.

Try to pull a knife on us, will you bitch?

Dante wiped the blood off his forehead, caught a whiff of the chloroform on the handkerchief, tossed it impatiently aside. This one was about to find out what making us this mad would cost her. He picked the body up under the arms and started to drag it into the shadowy alleyway and the door to the abandoned warehouse. He had scouted the area for weeks; no one ever wandered down here after nightfall. Plenty of privacy and absolute darkness, that's how he liked to work, and the warehouse was where he had planned to take this meat to the Green River, his valise already stowed inside waiting with his candles and his tools, and he already dreaming up even more elaborate punishments than usual for her foolish crimes. He might even go against his customary procedure; once he'd tacked her down and gagged her, he might just wait until she woke up before he went to work. Let her watch. Maybe he could even find a looking glass.

The body felt slight, feathery; he couldn't figure where she stored all that strength. Didn't matter: Meat, that was all she was now. He was an artist who worked in meat and this was his new canvas. His stimulation growing again after their little set-to at the thought of the fun to come.

Playtime; everyone come out and play. The Voices happy, caressing, pleased with his accomplishment.

"Hey! You there!"

Dante looked up. Shit! People running toward him, not fifty yards off: men, shadows tall against the buildings, at least three of them, maybe more. He scurried the meat into the cover of the alley, quickly running through his options.

"You! Stop there!"

He didn't need the Voices to make this decision; he dropped the body and ran as fast as he could. Whoever these men were, they hadn't seen him clearly; hard to give up a kill, all that legwork, but there would be other days and fresher meat, better than this. Heard footsteps enter the alley behind him as he turned into the street; at least one, maybe two men following, but he knew every building on every block, every doorway, window, twist and turn, part of his painstaking preparation: They'd never catch him now.

He turned two more corners, ran through an empty shotgun flat, dropped into another alley, pulled into the shadows of a doorway, and paused against the brick, motionless and alert; the knife appeared in his hand, broad and glistening. If anyone followed him there, they'd be smiling with their necks. He heard footsteps running past the alley, voices calling out to each other, doubling back, then receding. He waited ten minutes more than he needed to, then sheathed the knife; the way clear to home from here. They'd missed him.

What was that? Unmistakable: the hammer of a Colt revolver cocking right next to his head; the sharp poke of its barrel against his temple.

"Don't move, Mr. Scruggs," said a smooth voice in his ear. "I don't wish to shoot you after all the effort we've put into meeting you. Consider me your friend. Do you understand?"

The voice had an accent; what was it? German?

"Uh-huh."

"Good. You may turn your head now."

The voice definitely German; he'd commanded soldiers in his outfit, immigrants, sounded just like this fella. Dante glanced at the man with his good eye as he turned; he looked young, about his own age, tall, thick blond hair. Bright blue eyes. Big through the shoulders. Sharp looking; good suit. Was this one of the men who'd been after him? Dante didn't think so; this dude wasn't even breathing hard.

"What do you want, mister?" asked Dante finally.

Still holding the Colt to him, the man slid the nose of the barrel along Dante's forehead, down to his blank eye socket, where it rested. Slight smile on his lips. "You may call me Frederick."

"What do you want, Frederick?"

"Why, I want to help you, Mr. Scruggs."

"Help me? How's that?"

"Let me begin by saying I am an admirer of your work: I want to help you do your work."

"What do you know about it?"

"We have had our eye on you for some time now, Mr. Scruggs. And we have been most interested watching you advance in your . . . career."

"You have?"

"Oh yes. We take a great interest in the sort of work you do. And I must tell you, we like what we see. We like it very much."

"If you help me, like you say . . . what do you get out of it?"

"That is a fair question, Mr. Scruggs, and it has a simple answer: I will help you . . . because I want you to help me."

"How can I help you?"

"In ways you cannot possibly imagine. Why don't you come with me now, so we can . . . talk it over."

Something dark and insinuating and frightfully amused in Frederick's light eyes. The Voices weighed in: *We like this one.* Dante surprised: Unusual for Them to trust anybody he'd ever met so quickly. But he couldn't argue the point.

He liked him, too.

Doyle had been the first to cry out when they saw a man dragging a body into the alley ahead, and he was the first to reach her. Lionel Stern lit matches to give him some light and Doyle worked furiously to revive the woman in the plain gingham dress while Jack and Innes gave chase to her attacker. Presto pulled a rapier from his walking stick and searched the area; he lifted a bloodstained, chloroform-soaked handkerchief lying nearby and they realized she had nearly succumbed to its potent vapor. When he found the carpetbag in an adjacent warehouse, loaded down with rope, cutting tools, and crude surgical instruments, they realized with a shudder how near the woman had come to meeting an unspeakable end.

By the time the others returned, empty-handed, the woman's breathing had deepened and her pulse stabilized, but she remained unconscious and not entirely out of danger. Doyle could sense Jack preparing to argue that this should not interfere with their business, but before he could speak, Doyle insisted that they transport the woman to safe quarters at once. Jack offered no protest and Doyle realized that now he had received his confession, Sparks was reluctant to openly oppose him: Doyle held a trump card on Jack now, but he would have to use it judiciously.

Presto hailed a carriage; minutes later they took the rear entrance of the Palmer House, the four men surrounding Doyle as he carried the woman to an empty service elevator. As they exited the car and made their way down the hall to Doyle's suite, Major Pepperman had the misfortune to appear around the corner, his habitually eager expression changing to dismay.

"Thought I'd see if you're up for a nightcap," he said, faltering rapidly. "Brought a couple of newspaper men, waiting downstairs in the bar. . . ."

"Sorry, old man," said Doyle, smiling as he swept by him, the limp female body in his arms. "Some other time."

Innes unlocked the door. Doyle carried her inside and the others quickly followed; an unsavory-looking group at best. One of them dark as a Negro, dressed like a dandy; another wore a fearsome scowl and a scar worthy of a pirate. The door closed in Pepperman's collapsing face, his mind already composing the scandalous headline (HOLMES CREATOR CAUGHT IN LOVE NEST!) and personal ruination that would be sure to follow.

Doyle had been up to something untoward from the moment he arrived in America, Pepperman decided; the evasiveness, his impregnable reticence and persistent requests for privacy; why, the clues had been there from the beginning. What were Doyle and those men doing with that woman in his room? The Major was no genius but he could still add two and two together: The man was a secret deviant!

Waiting for the elevator, the Major lowered his shaggy head and banged it morosely against the wall. He had put up his own money to fund this tour, and until he realized some returns, he would have to do everything in his power to protect his expenditure; no one must learn of Doyle's loathsome habits, whatever they might be. Promoting a famous author—an *English* one, practically *reeking* respectability—had seemed such a safe investment at the time. Why hadn't he stuck to the circus?

Doyle laid the woman down on a sofa and afforded the men their first clear look at her: about thirty years of age, dark skin and hair, strong bones and features, not beautiful by any means, but arresting and handsome, a face hewn with resilience and fortitude.

"An American Indian," said Jack, as both he and Presto stared at her with something mysteriously close to recognition.

"Do you know this woman?" Doyle asked them observantly.

Jack shook his head uncertainly.

"How could I possibly?" said Presto. "Unless she's been to London and how likely is that? And yet, all the same, she does look familiar to me."

Doyle cracked open a vial of smelling salts under her nose; she jerked her head away, her eyes fluttered open. She stared in alarm as she saw the five male faces staring down at her. Doyle calmly reassured her and introduced the others, explaining how they'd found her in the street and where she was now, the sort of aftereffects she could expect from exposure to the drug. She listened attentively, her enormous self-possession reforming as she tried to patch the gaps in her memory: The image of her attacker's empty blue eye came back, staring into her, lifeless as a marble.

She said little, drinking water, surprised that she felt no impulse to bolt, but she did not sense danger from these men. Quite the contrary: By then she had picked out Jack and Presto and returned their inquiring gazes with equal curiosity.

"What is your name, miss?" asked Doyle.

She looked at his face before answering. "My name is Mary Williams."

"Have we met before, Miss Williams?" asked Presto.

The three of them, linked somehow. Did they know it was the dream?

"Yes," she said.

"Why do you suppose that is?"

She knew the answer; reluctant to voice it yet.

"Where are you from, Miss Williams?" asked Doyle.

She told them.

"You are American Indian, then."

"Yes; Lakota."

"Really?" said Innes, brightening. "How ripping."

Doyle gestured; Innes backed off.

"Had you ever seen this man who attacked you before?" Doyle asked.

"He has followed me since I got to Chicago."

"Do you know his name?" asked Jack.

"No. I know nothing about him," she said.

"Why didn't you go to the police?" asked Doyle.

"He had done nothing to me."

"Still, they might have helped—"

"I know how to protect myself."

The obvious answer hung in the air; she responded to it. "Tonight I made a mistake; my mind thinking of other things. It was the only moment he could have hurt me."

"The only one he needed," said Jack.

"If he comes again, I will kill him." Her tone left no reason to doubt her.

"Still, you are very lucky to be alive, Miss Williams," said Presto.

He showed her the contents of the carpetbag he'd found in the warehouse. She stared at the instruments of disfigurement without reaction. What she saw did not surprise her— nothing about that blue, blank-eyed nightmare would have—but she agreed that yes, she had been fortunate.

"If I may ask, under the circumstances, what were you doing out there tonight alone?" asked Doyle.

"Waiting for someone. They did not arrive. In my disappointment, I was not paying attention. That is how he caught me."

"Waiting for whom?" asked Doyle.

She looked back and forth between Jack and Presto. "I believe that I have been waiting for these two gentlemen."

The two seemed to receive this bombshell in stride; Doyle, Stern, and Innes looked shocked.

"You *believe* so?" asked Doyle. "On what basis? . . ."

"Let her speak," said Jack.

Walks Alone waited; yes, it felt safe to tell them.

"I have seen you in a dream," she said, looking right at Jack.

"Good night," whispered Innes.

"You know I am telling the truth. Both of you do," she said calmly, including Presto. "You know the dream."

Jack and Presto glanced at each other warily.

"Tell us," said Presto, testing her.

"A dark tower, in the desert. Tunnels beneath the earth; an altar or temple underground. Six figures gather; I am there. And so are both of you."

"Yes," said Jack.

"A black devil rising from the earth; a man. And he looks something like you," she said, nodding to Jack.

"Right. Scotch for me," said Doyle, moving to the bar.

"I'll join you," said Lionel Stern.

"Make mine double," said Innes to Doyle as he poured.

"You have had this dream," she said. "You have seen the tower."

Both Presto and Jack agreed.

"It started three months ago," she said. "Slowly at first; now it comes almost every night."

Jack nodded. Doyle watched him from across the room. Fire in his eyes again, feverish and disturbed, but still a sign of life.

"Two or three times a week," said Presto. "Wakes me in a cold sweat."

"Do you know what it means?" asked Jack.

"No," she said hesitantly; why frighten them with my interpretations?

Fortified with drink, Doyle moved back to them, unfolded Jacob's drawing from his pocket, and held it for her to see. "The tower in your dream; does it look anything like this?"

"Yes; this is the same."

Doyle looked back at Lionel Stern, who drained his drink and poured himself another with trembling hands.

"It also looks like one they have here in the city," she said.

"The tower is here? In Chicago?" asked Doyle.

"No; the one in the dream is like this but larger, built of black stone."

"What tower are you talking about?" asked Doyle.

"They call it the Water Tower. That's where I've been waiting for you. That's what the dream told me to do."

"The dream told you to wait for us?" asked Presto.

She nodded solemnly.

"Can you take us there?" said Jack, pressing forward.

"Yes; it's near where you found me; where you would have found me if I had waited a little longer."

"Let's go," said Jack, heading for the door.

"Miss Williams, you've been through a great deal; I strongly advise you to rest before—" said Doyle.

"No," she said with enormous authority as she rose to her feet.

On their way to the taxi stand, the odd sextet marched past the bar in the lobby of the Palmer House; Major Pepperman sat at a table near the door, force-feeding two reporters from Milwaukee stories about Dr. Arthur Conan Doyle's manly appeal.

"Say, isn't that him now?" asked one of the reporters, catching a glimpse of the man exiting the hotel.

"Couldn't have been," said Pepperman quickly. "Doyle's been asleep for hours."

"I think that was him," said the reporter.

"Not possible," said Pepperman, through clenched, smiling teeth.

When the two cabs stopped in front of the Water Tower, Doyle asked the drivers to wait as they climbed out for a look. Starkly lit by dramatically positioned gaslights, the Tower looked like a fairy tale castle rising from the darkness. Both Jack and Presto agreed it bore great similarity to the one from their dreams; Doyle took out Jacob Stern's drawing and they found many exact points of comparison as well.

"That explains the sketch," said Doyle, to Lionel Stern. "Your father must have seen this while attending the Parliament of Religions."

And yet Jack, Presto, and Mary Williams felt something wasn't right. The Water Tower was and wasn't the same; it seemed perhaps a model or template for the tower in the dream: one taller, darker, more ominous and forbidding. And there was no mistaking central Chicago for a desert. Their discovery delivered less than it seemed to promise, compounding the mystery and dampening their spirits.

What to make of the intersecting of their dreams? wondered Doyle. He had once investigated a case of three mediums in scattered parts of the world simultaneously picking up different pieces of the same spirit message, but each had received the information during trance states, not sleep, and it involved only a simple written message, not complicated imagery woven together with an apparently identical narrative.

From what they had learned, it seemed likely Jacob Stern had been party to the dream sharing. Why had these four been singled out to receive this particular message? Mary Williams seemed a likely candidate to possess the gift; Jack had never exhibited signs of mediumship, although his brother had occult powers and Jack's dabbling with drugs could have brought them on. But Presto bore no resemblance to the classic medium's profile: He was a lawyer, for God's sake, how much more earthbound could a man be?

The other common thread: The men each had some connection to a holy book of central importance to their religion or culture; Mary Williams had no involvement with such a book but she came from a people without a written language.

None of which answered the crucial questions: What was the meaning and purpose of the dream? What did it have to do with the missing books?

I may not have been given the dream, thought Doyle, but this much I can do: I must find the answer to those questions so they can finish whatever task this dream has called them to perform. . . .

Doyle turned to look at Sparks, standing apart from the others, staring silently up at the tower.

And unless I can find a way to bring Jack back to himself, he realized, they'll never make it.

A few blocks west of the Water Tower, as Doyle and the others studied its enigmatic facade, Frederick Schwarzkirk escorted Dante Scruggs into his fifth-floor office; the printing on the front door spelled only his name and a single word: COLLECTOR. At this late hour, Frederick's office was the only one in the building that showed any signs of life.

Inside the dimly lit suite, a swirl of activity: half a dozen men boxing up books and papers, carting them out to the hall. The men dressed in black and wearing gloves. The front room had been cleared except for a massive oaken desk in its center; on the desk a telegraph key and trailing from it a strip of paper bearing the dots and dashes of a received message.

"I have just returned from business overseas," said Frederick. "And as you can see, Mr. Scruggs, I am in the process of relocating my operation."

Dante nodded, smiled, and said nothing. As they rode over in the carriage, he had decided the fewer questions he asked Frederick the better; the man gave off an aura of confidence and power that made Dante feel dumb as a stump, but at the same time affectionately well cared for, like a favorite dog. And the Voices kept telling him not to worry; he could relax and trust that this man would carry him to safety. Dante felt as warm and snug in Frederick's company as a snake in a sleeping bag.

Frederick made no attempt to introduce Dante to the other men and left him momentarily alone to direct some of the work in the inner office, barking out sharp instructions in German. As one of the men passed carrying a box out to the hall, his sleeves rolled up, Dante noticed a strange tattoo on the inside crook of the man's left arm: a broken circle with three jagged lines darting through its borders.

Dante hopped agreeably out of the way to allow two more men through, pushing a stack of boxes on a rolling dolly. His movement put him close to the desk and the strip of telegraph paper, and he couldn't resist leaning over to take a peek at its hieroglyphs—he had worked as a telegraph operator during two of his army years. He could just make out the phrase BRING THE BOOK IMMEDIATELY when he heard a floorboard creak as Frederick reentered. Dante leaned away from the desk, looked down and studied his shoes, trying to convey a generalized innocence. Frederick walked past him and took a seat behind the desk.

"Naughty boy," said Federick, wagging a playful finger at him.

Dante giggled and smiled sheepishly, unable to conceal his guilt.

"You are a naughty boy, aren't you, Mr. Scruggs?"

"Yes, sir."

"Naughty boys sometimes get punished," said Frederick, picking up the telegraph strip and scanning it quickly between his slender fingers.

Dante felt confused and thickheaded, but he didn't seem to mind it much; there was no fear involved. When he finished reading the strip, Frederick set a match to it and dropped the burning strand on the floor. He toggled on the telegraph and tapped out a message; listening carefully, Dante heard him spell the words A GLORIOUS DAY before Frederick began to speak over the clack of the key, disrupting his concentration.

"You enjoyed being in the army, did you not, Mr. Scruggs?"

"Oh yeah. More than anything."

"Enjoyed that pride of authority," he said, with that same teasing smile; how could the man talk and send Morse code at the same time?

"Uh-huh."

"A sense of power."

"Yeah."

"Being a part of something larger than yourself; a sense of meaning in your life."

"Yeah, I liked that."

"A loyal soldier. Your every waking moment devoted to a purpose that served a design far greater than your ability to comprehend. Shoulder to shoulder with other men of like mind, marching forward, dedicated to serving the same high ideals."

"Huh?" This was getting a little rich for him.

Frederick laughed and smiled like a loving father. "You'd like to be a soldier in an army again, wouldn't you, Mr. Scruggs?"

"I guess so." Dante wasn't so sure.

"Not one ruled by a distant, unenlightened government, overrun with fat, incompetent commanders; corrupted cowards afraid of their own shadows. An entirely different sort of army, Mr. Scruggs, where you truly felt you belonged. Where instead of being punished for the unique qualities that make you who you are, you are rewarded for them. An army that would allow you, no, *encourage* you to continue your . . . personal work. You would like that, wouldn't you, Mr. Scruggs?"

Dante's eyes narrowed; a shudder of excitement ran to his groin as the sense of the man's tone, if not the words, got through to him. "Yeah. Yes, sir, I'd like that a lot."

"We recruit from all over the world," said Frederick. "Not many men meet our exacting standards. But after months of close observation, I can say with some confidence that you . . . measure up."

"How'd you find me in the first place?"

"We have eyes and ears in many places. If it is meant to be, the right person will catch our attention. He is observed, studied, as you have been. If he's found worthy, we move to the stage where you find yourself now."

Dante swallowed; he felt small, filled with wonder, as if an angel had reached down and touched him.

Frederick finished tapping out his message. He leaned down, ripped the telegraph wires out of the wall, and handed the key to Dante, "Put that in a box for me, would you please, Mr. Scruggs?"

"Sure, Frederick."

Dante looked around; there were no boxes left in the room. "Uh . . ."

"In there," said Frederick, pointing to the inner office, clearing a stack of papers from the drawers without looking up at him.

Dante nodded and carried the telegraph key through the door; he was immediately grabbed by a dozen grasping hands, lifted off the floor, and spread-eagled on his back across a desk. Dim light filtered through a slatted blind; Dante could barely make out their faces; no, they were wearing masks. Black masks; only their eyes showing through slits. A gloved hand smothered his mouth. Adrenaline pumped through his body; he struggled fiercely but couldn't move an inch, helplessly pinned.

Cows in the slaughterhouse, that's where his mind went; heads stuck through the rack, waiting for the sledge to cave in their skulls. What was that smell? Something pungent in the air; hot, sulfurous, like burning coals.

Frederick's face appeared above him; no smile now, fierce and purposeful. He reached down and pulled the knife from the sheath in Dante's pocket. The other men's hands were rolling up his sleeves, taking his pants down to his ankles. Squeals of terror came out of him; his bladder emptied involuntarily.

Frederick looked at the knife, read the manufacturer's trademark near the hilt. "Green River, Wyoming. How pleasing. The Green River knife is one of the best in the world. If this was a violin it would be a Stradivarius."

What the hell was he talking about? What did he want? What were they gonna do to him? Dante's eyes danced wildly around the room. Where were the Voices? Why couldn't somebody help him?

Frederick slit the buttons off Dante's union suit, spread it open, and ran the knife lightly over his privates.

"Have you even for a moment considered what the experience must be like for the women you've killed, Mr. Scruggs? What they must feel as you go about your work? The abject terror? Fear of dying? The pain as you make your first cuts? I have seen the bits and pieces of them you saved in your apartment; you are very fastidious about the parts you keep, aren't you? That interests me: One *collector* to another, what makes you choose? What draws you to keep one piece, discard another? The look, the feel? Is it the shape or the texture? The function of the part? Perhaps you don't know or haven't thought it through; yes, I think so. It's just magic, isn't it? The flesh is there, it speaks to you and you simply have to have it. I suspect this is how it's always been: When it speaks, you are bound to listen and obey."

Dante whimpered and moaned.

"Relax; isn't that what you always tell your girls in the beginning?"

He nicked him lightly with the blade; Dante felt a trickle of blood run down and pool between his thighs. Frederick leaned over next to his ear and spoke to him seductively, almost in a whisper. "Every pleasure has its price; every sin its reward. The rites of initiation are ancient and mysterious, as unknowable to us as the face of God. And yet we still obey them, because that is how the entrance into our brotherhood has always been achieved. You are baptized and reborn in the water of your own blood and fear. In no other way can you become useful to us; in only this way can you become more useful than you ever imagined. Be aware that death can always reach you; disobedience is not tolerated. Violence can be visited upon you with the speed of an idea. Your thoughts are no longer your own. Your mind and spirit belong to a higher power. Servitude has always been your goal, and now it becomes your reality. Trust that your life has brought you to this place in time, because that is what you wished for and all that it requires of you now is recognition and absolute surrender."

Frederick slammed the knife down into the table between Dante's legs, nicking his flesh again and starting a stronger flow of blood. "Be one of us and live forever."

Now a blinding pain seared into his left arm; Dante's eyes moved there, half-blinded with tears; smoke curled up from where the branding iron had left its mark on the bicep; as it lifted, he saw the burn; the burning circle broken by three jagged lines.

Dante fainted.

chapter eleven

A HALF-ASSED COLLECTION OF HUTS AND SHACKS THROWN up around the mouth of a failed silver mine comprised the city limits of Skull Canyon, Arizona. Population had boomed to a peak of 350 before the vein gave out and the railroad decided not to build a spur line station; these days permanent residents numbered exactly two: loco prospectors, sixty-five-year-old fraternal twins from Philadelphia, the Barboglio brothers, still working the shaft every day, living off the dust they could coax from its walls. The other ten were short-term residents, workers who cycled in and out of town, servicing the stagecoach stop and the fleabag Skull Canyon Hotel that provided sole lodging for travelers.

The population had swelled to thirty-one with the arrival the night before of the Penultimate Players—the hotel could only accommodate fifteen, so the stagehands and junior males spent the night sleeping in their wagons. Actually the number was thirty-two, if you included Frank McQuethy, who showed up just before dawn and found himself a notch in the high rocks that looked down on the canyon and hotel. Frank settled in as the darkness slipped away, close enough to see faces in the street through the scope of his buffalo gun, unhitched the safety, and waited for the Chinaman to show.

Five wagons parked behind the hotel; one carrying cargo. Horses stabled around the side. People started to stir as first light licked the top of the boulders on the rim; workers tossing out slops, carrying in wood, firing up the kitchen; smoke rose from the stovepipe chimney. Buckskin Frank pulled his saddle blanket tight around his shoulders and tried to stop his teeth from chattering, wishing he was huddled in front of that fire down below with a hot cup of Java in his hands. He was hungry, too, his stomach eating at him when he caught a phantom whiff of bacon on the breeze.

The desert had turned bitter cold on his ride. He couldn't shake it off the way he used to as a kid; this kind of cold lived in your bones. During the night, about halfway from Wickenburg, Frank had decided he was too old for this shit; maybe he should have headed for Sonora, after all. Despair swamped him; he couldn't count how many fine, clear mornings of his life he'd wasted in exactly this way, on the high ground, waiting for some unsuspecting fuckup to come out of a house or a cave or a teepee so Frank could pump a bullet through him; this sort of waiting led to the same morbid self-examination he'd just experienced five years of in the joint. No sir, this dry-gulching work did not fit him anymore; all he wanted at this time of the morning was a firm mattress and a warm pair of tits, and he kept himself awake with the thought that they might only be one shot away.

The first actors stumbled out of their wagons when the hotel rang the triangle for breakfast; the younger ones stretched and strutted and swaggered in that self-conscious, catlike way of people who were used to being noticed; even out here in the middle of East Jesus, hung over and pissing in the bushes, not even aware that Frank was watching, they acted like they were in front of an audience.

No Chinaman.

Half an hour passed; breakfast over, the stable hands walked out the horses, hitched them to the wagons, and the rest of the actors came out of the hotel. Frank studied each face carefully through the scope; four women, twelve men—all white—climbed into three of the wagons; one tall, fat, long-haired dude who acted like he was in charge took the reins of the one carrying what Frank guessed must be their scenery. The caravan seemed ready to roll but held up: the fifth wagon, smallest of the bunch, little more than a covered buckboard, remained empty.

Three last people walked out of the hotel; Frank inched forward, laid a finger on the trigger and glued his eye to the scope. A dark-haired woman—Christ, a real bright-eyed beauty—and a tall gangly man in a dark formal suit and between them a stooped figure with a long white beard in the queerest get up; a round furry hat, black suit, and heavy black coat. The two walked this old geezer between them to the last wagon and helped him climb into the back.

Something not right about this; Frank looked hard for details. Between the beard and the hat, Frank never got a clear look at the old man's face—there, as he stepped up into the back of the wagon and the coat moved, a dark stain on the side of his white shirt. Was that blood?

Should he take the chance? His finger tightened down on the trigger.

Think it through, Frank, said Molly's voice: You're still a convict and it ain't gonna help your case one iota to blow a hole through the wrong man in front of twenty witnesses. He eased back.

Raised voices. Frank swung the scope over; the long-haired blowhard jumped off the cargo wagon, waving his arms and screeching at the darkhaired woman; she gave him the business right back in his face. Frank couldn't hear the words this far away, but the tone of their voices reached him on the wind and Mr. Longhair was taking the worst of it. He finally tucked his tail between his legs and stomped back to his wagon, and the woman climbed into the back of the one where they'd stashed the old man. She had some spunk, this one.

The wagons began to roll out of the canyon and up the incline to the road leading west. The stable owner in Wickenburg who'd rented them the wagons had told Frank the actors were headed to a religious settlement out in the desert, a place called The New City, twenty-five miles north-northwest of Skull Canyon. Place just went up in the last few years, wasn't even on the maps yet, but growing fast. Folks out there weren't Mormons and seemed to be Christian; beyond that the man wasn't exactly sure what they were: good customers anyway, paid on time. Seemed harmless enough, a little eccentric maybe; building some kind of castle out of stone quarried in the hills.

If they followed his instructions and didn't get themselves hopelessly lost in the desert—a big if—the posse wouldn't arrive in Skull Canyon until late afternoon; Frank couldn't wait that long. Maybe the Chinaman wasn't with this bunch, but instinct told Frank he should get a closer look at the old man in the back of that last wagon; these were actors, after all, and actors could do things with makeup.

He had another reason to trail after them that he wouldn't admit to himself; he wanted a closer look at the other person in the back of that wagon. That dark-haired gal had set his fool's heart tripping like a snare drum. And she looked enough like Molly to be her sister.

Frank worked the kinks out of his back, rode down to the hotel, and asked a few questions; no one had gotten a clear look at the old man. He looked like a Jew, one of them said; an Old World type like he'd seen back east. What he was doing with a theatrical company in the middle of the desert nobody could say; the man had some kind of high fever and they'd been told to stay clear. Once in the hotel, he never came out of his room.

The black-haired woman? A real looker. She was taking care of him; her and that skinny fella. Somebody said they heard her name was Eileen.

Was there a telegraph office where these actor folks were headed? Yes, sir. Frank left a sealed message for the hotel to give the posse; when they arrived, they were to wait for him in Skull Canyon until he wired with further instructions.

And if any of the posse inquired, he'd be obliged if they'd tell 'em Buckskin Frank had rode off to the northeast, toward Prescott.

Frank fed his horse, treated himself to a cold breakfast, and then set out on the dirt road heading west to The New City.

At eleven o'clock that night, when Doyle, Jack, and company arrived at the offices of Frederick Schwarzkirk, they found the door open and the two rooms vacated. No less than four detectives in the group—Jack, Doyle, Presto with his lawyerly eye for detail and, in her own way, Walks Alone—pored over every inch of the place, while Innes and Lionel Stern stood watch outside in the hall.

The offices had been cleared out earlier that evening. Traces of burned paper in a trash can, a roll of telegraph tape in a drawer, the dusty outline of an object removed from the desk, snapped wires running out the baseboard; a private telegraph wire had been installed, Jack concluded, hooking into the lines outside, an illegal tap.

A uniform residue of dust on shelves in the inner room said the books stored there had never been moved until they were taken away; Presto suggested they had been stacked there purely for show.

From a smaller desk in the inner room, Mary Williams detected a smell of human urine. She also found traces of fresh blood in the wood, and even though windows had been left open, a disagreeable tang of charred flesh lingered in the air. Something hideous and repellent had taken place in that room within the last hour.

This office had obviously been maintained as a front to cover the activities of the men responsible for the theft of the holy books, concluded Doyle. And that implicated "Frederick Schwarzkirk" as the surviving member of the team that had attacked them on board the *Elbe*. What connection this might have to the communal dream—aside from the translation of the man's name, Black Church—remained out of reach. And their intensive search revealed no clue to which direction the man might have taken.

"Let's ask ourselves," said Doyle, as they stepped outside again. "These men are nothing if not thorough: If they're moving on, what loose ends have they left behind?"

No one said it, but the thought occurred to every one of them: We're a loose end; they may be watching us even now. The concrete canyon rising around them offered no security. They stepped back into shadow, raised their collars against the harsh wind blowing in off the lake.

"Rabbi Brachman," said Jack with alarm.

"They wanted to show him the false book," said Presto, finishing the thought.

"Doyle, you, Mr. Stern, and Miss Williams return to your hotel at once; secure the book," said Jack, showing a flash of his old command. "Presto, Innes, and I will pay a return visit to Brachman's temple."

Jack jumped into the first waiting carriage; Presto and

Innes followed. "Take the book to your room; don't open the door to anyone until we return."

Jack comes to life when there's an action to perform, thought Doyle. The rest of the time he's lost as a waxwork.

Doyle looked at Mary Williams as she climbed beside him into the second carriage, an idea taking shape in his mind.

A single lamp burned in a window on the floor above the pillared entrance to Temple B'nai Abraham.

"Those are Brachman's living quarters," said Jack. "The next window over is his library, from where the Tikkunei Zohar was stolen."

"Substantial-looking piece of business," said Innes, studying the building's Greek Revival facade.

"The thieves used a rear entrance," said Presto.

"That's where they'll try again," said Jack.

The three men stood in the shadows across the street. They had made one stop at their hotel, Jack running in to retrieve the suitcase he received from Edison after their visit to his workshop.

"Someone moving," said Innes, pointing to the lighted window.

A shape appeared between the lamp and window shade; difficult to distinguish, but it didn't look like the silhouette of an infirm seventy-five-year-old Orthodox rabbi. A tall figure, broad-shouldered.

Holding a large open book.

Jack unlocked the suitcase. Keeping it from the others' curious eyes, he removed from the case a heavy enlongated set of what looked like binoculars. A rounded steel frame extended back from the eyepieces, an armature that allowed the glasses to be worn on the head as a sort of helmet. Jack slipped them on; they had the unnerving effect of making him look like an enormous bug.

Jack watched the windows of the temple without comment. Innes and Presto exchanged an uncertain glance behind his back.

"Uh . . . see anything?" asked Innes.

"Yes," said Jack, scanning his head from side to side.

"Anything . . . in particular?" asked Presto.

Jack stopped. "Quickly." He took off the glasses, put them back in the suitcase, and closed it, frustrating Innes to no end.

"Follow me," said Jack.

They ran across the street and around the back of the synagogue to the rear door, where Jack removed a sleeve of tools from a pocket in his vest and handed the square box to Presto. Jack reopened the suitcase and took out a square contraption the size of a shoebox, with a round, silver dome attached to the front end and in its center a glass bulb. Hinged flaps that circled the dome could be manipulated to enlarge or shrink the aperture around the bulb. Holding the gizmo in one hand, Jack handed the suitcase to Innes.

"Point the opening towards the lock and hold it steady," said Jack.

Presto did as instructed. Jack narrowed the aperture, then threw a small switch on the side of the box; a low humming emerged, and moment later, a thin, wavering beam of white electric light poured out of the opening and lit up the area around the keyhole.

"Good God," whispered Innes. "What is that?"

"What does it look like?" said Jack, as he knelt down with his picks and went to work on the lock.

"Battery-powered?" said Presto.

"A flash-a-light," said Innes.

"As a matter of fact that's what Edison calls it," said Jack. With a soft click the lock yielded; Jack turned the knob and gently pushed the door into darkness, hinges creaking. "Switch off the light."

Presto turned off the device. Jack took out and put on the goggles again and peered in through the doorway.

"You don't suppose we should have just rung the door bell," whispered Innes.

Jack put a finger to his lips, asked for silence, and they crept slowly inside, Innes and Presto feeling their way along with a hand on the man in front's shoulder. Jack led them through the first room—a kitchen—and paused in an archway. Innes and Presto waited for their eyes to adjust, but the blackness stayed as impenetrable as the heavy silence surrounding them.

Jack took the box from Presto and briefly switched it on and off; in the instant of light, they saw a staircase in a central hall leading to the second floor. Double doorway off the hall to their left, a menorah beside it on the floor, the entrance to the synagogue proper. A foyer leading to the front of the temple straight ahead. Jack moved forward again, leading their fumbling procession to the base of the stairs; they stopped.

Someone still moving upstairs. Soft padded footsteps, measured paces; slippers brushing against carpet. Someone trying not to be heard.

Jack made himself understood with a touch that he wanted them to stay where they were. Then he started up the stairs without so much as a whisper.

Time stood still; Innes and Presto, reluctant to move a muscle, aware of each other's presence only by breathing. In need of orientation, Innes reached out and put a hand on the stairway wall; feeling around he found a round knob.

More footsteps upstairs, then a rush of them; something crashing to the floor, a struggle.

Innes turned the knob and the lights came on:

Two figures, all in black, hurtling toward them down the stairs, frozen for a moment by the light from a hallway chandelier.

Presto pulled the rapier from the sheath of his walking stick and charged up to meet them. The first man vaulted over the banister and landed catlike on his feet in the hall, heading for the door, carrying a loose black bag. Innes gave chase. The second pulled a knife from his sleeve; Presto thrust out the foil with great dexterity and ran the point clean through the man's palm, pinning it against the wall. The man in black dropped the knife; Presto leveraged his weight and punched the man in the jaw, knocking him back; his head clubbed hard against the balustrade and he lay still.

Innes sprinted out the front door moments behind the man

with the black bag, but he was nowhere to be seen. Innes let discretion serve as the better part of valor, went back inside the temple, and closed the door.

Climbing to the top of the stairs, Presto found a third man in black lying lifeless on the carpeted floor, head jutting at an odd angle from the top of his broken neck. His blade ready, Presto crept toward the half-open doorway, where the lamp they'd seen still burned.

Innes clenched his fists and stepped carefully over the inert man in black on the stairs. Two steps past him, the man leaped to his feet and went flying down the stairs; Innes hurled himself over the banister—so much for discretion— and landed square on the man's back, driving him into the wall. Squat and muscular, the figure stayed on his feet and whirled around wildly, a bull trying to dislodge a rider on its hump. Innes clamped a stranglehold on the man's neck— thick as a fire hydrant—and called for help.

"Hold on!" shouted Presto, coming down the stairs.

The man in black bucked backward, repeatedly slamming Innes against the wall, until they reached the open doorway to the temple and staggered down the center aisle, where they crashed to the floor, the man's compact weight falling heavily on Innes's midsection. The collision knocked every ounce of breath from his body; he wheezed and gasped for breath, crawling helplessly on hands and knees. By the time Presto reached him, the figure in black had fled behind the stage; they heard a crash of broken glass.

"Go," whispered Innes, waving Presto toward the back.

Presto switched on the flash-a-light and rushed after the man. He entered a storage room, crept slowly past the ark where the Torah was kept, and pointed the light at a billowing curtain. He stabbed the rapier into it, then drew the curtain aside to discover the smashed window through which the man in black had escaped.

Innes had sat up and regained his breath by the time Presto returned.

"You're fairly handy with that thing," said Innes, nodding at the blade as Presto slid it back into his walking stick.

"Champion of the épée at Oxford, three years running,"

said Presto. "Never ran anyone through with it before. Intentionally, I mean."

They moved quickly up the stairs and into the lamplit room.

Rabbi Brachman's body lay peacefully in a chair at his desk, slumped over as if while working he had gently laid down his head to rest. The burning lamp illuminated his open eyes, the white parchment of his skin.

Jack stood facing the body, studying the desk intently as the others entered. "Got away, did they?"

"Two of them," said Presto.

"Not without taking their lumps," said Innes, acutely feeling his.

"Assuming that's your work," said Presto, sliding the sword back into his walking stick. "The one in the hall."

Jack nodded.

"You got one?" said Innes. "How brilliant!"

"Didn't mean to kill him," said Jack coldly. "He's no help to us dead."

Innes noticed Brachman for the first time. "Good God, is he dead too?"

"The gift for deductive reasoning runs deep in your family," said Jack.

"Did they kill him?" asked Innes, too stunned to register the insult.

"Lethal injection," said Jack, pointing to a dim red mark on the Rabbi's arm. "The same method they used to kill Rupert Selig on board the *Elbe*."

"Poor old fellow," said Presto, genuinely saddened. "Twelve grandchildren, I think he said."

"Arthur was of the opinion that they scared Selig to death," said Innes.

"Arthur was wrong," said Jack impatiently. "The injection gives every appearance of a heart attack; that's what they want you to believe. Have a look at the one in the hall. And keep an eye out in case the others come back; I've got work to do in here."

"I'll take a moment first to honor the departed, if you

don't object," said Presto, brusquely. "He was a good man; he deserves some consideration of decency."

Jack stared at him. Innes couldn't tell if it was shock or affront.

"Or has it not occurred to you, Jack, that if we hadn't stopped to pick up your damn suitcase, Brachman might still be alive."

Jack stared at the floor, turning crimson. Innes was shocked by the intensity of Presto's anger; although he agreed it was justified, to express it in the presence of a corpse made Innes feel as if he were standing naked in front of his algebra class.

Presto gently closed Rabbi Brachman's eyes, shut his own for a moment, intoned a silent prayer, crossed himself, and then stalked out of the room. Innes made to follow him.

"Stay with me," said Jack.

"Really?"

"I need you."

Innes nodded slowly and put his hands behind his back, as he had often seen Arthur do—implying a deeper level of thought—and idled up to Jack's side.

"Were either of the men you chased carrying anything?" asked Jack.

"One had a black bag," said Innes, then realizing: "Do you think—"

"The false Zohar," said Jack, nodding. "They showed it to him, trying to coerce his opinion. So they have their doubts about its authenticity."

"Unlikely the Rabbi settled them, don't you think? He must have refused; I mean, why else would they kill him?"

"Because they heard us downstairs; and no, I don't believe he told them anything." Jack moved closer to the body, eyes open as a cat's, glittering with intensity. "Brachman was working at his desk when he heard them enter—fresh ink marks here, on the heel of his palm, the inkwell left open. What does that suggest?"

Innes paused thoughtfully. "That he was, as you say, working."

"No," said Jack, closing his eyes impatiently. "What does that say about the *state* of his desk?"

Innes studied the scene, nervous as a student at final exams. "There are no papers lying about. He may have hidden something?"

"In a place that even these professional thieves could not easily find. Where might that be?" asked Jack.

Innes gazed slowly around the room with furrowed brow, nodding thoughtfully and repeatedly, before admitting, "I haven't the slightest idea."

"Let's assume the Rabbi had, at best, ten seconds from the time he heard the men arrive to the moment they entered the room."

"Close at hand then; somewhere in the desk?"

"I've searched there already. Thoroughly."

"Loose floorboard? Under the carpet?"

"Less obvious than that," said Jack, watching him, arms folded.

I *am* being tested, Innes realized. Well, Arthur told me the man was peculiar. He studied the desk, glanced into its pigeonholes as if trying to sneak up on them unawares. Scrutinized the inkwell. Lifted the ink blotter; found a slit cut in its side.

"Aha," said Innes.

"No; looked there; empty," said Jack.

Innes stepped back to gain perspective, put his hands on his hips, and his right elbow knocked the lamp off the desk. It shattered as it hit the ground; small flames from the oil pooled on the floor. He stomped them out, nearly catching his boot on fire and plunging them into darkness again.

"Bother," said Innes, not at all comfortable being in the dark so near to a recently dead body. "Sorry."

Jack switched on the portable light, illuminating the broken shards on the floor.

"You've done it now," said Jack.

"I said I was sorry. . . ."

"No: you *found* them."

Innes looked down and saw papers among the pieces of the lamp.

"Well, it had to figure, didn't it?" said Innes, happy to take the credit. "I mean, the lamp right at hand. So little time."

Jack picked up the papers and studied them under the light: one a printed list of participants in the Parliament of Religions. The other a handwritten note.

"Everything all right?" asked Presto, reentering.

"Quite," said Innes, trying unsuccessfully to peer over Jack's shoulder at the note.

"What are you standing in the dark for?" said Presto.

"I was searching the lamp," said Innes. "Accidentally knocked it over."

"This man in the hall has that same scar on the inside of his left arm: a circle broken by three lines. What have you got there?" said Presto, moving closer.

"At the regrettable cost of Brachman's life," said Jack, pointedly, "the answer we've been looking for."

"I want your opinion of my friend Jack," said Doyle quietly.

Walks Alone looked at him for a long moment. Then she nodded. "He is very sick."

"Tell me how," asked Doyle.

She chose her words carefully before continuing; she sensed the concern this man had for his friend, and she did not want to upset him unnecessarily. "I can see the sickness in him: It is like a weight, or . . . a shadow in here." She pointed to her left side. "In him it is very powerful."

They were sitting before a fire in Doyle's Palmer House suite, Walks Alone cross-legged on the floor near the hearth, Doyle in a wing chair, savoring a brandy. An exhausted Lionel Stern lay asleep on the davenport, the crate holding the Zohar resting on the table between them.

"You sound like a doctor, Miss Williams," said Doyle.

"I was taught by my grandfather; he had strong healing power. But our medicine is very different from yours."

"In what way?"

"We believe sickness comes from the outside and enters into the body; it can hide there for a long time, and grow, before it makes itself known."

"How so? I'm a doctor myself," said Doyle, genuinely curious, deciding to confide in the hope of receiving the same. "That is, I was trained as one. And I do believe some people have an inborn talent for healing. I wish I could say I was one of them. I worked hard at medicine but it never came particularly easy to me."

"So you became a writer of books instead."

"One has to put bread on the table, don't they?" he said, with an apologetic smile.

"I am sorry I have not read any of them."

"Quite all right; it's a bit of a relief, actually. So, you are considered a doctor among your people, Miss Williams?"

Walks Alone waited again. She trusted this man for some reason; unusual for her to trust a white. He seemed as ignorant about her ways as all whites did, but he offered her a straightforward respect she was not used to receiving. He had strength but did not need to make a big show of it like so many whites did. She wondered if people were like him in his home country; she had never met an Englishman before.

"Yes," she said.

"And you can see so plainly that my friend is sick?"

"More: His life is in danger."

Doyle sat up straighter; he took her seriously. "So this is a physical illness."

"The sickness is in his spirit now, but will go into his body one day. Soon."

"Could he be cured before that happens?"

"I would need to see him more before I could say."

"Do you think you could help him?"

"I would not like to say now."

"How would you treat this sickness?"

"The sickness needs to be taken out of him."

"How would you do that?"

"In our medicine, as a doctor, you remove sickness from a person by inviting it to leave them and come into your body."

"That sounds as if it could be dangerous for you."

"It is."

Doyle studied her by the firelight; solemn and heartfelt,

staring at the flames. The modest, confident strength she radiated. He remembered Roosevelt's eye-popping diatribe against the American Indian and shuddered at the thick-headed compendium of clichés he himself had been carrying around about them. If Mary was any example, they were clearly different from whites—the product of a different culture, even a different race—but that was no reason to fear or despise her. And in spite of the bias of his conventional training, yes, he could believe she had the power to heal.

"What do you do with the sickness once you've taken it from them?"

"I send it somewhere; into the air, the water, or the earth. Sometimes into fire. It depends what kind of sickness it is. This is what we learn to do."

Doyle recalled Jack's stories about the En-aguas in Brazil. "You use various herbs and roots to help you, medicinal compounds."

"Yes," she said, surprised that he knew this. "Sometimes."

"What causes this kind of sickness? You say it comes from outside."

"When the world is made unsound, it creates more sickness. This goes out from the world and into the people."

"And how did the world become sick?"

"People have made it so," she said simply. "When the sickness goes into them, it is only returning to where it came from."

"So before man you believe that the world was whole?"

"It was in balance, yes," she said. Before the whites came, she thought.

He looked at her openly, honestly. "So if a person becomes sick, you believe it is only a reflection of what is already inside them."

"That is true most of the time."

"Miss Williams, I ask you to tell me plainly: Is there a chance that you can heal my friend?"

"That is difficult to say. I do not know if that is what your friend wants."

"What do you mean?"

"Sometimes a person will become attached to the sickness; sometimes they come to believe the sickness is more real than they are."

"Is that what has happened to my friend?"

"Yes, I think so."

"So he could not be healed. Not by anyone."

"Not when the attachment is so strong. Not unless he decides that is what he wants. He is too much in love with death."

She sees him clearly, that much is certain, thought Doyle. He finished the last of his brandy. Jack could certainly be diagnosed as mad by any medical standards. Whether any sort of medicine could bring him back remained to be seen.

A sharp knock at the door startled them. Doyle cautiously opened it a notch.

"See here, Doyle, we need to talk," said Major Pepperman. Judging by the lethal blast of his breath, he had been drinking heavily.

"Sorry, it will have to wait until morning, Major—"

Before Doyle could react, Pepperman had stuck a gigantic boot through the crack of the door and wedged it open. He took a step into the room, saw Walks Alone rising by the fire, Lionel Stern on the sofa.

"I knew it!" said Pepperman, pointing a finger at the woman. "You're up to something dastardly in here, Mr. Doyle; I must insist upon my right to be informed. . . ."

"Major, please—"

"Sir, I don't think you appreciate the risk I've taken in bringing you to this country. I have over five thousand dollars of my own capital invested in this enterprise, and if you are unable to fulfill the obligations of our agreement, it will leave me teetering on the brink of the abyss!"

"Major, I have every intention of fulfilling my obligation. . . ."

"I know exactly what you're up to!"

"You do?"

"Running around with shady characters at all hours of the night, smuggling unconscious women into your rooms; why, it's been all I can do to keep the house detective from breaking down your door!"

Pepperman strode about, gesticulating wildly. Doyle exchanged a helpless, apologetic look with Lionel Stern, who hovered protectively over the crate holding the Zohar. Walks Alone's eye drifted to the iron poker leaning on the hearth.

"I must have some assurance, sir; I must be provided with a proper guarantee or I shall be forced to submit this matter to the attentions of my attorney! We have laws about these things in America! I have a wife and five red-headed children!"

The door behind him opened. Jack, Innes, and Presto hurried into the room.

"Rabbi Brachman has been killed," said Jack, before noticing the giant pacing in the corner.

Pepperman took in this disturbing information, stopped dead in his tracks, and began to cry. "Murder. I'm ruined!" moaned Pepperman.

"Oh, my God," said Stern, sinking back down on the sofa. "Even the circus won't take me back now."

Presto went to comfort Stern, and Innes toward Pepperman, to restrain him if necessary, as Jack took Doyle aside.

"What is this man doing here?" asked Jack in a whisper.

"I'm not altogether sure," said Doyle.

"There, there, Major," said Innes. "Not as bad as all that, is it?"

"Reduced to promoting weightlifters and bearded ladies in a traveling freak show," said Pepperman, burbling through his sobs, dropping slowly to his knees and pounding his fists on the floor.

"Get rid of him, can't you?" asked Jack.

"He's very upset," said Doyle.

"I can see that," said Jack.

Walks Alone moved to the collapsed giant and took him by the hand; he looked up at her like a six-year-old mourning a dead puppy. She made a low soothing, murmuring sound, stroked his neck a few times, and Pepperman's sobbing slowly subsided. As he relaxed, she placed a hand on his forehead and whispered a few quiet words in his ear. Pepperman's eyes closed, his body slumped over to one side, and he was asleep before his head hit the floor. Loud snuffling snores ratcheted out of him, dead to the world.

"I've seen that done to snakes before," said Presto, in amazement, "but never to a human being."

"He should sleep now for a long time," said Walks Alone.

"What should we do with him?" said Innes.

"Drag him out to the hall," said Jack.

"The poor chap hasn't done anything wrong," said Doyle. "Let's put him on the bed."

It required all six of them to lift and carry Pepperman into the bedroom. Doyle threw a blanket on him, closed the door, and returned to the sitting room. Jack and Presto brought the others quickly up-to-date on the events at the synagogue; the men in black, their attempt to authenticate the book, the murder of Rabbi Brachman.

Never would have happened with the old Jack, Doyle couldn't help thinking: He would have anticipated their intentions, somehow prevented it.

"The same as the men on the *Elbe,* down to the mark on the left arm," said Jack. "It's a brand, burned into their skin, like cattle."

"The smell of burning flesh in that office tonight," said Walks Alone.

"Could have been some sort of initiation," said Presto.

"Let's attempt a summing up, then," said Doyle, trying to impose order.

Jack laid out two pieces of paper. "Before he died, Brachman concealed the information we asked for in his desk lamp, which Innes succeeded in finding."

"Nothing, really," said Innes modestly.

"This program lists the names of every clergyman who attended the Parliament of Religions. Brachman circled one name, a charismatic evangelist, an American: Reverend A. Glorious Day."

"A. Glorious Day?" said Doyle, a lump forming in his throat. " 'A,' as in Alexander."

"The preacher we saw in Edison's photos," said Jack.

"Who is this man?" asked Walks Alone.

"My brother," said Jack bitterly.

Doyle and Walks Alone exchanged a look: This is the source of his sickness. She seemed to understand.

"So we know Alexander was here in Chicago and we know the name he's using," said Doyle. "Can we establish any connection to the theft of the holy books?"

"The second piece Brachman left is this note, written moments before he died," said Jack, handing the note to Doyle.

Doyle read it aloud. " 'Mr. Sparks: I am able to recall meeting Reverend Day only once during the congress. Many scholarly seminars were held during the week of the Parliament; I presented a paper at one of these meetings, on the significance of sacred texts in the establishment of world religions. The Reverend Day came up to me afterwards, fervently interested, and asked a number of questions about these sacred books. . . .' The note ends here, abruptly."

"A sizable ink blot; he held his pen in place on the paper," said Jack.

"Because he heard someone moving outside his room," said Presto.

"So Alexander's interest in the books was born here, at the Parliament of Religions, while passing himself off as a preacher," said Doyle.

Jack nodded. "The first theft occurred six months later."

"The Upanishads, taken from the temple in India," said Presto.

"Then a month afterwards, the Vulgate Bible from Oxford," said Jack.

"And the Tikkunei, in Chicago, only weeks ago," said Stern.

"A trail that I'm confident would mirror the travels of this German collector," said Jack.

"Who, I think we can say with some confidence, is in the employ of your brother; during those first months after the Parliament he made contact with the Hanseatic League and commissioned the thefts," said Doyle.

"Exactly," said Jack.

"How would he have known about the League?" asked Stern.

"During his years in England, Alexander established knowledge of and contact with criminal organizations all over the world," said Doyle. "To conclude the League was among them is far from difficult."

"But why?" asked Innes. "Why does your brother want these books?"

Silence.

"That's a very good question, Innes," said Doyle.

"Thank you, Arthur."

"We can't answer that yet," said Jack, sitting apart from them.

"He hasn't attempted to ransom them, we know that much," said Presto.

"Perhaps he's searching them for . . . mystical information," said Stern.

"Hidden secrets," said Doyle. "Like the Kabbalah supposedly contains."

"Like that bit about how to build a golem," said Innes.

"Possibly," said Doyle.

"Stay away from that sort of speculation," said Jack sharply.

Silence again.

"Do we know where your brother is now?" asked Walks Alone.

"We know a telegraph line ran out of their office," said Presto. "Presumably that was their method of communication."

"Any way to trace the line?" said Doyle.

"Not now," said Jack.

"They would have used some sort of code," said Doyle. "And by now whatever link existed between them has surely been destroyed."

"The tower," said Walks Alone, with a flash of clarity. "That's where he is."

The thought startled everyone in the room, but no one quite grasped her point yet.

"The man in the dream, the one who looks like you," said Walks Alone to Jack. "Your brother; he was in Chicago; he saw the Water Tower, just as your father did before he made that drawing," she said to Stern.

"Good God," said Stern. "Maybe they met each other

here; my father and Alexander; they could have, couldn't they?"

"Possibly. Go on," said Doyle.

"What if your brother is building this tower?" Walks Alone asked. "Patterned in some way on the one he saw here."

"Schwarzkirk, the Black Church," said Presto. "It falls together."

"Somewhere out west," said Walks Alone. "In the desert we have seen in the dream."

"Maybe that's where my father's gone," said Stern, excitement rising.

"You're suggesting this black tower you've all seen is an *actual place,* not just a symbol from the dream," said Doyle.

"Yes," said Walks Alone.

"Why couldn't it be?" asked Presto, excited by the idea.

"I don't know; I suppose it could," Doyle admitted.

"And if it is, how hard could it be to find a building of such size and singular design?" asked Presto.

"Not hard at all," said Doyle. "We'll wire rock quarries and masonries in every western city."

"He'd need a huge number of skilled workers," said Presto.

"And an enormous pile of money," said Stern.

"Supply houses, construction outfitters . . ." added Presto.

"And newspapers; there'd be stories about such an unusual project," said Doyle. "Innes, make a list; we'll go to the telegraph office and start sending inquiries."

Innes took a sheet of stationery from the desk and began writing.

Doyle glanced over at Jack, sitting alone, staring at the floor, the only one not participating. "Can any of you remember more details from the dream that might tell us where the tower is?"

Jack did not acknowledge the question.

"Mary, you seem to have had the most revealed to you," said Presto.

Walks Alone nodded, closed her eyes, and directed her mind back into the world of the dream.

"Six people gather in a room under the ground," she said slowly.

"The temple; yes, I think I've seen that, too," said Presto.

"Each time the Black Crow Man rises from the earth, into the sky, out of the fire."

"Like the phoenix," said Doyle.

"Phoenix," said Stern.

His eyes met Doyle's as the thought struck them simultaneously.

"Phoenix, Arizona," said Doyle. "Send the first telegrams there—my God. I've just had a thought."

Doyle rummaged quickly through his notebook to find his sketch of the design they had found on the wall of Rupert Selig's cabin and the brand on the arms of the thieves. "We've been assuming all along that this design is an insignia of this league of thieves."

"What of it?" asked Presto.

"Perhaps we've been looking at it the wrong way," said Doyle. "Perhaps that's not what it is at all."

"What else could it be?" asked Innes.

Doyle turned the drawing on its side and pointed to it. "What does this look like now? These broken lines?"

"Dots and dashes?" said Presto.

"Morse code," said Innes.

"Exactly," said Doyle, laying it down flat, taking Innes's pencil. "Does anyone know what this translates into?"

Jack had moved across the room without anyone noticing. He stood directly over Doyle, looking down at the paper.

"The letter 'R' and a series of numbers," said Jack. "Thirteen and eleven on the middle line. Thirteen and eighteen on the last."

"It's not a date, then," said Doyle.

"Perhaps a geographical location, longitude and latitude," said Innes.

Jack shook his head. "Middle of the Atlantic Ocean."

"Maybe a biblical reference," said Stern. "Chapter and verse."

"Innes, there's a Bible in the drawer beside my bed," said Doyle, as Innes bolted for the door. "Don't wake the Major."

"How do we know which book of the Bible?" asked Presto, as Innes returned with a Gideon Bible and handed it to Doyle.

"One that begins with the letter 'R,' I suppose," said Doyle.

"Only three begin with 'R,' " said Innes from memory. "Ruth, Romans, and the Revelation."

"Ruth has only four chapters," said Doyle, quickly flipping to that section of the book. "And Romans only fourteen verses."

"What is the Revelation?" asked Walks Alone.

"The last book," said Stern. "A series of visions experienced by the Apostle John."

"A prophecy," said Jack, "of the Apocalypse."

"Here it is," said Doyle, finding the page. "Revelation, thirteen, eleven: 'Then I saw another Beast coming up out of the earth and he had two horns and spoke like a dragon.'

"And thirteen, eighteen: 'Here is wisdom: Let him who has understanding calculate the number of the Beast, for it is the number of a man: His number is 666.' "

chapter twelve

THE FIRST CHECKPOINT WAS FIVE MILES OUT FROM THE center of the town. Late afternoon by the time the Players' wagons reached it, desert all around, flat and desolate, sun hammering down like a blacksmith. Eileen was grateful for the extra canteens Jacob had filled before they left Skull Canyon; Kanazuchi went through two himself, silent as before, his movements spare and economical. His wound stayed clean, no festering; the strange man seemed to be using the energy he conserved to consciously will himself to heal and damned if it wasn't working; his pallor gone, breathing steady and strong.

At the moment, Eileen felt more concern for Jacob, driving their wagon all day in the blinding heat; she spelled him at the reins for a stretch until the swelter drove her back under the cover of the canvas. She knew the poor man had to be exhausted just from the tossing and jolting the rough road gave their buckboard—his face scarlet, sweat soaking his shirt—but he never complained, cheerful and buoyant as ever, making it impossible for her to give in to her rising sense of apprehension.

Damn Bendigo anyway for marching them out across a desert in the heat of the day; their first performance wasn't until tomorrow night, they shouldn't have attempted this crossing until the sun went down; the road was well marked and the wagons all equipped with lanterns. But heaven forbid they should show up late for a free meal; Rymer might lose a nickel.

Winding down from the foothills of the Juniper Mountains and into the sands of the eastern Mojave, their caravan had just passed through an eerie formation of spiraling vertical pillars, etched out of limestone and silt, rising from the flats like a forest of rock. The wagons rounded a corner in the densest part of the stand and came to a crude gate fashioned from large cut logs, the first sign they'd seen of human hands in hours. A small hut, built from the same wood, apparently empty, stood to the side.

A sharp whistle blew.

Out of nowhere, a dozen heavily armed men—people; Eileen realized half of them were women—appeared on every side and above them on top of the pillars, rifles cocked and trained on the wagons. They wore light cotton pants, heavy steel-tipped boots, and identical collarless white tunics; each one equipped with a belt of bullets slung around their waists.

Something else odd about them: They were all smiling.

A tall woman, the only one without a rifle—she wore twin-holstered sidearms and a whistle around her neck—stepped forward to the gate and spoke to Rymer in the lead wagon.

"Welcome to The New City, friend," said the woman cheerfully in a loud, clear voice. "What is your business with us today, please?"

"We are the Penultimate Players," said Bendigo, with a grand sweep of his Tyrolean hat. "Theatrical vagabonds. Come to entertain, amuse, and, one hopes, humbly, to please."

The woman smiled at him. "One moment, please."

She opened and consulted a list in a leather-bound folder she carried and apparently found a corresponding entry.

"And your name, sir?"

"I am Bendigo Rymer, director of our happy band; entirely at your service, madam."

"How many in your party, Mr. Rymer?"

"We are seventeen, uh, nineteen of us, in all."

"Thank you, sir; you are expected," she said, closing the book. "We will have a look in your wagons, and you can go right on in."

"By all means," said Rymer. "We have nothing to hide."

The woman gave a signal, and the guards on the ground moved swiftly forward, throwing open the wagon flaps, while the ones stationed on the pillars held their rifles pointed and ready.

"Good afternoon," said Jacob to the handsome young black guard who took hold of the bridle on his mules.

"Good afternoon, sir," said the man, well-spoken, smiling broadly.

"You have a tremendous amount of heat out here in your desert this afternoon," said Jacob, mopping his brow.

"Yes, sir," said the guard, still smiling, never taking his eyes off him.

The canvas yanked away from the rear of their buckboard: Kanazuchi had pulled himself into a sitting position, swords hidden under the skirt of his coat. Startled, Eileen turned to look at the face of the guard; a slight young woman, no more than twenty, pony-tailed and freckle-faced, but she moved with the sharp assurance of a well-trained soldier. Her eyes darted methodically around the empty wagon—what is she looking for? Eileen wondered—and settled on Kanazuchi for a moment. He nodded and smiled, betraying no uneasiness. The girl smiled in return, a gaptoothed grin that suggested no undue curiosity.

"Hello," said Eileen.

"Have a glorious day," said the girl, and dropped the canvas cover.

The guards on the ground stepped back and signaled to the woman at the gate; she leaned on a stone counterweight and the log barrier rose up smoothly, clearing their path.

"Please proceed, Mr. Rymer," she said to Rymer. "Do not attempt to leave the road. When you reach The New City, someone will meet you with further instructions."

"We are most grateful, madam," said Rymer.

With sweat covering his body, Bendigo congratulated himself on the unflappable coolness of his performance—authority figures outside the theater paralyzed him, particularly when heavily armed—but the woman hadn't noticed even the slightest uneasiness. What an actor he was! He urged his mules through the gate. The other wagons quickly followed.

"Have a glorious day!" said the woman at the gate, smiling and waving at each passing wagon.

"Thank you," said Jacob, returning her wave. "You, too!"

Eileen peeked out of the back as the log gate closed behind them; the guards on the pillars watched them roll away, rifles still in hand, while the others disappeared back to their hiding places.

"What do you make of that?" asked Eileen.

"I detect the fine hand of religious fanaticism," said Jacob from the front seat.

As he joined her to look through the flap, Eileen noticed a profound change in Kanazuchi; he looked revitalized by their encounter at the gate—focused, senses keenly attuned, his movements regaining their catlike precision and alertness. Although she felt no threat to herself, for the first time she felt a reason to fear him: He seemed more animal than man.

"Strange, weren't they?" she asked.

"Serious people," said Kanazuchi.

"Seriously happy."

"No," he said, shaking his head slightly. "Not happy."

From the checkpoint forward, the road improved dramatically; hard packed dirt graded and leveled on top of the sand, nearly eliminating the rocking of the wagons. Across the dry flatlands to the rear, a distant rhythmic pounding faintly reached their ears. Eileen shielded her eyes and peered out in that direction but could see nothing on the heat-distorted horizon.

"What is that?"

"They are putting up fences," said Kanazuchi. "Barbed wire."

"Who is?"

"The people in white."

"You can see that from here?"

He didn't respond; Kanazuchi discarded Jacob's round hat, removed the long black coat, and began to strip off the motley patchwork beard.

They were getting close.

Time to reassume his own identity.

By nine o'clock that morning, the Chicago Western Union office had received a flurry of responses to their late-night

barrage of telegrams. Attaching the name Arthur Conan
Doyle to the inquiries greatly increased the alacrity and den-
sity of detail in the returns, particularly from newspaper ed-
itors, most of whom confessed they couldn't help with the
requested information but were unable to resist firing off a
question or two about the uncertain fictional fate of you-
know-who.

As they had suspected, the most promising results came
back in a lengthy reply from the *Arizona Republican* in
Phoenix, the Arizona Territory's first newspaper.

The editor wrote that local attention was growing in the
direction of a recently found religious settlement a hundred
miles to the northwest. Called itself The New City, built on
private property; its founders had bought over fifty square
miles of surrounding undeveloped land. Clearly they had a
lot of money to throw around; speculation about The New
City's wealth centered on the possible striking of some fab-
ulous silver lode.

Every one of the paper's repeated attempts to research a
story on the place had been politely but firmly rebuffed;
folks wanted to hang on to their privacy out there for some
reason. That attitude didn't raise a sea of red flags in this
sparsely populated corner of the world; a lot of people came
west in search of that same commodity.

One of the reporters the *Republican* sent out that way had
found The New City so much to his liking he decided to stay
on. They hadn't heard a single word from the man after a
telegram announced his resignation—in which he described
the place only as a "kind of Utopia"—but that didn't surprise folks at the paper much: He was a bachelor fellow
from Indiana, an odd duck who'd never quite fit in.

Neither were utopian social experiments that great a rar-
ity in the development of the American character, noted
Doyle. Over a hundred had sprung up all over the country
since the Civil War, the most noteworthy being the Oneida
Community of Perfectionists in upstate New York; known
for the fine silverware they produced but even more for their
bold rejection of marital monogamy. At the opposite end of
the sexual spectrum were Mother Ann Lee's Shakers of the

Millennial Church, strict celibate abstainers who had set up shop in more than thirty different locations from Massachusetts to Ohio. How they planned to perpetuate themselves without benefit of biological reproduction didn't seem to worry them since Mother Lee had prophesied the end of civilization within their lifetimes; chastity ensured them that theirs would be the only souls allowed through the Gates of Heaven. Why the Shakers then devoted themselves to building such sturdy, built-to-last crafts and furniture when there wouldn't be anyone left to appreciate them was a question they never got around to asking.

Arizona's attitude toward The New City could best be described as "live and let live," wrote the editor. A number of Mormon settlements had established themselves in that same northwest quarter of the territory over the last few years, and they kept to themselves as their creed dictated without raising any eyebrows; why, the entire state of Utah had sprung up around the Mormons and the fortunes they'd made in their ranching and mining enterprises. Far be it from the politicians of Arizona to turn their back on such rich potential revenue out of small-minded religious prejudice.

So: Economically self-sustaining and socially self-governing, what business was it of anybody's if these people of The New City wanted to live according to their own beliefs, whatever they might be? (No one seemed to know a thing about that.) And if any financial benefits trickled down to the surrounding area in which they chose to establish their community, as they so obviously had to the *non*-Mormons of Utah, so much the better. Absolutely consistent with the American guarantee of religious freedom, that was the *Republican*'s editorial position on the subject.

Hustling to a local bookstore and returning with a detailed map of the Arizona Territory, Innes charted The New City's location as described by the editor directly in the heart of the eastern Mojave Desert.

So far so good. The issue of what they should do in response was definitively settled by one last nugget from the *Republican*. Rumor had it the citizens of The New City were building a tabernacle to rival the one the Mormons had recently completed in Salt Lake City. No one at the paper had actually laid eyes on the place, but it was going up fast and was supposedly being fashioned from black stones drawn from quarries in northern Mexico.

The black church.

After leaving the telegraph office, Doyle returned to the Palmer House and delivered a promissory note of $2,500 to Major Rolando Pepperman, guaranteeing Doyle's participation in the remainder of his tour after a two-week delay. Needed, he told the Major, for the resolution of unspecified personal difficulties. Confined to his bed, hung over and glum, Pepperman accepted Doyle's offer without question, fully expecting never to see the man again, and with a resigned feeling of relief. The Major had already made up his mind; if they would have him, he was going back to the circus.

Because no connection to The New City had been established, the editor of the *Republican* did not mention in his telegram the story dominating their local headlines, that of the decapitating fugitive Chinaman, Chop-Chop—he'd coined the nickname personally; one of his finer editorial hours.

If he had, Doyle, Jack, Innes, Presto, Stern, and Walks Alone would have made their way to the Chicago train station and purchased their one-way tickets to Phoenix with even greater urgency.

The night before, while visiting the dream again, Walks Alone had been able to distinguish one of the faces of the other three figures that had joined them underground:

An Asian man, who held in his hands a flaming sword.

By the time Dante Scruggs knitted his savaged wits back into something close to working order, he realized he was riding a train. A private compartment, daylight outside the windows, moving through open countryside; farms, fields of wheat. Three other men sitting with him, dressed in suits, vaguely recognizable: He'd seen them all in Frederick's offices the night before.

The men who'd hurt him.

They watched Dante closely as he came around, with interest but without emotion or friendliness. The three looked different from one another but seemed the same in behavior, gesture, each of them pulled taut as a bowstring, containing a violence that threatened to spill over at the slightest provocation. Dante understood what that feeling was all about.

"What time is it?" asked Dante.

The three men stared at him; finally one of them pointed to the watch pocket of his vest.

Looking down at himself, Dante realized he was similarly dressed, like a traveling businessman. Dante put a hand into his own vest pocket, pulled out a watch, and opened it.

Two-fifteen.

He replaced the watch. Felt a dull throbbing on the inside of his left arm, then, remembering the brand they'd inflicted on him there, decided not to touch the area or draw their attention to it. Who knew what else they might do to him?

Why couldn't he remember anything after the searing pain of those moments? Their hands holding him down; Frederick's face looming over his, speaking softly, hypnotically. He had obviously blacked out but more than twelve hours had passed since then. Had they given him some kind of drug that erased everything else from his mind?

He wanted to ask a hundred questions, but fear kept him quiet. Something else rose up unexpectedly: a feeling of kinship with these men. Dante had seen the marks on their arms; obviously they'd all experienced what he'd gone through last night—the suffering and terror of that nightmarish initiation. It united them in a way that meant more than friendship; he didn't need friends, never had.

Fellowship, that was something else again.

What had Frederick said to him?

An army. These were soldiers, as he had been once and was now again.

Fighting men. The idea grew on him.

What had he hated about the regular army, anyway? The small talk, petty complaints, and laziness of the average volunteer, their stupidity and lack of discipline. Any behavior that distracted from what he saw as their primary business: killing.

That didn't seem to be a problem with these men. Dante felt himself relax. Maybe Frederick was right. Maybe he did fit right in.

The door opened; the two men nearest to it got up and went outside, as Frederick entered and took a seat directly across from Dante. At the sight of Frederick's handsome smiling face, Dante tensed up again, his heart raced, his palms went moist.

"How are you feeling?" asked Frederick warmly.

"Okay," said Dante. "Real good."

"Any discomfort?"

Dante shook his head.

"Any . . . second thoughts?"

"No, sir."

Frederick stared at him until Dante had to look away. Frederick put a friendly hand on his knee, rubbed it intimately. Dante blushed, looked up at him, and grinned.

"You'll do just fine," said Frederick. "With your background, the training shouldn't prove difficult."

"Training?"

"Shouldn't take long, either. You've been a leader of men before. You may even be officer material."

"Whatever you say."

Frederick leaned back and studied him. "Hungry, Mr. Scruggs?"

"Yes, sir," said Dante, realizing. "Real hungry."

Frederick gestured; the man remaining in the compartment pulled down a wicker basket from the luggage rack, set it on the seat beside Dante, and snapped it open, revealing a mouthwatering selection of sandwiches, fruit, and beverages.

"We are careful about what we eat," said Frederick. "Good food. Nutritious and well balanced. No liquor is allowed."

"I don't drink, anyway," said Dante.

"That's fine. An army travels on its stomach, isn't that right, Mr. Scruggs? Help yourself."

Dante could hardly recall ever feeling so ravenous; he devoured three sandwiches and two bottles of ginger ale without saying a word, wiping his mouth across the sleeve of his new jacket, shameless as a starving dog. Frederick leaned back in his seat, folded his hands neatly, and watched Dante eat, a sly smile playing across his strong features.

As Dante finished eating and let out a resounding belch, at a signal from Frederick the third man replaced the basket in the rack and left the compartment. Frederick delicately held out a napkin; Dante stared at it for a moment before realizing what this was, then took it and cleaned off his dripping mouth and chin.

"Are you curious about the group you've become part of, Mr. Scruggs?" asked Frederick, with that teasing smile again.

"I figure my job is," said Dante, pausing to bring up another burp, "do what I'm told and don't ask questions."

"Good. For instance, you do not need to know what we call ourselves, because it is not a question you will ever be required to answer."

Dante nodded.

"You will never be told anything unless we determine that you need to know it. Do you know where we are going now?"

"West somewhere," said Dante with a shrug, observing the position of the sun out the window.

"Quite perceptive; but beyond that, do you *care* where you are going?"

"No, sir."

"We are great believers in discipline, Mr. Scruggs. Discipline of behavior; discipline of the self. It is essential to our work that people should not take any notice of us. Imagine, for example, that a job you were involved with required you to dine in a fancy restaurant and it was important for you to blend seamlessly into that crowd."

"Okay."

Frederick leaned forward and whispered, "Do you think that would be possible, Mr. Scruggs, if you were to exhibit the table manners of a pig rolling around in its own shit?"

Dante felt the blood drain from his face; Frederick still smiled at him.

"No, sir."

"This is why we learn to train our minds; and why we believe every personal failing must be so severely punished. This is how we *learn*."

Sweat trickled down the back of Dante's neck. Frederick reached over and patted Dante's leg.

"Don't look so worried, Mr. Scruggs. I hadn't made you aware of our standards and you were so very hungry. But having had this conversation, I won't expect to see such a disgusting display from you ever again. Will I?"

"No, sir."

Frederick gave Dante's thigh a reassuring squeeze and leaned back.

"We recognize that each of our men is uniquely qualified to do our work, and if he pleases us, he should be uniquely rewarded. You have developed your own particular interests in life, Mr. Scruggs, apart from ours; we feel that if you have fulfilled our needs to a high level of satisfaction, we should in turn provide you with an opportunity to satisfy yours."

"Okay." What did he mean?

"Do not be deceived; this generosity springs from a selfish foundation: It has been our experience that giving a man what he wants when he pleases us will only provoke him to work that much harder in the future. It is an *investment*. Do you follow me?"

"I'm not sure."

"An example would be in order. Let's imagine that we have given you a difficult assignment to complete and you have performed it flawlessly. What might you expect from us in return?"

Dante shook his head.

Frederick, all-knowing, snapped his fingers; one of the men opened the door from the corridor outside and in walked a plump, attractive young woman, a strawberry blonde, provocatively dressed, carrying a small valise.

"Yes?" said Frederick to the woman.

"Pardon me, gentlemen, I don't mean to intrude," said the woman, obviously nervous.

"How can we help you, miss?" asked Frederick politely.

"I found this case, you see, under my seat in the next car over?" she said, in a grating midwestern drawl. "And the fella outside—your friend, I guess, he was sitting across from me—he said he thought it belonged to one of you gents in here. So he asked if I wouldn't mind bringing it back myself."

"How very kind of you," said Frederick. "Did our friend offer you anything for its safe return?"

"Sort of," said the woman, blushing.

"How do you mean?"

"He said one of you fellas would give me ten dollars if I did it."

"He would be right," said Frederick, taking out his bill-fold. "Forgive my manners, won't you join us for a moment, miss? It must be more comfortable in here and we really are most grateful."

"All right," she said, still standing, awkwardly holding the valise.

The man in the hall closed the door behind her, leaving her alone with Dante and Frederick.

"Here then, Mr. Johnson," said Frederick to Dante, "why don't you take your case back from the young lady?"

Dante glanced at Frederick in confusion.

"Oh, is it yours?" said the woman, holding it out to him.

"Thank you," said Dante. He accepted the case from her, holding it stiffly in his lap.

Frederick patted the seat beside him and the young woman sat down, as he slipped a ten-dollar bill from his billfold.

"As promised," said Frederick.

"Thank you very much, sir," said the woman, taking the money, eyes downcast, embarrassed.

"No, thank *you,* my dear," said Frederick. "Mr. Johnson, perhaps you should examine your case and make sure everything is in order."

Dante nodded, set the case flat across his knees, and carefully unfastened the twin clasps.

"If you don't mind my asking, are you traveling alone, miss?" asked Frederick. "What is your name, by the way?"

"Rowena. Rowena Jenkis. No, I don't mind. And yes, I am," she said. "Traveling alone, that is."

"I see," said Frederick, smiling warmly. "You're a very pretty girl, if you don't mind my remarking."

"No, I don't mind at all."

"Are you a prostitute, by any chance, Rowena?"

The girl looked stricken; her hands tensed into fists and she glanced nervously at the door. Frederick studied her reaction carefully.

"Please, I don't mean any offense by the question," said Frederick pleasantly. "And I certainly hold no ill towards you if you are. We're all very open-minded here. It's only an observation. To satisfy my curiosity."

She looked rapidly back and forth between them. "I guess I done some of that, yeah," she said, her hands relaxing, stroking the silky mohair seat.

Dante opened the case; inside, laid out meticulously on a bed of black velvet were arrayed two rows of new, gleaming, stainless steel surgical instruments; scalpers, spreaders, saws.

"Is everything in order, Mr. Johnson?" asked Frederick.

"Oh yes."

"Nothing missing?"

"No," said Dante. "Everything's fine."

"Good."

Dante slowly fastened the case and looked up at the girl.

She smiled at him; the one with the accent seemed a bit sophisticated and intimidating for her taste, but she liked this boyish-looking blond. She thought she could have some fun with this one, bringing that little boy out in him. He had a real friendly face—she was severely nearsighted but hated wearing glasses—but there was something funny about his left eye: What was it?

"May I offer you a drink, Rowena?" asked Frederick, bringing down the picnic basket. "Perhaps something to eat. We've brought along some lovely sandwiches."

"That'd be just wonderful, thanks," said Rowena, snuggling back into her first-class seat.

Rowena hadn't been looking forward to moving to Kansas City one little bit; she knew the house she was going to work in there was nowhere near as nice as the one she'd just left in Chicago, and she hated having to get to know a whole bunch of new girls all over again.

But judging by the size of the bankroll in this fancy gent's billfold, she had a feeling this trip might turn out all right after all.

By midafternoon, Buckskin Frank had made up the actors' head start. For all his years riding through the region, he'd never been out this far before; not even Apaches had much use for the place. The heat was brutal once you hit the sand, but he knew how to pace a horse through it; he'd done it a hundred times in other wastelands, and he stopped every hour to water both himself and the horse; he'd always taken good care of his animals. They seemed more deserving of kindness than most people he'd known and returned it more faithfully.

The road was easy to follow and their tracks were fresh. He stopped on top of the last bluff before the road dipped down for good into the flats; another fork intersected with the road a quarter mile below, the only other one he'd come across since Skull Canyon, snaking off to the southwest.

There: Dust kicking up on the main road ahead; Frank took out his field glasses.

His first sight of the actors, five wagons rolling out of a cluster of tall rock. The last wagon had its flap open but he couldn't see any—What was that?

He swung the glasses back from the theatrical troupe and focused in: Looked like a gate across the road, this side of the wagons, about a mile off. Small cabin; telegraph lines running off, following the road ahead. Figures moving, but he was unable to pick out any details from this distance through the heat waves.

His eye caught another cloud rising from that secondary road to his left; he moved the glasses over.

Conestoga wagons, a longer string, maybe ten of them, closer than the other group, heading toward the intersection beneath his position. Drivers wearing white shirts, a second white shirt riding shotgun.

What was in the wagons?

Crates, long crates, piled high in every one.

He knew that shape.

But it made no sense; these were clearly civilian drivers. Couldn't be, could it? To be sure of it, he'd need a closer look.

Not that this was his business, he reminded himself, but if anything was going to complicate taking down the China-man, he had to make it his business.

Frank figured ten minutes before the wagons reached the intersection. He kicked into a gallop to the bottom of the bluff, then left the road and picked his way through the sand to the first outcroppings of rock formation. Strange shapes rising, a maze of twisted pink and white columns like a stand of petrified trees. He tied off his horse out of sight, took his rifle, and went looking for high ground.

The wagons were still a few minutes away, approaching along the main road from the left. As he advanced, he heard movement echoing ahead out of the rocks, then a rhythmic beating sound, followed by voices.

Singing?

Frank crept onto a large boulder and edged over to its rim, giving him a view of a small natural clearing set in the mid-dle of the formation.

A dozen of those same white-shirted people he'd spotted on the wagons, sitting in a circle in the clearing, clapping their hands and singing "Rock My Soul in the Bosom of Abraham."

Young faces. Smiling to beat the band. Two of them black, one Mexican, at least one Indian. Half of them women. Bandoliers around their waists, sidearms. Rifles stacked against the rocks; repeaters, serious guns.

What the hell sort of Sunday school outing was this sup-posed to be?

Frank jerked back away from the edge when he heard a footstep scuff the dirt behind him. He turned slowly; another one of the white shirts, a blond-headed kid, barely out of short pants, patrolling the narrow passage between the rocks below, a rifle in his hands.

A pebble rolled off the boulder and hit the ground near the boy's feet; the boy stopped and kneeled down.

Frank froze; *if the kid glances up, he'll be looking right at the soles of my boots. And two seconds later he'll be wearing a footprint on his face.*

The boy didn't move.

Frank held his breath. *What the hell's he doing? If I was his age, I'd be sneaking a smoke, trying to talk some girl out of her petticoat.* The boy crossed himself—he'd been *praying*—stood up, smiled to himself, and moved along, away from where Frank had tied his horse.

Frank exhaled slowly, then counted to a hundred. Singing and clapping continued from the clearing, the same song, over and over again. No one in a white shirt came looking for him. He slipped off the rock and moved silently back to his horse.

This was too weird.

A strong instinct came up inside him: If you want to head to Mexico, Frankie boy, now's the time.

The wagons had progressed along the main road, level with his position now. Frank moved to the edge of the rocks, less than fifty yards away, rested his arms in a crevice, and trained his glasses on the caravan.

On the long crates in the back of the wagons.

He examined each load carefully as they passed by; yes, each bore the same stenciled stamp on the boxes that he thought he'd find: U.S. ARMY.

Those were Winchester rifles in those crates. Standard military issue.

Hundreds of them.

THE NEW CITY

"Praise God. Hallelujah; isn't it a glorious day?"

"Thank you, Brother Cornelius; it is indeed a glorious

day," said the Reverend as he stepped out of his House for the first time that day—it was already hours past noon—and onto the planked sidewalk on Main Street. He squinted against the bright sunlight; hot, dry air blasting his lungs; worrying again where he would find the energy to fulfill this day's obligations.

If only they knew what I wanted from them, thought Reverend Day, wearily looking out at the crowded street. *How many would stay? How many would turn and run?*

"Tell me, Brother Cornelius, has it been a good day?"

"A glorious day, Reverend. Praise the Lord," said Cornelius Moncrief, who had been waiting for the Reverend without complaint for over two hours, as he did most every day.

"I'm pleased to hear it. Walk with me a while, Brother?"

They fell silently into step together; the enormous hulking man in the long gray duster—The New City's recently appointed Director of Internal Security—slowing to keep pace with the stooped, hunchbacked preacher, his silver spurs jangling to the rhythm of his limp. Citizens in the street smiled and bowed low to Reverend Day, offering devotions as he passed; the Reverend waved kindly to each member of his flock, a blessing never far from his lips.

Terrified of me; keep up the good work.

"The love of our people is a wonder. Truly a gift from God," said the Reverend, as they left Main Street and made the turn toward the tower.

"Most truly, Reverend."

"And have I mentioned to you, Brother Cornelius, how grateful we are for all your hard labor on behalf of our Church?"

"You're too kind, Reverend," said Cornelius, feeling the same swelling in his chest that arose whenever the Reverend spoke kindly to him, as if he was about to bust out laughing or crying and wasn't sure which.

"Brother, you have returned my faith in you a thousand-fold; you bring to the hearts of our Christian soldiers a fighting spirit, inspire them to take up arms with joy and great zeal, marching forward as one, for the protection of our Flock and the destruction of our Enemies."

Tears flowed freely from Cornelius's eyes; he stopped in his tracks, too overcome to look at the Reverend or respond, bowing and nodding his head. Reverend Day watched him weep, patting a compassionate hand on the man's massive shoulder. *No matter how many times I sling this line of bullshit at them, they wolf it down like a pack of starving dogs.*

"There now, Brother Cornelius," said Reverend Day, chucking him under the chin. "Thy tears are like the gentle rain of Heaven, that give life to this dry and dusty plain; and flowers bloom where once there was a desert."

Cornelius looked at him, a shy little smile breaking through his tears.

Time for a taste of the Sacrament, thought Reverend Day.

The Reverend hooked Cornelius with his look and turned on the juice, pumping a few measured jolts into him; he watched carefully as the Power drilled into the man's core and went to work, warping his thoughts to suit the Reverend's needs.

A dark shudder ran through his nerves; he loved administering the Sacrament, the delicious sensation of reaching inside them, the intimacy of the contact, caressing the nakedness they so obligingly exposed. These moments of private violation through their eyes were the ones he lived for.

When he saw Cornelius's pupils glaze over, the Reverend pulled back the tendrils of the Power, folded them into place like a Murphy bed, and snapped his fingers in the man's face. Cornelius blinked, the connection broken. His eyes rolled in his head like runaway marbles.

After years of trial and error, the Reverend had learned to regulate his congregation's exposure to the Power, entering them with the delicate touch of a surgeon; dose them correctly and they went pliant as rag dolls for days, a drunkard's grin pasted to their skulls. Give them too little and their minds gradually returned; too strong a measure and drooling into a cup became a full-time occupation. There were more than a few of those failures planted in shallow graves outside the City.

He had to walk a razor's edge with Cornelius; the man's will was strong so he required more juice than most to keep him in line, but the Reverend couldn't risk frying his nervous system. He needed this one. Cornelius had in short order transformed an undisciplined bunch of green recruits into an army; no one in town could match his leadership and tactical skill, tempered by such gleeful barbarism.

And it all took so much effort; Lord, he was tired.

Cornelius opened his eyes. Good, the man was back in his body. Now some Scripture to lead him out of the fog:

"Incline your ear and hear the words of the wise," the Reverend whispered.

Cornelius eagerly leaned down close to him.

"Apply your heart to my knowledge; I have instructed you today so that I may make you know the certainty of the Words of Truth. Hear, my son, and be wise; because only through wisdom a house is built and only by understanding is it made to last."

His eyes focusing again, Cornelius nodded slowly; complete devotion and absolutely zero comprehension.

That's right, you muttonhead, thought the Reverend, watching closely. *Message received.*

"So," said Reverend Day, walking ahead, back to business, "what *good* news have you for us today, Brother?"

Cornelius wavered a moment, found his balance, and then fell into step like an obedient cur. "That troupe of actors came through the East Gate, right on schedule," said Cornelius, waving a telegram.

"When?"

" 'Bout an hour ago; should be driving into town any time."

"Isn't that wonderful?" said Day, genuinely enthused. "We can look forward to some lively entertainment. Do you realize how long it's been since I've attended the theater?"

Cornelius frowned. "No?"

Hopeless. Well, never mind.

"Welcome our new arrivals for me and invite them to dinner tonight as my honored guests."

"Sure, Reverend," said Cornelius, pulling out another telegram. "And more good news, sir; our new rifles just came through the Gate, too."

"Marvelous, Brother."

"If it's okay with you, sir, I'll have 'em sent to the warehouse so I can inspect the shipment myself."

"Yes, do that, would you? Now tell me, Brother Cornelius, does the training of our militia go well?"

"Reverend, the way our Brothers and Sisters are giving themselves over to it is an inspiration," said Cornelius, eyes misting over again.

"Fine. How's their *marksmanship*?"

"Better every day. And when these new rifles are handed out, it'll get even stronger."

"Good, excellent . . ."

Cornelius's voice caught in his throat, choked up again. "Reverend, I have never been so proud of such a fine group of young people. . . ."

"That's fine," said Day, cutting him off with a sharp chop of his hand, weary of the man's relentless blubbering, so pathetic in a man his size.

They had reached the base of the tower, workers scattering out of his way as he passed. Day stepped into the shadows of the tower, finding relief from the sun under the only shade in sight. As he took off his hat to wipe the sweat off his brow, an electric twitch ran up the stiff length of the Reverend's spine. He recognized the signal immediately, the aura already tightening like a steel band around his forehead.

This was a bad one.

Day felt a trickle of blood flow from his nose. He turned away and covered his face with a handkerchief. *Have to hurry now, not much time.*

"Excuse me, Brother, I must attend to my meditations," said Reverend Day, waving his hat, shushing him away. "Off you go. Back to work."

Cornelius obsequiously struggled against tears, nodded, and trotted back toward town, glancing over his shoulder for reassurance. Reverend Day waited for his first look, waved once, then hobbled around to the side of the cathedral.

Workers scurried off as he approached. Alone, he fumbled the ring of keys from his pocket and undid a padlock securing two steel flaps cut into the dirt. He lifted a flap, dropped it to the side, and straightened to catch his breath before descending.

Handkerchief turning red in his hand, blood flowing freely.

He took the stairs down into the earth, inserted a key in the black onyx door; the lock yielded with a deep, satisfying snick. He pushed lightly; the immense panel, a marvel of construction and design, pivoted on gimbaled hinges and swung open like a gentle breeze. Reverend Day stepped into the cool air of the sepulcher, then closed and locked the door behind him.

As he stepped quickly through the octagonal foyer, sconces of steel and glass lit his way through a maze of labyrinthine passages carved from barren rock. One hand trailed along walls polished to a silky perfection, boot heels snapped sharply on black marble, following the winding path that only he knew by heart, down into the belly of the church, light growing dim, echoes of his footsteps sounding deeper.

At the second door, he applied the black stone key and entered his private chapel. In addition to Day's, only the eyes of the stonemasons and coolie demolition team who had completed this part of the work had ever seen this private sanctum; they were all buried here now, under the black hexagram mosaic on the white marble floor.

Rougher hewn than the passageways, the rock walls gave off a moist, earthy air; this was the way he wanted it, damp, musty, closer to the heart of the earth. Reverend Day limped around the edge of the hexagram, glancing up at the intricate grillwork in the ceiling, stopping to inspect one of the six small silver caskets on pedestals set at the points of the star.

He opened the casket and let his fingers caress the parchment of the ancient book inside. A folio copy of the Koran. A freshet of blood fell from his lip onto one of its pages. As his blood touched the paper the Power roiled inside him like steam in a dynamo, threatening to burst his skin. He jerked his hand away from the page before damage was done.

Yes; the room worked perfectly, just as the Vision had revealed; it amplified his Power like sunlight through a magnifying glass.

He stopped at the last casket: the only empty one.

One more book and I can complete the Holy Work. And Frederick is on his way with it now; I'll have it within days.

Colored lights flashed around the corners of his sight—ribbons of reds, greens, violets—signaling the onset of the Vision.

Throbbing in his head like a drum, blood pouring from his nose, the Reverend staggered to the center of the star, moaning softly. His hands hung freely at his sides; tingling ran down his arms and legs, horror and wonder filling his insides as the Vision came close. His gaze drifted to the corner of the room where the pit descended; the abandoned mine shaft he'd found waiting here as the Vision had indicated: black, hollow, bottomless. A gust of wind from the depths rustled his hair, its emptiness promising the consummation of his thousand darkest dreams.

The Reverend's eyes rolled back as the Vision seized hold of his muscles and threw him to the floor, legs kicking furiously, fists clenched, arms lashing out in fitful spasms, head thrashing from side to side, bucking against the floor, spittle foaming at his lips, violent, pitiable animal cries strangling his throat.

But his mind stayed clear. An explosion ripped through his center.

The Light from Below, holding him.

And through the folds of its bright embrace, even in the grip of his horrible ecstasy, rumbling from the pit he heard a whisper of the Beast.

book four

THE NEW CITY

chapter thirteen

*A*S THE SUN SETS, OUR TRAIN IS CROSSING THE MISSISSIPPI RIVER near St. Louis. We departed Chicago at noon; if we meet our connecting train without delay, the journey to Flagstaff, Arizona, will take twenty-four hours. At the station there, a chartered train will be standing by to transport us to the city of Prescott, according to our map less than sixty miles from the location of The New City. How long the ride there will take depends on factors we cannot yet determine: terrain, weather, the quality of roads. Suffice it to say we will make our way as swiftly as humanly possible, and then see what we shall see. Not quite the deluxe excursion of the West Teddy Roosevelt had in mind.

Presto has generously agreed to provide the necessary funding from his apparently limitless reserves; he has hired three private sleeping compartments for the six of us on board. We must all try to rest during this leg of the journey; as difficult as that seems, it may be the last good opportunity we have.

The others are forward in the dining car. JS remains alone in the compartment next to mine. Since his recent confession to me on the train, he has retreated steadily deeper into silence and brooding melancholy. I wish I could say he was preparing for what he senses is to come; I'm more inclined to think what we're witnessing is the slow, strangling death of a personality. Even the realization that his brother survived has not restored the same sense of purpose to him; it is a black and solitary light that burns in Jack's eyes. And after all the man has endured, I do not know how much more any soul can bear.

These three we travel with—Jack, Presto, the Indian woman Mary Williams—and the absent Jacob Stern have been given a responsibility by the common dream that remains out of their reach, one that for whatever reason Innes and I do not explicitly share. But we each have our roles to play and if mine is to act the detective to uncover their true purpose, that is more than enough. I suspect, however, that a more valuable contribution would be to find a way to return Jack to some measure of himself before the final confrontation. Without Jack at the top of his game, whatever lies ahead for these people can end only in disaster. Our time is short; there is only one card left I can think of to play.

Tonight.

The black tower came into view as their wagons skirted the last cluster of rocks and rounded the turn into the settlement; they could see figures milling like ants around the scaffolding that enveloped its central tower as it rose over two hundred feet above the desert floor. Construction was still a fair way from completion—even from this distance sections of its facade appeared to be little more than a shell.

But for all that, to come upon such a stark, incongruous spectacle thrusting skyward from the heart of a wasteland took their breath away.

"That's what you saw in your dream?" asked Eileen, moving up beside Jacob on the driver's seat.

"Close enough," said Jacob, mouth going dry, heart thumping against his ribs. The sight seemed to paralyze him.

"You too?" asked Eileen.

Peering out from the shelter of the canvas flap, Kanazuchi nodded.

"Okay," said Eileen slowly, trying to center her mind on practical concerns. "What do we do now?"

"I haven't the slightest idea," said Jacob.

"But—But you said you'd know what to do when you saw it."

"Give me a moment, dear, please. It's unnerving enough to come across something like this to begin with. Without even considering the implications of . . . of what . . ." He faltered badly. She noticed the reins trembling in his hands.

Good God, I've made a terrible mistake, Eileen realized. I've been assuming the poor man had some sort of plan, that if what they had dreamt about turned out to be true, he would be able to lead us through whatever followed, but he's frightened and fragile and may have no better idea about how to proceed from here than I do.

"Of course, Jacob," she said. "Bit of a stunner, after all. We'll just have to see, won't we?"

He ran a hand nervously over his chin and couldn't seem to tear his eyes off the tower. She handed him a canteen and held the reins for him as he took a long drink.

"I'm so thirsty," he said quietly and drank again.

A groaning of wood from the wagon's interior. Eileen peered back through the flap; Kanazuchi had ripped up one of the planks in the floor bed with his bare hands. Reaching down, he laid his long sword inside the cavity beneath the boards.

"What are you doing?" she asked.

He didn't answer. She noticed he had changed back into his black pajamalike coolie clothes; Jacob's clothes lay folded in a neat bundle. Kanazuchi replaced the plank, concealed his second smaller sword, no more than a long knife, in the waist of his belt, then moved next to them at the opening.

"Jacob," he said quietly.

Jacob turned abruptly to face him, sweat running off his brow, fear lighting his eyes, his breathing rapid and shallow. Their looks engaged. Kanazuchi reached out a hand, and with the tips of his fingers touched Jacob gently on the forehead. Jacob's eyes closed and Kanazuchi's features settled into an expression Eileen had never seen him wear in the short time she had known him; no less feral and alert than before but tempered by a softening of character that suggested deep kindness and a wellspring of compassion.

How completely unexpected, thought Eileen. But then the man claims to be a priest, doesn't he?

Jacob's breathing slowed and settled; the bunched lines on his forehead smoothed. After a minute of this contact, Kanazuchi took his hand away and Jacob opened his eyes.

They were clear again. The fear was gone.

"Remember," said Kanazuchi.

Jacob nodded. Kanazuchi started toward the back; boldly, Eileen reached out and took him by the arm.

"What did you just do?" asked Eileen.

He studied her for a moment; she felt no danger and saw depths in his eyes, realizing how much of himself he kept concealed.

"Sometimes we must remind each other," said Kanazuchi, "of who we really are."

He bowed his head slightly, respectfully. Eileen released her grip. Then, moving like a shadow, Kanazuchi slipped silently out the back of the wagon. Eileen watched him sprint across a stretch of desert and disappear behind a stand of rocks. She looked carefully but did not see him again.

"What did he just do to you?" she asked Jacob.

"If I didn't know any better, and I do, I would say it was something along the lines of . . . a laying on of hands," he said, climbing into the back.

"Fiddlesticks."

"Now, now; just because a man carries a sword doesn't mean he's a bad person."

"He chops people's heads off."

"My dear lady, we shouldn't impose the values of our culture onto a person from one so completely different from our own, should we?"

"Heaven forbid. And just to show how open-minded I am, maybe I'll take up head shrinking as a hobby."

"I'm sure he could furnish you with a regular supply for practice," he said laughing. "Excuse me, Eileen; before we arrive, I think it best if I changed back into my own clothes. You're supposed to be carrying a sick old rabbi in this rattletrap." He closed the flap and picked up a few wispy scraps of hair from the floor of the wagon. "The beard, I'm afraid, is a total loss."

"If anyone asks, tell them it's a side effect of your disease."

She cracked the reins, urging their mules to catch the other wagons. Moments later, from the back she heard Jacob whistling happily away.

What a remarkable change had come over Jacob since Kanazuchi attended to him, wondered Eileen. But they were both priests and they shared that strange dream; perhaps that meant they had more in common than she could possibly imagine.

"Seems we have company," said Jacob, looking out the back of the wagon. Clouds of dust rose in the far distance on the road behind them; another string of wagons.

Moments later a convincing, albeit beardless, rabbi again, Jacob rejoined Eileen, took the reins, and enjoyed his first look at The New City. The town lay half a mile ahead; twin rows of sturdily constructed clapboard buildings lined either side of a main avenue that terminated at the tower construction site. Only a few of the buildings grouped near its midpoint carried a second story; from there ramshackle houses, little more than shacks, spread out in a disorderly sprawl that extended as far as they could see. The hump of a domed barnlike warehouse, the only other sizeable structure, rose out of their midst to the south.

"My," said Jacob. "These people have been very, very busy."

Directly ahead another guardhouse stood in their way. High barbed wire fences ran away from it in both directions and encircled the settlement, leaving a broad bare hundred-yard stretch of desert between the fence and the city limits. Armed guards wearing the same white tunics moved out from the gate to meet them as the wagons approached.

"Jacob, I don't mean to be a bother. . . ." She was chewing her lip.

"Yes, dear."

"Have you had any more thoughts about my original question?"

"I have, actually; I suggest we smile a great deal and do exactly what is expected of us, while patiently acquiring a sense of the town and who is in charge. You are scheduled to perform here for a week, yes? So we have some time, and as welcome guests this may require less effort than you might suppose. Particularly for someone so effortlessly charming as yourself."

"Okay." Not bad so far.

"Then, very quietly, we should try to find out where they are keeping the books."

"And then? . . ."

Jacob turned to her and smiled. "Please, my dear, a little forbearance; I'm having to improvise here."

"Sorry," she said, striking a match and lighting a cigarette. "Part of my training; I like to have all my lines before I walk out on stage."

"Perfectly understandable."

"And him," she said, nodding toward the rocks where Kanazuchi had disappeared. "What about him?"

"I assume our mysterious friend will proceed along similar lines. We know he's left his weapon here in the wagon; at some point, he'll certainly come back for it."

"We can't very well sit in the wagon all night waiting for him. . . ."

"If he needs us for any reason, he seems more than capable of finding where we are."

Eileen inhaled deeply, let out a cloud of smoke. The guardhouse less than fifty yards off, white shirts fanning out to meet Bendigo in the lead wagon.

"We could die in there," she said.

"The thought had occurred to me."

"It feels sort of ridiculous under the circumstances. Even more than usual. Putting on a play."

"One could also die in bed tonight or have a horse fall on him, or God forbid be struck by lightning from a clear blue sky," he said gently. "That doesn't mean we shouldn't go on living."

She looked at him, chucked her cigarette away, and put her arms around him, laying her head on his shoulder. He touched her hair tenderly. She liked the way he felt and wanted to cry but fought off the tears, reluctant to appear weak.

"Don't go and die on me just yet, all right?" she said. "We've only just met, but I'm growing rather fond of you, you old bag of bones."

"I will try to cooperate. But only because you insist," he said with a laugh.

The wagons ahead slowed to a stop; Rymer, standing up and waving his hat, had a brief exchange with the guards before the gate was raised and the wagons waved through.

"You're supposed to be sick," she reminded him.

Jacob handed her the reins and took his place in the rear before they reached the gate. Eileen returned the enthusiastic waves of the smiling guards as they passed under a sign that read WELCOME TO THE NEW CITY.

"Hello. Hello," she called to them, then muttered through her dazzling smile, "Nice to see you, too, you right bunch of sods. Keep smiling, that's good, you deranged pack of prairie weasels."

The troupe drove through no-man's-land and down Main Street. Facades of all the buildings flanking them sparkled with fresh coats of whitewash; bright flowers in boxes underlined every window and chintz curtains softened their interiors. Plain well-crafted signs announced each building's purpose: dry goods, dentist, silver- and blacksmith, hotel, variety store. Smiling citizens stood outside each establishment on the scrubbed, planked sidewalks and waved happily to the passing wagons. Their shirts gleamed an immaculate white; they all looked healthy and clean.

Ahead on the left a crowd had gathered under a marquee outside the opera house, where a banner read: WELCOME PENULTIMATE PLAYERS. A joyful cheer went up as the wagons rolled to a halt next to the theater entrance and the ovation continued as more people ran down the street to join the throng, all wearing wide grins and the same white tunics.

Bendigo Rymer stood up again on his perch, waved his hat all around, and bowed deeply in every direction.

The sot's convinced they're all here to welcome him, thought Eileen. Like he died and went to heaven.

"Thank you! Thank you so much," said Bendigo, unheard

above the cheering, his eyes awash in tears. "I can't tell you how much your being here to meet us means to me: such a wonderful, generous reception."

"I don't believe that I have ever seen a man so desperately starved for affection," said Jacob with quiet wonder.

"Count that as a blessing."

The rest of the players were poking their heads out of the other wagons with similar confusion; so far all they'd done was drive into town; what would this crowd be like when they actually gave a performance?

The cheering died instantly as a huge man in a long gray duster, the only person they'd seen in the city not wearing a white tunic, strode out of the pack and approached Bendigo's wagon, accompanied by a frowsy woman carrying an open notebook.

"Welcome to The New City, my friends," said the big man.

"Thank you, I—" started Bendigo.

"Isn't it a glorious day?"

"Indeed, indeed, sir, the likes of which I have never—"

"Are you Mr. Bendigo Rymer, friend?" asked the big man.

"The same, sir, at your service . . ."

"Would you step down and have your people come out of the wagons and get together here for me, please?"

"At once, sir!" Bendigo turned to the other wagons and clapped his hands. "Players! Front and center, double time, all together!"

The actors and stagehands gathered beside Bendigo; utterly silent now, and still smiling, the crowd pressed in surrounding them. Eileen helped Jacob out of the back of their wagon and, making it appear as if he was still quite infirm, helped him walk haltingly to the front.

"May I humbly present, for your employment and delectation, Bendigo Rymer's Penultimate Players," said Bendigo, doffing his stupid green hat with a flourish.

The big man carefully counted heads. No one in the crowd moved or whispered. He looked down at the woman's notebook, then counted heads again, finished, and frowned.

"Supposed to be nineteen of you," he said to Bendigo.

"Pardon me?"

"S'only eighteen people here. You said nineteen at the gate. You got an explanation for that, Mr. Rymer?"

Rymer gulped and looked around, caught Eileen's eye, and briefly registered the sight of Jacob without his beard. Eileen saw the man's puny mind working like a hamster on a wheel. He took a step toward the big man, folding his arms, assuming a completely unauthentic camaraderie.

"Yes, of course, it's quite simple really Mr. . . ."

Bendigo fished for a response; the big man stared at him and smiled.

"Uh, my good sir. You see . . . this gentleman here," said Rymer, turning and pointing at Jacob, "joined our company in Phoenix, when he took ill, and I must have neglected to include him in our number."

"Then that ought'a be one more, not one less," said the big man. "Shouldn't it?"

Bendigo's smile froze on his face, stricken and fresh out of bright ideas. Eileen walked quickly forward to them.

"I'm sure I can explain," she said calmly. "We did have another gentleman with us when we left the station in Wickenburg, a doctor who traveled along for a while, to make sure our friend made a proper recovery."

"So where'd he go?" asked the big man.

"He rode back yesterday; he'd brought his horse along, tied to the back of our wagon; the last wagon, you see, trailing quite a ways behind the others—I'm afraid driving a team of mules is somewhat new to me—so Mr. Rymer must have failed to notice when the doctor took his leave."

"That's it, of course," said Rymer, sweat greasing his forehead. "The extra man."

The big man looked back and forth between them, smiling, betraying no reaction. Eileen noticed pistols strapped to the belt under his coat and the handle of a shotgun protruding from a deep inside pocket.

"So this man here," he said, pointing at Jacob. "He's not one of you."

"No, no, not at all," said Rymer hastily.

"He's a *friend*," said Eileen.

"What's his name?"

"His name is Jacob Stern," said Eileen.

The big man gestured to the woman; she wrote the name down in her notebook. Then she turned the page.

"I need the names of the rest of your people now," said the big man.

"Of course, sir," said Rymer, fumbling out a list.

"What's your name?" asked Eileen.

"What's yours?"

"I asked you first," she said.

Bendigo turned and shot her a dirty glance; Eileen half expected him to kick her in the shin.

"Brother Cornelius, ma'am," said the man with a menacing smile.

"Eileen Temple," she said, extending her hand. The big man looked down at it, slightly off balance, then shook it lightly. "Quite a beautiful town you have here, Brother Cornelius."

"We know," said Cornelius.

"Would you please stop?" whispered Bendigo to her under his smile.

"You'll be staying at the hotel, just down the street," said Cornelius. "We'll escort you there after you take your stuff into the the-a-ter."

"Marvelous, so looking forward. I'm sure it's an absolutely splendid facility," gushed Bendigo.

"You tell me," said Cornelius. "You'll be the first to use it."

He gestured roughly; the woman handed Rymer a stack of leaflets.

"These are the rules in The New City," said Cornelius. "Please give one to each of your people. Ask them to obey. Our rules are important to us."

"Of course, Brother Cornelius," said Bendigo.

"Reverend Day would like to invite you to be his guests at dinner tonight," said Cornelius, with a look at Jacob. "All of you." He gave a sharp look at Eileen; she glanced away.

"How absolutely splendid," said Rymer. "Please tell the

Reverend we would be most honored to accept his invitation. What time would—"

"Eight."

"And where would—"

"We'll come get you," said Cornelius. "Have a glorious day."

He walked back into the crowd out of sight. Giddy with relief, Rymer handed out the fliers to the company. Cheerful volunteers came forward from the crowd to help the stage-hands unload their cargo.

Eileen realized she had never seen so many people of so many different races harmoniously grouped together before.

Something was dreadfully wrong here.

Kanazuchi watched their exchange from rocks above and outside of the fence to the east of town. With the naked eye, he could not make out their words from this distance, but he could read expressions and gestures like printed characters. It told him this:

The white shirts moved as one body, like insects in a hive.

No one of the white shirts realized yet that anyone else had been on board the last wagon; the stupid actor in the loud green hat had nearly given him away until Eileen stepped forward.

The big man, the one who'd asked the questions, was dangerous. Because of this man's attention, Jacob would soon be in trouble; he could not allow anything to happen to the old man. When the moment came, Jacob would be needed; for what exactly, only time would reveal.

Kanazuchi recognized he could do nothing until nightfall, four or five hours away. Regular armed patrols moved below him on either side of the fence; he would observe them for a while to understand their patterns.

After the actors unloaded their cargo, he watched them drive the wagons to a stable on the southern side of town: The Grass Cutter was safe for now and he knew where to find it.

He turned and studied the tower he had seen in the vision. Watched the workers swarming around its base.

When darkness came, that was where he would begin.

*   *   *

Innes burst into the compartment, holding a telegram. "I've secured horses, maps, weapons, and supplies; they'll be waiting for us at the station in Prescott." He handed Doyle a copy of the manifest he'd drawn up. "Took the liberty of putting this together; if there's something else you think we need, there's still time to wire ahead for it."

The boy's military stripe coming to the fore, thought Doyle with no small satisfaction as he glanced at the list.

"More than adequate," said Doyle, handing it back.

"Repeating rifles; I assume you both know how to shoot," said Innes, looking around at Presto and Mary Williams.

They nodded. Presto resumed the story he was relaying to Doyle; Jack's behavior at the time of Rabbi Brachman's death.

"Are you sure the man can be trusted?" asked Presto. "He seems to have an alarming disregard for human life."

Doyle looked outside at the moonlit plains rushing past the window.

"Leave us a moment would you?" asked Doyle of the other men.

Innes and Presto exited the compartment; Doyle turned to Mary.

"You have a connection to Jack. Through the dream."

She nodded, her eyes not leaving his, steady and strong.

"I've done all I know how to do for him. My diagnosis . . . offers no solutions. Do you have an idea about the reason for his illness?"

"Sometimes people are attacked by . . . an outside force."

"What do you mean?"

She hesitated. "Evil."

"Do you believe evil exists? As a separate entity?"

"That is our teaching."

Doyle took a deep breath, stepping off into unknown territory.

"Then if you're going to try and heal him," he said to the Indian woman, "you'd better get on with it."

She looked at him solemnly, nodded once, and moved to the door.

"Anything I can do?" asked Doyle.

"No," she said and quietly left the compartment.

Buckskin waited until the light faded from the western sky before he left the shelter of the rocks. The singing from the hollow stopped before dark and the kids in the white shirts lit a big campfire as the cold came on. Before the moon rose up, Frank led his horse across the road, away from the guardhouse, where lamps were still burning, and along the perimeter of the fence.

Ten double strands of barbed wire had been slung between posts drilled twenty paces apart; sunk deep in the sand, filled with mortar, built to last. The wire was a mix of Ric Rac and Hollner Greenbriar, two strands with a serious bite; a run-in with this much of the stuff could cut an animal, or a man, to shreds. These folks knew how to build a righteous fence, he had to give them that; must be some ranch hands among the gospel thumpers. But were they raising cattle in there? This wasn't grazing country; three strands of wire was enough to do the job on any range, and no fence he'd ever seen needed to run seven feet high to contain a herd. No; this fence had been put up for keeping something *out*.

Every half mile inside the lines, they'd added a watchtower, a covered platform twenty-five feet high with a ladder running up to a cabin. Manned by white-shirted guards toting Winchesters; Frank had to ride back a few hundred yards from each one to stay out of their sight.

A few miles along, coming back to the fence after skirting a tower, he saw a field of light shimmering five or six miles ahead across the sand; a good-sized town, the center of this strange settlement. If the Chinaman had been hiding in one of the actors' wagons, that was where he'd be now.

Frank sat still in the saddle, shivering in his coat, and studied the situation. The fence ran on ahead to the left out of sight; he had no reason to believe it wouldn't complete a ring all the way around the settlement. They'd most likely included another couple of gates somewhere along the loop, which meant he could try to ride past the guards there or cut his way in anywhere on the fence. How he was supposed to ride back out again with a dead Chinaman strapped to the butt of his horse was a different story.

Mexico, on the other hand, lay two easy days' ride south, and there were no fences or guards anywhere between here and there. He could shave off his moustache. Lighten his hair with some lemon juice like he'd heard about in prison.

That dark-haired gal was inside there, too. As he thought of her, the sight of Molly Fanshaw's body lying on that Tombstone street two stories below him with her sweet neck broke came back. The empty whiskey bottle in his hand . . .

He shook it off; his face tightened painfully.

Bad enough living in a cell with those memories; on the outside, there's a thousand reminders of your every failing. And as it turns out, a whole lot more disgust about your old selfish ways than you ever knew was inside you, ain't there, Frankie boy?

Was that Molly's voice or his own? He'd been hearing Molly more and more inside his head. Helpful words, teasing and gentle, the way he liked to remember her. Did that mean he was just turning soft or going crazy? Was she dead and gone or riding shotgun in his mind?

Shit. Did it matter?

His eyes picked up light and movement inside the fence to his left; what was that? Long way off. He took out the field glasses, scanned for the flickering he'd seen.

Torches. A wide column of white shirts giving off a faint glow in the early moonlight. Carrying rifles, parade formation, a hundred of them at least, and a big man in a long duster riding alongside, watching like a drill sergeant.

Whatever the hell this added up to, it was a damn sight worse than some crazy Chinaman running around with a meat cleaver.

The dark-haired gal was in there.

Frank began to reach for the wire cutters in his saddlebag but stopped short when he heard Molly's voice:

You want to think you're doing it for the girl, that's fine, Frankie. But let's be clear about something: You got some serious scores to settle up with yourself first. You can go right ahead and make a martyr of yourself, Buckskin Mc-Quethy, but nobody's insisting you have to be an ox about it. Cut your way through that fence and in ten minutes you're like to have a hundred rifles staring at your face. And be honest, Frank; talking your way out of trouble ain't never been your long suit.

Never could sneak a nickel past Molly; she knew him inside and out.

Frank turned his horse and rode down the fence line, looking for the next gate.

As Buckskin Frank bunked down outside to wait for the sunrise, Kanazuchi was using his hands to separate two strands on the inner fence. His long knife would have cut through the wire without trouble, but he couldn't leave tracks, and with only five minutes between patrols, he couldn't hesitate; the moon would be high soon and take away his only advantage.

He pulled open the wires like strings of a long bow and slipped smoothly through the narrow opening. The wound on his left side throbbed painfully as he called on the muscles around it to complete the difficult maneuver, careful not to snag his shirt on the razor-sharp barbs; if this had been his fence, he would have coated them with poison.

Easing the wires back into place, he erased his footprints in the sand and set off at a dead run for the nearest shelter, a shed one hundred yards away across open ground. If a patrol had been watching all they would have seen was a blur.

Folding into the shadows against the wall, he opened his senses; sounds from all over the town reached him here, two blocks off the main street. One-room shanties built nearly on top of each other stretched out in every direction; wood fires burning in stoves, smoke rising from crude chimney pipes. Food cooking. Chickens in backyard coops. Horses moving in stalls of a nearby stable. Smell of urine from a nearby latrine. Someone passed by; a white shirt, carrying yoked pails of water. Kanazuchi erased himself in the darkness. Waited for the footsteps to recede.

The tower stood half a mile off, its blackness carving an

even darker hole in the night sky. Construction continuing; bright lights, hammering and scraping of rock. He could pick his way among the shacks to get there, avoiding the main street altogether.

He dodged down alleys, retreating into hollows and shadows whenever anyone approached. Occasionally he caught glimpses of the white shirts in shacks through open windows, sitting motionless before their fires, silently at tables, lying on crude cots with their eyes open. As he stepped through a narrow gap between houses, he heard weeping: Through an open door he saw a woman sobbing, curled up on the floor; a man sat at a table, ignoring her, quietly eating from a bowl.

No dogs bothered him as he moved between the shacks; these people kept no pets. Strange in a community this size. And he heard no laughter; always a keynote in the night sounds of any city; families, lovers, people gathering, drinking. None here. Something else missing: He had seen no children. Many couples, but no children.

Turning a corner, he came face-to-face with the youngest person he'd seen, a boy perhaps fifteen, wearing the white shirt and carrying a bucket of slops. Neither of them moved; the boy stared at him without interest, dull and lifeless, then turned and trudged away.

Kanazuchi picked up a rock from the ground, glided around the next building, and waited; moments later, two adult males appeared from the direction the boy had gone, carrying cudgels and lanterns, raising them high, searching for an intruder. Kanazuchi threw the rock far in the opposite direction, rattling a tin roof; the men turned and headed toward the noise.

Soon Kanazuchi reached the edge of the settlement; a quarter mile of open ground inclined up a gradual rise to the construction site. The church's two wings extended out from either end of the building, in the shape of a capital "E" laid on its side; above its center section rose the black tower from his dream.

Spiraling minarets adorned the spired reaches of the structure; walls covered by a mass of irregular forms and shapes he could not distinguish from so far away. Stonemasons chiseled away at these forms from scaffolds wrapped around the wings.

The tower in the middle, as high as the building was long, looked closest to completion. Oblong slits perforated a bulging capsule at its peak, perhaps a bell tower, a black slate roof above.

Immense, narrow doors yawned open at the tower's base; sheets of suspended linen prevented Kanazuchi from glimpsing its interior. Paths in the dirt circled the church and led out to work and supply stations; quarried squares of rock, a lumber mill, tool sheds, firing ovens for the bricks. The entire site teemed with an army of workers. He saw no overseers in the group; each man and woman seemed purposeful and self-directed.

A quarter mile behind the building rose a sheer mountain of smooth rock, a pale monolithic dome reaching twice again as high as the central tower. When viewed straight on, the rock provided a dramatic backdrop that accentuated the tower's stark visage. Between the construction site and the rock lay its rear entrance, less heavily trafficked.

He waited for the moon to drift behind a cloud, then left the cover of the shanties, moving into the open, away both from the tower and the town, then circled back to the outcroppings of the massive rock formation. The back of the church came into view; nowhere near the same level of activity back here. The rear facade exhibited nothing like the front's refinement and detail; its builder had designed his church to be viewed from the front.

Kanazuchi observed the workers' routines as white shirts periodically pushed wheelbarrows of debris out the back entrance, dumping their loads into a widespread area of waste a hundred paces toward the dome. He crept down to the edge of the site and concealed himself behind a mound of dirt.

When the next worker approached, Kanazuchi waited until he lifted the barrow to empty it, then snapped his neck with a single blow and dragged the body behind the dirt. He stripped the dead man's clothes, put them on over his own; white tunic, pants, and boots. A rough cotton weave, the pullover shirt had an open collar and hung to the middle of his thighs, leaving room for him to tuck the long knife, the *wakizashi*, in the back of his belt. Pulling down the dirt with his hands, he quickly buried the body.

Retrieving the wheelbarrow, he encountered a second worker arriving with another load; the pale, slender young man dumped out his barrow, hardly noticing him. Kanazuchi grabbed the handles of his wheelbarrow and followed the man along the path back toward the rear doors. As they approached, the immense scale of the black cathedral came clear to him; the largest building he had ever seen. From its base, Kanazuchi looked up and could not see the summit of the central tower.

They entered down a ramp of wood set on a flight of stairs lit by torches in brackets on the walls. Workers were laying sheets of slate on one section of floor. Others chipped away at arches and portals; some applied mortar to cracks between the blocks of stones. Kanazuchi pushed his wheelbarrow into the central chamber of the church, unable to distinguish the high reaches of the walls rising above him in the dim light. But he could feel the cold, black sense of dread in the room.

He remembered drawings the priest at their monastery had shown him of European cathedrals and thought they must feel similar to this place; cold and threatening, designed to frighten and browbeat its worshipers. In his land, churches were gentle buildings, tied to the land around them, built to inspire harmony and inner peace. He wondered again what sort of god they followed in these Western countries that needed so badly to be feared.

In his vision, Kanazuchi had been shown a chamber buried below the main hall of the tower, a room where he had seen the Chinese men working. Perhaps it lay somewhere beneath where he was standing now; the debris behind the church could have come from such an excavation. If the room did exist, he needed time to search out its entrance.

A row of rectangular gaps in the walls on either side of the hall awaited windows, but stained glass had been installed in one opening; a round window directly above the rear doors was illuminated by a bright beam of moonlight that projected the image in the glass onto the black stone floor:

A perfect red circle of light, pierced by three jagged bolts of lightning.

He noticed the floor sloped in a gentle concavity toward its center, where this red circle projected. Kneeling to look closer, he saw that narrow gutters had been carved in the stone throughout the room, leading down to a network of connecting grills in the lowest point of this subtle basin. A cool wind blew up through the grillwork from below.

As Kanazuchi reached to examine the grills, bells in the tower above him began to ring, creating a deafening din inside the building. At the first strokes, the workers around him immediately stopped what they were doing, laid down their tools, and moved toward the front of the cathedral. Kanazuchi followed, mixing in with the workers as they funneled through the open doorway. He hid himself in their midst, a hundred of them, as they massed silently before the entrance; he spread his senses into the crowd around him and realized with a jolt: Only one mind at work here. No thoughts, no noise, no inner voices. One mind directing all these bodies.

Foremen dressed in black appeared on either side, armed with rifles. Looking ahead, Kanazuchi saw another equally sized group of white shirts approaching from the west: the next shift. More brown, black, and yellow faces than white, he noticed; the same as those around him.

The two work details moved past each other, exchanging only vacant smiles. The new group entered the church and the sounds of methodical labor resumed. Kanazuchi's shift marched half a mile west, splintered into smaller groups, and entered three low buildings; workers' residences. He obediently trailed the ones before him into their dormitory under the watchful eye of stationed armed guards; none paid him any attention.

Rows of double bunks lined the room's interior, accommodations for forty, both men and women. Exhausted workers dropped into the first bunk they came to; many fell asleep instantly.

Kanazuchi climbed into an upper bunk. The building closely watched from every side by guards. No other options; with the wound on his back still healing his body needed rest: He would sleep for a while.

The Reverend A. Glorious Day arrived an hour late for dinner. By then the actors, as was their custom, had long since consumed every edible substance placed within arm's reach. After passing what remained of the afternoon quietly at their hotel—the printed rules stated no one from outside the community could wander around town without an escort and none had been offered—the Penultimate Players had been summoned precisely at eight o'clock and led straight to the Reverend's private residence.

The House of Hope, announced the sign outside the large adobe hacienda, the most elegant of the buildings lining Main Street. Its dining room, like the rest of the quarters they caught a glimpse of on their way in, sported an odd mélange of lavish decorative styles—plush Victorian chairs, light Norwegian hutches, Persian carpets, oriental statuary—as if a dozen millionaire's households had been scrambled and redistributed.

Silent, cheerful, and attentive white shirts served a dinner of satisfying fare spiced with a Mexican accent. At its conclusion, Rymer seized the floor and proposed a toast with the fine red wine they were drinking—although alcohol was forbidden in The New City, according to their fliers, the House of Hope apparently had a separate set of rules. Rymer spent the last five minutes of his oratory congratulating his own great good sense on having brought the Players to this obviously enlightened outpost of civilization.

"Bravo, Mr. Rymer; your graciousness is exceeded only by your epic loquacity."

They turned. Reverend Day stood in the open doorway; he'd been there throughout Bendigo's lengthy testimonial, but no one in the company had seen or heard him enter.

Bendigo bowed deeply in the Reverend's direction, almost certain that he had been complimented.

"Now you really must explain for me," the Reverend went on, "how ever did you arrive at such a fascinating name for your little troupe?"

"Because if I do say so myself," came Rymer's reply, screwing himself up to his full sixty-seven inches, "we pride ourselves on providing our audiences with the penultimate in theatrical experience."

"Is that so?" said the Reverend, lowering into his seat; Eileen to his right, Bendigo to his left, then Jacob Stern. "Are you by any chance aware that the definition of *penultimate* is 'next to the last'?"

The self-satisfied grin on Rymer's face froze like a flower in a hail of sleet; his brain locked to a dead stop.

This one will be easier, realized Day, *than taking candy from a dead baby.*

Eileen appreciated the Reverend's jab, but as he sat down beside her and she got a first good look at him, the breath caught in her throat.

Her first thought: This man is dying.

The Reverend moved like an insect, stiff and mechanical, as if a steel rod had assumed the place of his spine. A dark suit hung on his thin body like limp masted sails. A spiny hump rounded his left shoulder and his left leg appeared to have withered. His hands were long and slender, loosely limbed, and covered with coarse black hair; they looked like the hands of an ape. The man's face appeared skeletal: a high domed forehead rising above deep-set luminous green eyes, cheeks collapsing above a white bony jawline. Black and gray tangles of lank hair fell from the crown of his head to his shoulders. Lumpish blood vessels coiled around the sides of his forehead, pulsating dimly. Bright, livid scars crisscrossed his stark marbled skin, as if he'd been cut apart and inexpertly reassembled.

I know this face, she said to herself. I've seen it before; I don't know where or why, but God knows it's not one you'd soon forget. She thought of bringing it up, but strong instinct warned her not to speak to him.

The Reverend made no attempt at introductions; he knew the names that were important to him, everyone quickly figured out who he was, and the actors all lost their voices the instant he appeared. His voice oozed with a deep southern accent—or was there a hint of British underneath?

Unaware of Eileen's spark of recognition, Jacob realized he had met this man before as well and he remembered where exactly: the Parliament of Religions, last year, in Chicago. But it was clear to Jacob, now shorn of his beard, that the Reverend Day could reclaim no memory of him; his magnetic eyes studied Jacob carefully but without a trace of identification.

His eyes are deadly, realized Jacob, glancing down at the last of his apple pie, heart accelerating. He had encountered people before whose will exerted a palpable force; this man projected it through his eyes like the flex of a muscle. Mustn't look in those eyes; he wanted to warn Eileen.

"And how are you feeling this evening, Mr. Jacob Stern?" asked the Reverend. "I understand you were taken ill somewhere along your journey."

"Much better, thank you," said Jacob, hoping Eileen would look at him; she was fixed on Reverend Day.

"You are obviously not a member of this company; may I ask what brings you to our corner of the world?"

"You could say I was a sort of tourist," said Jacob modestly. "A man enjoying his retirement, setting out to see the West . . ."

"What sort of community is this anyway?" asked Eileen, unable to stay her curiosity. "I'm assuming you're in charge here, so I mean, what's the point of it all? What's the purpose?"

Reverend Day turned to her for the first time, and she felt the force of his gaze hit her like a physical blow; his expression appeared casual, even friendly, but the power in his eyes sickened her, turning her stomach. The blood drained from her face; she had to look away.

"To serve God, Miss Temple," said the Reverend modestly. "And his son and Savior, Jesus Christ. *As should we all*. I'm sorry, weren't you given a copy of our flier? It contains all the basic information one should know about us. We hand one out to each of our visitors when they arrive."

He wants me to look at him, realized Eileen; he wants me to and I mustn't; I can feel his mind scratching at me like a spider trying to find a way to crawl inside my head.

"Forgive me for making the observation," said Jacob, keenly aware of her distress, trying to pull the man's attention off her, "but it seemed to me your flier was more concerned with the many things one *shouldn't* do."

Day turned slowly back to Jacob; his look hardened, just short of anger. "You might recall, sir, that even God gave us his thou-shalt-nots."

Doesn't like to be contradicted, thought Jacob. Certainly he's not used to anyone taking exception with him—and with eyes like those in his head, who in his right mind would want to? Well, go ahead and do your worst to an old man, you monster, but harm a hair on this woman's head and I'll make you regret the day you were born.

"Only ten of them," said Jacob. "You've got fifty."

"Strict obedience to God's will is a difficult and challenging path for any man to follow," said Day. "We make no claims of perfection, Mr. Stern, we merely strive for it."

"The world would applaud you for it. Why hide yourself away like this?"

"The world . . . is a wicked place, as I am sure in your travels you have not failed to notice. Our hope is to build a better world for ourselves within the confines of our City. That's why I call my home the House of Hope. And we expect visitors to respect our efforts, and our values, even if they don't necessarily agree with them."

"Respect, certainly," said Jacob.

Don't provoke him, Jacob; ease up.

The Reverend's eyes stayed fixed on Jacob, kindling a realization and deeper interest. "Are you by any chance a man of God yourself, Mr. Stern?"

Jacob's eyes met Eileen's briefly; now she was trying to warn *him* off.

"You might say so," said Jacob. "I'm a rabbi."

"Of course, now it makes sense to me," said Reverend

Day. "We have more than a few of your Israelite brethren among our number here, along with all the other failed faiths—converted, of course, to our way—but at one time sharing your beliefs."

"Win a few, lose a few," said Jacob, with a shrug.

The Reverend smiled patiently. "I would not wish to impose upon my guests the rigor of a theological debate, but perhaps *you* would care to sit with me, tomorrow, Rabbi Jacob Stern, and discuss our . . . differences."

"I welcome the opportunity, Reverend. But I must warn you that converting to Judaism is a very serious undertaking."

"In the service of God's Holy Work," said Day with a smile, "that is a risk one must always be willing to embrace."

Reverend Day turned back to Bendigo Rymer, who had been sitting motionless throughout and who now, blinking his eyes rapidly, appeared to emerge from a deep hypnotic trance.

"I trust you found our humble theater to your liking, Mr. Rymer," said Day, rising to his feet.

"Yes; wonderful, sir," said Rymer, deeply moved by the man's solicitude. "Marvelous facilities; thank you ever so much."

"Splendid. I cannot tell you how greatly we look forward to your performance tomorrow night," said Day.

Reverend Day bowed stiffly and quickly left the room. Jacob put a hand to his forehead, trying to contain the throbbing pain that suddenly collected there; Eileen moved to him in concern.

The rest of the Players, who felt as if they'd been holding their breath for an hour, let out a collective sigh of relief.

Walks Alone knocked softly on the train compartment door. No answer. She reached to knock again, and Jack Sparks threw open the door, a pistol in his hand, furious at the intrusion. She remained calm and waited for him to speak.

"What do you want?"

"May I come in?" she asked.

"Why?"

She looked at him, pushing gently through the wall of anger he had built around himself. Jack dropped his look, tucking the gun back in his belt. He held the door open for her; closed and locked it after she entered.

She sat, carefully controlling her breathing in order to send no harsh signals into the room; after a few tense moments, Jack sat across from her.

"I want to tell you about my dream," she said.

After a few moments: "Go ahead."

He watched her with a cold, impatient scowl. She took another deep breath; how she began was most important.

"In my dream the earth is my mother; my father is the sky. They are apart but they live side by side, touching each other along the horizon, in balance. Because they are in harmony, the animals are born into the world, each in the image of the gods who share the heavens and the earth. The people are the last creatures to appear, they take the longest to create."

"Why?"

"They carry the most responsibility. . . ."

"What does that mean?"

"They are the only ones who are given both light and darkness. Animals obey their gods without questioning; they know only goodness; the people are the only ones who must listen to both sides. They are the only ones who must decide."

"Decide what?"

"Which side is stronger in them."

She met his eyes briefly; anger flashed in him before she looked away.

"Did *he* send you here?" said Jack, jerking his head at the wall he shared with Doyle's compartment.

"I am only telling you my dream," she said simply, waiting.

"All right," he said finally.

"In my dream, the people have fallen from balance; they have forgotten that they were born from both earth and sky. Their minds grow strong but their hearts are closed; they have lost respect for the other animals and their gods. The people now believe they found their own way to the earth and that they are here alone, separate from the rest of creation. Their minds are strong, but by deciding to follow this path they have turned away from truth.

"This creates an emptiness in them. Into this emptiness come thoughts from the mind, thoughts that speak without the voice of the heart. Thoughts of power and controlling others. Darkness. This is how the wound begins to open."

"The wound?"

"The wound in the earth. The wound we have seen in our dream."

"In the desert."

She nodded. "What the people need is a healing, to bring the heart and mind together; what the mind tells them is that they need more power, and in this way the wound grows deeper. I am only telling you my dream."

Jack's look softened, interest creeping into his eyes, fighting the pain.

"In the dream we share, a tower has been built in the desert," she said, feeling confident enough to include him now. "My people use the medicine wheel to open their hearts and hear the voices of our gods; although we call out to the sky to hear them, we know the gods live inside us and that is where we must listen."

"And the tower?"

"This tower is like our medicine wheel, except it calls out to the darkness. A wound is open beneath it in the earth and the Black Crow Man asks the darkness to rise out of the wound and send its power over the earth."

"And this is how the darkness wins," said Jack.

"This is how time ends. This is how the people are destroyed; because they have opened the wound and allowed the Black Crow Man to invite this darkness into the world."

"Who is this man?"

"In each of us, the false voice of the mind. In the dream he is the one who leads the people to the wrong path and calls out the darkness from deep inside the earth."

"And in the real world," said Jack, "he is my brother."

She hesitated. "I believe that is so."

"Who are the Six?"

"The ones who are called to stop him."

"Called by whom?"

"That is not for us to say."

"But you and I are among them."

"We were given the dream. Yes, I believe that was the reason."

Jack sat silently, face contorting as he struggled with waves of emotion. She watched compassionately but made no movement toward him; he would have to reach for her.

"How? How can we stop him?" asked Jack, raw fear on his face, voice breaking. "I've tried before and I've failed. I've failed myself as well. I've let the darkness in." His voice fell to a whisper. "I'm afraid. Afraid that I'm not strong enough."

Walks Alone took another breath and looked at him directly for the first time; this was the moment.

"You must heal yourself. Before you try again," she said.

He stared at her, the last armor of protective rage melting away, vulnerable and real, tears pooling in his eyes.

"I don't know how to begin," he whispered.

"But you will try to stop him, anyway."

"Yes."

"Then you will fail again. Is that what you want?"

"No."

"You have no choice then."

He shook his head, agreeing. Tears ran freely down his cheeks.

She took his hands and held them tight. He looked at her.

"I will help you," she said.

The first scream from the adjoining berth woke Doyle instantly from a restless sleep. He rushed out his door, followed quickly by Innes; both men paused and listened at the door to Jack's compartment. A rhythmic chanting reached them, the woman's voice, and the musky odor of burning sage. Falling and rising above the chant they could hear low moaning, then another protracted scream that stood their hair on end.

"Good Christ," said Doyle.

"Sounds like he's being roast on a spit," said Innes.

Doyle pushed through the door; the sight greeting them stopped them in their tracks.

The cramped room blisteringly hot. Jack lay flat in the narrow space between seats, Walks Alone kneeling beside him. Jack unconscious, naked to the waist, his torso daubed with diagonal streaks of red and white paint; Mary Williams, wearing a loincloth and halter top, displayed some of the same colors patterned on her face. Smoke from two smudge pots, burning sage, choked the close air. A long wooden pipe lay on one of the seats and a four-foot length of willow stick, topped with an eagle feather, rested on the floor near Jack's head.

Both of them drenched with sweat, Jack writhed in agonizing pain as she rotated her hands, as if rapidly kneading dough, above his rib cage. Lost in fevered concentration, her features tense and sculpted, repeating over and over again the same incomprehensible incantation, she did not even glance up at the Doyles' arrival.

Another dreadful scream broke Jack's lips and his body bridged off the floor, taut as a bowstring. Realizing his cries could be heard up and down the length of the car, Doyle thought to close the compartment door, but he could not respond to the impulse when he saw something appear in her hands as she quickly raised them from Jack's chest:

A wobbly transparent mass of pink-and-red tissues about the size of an oblong grapefruit, a hot black jellied nugget burning in its center, mottled all around with curved bands of a sickly gray substance that like ribs seemed to give the object structure.

Something fetal, a larva, more insectoid than human, thought Doyle. He turned to Innes; his face had gone white as an egg. Doyle felt strangely reassured; at least Innes was seeing it, too.

The woman's hands continued to agitate, vibrating at such an impossibly high rate it made it difficult for them to determine whether the queasy handful was being shaken by her or animated by its own odious energy. Part of their minds questioned whether she held anything in her hands at all.

Jack's body collapsed hard onto the floor.

Doyle grabbed Innes and pulled him back out into the hall, closing the door quickly behind them. They stared at each other in shock, Innes blinking rapidly, his mouth working but producing no words.

Doyle raised a finger to his lips and shook his head. Innes walked immediately back to their cabin and retrieved a bottle of whiskey from his bag. Sitting down across from each other on their bunks, the brothers plied themselves with measured, medicinal doses and waited for the whiskey to expunge the repellent memory from their brains.

They said nothing further about it; no more cries were heard from next door during what little remained of the night.

SKULL CANYON, ARIZONA

The posse had already spent one hell-raising evening overrunning the Skull Canyon Hotel, and as the liquor began to flow on this second night, it seemed unlikely the town could contain them much longer.

The group was currently suffering a heated division about which menace to society they should hunt down first: the Chinaman or that back-stabbing, snake-eyed, double-dealing, son-of-a-whore convict Buckskin Frank McQuethy. But they were agreed that whichever one of these running dogs they caught up with first would get fitted for a hemp necktie pronto and swing from the nearest tree.

Sheriff Tommy Butterfield felt the most personal sense of betrayal; he'd gone to bat with the governor about Frank, for Christ's sake. Put his trust in the man, laid his own political future on the line, and this was how Buckskin repaid him: a note pinned to a stable wall and vanishing into the night. The rat bastard could be halfway to Guadalajara by now. Tommy had been able to persuade the posse to ride on to Skull Canyon according to Frank's instructions that morning, but when they got there and found him gone again, the call for retribution turned into a chorus.

Throughout the next day, the talk grew meaner and the interrogation of the hotel staff rougher, until finally one of the clerks admitted that Frank had not gone off toward Prescott as they'd originally told the posse—according to Frank's orders under a severe threat of death, he was fast to add—but had been seen riding west toward that religious settlement. Where the actors and Chop-Chop the Chinaman had been headed in the first place. Now the room really fell into an uproar.

We'll ride there tonight, went the prevailing sentiment, ride in shooting and root out both of 'em; God take pity on anybody who stands in our way. All that remained was figuring out how to find the place.

That's when the gentleman who'd been sitting quietly in the corner with his four traveling companions spoke up for the first time.

We know that road, offered the gentleman. In fact, we're headed that way ourselves, and we would be more than happy to show you the way.

Right now?

Yes, we were planning to leave tonight, the man explained. And we know a good campsite along the way should you decide to break up the ride.

What's *your* business in this religious place? somebody asked.

We're Bible salesmen, said the man, and sure enough one of his companions showed them a valise that was chock-full of holy books.

A caucus ensued among the posse's elders; these fellas looked legit, sharply dressed and groomed, obviously God-fearing men, and they seemed to know the territory. The verdict came back fast and unanimous: The posse would ride with them at once.

By the time the thirty-eight amateur lawmen had assembled outside, the five Bible salesmen were saddled up, ready to go. None of the vigilantes overheard their leader, the man who'd spoken up first inside, the handsome one with the slight German accent, say quietly to his companions:

"Wait for my signal."

to you. None of the fighters overheard it all leader, the man
would draw him up that made; the confidence and with the
silent column came a moment's embarrassment.

chapter fourteen

FRANK WAITED UNTIL FIVE MINUTES PAST SUNRISE TO RIDE
up to the gate; a man and woman wearing identical white
shirts, both carrying Winchesters, stepped out of the guardhouse to meet him.

"Welcome to The New City," said the woman.

"Nice to be here," said Frank.

"Isn't it a glorious day?"

"Seen worse," said Frank.

"What is your business with us today, sir?" Both of them
smiling.

"Figured on joinin' up," said Frank, grinning right back at
them.

"Joining . . . up?" asked the woman.

"Yup."

Their smiles wore down around the edges; they glanced at
each other uneasily.

"Joining up," said the man.

"Yup."

"Excuse us a moment, please, sir," said the woman.

The two moved back into the guardhouse, whispering to
each other; Frank could see the man through the window,
working a telegraph key. Looking up, he traced the suspended wire following the road toward the distant town. He
took out his field glasses and trained them east, where he'd
seen the military maneuvers taking place during the night;
looked like a firing range set up there, sandbags and targets.

Frank heard the telegraph key clicking; an answer coming
back. He tucked the glasses away as the guards moved back
outside, all smiles again.

"You may ride on ahead, sir," the woman said to him.
"Please stay on the road at all times. When you reach The
New City, someone will meet you with further instructions."

"Have a glorious day," said the man.

Frank tipped his hat and urged his horse forward. The gate closed behind him. The road was simple but well maintained: flat stones laid down in orderly rows, wide enough for a wagon, cutting straight through the shifting dunes. Smoke rising from chimneys in the distance. As he rode the five miles to the next gate, a black stain that came into view in the distance turned out to be a gigantic black tower. Once he realized what he was looking at, Frank stopped; he heard Molly's voice again:

Looks like you wandered into the middle of somebody's nightmare now, Frankie; don't know whose exactly—ain't yours, 'cause I'm not in it. What you gonna do?

You know me, Molly; in for a penny, in for a pound.

A vast shantytown spread out ahead of him. Surprising; from the outside he'd figured The New City would be all picket fences, shade trees, and freckle-faced kids; this looked more like one of those dirt-poor slums he'd seen squatting outside big cities in Mexico.

He moved on. Smiling faces waved him through a second gate. A pretty young girl met him on horseback at the guardhouse and escorted him to a stable just off the town's main street. Looking through an arch to a courtyard in back, Frank spotted the actors' wagons grouped against a wall.

He'd come to the right place, that much he could bank on.

A group of five smiling young people in white shirts, none of them older than eighteen, blacks and whites mixed together, eagerly greeting him as he climbed off his horse. A stable hand led the horse, and his Henry rifle in its saddle holster, away. They pressed a printed flier into his hands— "The New City Rules for Our Guests"—and asked him to surrender his sidearm.

"No weapons are allowed in The New City," said one of the shirts, pointing to Rule 14 on the sheet, which was nearly as long as his arm.

Frank saw no percentage in arguing and handed over his Colt.

"I'll keep the holster, if you don't mind," said Frank.

"We don't mind at all, sir," beamed one of them.

"Good," said Frank.

'Cause I'm probably gonna need those bullets for the gun I hid in my boot.

"Would you please take off your hat and put your hands over your head, sir?" asked another.

"Why?"

"So we can give you your shirt," said another.

Two of them opening one of the white shirts, ready to slip it over his head. Frank thought this over for a second and decided it pissed him off.

"No thanks," he said.

He handed back the list of rules and walked out of the stable. The welcoming committee trailed after him like a flock of anxious ducks.

"But everyone who wants to join us has to wear their shirt, sir. . . ."

"It says so right here in the rules."

Frank turned onto Main Street and kept walking; the avenue and the planked sidewalks crowded with busy, smiling people, all wearing the same white shirt. More than a few Chinese faces in the mix, Frank noticed. None that answered right off to the Chinaman's description, but enough of them to encourage the idea that Chop-Chop might not be far off.

Frank stopped, struck a match off a pillar, and lit up a cheroot. The five shirts following him whispered among themselves, confused; finally one of them, a bespectacled black kid, stepped forward.

"I'm sorry, sir, there's no smoking allowed in The New—"

Frank turned and shut him up with a look.

"How much you kids want to go fishing?" asked Frank, reaching into his pocket for a handful of silver dollars. "A buck apiece, how 'bout it?"

The six stared at him and each other in shock.

"There's no money here in The New City, sir."

"We have everything we need."

"All our needs are provided for."

"That figures," said Frank, putting the coins away.

"It's important for everyone to follow the rules."

"Sure it is, kid, or what you got is anarchy and that's no way to run a railroad, is it?"

They looked at him blankly until the somber, round-faced black kid, who was emerging as their leader, picked up the thread of their argument.

"Especially if a person wants to join. They told us you wanted to join."

"They did, did they?"

"You do want to join us, don't you, sir?"

"I'm thinkin' about it," said Frank, looking off up the street. A poster outside a large building ahead on the right caught his eye; bright colors, big print. He walked toward it.

"Because we have strict rules about people wanting to join us," said the black kid, continuing to tag along.

"Somehow that doesn't surprise me."

"We really need you to follow the—"

"What's your name, kid?"

"Clarence, sir," said the black kid.

"Tell you what, Clarence. Why don't you cut the crap and give it to me straight so I can make up my own mind? Who's running the show here?"

"Excuse me?"

"Who's the head honcho?"

"Our leader?"

"Who wrote the rules?"

"Our leader is the Reverend Day."

"Reverend A. Glorious Day," said another, enthusiastically.

"What's the 'A' stand for?" asked Frank.

More blank stares.

"What's so all-fired special about this Reverend Day?" asked Frank.

"Reverend Day speaks to the Archangel," said Clarence.

"He brings us the Word of our Lord."

"Through the Reverend we see Him—"

"We *commune* with Him, Brother Tad," corrected Clarence.

That stopped Frank dead on the sidewalk. "You what?"

"We commune with the Archangel."

They were beaming at him again like lunatics.

"Which Archangel is that?" asked Frank.

"We don't know his name, sir."

"He's just the Archangel."

"He sits at the left hand of God," said Clarence.

"That's what this Reverend Day tells you?"

"Oh yes, he knows the Archangel well. . . ."

"But we know Him, too, here, in our hearts," said Clarence. "When we have communion with Him."

"Whereabouts does all this communing take place?"

The white shirts smiled at each other like the answer was so obvious.

"All around."

"The Archangel is everywhere."

"We hear his voice wherever we go."

"We're never alone. . . ."

"You mean to say that, right now for instance, you hear a voice telling you what to do?" asked Frank carefully.

"Yes, sir; through Reverend Day the Archangel is always with us."

"Praise the Lord."

"Hallelujah."

"Okay," said Frank, nodding slowly, looking at all the smiling white shirts passing by on the street, more wary now that he realized he'd wandered into an insane asylum.

"And you'll hear the Archangel, too, sir, once you join us."

"After you meet Reverend Day, you'll understand."

"All the people who want to join us meet Reverend Day. . . ."

"What's the tower you're building over there for?" asked Frank.

"That's the Tabernacle of the Archangel, sir."

"So it's a church."

"Much much more than that, sir."

"When the Holy Work is finished, that's where the Archangel will appear," Clarence piped in eagerly.

"The Reverend says the Holy Work is near."

"It won't be long now."

"What a glorious day that will be!"

A chorus of hallelujahs followed.

Jesus Christ, thought Frank, they're crazier than a bunch of drunken monkeys at a taffy pull.

"Let me ask you something, Clarence," said Frank, putting a hand on the boy's shoulder and pointing to a poster for the Penultimate Players beside them on the wall. "This play is being put on tonight; have I got that right?"

"Oh yes, sir."

"And the actors for this thing, are they staying here in town?"

"Yes, sir; they're over at the hotel," said the black kid.

"Where would that be?"

"Just down the street."

"That's where all our visitors stay."

"That's where you'll be staying, too, sir."

"Well, why didn't you say so in the first place—"

Interrupting them, a commotion in the street: five men on horseback galloping up to a building across from them, scattering people out of their way. Unlike any other building on the street, a big adobe, like a ranchero's hacienda. A sign in front: The House of Hope.

Shouts from the riders; huge man in a gray duster coming down the steps of the House of Hope to meet them: the same man Frank had seen with the troops last night in the desert.

The five men well-dressed; dark clothes, covered with dust from a hard ride; one of them injured, the others helping him off his horse. Bloodstained bandage around what looked like a gunshot wound to his thigh. A tall, blond fella, the lead rider, hint of a foreign accent in his voice, shouting to the big man.

Something about a posse.

Shit.

The big man barking instructions; white shirts leading their horses off. Others wearing all black running down from the House of Hope to help carry the wounded one inside. One of the riders, a smaller blond, lifting a briefcase from his saddlebag before trailing the rest of them in. Over in less than a minute. Activity on the street returned instantly to normal; not a soul stopped to wonder or gossip about what they'd just seen.

Like no small town I've ever seen, thought Frank; a little excitement like that would set most folks off gabbing for an hour at least.

He watched the big man climb back up the stairs to the House of Hope and the realization nearly knocked off his hat.

He knew this fella from somewhere. Where was it?

Jesus, that was it: Cornelius Moncrief.

Head-buster deluxe for the railroad. Ten years ago, Moncrief came into Tombstone and nearly beat this poor little accountant fella to death in the middle of a full saloon. Claimed he'd run off after embezzling twenty thousand dollars from the home office. If it was true, Frank and the other deputies couldn't find any cash in the poor bastard's possession, but he refused to press charges so they couldn't stick Cornelius for the assault. And they could tell from Moncrief's attitude that he knew his position with the Southern Pacific brass made him untouchable.

Frank had escorted the big man to the edge of town on Wyatt's instructions and invited him to never set foot there again. Cornelius just laughed in his face and rode off; he was crazy and he liked to hurt people. That's why he lingered in the memory.

What the hell was he doing here?

"You'd better take me to the hotel," said Frank.

Kanazuchi slipped away from the workers' shacks after walking out to use the latrine. The guards weren't as sharp-eyed in the morning and they'd been busy doling out the workers' breakfasts, bowls of oatmeal and a crust of bread served in a mess hall between their huts.

Making his way through the shanties, Kanazuchi adopted the passive smiling face the white shirts wore and no one gave him a second glance. In the daylight, he saw that none of these buildings off the main street had been given paint or whitewash. No flowers or decoration. Only four thin walls and flat corrugated tin roofs. Filth and despair. The one attractive street served as a false display, to impress visitors. Or to keep the citizens in order.

His dream had told him he would find the Kojiki and the other holy books in the chamber below the church, but his mind had not found a way around the problem the church presented; how to search for an entrance with shifts of workers swarming over the area both night and day.

The rounded roof of a tall building to the south caught his eye and he moved in that direction. Along the way, he heard the sounds he had missed the night before:

Children's voices. Laughter.

He followed the sound to an enclosed compound, ringed by a fence of knotted barbed wire. Inside the circle, children were playing games in the dirt, over a hundred of them, running, tossing balls back and forth. Boys and girls, different races. None older than eight or nine. Low buildings lined the far side of the circle; their living quarters. A row of adults stood around the perimeter, not participating in the play, encouraging, or even supervising. Just watching.

Kanazuchi had seen enough now to realize the people in this city lived and moved under the most powerful form of mind control he'd ever witnessed; trying to probe beneath the surface of the workers' consciousness proved useless. How or why this group illusion gripped them so fiercely he could not determine; a blank, impenetrable wall had been built around their thoughts. But he sensed that the energy controlling these people was already beginning to decay.

And for some reason, these children were still free, even happy. Living together, apart from their families.

They are just waiting for them to reach the right age, Kanazuchi realized. Like ranchers raising a herd of livestock.

One of the children, a tiny curly-headed girl, chased a bright red ball to the edge of the fence. It rolled underneath the strands and stopped at Kanazuchi's feet; he picked up the ball and held it out to her. She looked at him coyly; he made the ball disappear with a deft sleight of hand, then reached through the fence and produced it from behind the girl's ear. She accepted it with a delighted gasp of astonishment and ran off laughing toward the others.

One of the adults inside the fence had noticed their inter-action; Kanazuchi raised the dead smile back onto his face, waved blandly, and walked away.

A two-story warehouse drew into sight, standing apart from the shanties in a clearing. He waited for the area to empty before crossing to its walls. Barn-style double front doors slightly open; two yawning whiteshirts patrolling with rifles. Kanazuchi walked slowly around to the rear, where he found a single door. Tried the handle, twisted quietly with all his strength until it yielded, then slipped inside.

Stacked wooden crates covered with canvas and tied to the ground by rope occupied most of the open floor space. Kanazuchi walked between rows piled as high as his head. Out of sight of the front doors, he cut the rope holding one stack and wedged open the crate. A dozen rifles inside, his estimate, more than a thousand rifles in the room.

A row of irregular shrouded shapes stood across from him; he lifted the canvas. Four round-barreled guns mounted on sturdy tripods. Countless smaller boxes stenciled with the word GATLING and filled with coils of linked ammunition belts piled nearby. He had never seen one before, but he had heard of such weapons: machine guns. He had also heard it said that one man armed with a machine gun in open ground could kill a hundred in less than a minute.

Sound nearby; a gentle rasp of snoring. He traced it to a white shirt sleeping on the ground three rows away, rifle beside him. An Asian face.

Chinese.

Kanazuchi picked up the rifle, reached down and tickled the man's nose with the tip of the barrel. He woke sluggishly, offering no reaction, even with the gun staring him in his face.

"Why are you sleeping on duty?" asked Kanazuchi in Mandarin.

"Will you report me?" the man answered flatly.

"What if I had been an intruder?"

"Don't talk in that language," the man said in English. "It is against the rules."

"I will report you if you do not answer my questions," said Kanazuchi in English.

"You should report me. I have broken the rules. I should be punished," the man said almost eagerly, the first emotion he'd exhibited. "That is your responsibility."

"Do you know what will happen to you?"

"I will be sent to the Reverend."

"What will the Reverend do to you?"

"I will be punished."

"How?"

"You must tell them what I have done. That is the rule. If you do not tell them, then *you* have broken the rules. . . ."

Kanazuchi grabbed the man's throat, cutting him off.

"When did you come to this place?" Kanazuchi asked in a whisper.

The man stared at him, not even bothered by the constriction to his breathing.

"How long ago did you come here?" asked Kanazuchi.

"Two years."

"There were men here who worked with explosives, Chinese; did you know them?"

The man nodded.

"They worked for the railroad; did you work for the railroad, too?"

The man nodded again.

"Where are they now?"

"Gone."

"They built something here, a room underground, under that church, do you know where this room is?"

The man shook his head. He told the truth.

"Is the Reverend the man they have built this for?" asked Kanazuchi.

The man nodded again. "Everything is for the Reverend."

"Where is the Reverend now?"

The man shook his head.

"Tell me where he is or I will kill you."

The man shook his head again, a reptilian cold possessing his eyes.

"You are not one of us . . ." the man said.

He tried to cry out; Kanazuchi gripped his throat harder before a sound could escape and crushed his windpipe. The man collapsed like a broken puppet. Kanazuchi dragged the body to the edge of the room, emptied one of the rifle boxes, stuffed the dead man inside, and covered the box with canvas.

No movement from the front; the guards had not seen or heard him. He retraced his steps to the back door and left the warehouse.

His briefcase resting on his lap, Dante sat outside the office door and waited as Frederick had ordered him to do. The men they'd traveled with were elsewhere in the house attending to their wounded comrade, struck by a stray bullet as the last of the posse was going down. They'd ridden hard nearly two hours straight after that, all the way to The New City. Dante was still reeling from all he'd taken in since they arrived.

Through lace curtains, he could look down on Main Street; its clean white simplicity reminded him so much of the home he'd always wanted that he hoped he would never leave. He had nearly given up dreaming that such a nice friendly place could even exist. But this was the House of Hope, wasn't it?

He could smell pies baking in the house, apple and cherry both, his favorites. He wondered if they would give him vanilla ice cream with his pie; yes, probably so. He wondered when they would let him have one of the uncommonly attractive women he had seen in the street. The Voices in his head had never sounded so happy.

We want to eat everything, everything, everything.

He was startled out of his dreamy mood by angry voices coming from the office; the man he had heard them call the Reverend was yelling at Frederick, something about a book that Frederick had brought with them.

"Useless! This is *useless*!"

The book they'd brought with them came flying through the doorway; its spine cracked as it hit the far wall.

"How could you be so blind? How can I finish my Work

without the real book? What do you expect me to use in its place?"

Dante couldn't make out Frederick's response, only the more reasonable tone of his voice.

"Oh, really? Left a trail of crumbs, have you? And how can you be so bloody certain they'll bring the real one with them?" said the Reverend. "How can you be sure they'll even *follow* you?"

Another smooth reply from Frederick.

"NO!" the Reverend screamed. "You'll not collect one *penny* until that book is in my hands."

Again Frederick replied in the same soothing manner; over some minutes the Reverend's anger subsided and his voice calmed to Frederick's level. Dante felt relieved; he didn't like the idea of anyone being so angry at Frederick; it made his new world feel as brittle as a hard-boiled egg.

Moments later the door opened; Frederick smiling, waving him inside. Dante entered the office.

The Reverend Day stood in front of his desk, smiling too, anger gone, holding his arms out to welcome Dante.

Frederick walked him across the room, gripped Dante by the hands, rolled up his left sleeve, and showed his brand to the Reverend, who nodded in kind approval.

"Why don't you show the Reverend your new tools, Mr. Scruggs?" Frederick whispered in his ear.

Dante opened his briefcase; he felt a twinge of embarrassment when he realized he hadn't had time to clean off all the blades after they'd finished with the posse. Halfway through, he realized he didn't like working on men nearly as much, remembering with a thrill the chubby blond girl from the train—in a jar in his suitcase he'd saved two choice pieces of her that he hadn't even had time to appreciate yet—but he guessed it was still better than dumb animals or insects. Men were better than nothing.

Somehow when Dante looked into the Reverend's eyes, he felt all of his secrets were understood. No need to explain himself or feel ashamed. This was the man in charge, their general, and he was more bighearted than any soldier could ever hope for. Just as Frederick had said he would be.

And the Voices liked this man even more than they'd liked Frederick.

"You know, it's so interesting, I believe we have a first," said the Reverend to Frederick, still gazing at Dante.

"What is that, sir?" asked Frederick.

"This one doesn't even need to be Baptized," said Reverend Day, reaching out and lightly stroking Dante's fuzzy cheek.

"We agreed you were not to work your 'sacraments' on any of my men," said Frederick tensely. "That was our arrangement."

"Don't work yourself into a state, Frederick," said Reverend Day, his eyes caressing Dante. "When the boy's already been so touched by grace it would only be gilding the lily."

Their train pulled into Flagstaff, Arizona, ten minutes ahead of schedule; when Doyle, Innes, Presto, and Lionel hurried onto the platform, they found two officials of the Santa Fe line waiting to escort them three tracks over to their chartered express; an engine and tender pulling a single passenger car, bound for Prescott.

Walks Alone held on to Jack's arm, lagging behind the others. They were the last to step down from the train. She had not left his compartment once since Doyle and Innes had burst in on them the night before. None of the others exchanged a word with either of them, and even now, transferring to the other train, neither of them met anyone else's eye.

Blistering heat from the noonday sun. Jack looked pale and depleted, hardly enough strength to put one foot in front of the other, all his energy directed inward. She appeared to be equally exhausted and her focus centered solely on moving Jack to the second train.

If she followed the procedure she described to me, then she's invited his illness into her body, thought Doyle as he watched her. If that was true, he shuddered to think what she was fighting against now. He noticed she still carried the stick topped by the eagle feather in her hand.

What if she's failed? What if they're both incapacitated? What do I do then? I can't slay another man's dragons.

"Not the most advantageous time for romance, wouldn't you say?" whispered Presto to Doyle.

"Good God, man, what makes you say that?"

"She was in his compartment all night. At one point I thought I heard a . . . cry of *amour*."

"You did hear a cry. *Amour* had nothing to do with it," said Doyle.

Love, maybe, but not passion. And the indescribable way in which he had seen that power being employed was not something he felt willing to share with anyone.

Innes broke in to hand Doyle another wire confirming all the supplies he had requisitioned would be waiting when they arrived in Prescott. After supervising the storing of their luggage, Innes climbed on last in time to see Jack and Walks Alone disappear into one of the car's closed compartments.

"Hasn't pulled any more strawberry shortcakes out of his ribs today, has she?" he asked Doyle quietly.

"Let's hope the one was sufficient," whispered Doyle, raising his finger to his lips again.

Five minutes later their train was steaming its way south. Two hours to Prescott.

"I don't like the idea of you going there alone," said Eileen.

"I tend to agree, my dear, but it didn't sound like an invitation I could reasonably turn down," said Jacob.

"You're not well; you should be resting."

"Now you're sounding like my late wife: Jacob, come to bed, you'll ruin your eyes reading in that light."

"You probably didn't listen to her, either."

Jacob stopped by the door in the lobby and took her by the hand.

"I always listened. So far I've outlived her six years."

"Don't go," she said quietly.

"This is what I've come for. I should make such an effort only to turn back at the threshold?"

"Then let me come with you."

"But my dearest Eileen, you weren't invited."

"I'm sure the Reverend won't mind."

"No. I mean, by the dream."

She looked into his eyes, saw the joy and determination shining through; no trace of fear. A tear formed in her own eye.

"Please. Don't die," she whispered.

He smiled, gently kissed her hand, turned, and pushed out onto the street through the swinging doors.

Just like a cowboy, he thought, as he straightened up and headed toward the House of Hope.

Eileen dried her tears, not wanting the actors gathering in the lobby to see her in such a state. They were already moving toward the theater, a scheduled rehearsal only a few minutes off.

A man stood up across the lobby and strode toward her, taking off his hat. Wearing a fringed yellow leather jacket, boots, chaps on his pants; he looked like an actor in a western melodrama. At least he wasn't wearing a white shirt. But five worried youngsters in white shirts immediately followed the man over to her.

"Ma'am, might I have a word with you?"

A tall one. And handsome wasn't the word for it. And good Lord, what a voice, like a low note on a cello. She instantly revised her first impression; she'd been spending far too much time in the company of actors. The way he moved, the way he carried himself; this man was a real cowboy.

She pulled out a cigarette, her favorite stalling technique; he had a match struck off his thumbnail before she could pull one from her purse.

"What about?"

"Would you mind stepping outside a moment?" he said, with an explanatory shrug in the direction of the five white shirts.

"Gladly."

He held the door for her as she exited, then turned to block the shirts when they tried to follow.

"You kids stay put," he said.

"But we're supposed to see you to your room. . . ."

"Here's a buck," he said, flipping them a coin. "Go buy some lollipops."

"But, sir—"

"Clarence, if I catch you trailing after me one more time, I will personally kick your rear ends into the middle of next July."

Frank shut the swinging door firmly in their faces, put on his hat, and fell into step beside Eileen on the sidewalk.

"You're name's Eileen, isn't it, miss?"

"Yes."

"Mine's Frank."

"Frank, I have a feeling you're not interested in my autograph."

"No, ma'am. Could I ask how long you planned on staying in this booby hatch?"

"The play's scheduled to run for a week; why?"

"To put it plain, we're sitting on top of a powder keg and it's about to blow."

They were drawing stares—two tall, attractive, nonconforming strangers—from white shirts passing on the street.

"Keep smiling at 'em," whispered Frank.

"Makes you wonder what they're so damn happy about," she said, smiling and nodding pleasantly. "They've kept us under lock and key since the moment we arrived. Not that that's such a bad idea with actors. How long have you been here?"

"About an hour."

"Do you have any idea what the hell is going on?"

"They're stealing rifles from the U.S. Army, for starters."

"Rifles? For *these* people?"

"And every last one of 'em's a few shovels short of a funeral."

A stout middle-aged black woman approached and planted herself in their way, holding out a copy of the printed regulations. "Excuse me, friends," she said with a deranged grimace, "but it is against the rules for visitors to walk around The New City without an escort."

"Thank you, ma'am; the Reverend told us it was okay," said Frank, smiling right back at her.

"We just spoke with him," said Eileen, grinning like an idiot. "He sends his love."

The woman stopped in her tracks, poleaxed; they stepped around her and continued on.

"No smoking, either," the woman called after them, less confidently.

Eileen waved and flicked her cigarette over her shoulder.

"So I wanted to suggest," said Frank, "that if you had a mind to remove yourself from the premises before Uncle Sam comes looking for his guns and the shit starts flying—excuse the expression—I'd be more than pleased to get you the hell out of here."

She stopped to look at him. Yes; genuine American sincerity.

"That's a very kind offer, Frank."

"My pleasure."

"But I'm afraid I can't leave at the moment. Not without Jacob."

"The old man."

"He's not that old. Does he look that old to you?"

"He's not your husband, is he?"

"No."

"Good," he said, with the first authentic grin she'd seen since they'd left the hotel. "Then we'll bring Jacob along."

"I'm afraid it's not going to be as simple as that," she said.

He looked at her. "Not for me either, exactly."

She glanced around at the white shirts on the street, gestured discreetly, and they moved around a corner into an empty alley.

"You start," she said.

Frank pushed his hat back and hooked his thumbs on his belt. "I'm gonna have to ask you about the Chinaman."

She squinted her eyes and studied him again; for such a good-looking man, she had to admit, his character didn't seem all that deficient.

"Have you had any unusual dreams lately, Frank?"

Frank thought for a moment. "No, ma'am."

"Then first I have to tell you a very strange story."

"Come in, come in, Rabbi Jacob Stern," said the Reverend, waving an arm toward a velvet sofa in the corner of his office. "Delighted to see that you could join me today."

"I was able to find time in my busy schedule," said Jacob.

The Reverend did not rise from the desk or offer to shake his hand; Jacob took a seat on the sofa beside a large globe resting on an oak stand. Aside from a gilded Byzantine icon on the wall behind the Reverend's desk and a King James Bible lying open on a reading stand, nothing suggested that this served as the office of a cleric. Furnishings plush, even opulent, like a picture Jacob had seen of John D. Rockefeller's study. The air felt heavy and cool. Thin strands of brilliant white light cutting through wooden window blinds into the shadowy room were the only reminder that the house rested in the middle of a desert. Motes of dust spiraled up from the heavy Persian carpet and danced in the beams. His eyes adjusting to the half-light, Jacob couldn't see the Reverend distinctly in the darkness behind his desk.

"A very comfortable room," said Jacob.

"Do you like it? I had them build my House with the thick adobe walls that are such a characteristic feature of the local architecture; it keeps the heat at bay until well into the afternoon. The furniture is all donated, by the way, gifts from my more generously endowed followers. I don't believe a man of the cloth should receive a regular salary, do you, Rabbi? I think it violates the sacred trust between God and his . . . . representatives."

"All very well for God, but a man's got to eat."

"Tithing; that's the answer, and of course, like most common sensible ideas, it's been with us for hundreds of years. Everyone in the community making the same sacrifice—or shall we say contribution—setting aside a portion of their earnings to support the shepherd of their spiritual flock, be it preacher, priest, or rabbi."

"Ten percent is the usual figure," said Jacob.

"I've made the tiniest innovation," said the Reverend, leaning forward into a scallop of light. "I take one hundred percent."

Day's eyes crept into view for the first time in the hot slice of sunlight. Jacob felt them reaching out at him like oiled tentacles and looked away. He swallowed hard. His heart skipped a beat.

"I had the great fortune to baptize a steady stream of millionaires into our church early on in my ecclesiastical career. I can't tell you the tithing was entirely their idea, but once the suggestion entered their minds it met a remarkable degree of receptivity. And I discovered there is an extraordinary surplus of wealth in these western states; shipping, cash crops, silver, oil. Millionaires are hardly the rare bird you find in the East—to be blunt, out here they are practically a dime a dozen. And despite all this talk about camels and the eyes of needles, I have found that a rich man is just as desperately in need of salvation as any destitute sinner."

"They're still with you, these former millionaires."

"Oh, yes. Right here, in The New City," said Day, neglecting to mention how the sight of these former captains of industry and their pampered wives mucking out the latrines still filled him with happiness. "And if you were to ask them, well, I'd be shocked if to a man they didn't say that their lives were one hundred percent richer today."

"One hundred percent."

"So much senseless heartache, the strictly material life. So much disquiet and worry about holding on to what you've accumulated. Straining to make its value grow beyond any reasonable fulfillment of one's needs. And what a powerful joy to be released from that suffering and rededicate oneself to a life of spiritual simplicity."

"Must be a terrible burden, all that money," said Jacob, looking around at the riches in the room. "Tell me, how do *you* manage it so well?"

"I consider myself blessed, I really do." Reverend Day stood and limped slowly around his desk toward Jacob. "Enormous wealth seems to place no untoward weight upon my soul whatsoever. It rests on my broken shoulders like a hummingbird." He waved his hand through a ray of light and the dust ducked and swirled.

"What's your secret?"

"I claim nothing for myself. I am a servant, not a master. I live to fulfill my obligation to God, and what earthly goods pass through my hands leave no stain. Ask what all this money means to me and I would tell you truly, Jacob Stern, that I cannot tell a silver dollar from a buzz saw. Money is merely a tool given to me to complete the Holy Work."

"The Holy Work . . ."

"Why, The New City. Our cathedral. Everything you see around you."

"And its purpose?"

"To bring man closer to God. Or should I say to bring Him closer to man. . . ." The Reverend stopped himself and smiled curiously. "You're filled with questions, aren't you? Why don't we speak more . . . directly?"

"What about?"

"I know you, Jacob Stern," said Day, taking a seat across from him. "I admit I could not place you at first; you've shaved your beard, old man. The Parliament of Religion, last year in Chicago, yes?"

Jacob felt the throbbing in his chest approach like the footsteps of a giant. He nodded.

"You are no pleasure-touring retiree. You are a scholar in Kabbalah, as I recall, and one of the foremost. Kabbalah is one of the holy books I've been attempting to decipher since I began my serious collecting. So naturally I am very curious to know, Rabbi Stern, just exactly . . . what . . . you are doing here?"

Jacob felt a wave of energy slide around his head and chest like a slick spineless insect, probing for a weakness. He summoned his strength, erecting a barrier of thought to hold off the gnawing insinuations. His life felt as fragile and indefensible as the dust drifting in the mottled air.

"I believe I asked you first," said Jacob.

"Fair enough," said Reverend Day. "We have time; you don't have anywhere you have to be." He laughed, a first hint of cruelty.

"I'm listening," said Jacob.

Reverend Day leaned forward and spoke in a theatrical whisper, like an adult telling a child a bedtime story. "One day, a man awakens and discovers burning inside himself a light. A tremendous well of Power. Call it a spark of the divine, whatever you prefer; he has been touched by grace."

"It's been known to happen," said Jacob.

"In time he learns to use the Power—no, that's not right: He learns how to *enable* the Power to perform its sacred work through him; a more modest way of putting it. From that moment, the Light guides his every thought and action, directing the man to gather about him a congregation and lead his people away from the corrupted world of man. Into the desert. To build a new Jerusalem. The Power provides him with a Vision to show how and where they should remove themselves; a dream about a black tower, his church, rising from the sand."

"You've had a dream like this?" asked Jacob, looking up in surprise, then willing his eyes back down to stay focused on the dust.

"Nine years," said the Reverend. "Since the day I woke and found myself lying in a filthy ditch by the side of a river. In Switzerland, of all places. No memory of who I was or any single detail of what my life might have been before. All I possessed was this dream. This Vision. And I paid a terrible price for my enlightenment. My body crippled, many times worse than you see the poor self now: a year to heal, two before I could walk. Was it worth it? Without hesitation I would have to tell you: yes.

"Go to America, my Vision commanded, and plant your seed in the sand. Who was I to argue with such an authoritative voice? Nothing, a speck of dust. And so, without benefit of clergy, I took up the cloth," said Day, gripping his frock coat by the lapels. "Actually I took it off a Baptist preacher I killed in Charleston, South Carolina. A perfect fit, not a single alteration, and I'm not such an easy man to dress what with my various . . . irregularities. Clothes do make the man, in the end. What do you think, Rabbi? Am I not the very model of a modern evangelical?" He hummed a snatch of Gilbert and Sullivan and laughed.

"So your vision led you to this place," said Jacob, struggling to concentrate and keep the man on track.

"With the aid of the millionaires I won to my side between Charleston and here—New Orleans proved particularly fertile ground, by the way; combine dissolute living with new money and they practically *beg* you for absolution. With their generous contributions, before long The New City brought life to this barren plain. You can well imagine the attention to detail required to birth such a child of the imagination; architecture, social organization, supply lines, local government. Years flashed by with hardly a spare moment for the theological.

"Until one day I looked up to see our little town coming along so splendidly; nearly a thousand of us, more flocking to our side as I toured the western coast, preaching from the back of a wagon . . . and I realized how thoroughly I had neglected to develop the *scriptural* foundation of our community. Our spirit was willing but the flesh was . . . ignorant.

"So I made a pilgrimage. Chicago, last year, to mingle with my fellow clergy. What an assembly of knowledge, what an inspiration! I can tell you truthfully, Rabbi, the Parliament of Religions changed my life. My path was revealed to me and it was a daunting one: I needed to study and root out the *prima materia* of all the religions of the world, then unite their separate truths in the name of the one true Vision which I already possessed but lacked the ability to articulate.

"So I began my collection of the world's great holy books and the study of their secrets. One of the first ideas you acquire is that there is no such thing as coincidence. And I must tell you, Jacob Stern, that your appearing in The New City at this moment is remarkably fortuitous."

"Why is that?"

The relentless pounding in Jacob's head nearly drowned out the sound of Reverend Day as the man drew his chair closer. A nauseatingly ripe smell of lush rotting flowers blossomed in the air.

"Because I believe you have been sent to me so that we can complete this great Holy Work together. That is why you are here. That is why you have shared my dream about our church."

"What makes you so sure I've had the same dream?" asked Jacob.

"Please, let's not be disingenuous; I know many things about you and I have no doubt you are a wise enough man to figure out the 'why' of it."

The Reverend casually waved his arm; Jacob felt hot liquid running from his nose and raised his hand to it: blood. He looked up, feeling dizzy, narrowly avoiding the Reverend's eyes. But he saw it, there, trickling down the man's lip, his own blood as well.

Jacob nodded again; the "why" didn't matter. The only important question was "how": how to stop him.

"You can see that with all my responsibilities here I have found it impossible to consider any of these people *colleagues*," said Reverend Day, voice rising with excitement, oblivious to his own bleeding. "I knew you would come; it was foretold in the dream."

"What do you expect me to do?"

"So long since I've sat with anyone qualified to appreciate my discoveries. I hardly know where to begin. Let me share with you what I've concluded from my studies and tell me if you agree."

"All right."

Rotting flowers permeated the air; Jacob breathed through his mouth, staring at the floor, feeling the Reverend's eyes slowly pick apart his defenses.

"In Hebrew scriptures there is no direct mention of God; many other names are given Him, but the *Ain Sof,* the Godhead, the source of all creation, is never named directly, because its identity lies beyond human comprehension. Correct me if I'm wrong."

Jacob nodded in agreement; the pain increasing dreadfully. He put his hands to the side of his head, focused on the dust swirling in the wake of the man's gestures.

"The absence of God is darkness. Darkness is considered Evil. Before light came into the world, before good existed—because God is good—there was only darkness. We know God gave man a free will because He wanted us to live freely upon the earth. But to be *truly* free means that we must defy what is traditionally called God's will; do you see? By defying God we become more godlike. That was his original intention in creating us. And in order for man to live the way God intended, Evil had to exist in the heart of man from the beginning, because without the possibility of Evil, of *choosing* between these two paths, he has no free will to exercise.

"Therefore . . . *Evil was God's original gift to man*. Are you with me so far, Rabbi?"

Somehow Jacob found the strength to shake his head, the pounding now joined by a grating rattle in his ears that obliterated everything but the Reverend Day's voice.

"Evil has a purpose, yes," said Jacob, "but only so man can struggle with his brokenness. Move himself towards becoming whole again."

"Yes, that is one way open to us, I agree. But clearly there is another path to godliness; through the pursuit of this power we call Evil," the Reverend continued feverishly. "I grant you, not one for most men to follow. Only for those few that have fallen into darkness, been corrupted by it, and found the strength to rise again . . ."

"This is not a path for human beings," said Jacob, his voice sounding distant and tinny.

"My point exactly," said the Reverend, with a broad smile, blood running down between his teeth. "This less-traveled way is the path of *emulating* God, not obeying Him. To become godlike by seeking Power and moving beyond consideration of Good and Evil. To move closer to God than man has ever dared by challenging and combating His authority."

"You cannot defeat God," said Jacob, feeling an immense weight crushing his limbs, pressing down on the back of his neck.

"Oh, do you think so? Then let me ask you this; in order to follow the path of good, the path of *God*, the path most human beings blindly follow, this is why the great holy books came into the world. That is the common wisdom, yes? Given to us as the Word of God; a series of manuals for living, spiritual handbooks detailing the Laws of God, handed down to man through the prophets of the world religions."

"Yes, yes."

"Then we may say that God is *in* those books, is He not? God appears to us in His words and His Laws which limit and define us. This is the way God comes closest to manifesting in our physical world."

"Agreed."

Reverend Day leaned in, only an inch away from Jacob's face. "Rabbi, how can we be so certain that man's destiny is—not to *obey* God's will—but to free ourselves from Him? Why should we continue to live under the unquestioned assumption that the plan God outlined for us in these books was the *right* one?"

"That lies beyond our capacity—"

"But He gifted us with free will; how can we be sure His true intention isn't for us to rid the world of His influence and by so doing evolve into gods one day ourselves? What if this liberation turns out to be the true function of the Messiah that the books refer to?"

"I don't understand," said Jacob, clinging to consciousness, darkness closing around the edges of his sight, tears falling from his eyes.

"This will sound like a blasphemy to you; imagine that our so-called *Deity* is, by cosmic standards, nothing more than a foolish, undeveloped *pup,* as plagued by doubt, as troubled and unsure of His own intentions, as any man on earth. Imagine a being like this, no longer able or willing to reliably guide us, a parent losing control of its children as we outgrow the need for His protection. . . ."

"That is not for us to know."

"But I disagree. Look at the evidence, Jacob. Look at the wickedness of this world: sin, violence, corruption, warfare. Would you call the 'Creator' of such a hellish inferno infallible? Are His ways and methods so beyond our reproach? I think not."

"Those are the works of man, not God . . ." Jacob protested; his heart raced dangerously, tripping out of control.

No longer listening, Reverend Day reached out and gripped Jacob's wrists, his voice digging in like a knife.

"I believe that it is man's true purpose to *eradicate* God's Laws on earth, to free ourselves from the limitations He imposed a thousand ages ago. The irony is this so-called God knows He's failed, even if He won't admit the thought into His own mind. And I have come to realize that this final act of rebellion, casting God out of our world, is the very reason why God *himself* created man—to defeat and surpass Him—even if He won't acknowledge it."

"How?"

"By destroying God's presence on this earth," said the Reverend in a violent whisper.

"But how would you—"

"The plan for destroying Him has been lying hidden in His books from the beginning. He put it there Himself, I've decoded the information: and I've built a chamber beneath my church according to His sacred specifications, to amplify the Power of the action."

"What action?"

"It's so simple, Jacob: *He wants us to burn the books.*"

Jacob stared at the ground, shaking his head, trying to shield himself against the madness.

"Burn the books! Destroy His Laws, erase His presence from the earth! That's the great Holy Work for which God created man in the beginning. And doing it will set free the Messiah who can lead us the rest of the way to our final freedom. The one, true Messiah."

"You?"

Reverend Day laughed, blood running from his ears, his nostrils, red flecks forming in the corners of his eyes. "Heavens no; I'm just a messenger. Our Messiah is the one angel too pure and selfless for the likes of God; the Archangel He bound in chains, cast out of heaven, and consigned to the pit, for fear that in his righteousness he would one day reveal to man his real and higher destiny.

"We will complete the Archangel's work here, that's the purpose of our City. We will destroy the books and break the chains that bind our Messiah in darkness. That's the divinity of the dream, why we've been gifted with the Vision. That's why . . . we . . . we . . ."

Reverend Day rose abruptly to his feet, severe shaking agitating his limbs. Jacob felt as if his own skull were about to burst, the smell of rot sickening him.

He looked at the Reverend; the man's eyes rolled back in his head, a harsh gibbering burst out of his throat, his body stiffened, and he fell hard to the carpeted floor, dust explod-

ing into the light, his arms and legs flailing like a landed
fish, blood streaming from every orifice in his face.

The pressure in Jacob's head let up as if a valve had been
shut off. His eyesight returned to normal, the throbbing re-
lented, and he registered the sight of the Reverend on the
floor before him.

A grand mal seizure, realized Jacob. The man's an epileptic.

And his power can't penetrate the veil of the attack.

Jacob gripped the edge of the sofa as he realized what he
must do. Where would he find the strength? The man had
nearly killed him without even looking him directly in the
eye. Jacob wobbled to his feet; the seizure showed no sign
of abating, but there was no telling how much time he had.

He searched the room and his eyes settled on a crystal pa-
perweight, an orb wrapped in vines of glass resting on the
desk. Jacob staggered to the desk, gasping for breath. He
hefted the crystal with both hands; yes, heavy enough.
About the size of the steel balls the Italians bowl with on the
Greenwich Village green.

Two steps back, standing over the Reverend, looking
down at him; a lessening in the attack's intensity. Jacob frantically tried to find his balance, took a deep breath, and lifted
the crystal over his head.

A rush of vertigo; too much effort. Vision darkened
alarmingly, he lowered the ball, dropped painfully to his
knees. Blood and sweat pouring down his face; he rested the
ball on the floor, wiped his brow with his sleeve.

*Keep breathing, old man; if it's the last thing you ever do,
make your life count for something and wipe this abom-
inable insult to God's grace off the face of the earth.*

The Reverend's awful shuddering subsided further, his
tongue protruded from the side of his foaming lips. He
moaned unconsciously.

Finish it, Jacob; put the wretched animal out of its misery.

Jacob edged closer to the man and raised the ball again.
He paused, waiting for the Reverend's head to settle so he
could bring the weight down squarely on his forehead.

The Reverend's eyes opened, instantly aware and alert,

locking onto Jacob's, as if he'd been watching all along from the shadows of his fit.

Jacob looked away and struck at him with the ball.

Too late; a wave of pressure nudged his aim slightly to the side; the ball smashed harmlessly into the carpet an inch from the Reverend's skull.

Day's hand snapped up and grabbed Jacob's wrist in a vise, snapping a bone. With his other hand, he wagged a chiding finger in his face.

"Naughty, naughty," whispered Reverend Day, pale and frightful as a corpse.

He gestured sharply; the ball flew from Jacob's hands and crashed against a far wall, shattering, an explosion of glass.

Day gestured again; Jacob rolled back and fell against the desk, pinned there helplessly, unable to move a muscle.

"The Hindus have an interesting theory," said the Reverend, as he advanced on him. "They believe God speaks to them . . . through the *eyes*."

chapter fifteen

Aᴌᴛʜᴏᴜɢʜ ᴅᴇꜱᴛɪɴᴇᴅ ꜰᴏʀ ᴀ ʙʀɪɢʜᴛ ꜰᴜᴛᴜʀᴇ ᴏɴᴄᴇ ᴛʜᴇ north-south lines in the territory connected through its terminus, Prescott, Arizona, had still not grown beyond much more than a whistle-stop. Doyle's charter was the only train in the yard when it arrived late that afternoon.

Six sturdy horses and two pack mules waited for them at the supply depot, along with the supplies Innes had ordered: maps, rifles, ammunition, medical kit, and a week's stores of food and water. The retired prospector behind the counter had been outfitting mining expeditions for fifteen years, even an occasional Englishman or two among them—the Arthur Conan Doyle name meant nothing to the old man; he wasn't a reader—but he had never seen an odder or more purposeful bunch than the one doing business with him now.

A younger man, whittling a stick near the cracker barrel, watched them finish their transaction, then got up and walked slowly over to the telegraph office.

As Doyle left the depot, he saw Jack and Mary Williams stepping down, once again the last to leave the train. Her energies seemed to have revived, color returning to her face, and she had changed into riding clothes and boots. Jack still looked as blank as a slate. She left him sitting on a rock outside the corral, holding a blanket tight around his shoulders, Edison's suitcase between his feet, as she went about the bridling of their horses.

Seizing the opportunity to question her alone, Doyle stole up alongside and whispered, "How is he?"

"Too early to say," she said, not looking at him, strapping a canvas valise to her saddlebag.

"But do you think it worked?"

"The healing was difficult."

"I could see that. Takes a while to recover, does it?"

"Sometimes there is no recovery," she said, glancing at Jack, huddled under his blanket, staring at the ground.

"When will we know?"

"That is up to him," she said, trying to close the door on the subject.

"Awfully indistinct, finally, isn't it? Your medicine," said Doyle in a flush of irritation.

"No more than yours."

She turned to him; he saw the effort and strain so clearly etched on her face and felt instantly remorseful.

"Hope we didn't disturb you last night," said Doyle.

"When?"

"We heard a scream; we came into the compartment."

"I do not remember," she said, looking at him directly.

He decided she was telling the truth.

"Mary. Can you tell me any better now what you think was . . . wrong with him?" he asked.

"I do not know how to describe it in your terms."

"In yours, then."

She paused.

"His soul was lost," she said forthrightly.

"Can you tell how, exactly?"

"The soul is able to travel far but must then find its way back. The way back into his body had been blocked."

"Blocked?"

"When the soul leaves, its place can be stolen."

"By what?"

"By a *windigo*."

"A what?"

"A demon."

The memory of the fleshy mass they had briefly glimpsed in her hands flashed before his eyes. He felt helpless, bumbling, and somewhat ill.

"How?"

"Does it matter?"

"Suppose it doesn't," said Doyle. "I've never seen anything like what we saw in that room last night."

She looked right at him again. "Neither have I."

"Mary, I—"

"My name is Walks Alone."

Doyle nodded, appreciating the confidence he knew her disclosure conveyed. "If there's anything I can do . . ."

She shook her head. "It's up to him now."

Before he could ask her anything else, she led the two horses to Jack. Doyle watched her guide him slowly to his feet and up onto the horse. He did not look at her and still moved and responded to her touch like an obedient sleepwalker. Any thought taking place behind his clouded eyes remained obscure to observation. Doyle walked back toward the others.

Lionel Stern was the only stranger among them to horseback; they decided to put him on a large sedate gelding and let him bring up the rear. He was standing outside the corral, holding the reins out at arm's length, staring uneasily up at the animal.

"On principle," Lionel said to Doyle as he passed, "I'm against the idea of sitting on anything that's larger and stupider than I am."

Innes had seen to the purchase and the packing of the mules and with Presto was now studying a map laid out across a rock.

"The old fellow inside said we'd find a road, about here, that's not on the map," said Innes, drawing in an east-to-west line.

"What sort of road?"

"The nutters put it in themselves; it's supposed to take us directly to their settlement," said Presto.

"How long?" asked Doyle.

"If we ride straight through, perhaps late tonight."

"What's this place, Skull Canyon?" asked Doyle.

"Stagecoach stop. We'll cut down through these hills and pick up the road ten miles west of it," said Innes, very much at home in the world of maps and tactical options.

"The old man said that over the last few years, they've had a steady stream of people passing through on their way to The New City," said Presto.

"Wide-eyed fanatics, the lot of them," said Innes. "He also told us they had five men come off a train and retain some horses early yesterday."

"They answer splendidly to the description of Frederick Schwarzkirk and company," said Presto, lowering his voice, with a glance at Walks Alone. "Including one with a rather unmistakable solid-blue glass eye."

Doyle's brow furrowed; he hadn't even considered that the attack on Walks Alone might be somehow connected to the league of thieves.

"Alarming," he said.

"Yes," said Presto, with a glance at Innes. "We thought so, too."

A loud crash from nearby; Lionel's saddlebags had fallen to the ground, and he was sitting upright on his horse, clutching the rear lip of the saddle, facing exactly backward.

"I may need a little help with this," said Lionel.

Frank could see the House of Hope from the window of his second-floor hotel room. Neat lines of cigar ash had accumulated on the windowsill; he'd been watching the front door of the place for an hour, as he had promised Eileen he would do when she left for the theater.

Jacob had not returned from his appointment with Reverend Day. Eileen marched over there to look for him at six o'clock and was turned away; their meeting was still going on, a black shirt told her; they did not wish to be disturbed. Her instincts advised her differently and she returned to the hotel in a tizzy. Frank calmed her as best he could and gave his word he would find Jacob and meet her at the theater after the show.

Not that he didn't have enough to worry about. The Chinaman had been in their wagon all the way from Wickenburg, she'd told him, including that morning Frank had seen them in Skull Canyon; he'd had the killer square in his sights and let him off the hook. Now Chop-Chop was probably on the loose inside The New City—Kanazuchi was the man's name; he was some kind of priest, from Japan, not China—and if the rest of what Eileen had said was to be believed, both he and this Jacob fella had been drawn out here by a nightmare both men were having about that big black tower.

In the old days, that alone would have been enough to drive him back to drinking.

One part of his dilemma had turned crystal clear, however; if he planned on making any serious time with Eileen—and he did, more than ever, after talking to her—putting a bullet through this Japanese would knock his chances down to less than zero. Which amounted to as big a rock and as hard a place as Frank could ever remember finding himself between.

He looked at his watch sitting open on the sill: half past seven. The play was supposed to start at eight. He wanted to take a stroll around the House of Hope but needed to wait until dark. He wanted just as much, if not more, to see Eileen on the stage.

Another angle had been taking shape in the back of his mind; it held out the prospect of a better outcome but carried a higher risk. He'd need his Henry rifle to pull it off and he'd more than likely get himself killed. Naturally that's the one he was leaning toward.

Frank put on his hat, walked out of the room, and peeked from the top of the stairs. Clarence and the nitwits still waited for him in the lobby. He tried doors along the hall until he found an open one, slipped out a window, shimmied down a rain gutter into the empty alley, and made his way to the intersection with Main Street; as evening came on, a large crowd of white shirts gathered outside the theater.

Seeing Eileen perform in this or any other show would have to wait. But it was about the best reason he could come up with for staying alive.

From the edge of the shantytown, Kanazuchi watched the last of the white shirts enter the theater. Torches burning in the brackets out front were beginning to work against the gathering dark. He waited five more minutes, then walked across the empty street and down an alley toward the stables.

He had learned that Reverend Day lived in the adobe house across from the theater. This man would know the location of the underground temple and the books, of that much Kanazuchi felt certain; he was probably the man who had arranged the theft of the Kojiki.

Kanazuchi had waited hours for the Reverend to come out

of the place the white shirts called the House of Hope; there had been no sign of him. The house was heavily protected, and its guards, all dressed in black, were more dangerous and better armed than the white shirts he had seen. To get inside, he would need the help of the Grass Cutter.

Curious: While watching from this vantage point, a short time after he began, Kanazuchi had witnessed a clear disruption in the white shirts' concentration, as if the control they moved under had suddenly lapsed. Some stopped dead in the street, others fell to their knees; a few appeared to be in severe pain. Minutes later, the control resumed and the white shirts instantly went on about their business as if nothing had happened.

No one approached as he entered the stable; the barn appeared to be empty. By the light of a single burning lantern, he entered the rear courtyard where the actors' wagons stood. He stopped and listened: no one there. Kanazuchi slowly parted the canvas on the back of the wagon he had ridden in and found himself staring down the barrel of a rifle.

"Eileen said not to kill you," said the man kneeling inside.

The hammer already cocked; finger edging down on the trigger.

If I attack, the bullet will still strike, Kanazuchi realized.

"I don't want to," said the man. "But I will."

Kanazuchi looked him in the eye. A serious man. He was good; nothing had given away his presence in the wagon. He knew how to hide and he undoubtedly knew how to kill.

"What do you want?" asked Kanazuchi.

"They've got Jacob. Eileen said you need him for something and that you'd want to get him back. That true?"

"Yes."

"Then I need your help."

Kanazuchi nodded. The man uncocked the hammer but did not lower the rifle.

"Where is he?" asked Kanazuchi.

"That big adobe."

"We must get him out."

"That's what I was hoping you'd say. Looking for this?"

The man tossed the Grass Cutter toward him; Kanazuchi caught the scabbard and pulled the sword in one blindingly fast move. The man's grip on the rifle didn't flinch.

"My name's Frank," said the man.

"Kanazuchi," he said, with a slight bow.

"Kana . . . that mean anything in English?"

"It means hammer."

"Well, what do you say, Hammer," said Frank, finally lowering the gun. "Let's go raise a little hell."

Kanazuchi stood aside as Frank climbed out of the wagon. They looked at each other warily, a perceived sense of professional kinship and common cause delicately balancing the scales against powerful self-preserving instincts. Each waited for the other to make a first move; then, like dance partners, both turned and walked in step toward the stable.

"Took my sidearm when I rode in but they left the rifle with my saddle gear. They didn't look for the one in my boot," said Frank, touching the butt of the spare Colt in his holster.

"Mistake."

"This town's sicker than a bag of drowned kittens."

"It is like a clock; wound up, running down."

"Getting sloppy," said Frank, nodding. "You feel it, too."

"Yes."

"This freak show's coming to a head," said Frank.

"Remove the head, the body will fall."

"Now there's something I know you're good at."

"Sorry?"

"That's sort of a joke, Hammer."

Kanazuchi thought for a moment, then nodded. "I see."

They stopped just short of leaving the alley at the edge of Main Street. Ghostly laughter followed by applause drifted toward them from the theater, then faded to an eerie silence. Lights burned in windows on both floors of the House of Hope; they could see at least six of the guards in black patrolling its broad front porch.

Frank struck a match on the side of the barn and lit a cheroot. "Figure this Reverend A. Glorious Day's the one we want," said Frank.

"Twelve men guard the house; only three in back," said Kanazuchi, watching their movements.

"Move around much?"

Kanazuchi nodded. "They change every hour."

Frank glanced at his watch. "Had a notion about how we might get inside."

Frank explained as they crossed Main Street. Kanazuchi agreed. They turned down an alley and approached the back door of the House of Hope.

Three guards sitting on the porch armed with Winchesters and Colts. Frank walked five steps ahead, hands over his head; Kanazuchi behind him—Frank's pistol in his belt, the Grass Cutter out of sight down the back of his shirt—pointing the Henry rifle between Frank's shoulders.

The guards stood up. They wore loose black clothes; their eyes clear and alert. Not the same group of men, but their manner reminded Frank of the ones he'd seen ride up to the House earlier that day.

"I found this man walking in the stable," said Kanazuchi.

"I already told you, you stupid slant-eyed son of a bitch," said Frank, staggering and slurring his words, "wanted to make sure they were taking care of my horse—"

"Be quiet," said the lead guard.

"He had the colic few weeks back, can't be too careful; those damn kids weren't even tending to—"

Kanazuchi smacked the back of his head with the rifle butt; Frank stumbled and fell forward on the stairs.

"He told you be quiet," said Kanazuchi.

All three guards looked down at Frank curiously, rifles lowered. Frank curled his hands near his stomach and moaned as if he was about to be sick.

"He's one of the visitors," one of them said.

"Yes. He has been drinking," said Kanazuchi.

"Take him to corrections," said the lead guard.

Two of the guards reached down to grab Frank by the arms just as he slipped Kanazuchi's long knife out of his shirt; as they stood him up Frank drove his shoulder into the chest of the lead guard, knocking him back hard into a column, then grabbed him around the face and plunged the knife in behind the man's left ear. He died without making a sound.

From behind, Frank heard two sounds like a rush of rain-water; when he turned, the bodies of the other two guards were falling to the porch and their heads were rolling down the stairs. Kanazuchi's sword was already resting back in the scabbard.

Damn. This guy knew his stuff.

Kanazuchi tossed Frank his rifle; Frank cocked it one-handed, then exchanged the long knife for his pistol. Kanazuchi slid the *wakizashi* into its scabbard; Frank hol-stered the Colt. They moved to either side of the back door and waited.

"Didn't have to hit me so hard," whispered Frank.

"More authentic."

"Glad I wasn't playing dead."

No one came; none of the guards from the front had been alerted by the skirmish. Frank tried the door; it opened.

Dim lamps lit the interior hallway. Thick carpets muffled their steps. Plush furnishings throughout the house, oil paintings on the walls, a crystal chandelier hanging over the stairs in the front entryway. Not a spittoon in sight. Fancier than a St. Louis whorehouse.

They heard a raised voice in a parlor to their left, crept up on its partially open sliding doors. Inside, four more of the black shirt elite being jawed at by an obvious superior, a tall, blond fella with a foreign accent; the same bunch Frank had seen arrive that afternoon.

". . . the wire says they got off the train in Prescott and left on horseback this afternoon. Look for them on the eastern road. Five men, one woman. They should be carrying a book with them. Let them ride through; take them when they pass the gate. The Reverend won't release our money to us until he has that book. Go."

The four men started for the sliding doors; Kanazuchi and Frank slipped across the hall into a dark room as the men moved off toward the front of the house.

"Not you, Mr. Scruggs."

One of the four, a baby-faced man carrying a briefcase,

stopped obediently; the blond man put an arm around his shoulder and walked him toward the door.

"You stay with me," said the tall one.

Frank and Kanazuchi waited until they heard the front door close before stepping back into the hall. Through curtains they could see the guards patrolling the front porch. Keeping one hand on the pommel of his sword, Kanazuchi nodded toward the stairs; Frank acknowledged and they went up; stopped on the landing when they heard the creak of a floorboard above. A black shirt came into view, looking down over the balustrade to the entrance hall below.

Kanazuchi whipped his arm forward and the handle of his knife appeared in the guard's throat; he slumped to the floor, silently clawing at the blade. Kanazuchi took the rest of the stairs in three steps without making a sound, put a foot on the guard's neck and snapped it.

This guy really knows his stuff, thought Frank.

Frank followed him up. They entered the first door to their right off a central hall. Kanazuchi closed and locked the door behind them. Brighter light. A lived-in feel, more than the other rooms they'd seen. Book-lined shelves. Work on a desk. A large globe. A Bible, open on a reading stand.

"Reverend Day," said Kanazuchi.

Frank knelt down to examine dark stains on the carpet.

"Blood here," said Frank. "Fresh; maybe two hours."

"Jacob," said Kanazuchi, looking at broken glass littering a corner.

"Looks like he put up a fight. They dragged him out . . . this way," said Frank, following the smeared trail of blood; it stopped abruptly before a blank panel of wall.

Both men studied the wall.

Shouts from the back of the house, relaying quickly around to the front, an alarm; someone had found the bodies.

Frank and Kanazuchi looked calmly at each other. They heard footsteps pounding up the stairs outside but neither man hurried. Frank traced a barely visible seam running parallel to the line of the rose-colored wall paper. Kanazuchi discovered a discolored spot on the paper, slightly darker from an accumulation of skin oil. He touched his finger to the spot and pushed; a catch released and the wall panel swung open along the seam, revealing a narrow passage.

The doorknob to the office behind them rattled; the lock held. They heard a jangle of keys. As a key was inserted, Frank dropped to one knee, fanned the handle of the rifle, and emptied the fifteen shots in the Henry's chamber through the door in under five seconds, followed by six from his Colt. Kanazuchi ran to the door and opened it.

Four black shirts dead in the hall outside.

This man is good, thought Kanazuchi.

More shouts outside and below, reacting to the gunfire, the alarm spreading beyond the House. Frank followed Kanazuchi into the concealed passage. Scuffed bloodstains led them down a flight of stairs, through a short corridor, and out a one-way door into the pantry of the House's kitchen. They paused in the darkness; Frank calmly reloaded. Footsteps and raised voices multiplied around them.

"The Reverend is not here," said Kanazuchi.

Frank snapped the filled chamber back into the Colt. "No shit."

"They took Jacob out that door." Kanazuchi pointed to the door where the stains ended. "I could not see it from my position."

"Well," said Frank, hearing movement upstairs in the passage behind them. "We can't stay here."

They stepped silently across the kitchen and out the door, through a small storage room and into a narrow alley on the north side of the house. Bloodstains and footprints ended, impossible to track farther in the dark. There was no one in the alley, but they heard a mob running toward the House of Hope from every direction. A bell started ringing at the top of the black church.

Kanazuchi led them into the tangled shanties, and they ran from the rising commotion until they left it in the distance. The huts were empty; most of the town was in the theater watching the show. The two men ducked under a shabby tin lean-to.

"Good news is," whispered Frank, "they don't know what we look like."

"Every one of them will search for us," said Kanazuchi, his expression never changing. "We don't know where Jacob is."

"That's the bad news."

Moving as steadily through the rough terrain as Lionel's riding skills would allow, they found The New City road shortly before seven o'clock. Innes took the lead, reading their map flawlessly; Walks Alone guided them through two uncertain stretches. Doyle watched Jack throughout the ride for any signs of life beyond subsistence. None appeared. He gave no response to Doyle's questions, eyes focused on the horizon, face emptied of expression.

Open desert stretched out before them, and as the moon rose in the clear sky, they accelerated their pace to a steady gallop, Lionel clinging to the lip of his saddle for dear life. Two miles along, the horses shied severely, nearly throwing Innes; something spooking them off to the right. Doyle saw dark wings circling above them in the moonlight.

"Night owls?" he asked.

Walks Alone shook her head. She dismounted and moved through a narrow path in an outcropping of rock to their right. A call came for them to follow; the party dismounted, walked their horses in through the passage. Fifty yards on, the horses balked at the final opening. Jack and Lionel stayed behind; the others crept through the rest of the way, weapons drawn.

The full force of the smell hit them as they cleared the rocks. Three dozen vultures scattered.

An afternoon in the hot sun had ruined the thirty-eight corpses in the clearing beyond the terrible outrages already committed on them. Most of the men had been shot; a dozen had suffered under knives. Carrion birds had done the rest of the damage.

Glad we got here after dark, thought Doyle; the blood looked black in the moonlight, abstract.

"Don't touch any of them," said Doyle.

Doyle looked to his left. Jack had come through the rocks and was standing off to the side, staring at the mangled bodies. His features contorted, animated by the beginnings of thought and, Doyle thought, the first stirring of rage. Something fierce in him, triggered by the smell of blood.

Doyle stepped forward and picked up a badge lying in the sand.

"Deputy," he said, reading the badge. "Phoenix."

"They're all wearing them," said Walks Alone, wading in farther.

"Lionel, stay where you are," said Doyle, kneeling to examine a body and seeing him appear in the opening.

"What is it?" Lionel asked.

"Just stay there."

"Most of them middle-aged, obviously sedentary," said Doyle.

"Does this make any sense to you?" asked Presto.

"They don't look like lawmen," said Innes.

"They're not. They're volunteers," said Doyle, studying a bloodstained piece of paper he had plucked from inside one victim's coat. "A posse; I believe that's what you'd call them. Looking for this man."

Doyle held out the flier, Presto lit a match, and they saw a crude pen and ink sketch of a diabolical-looking Asian man above a brief, lurid description of his alleged crimes.

" 'Chop-Chop the decapitating Chinaman,' " read Innes.

" 'Wanted for ten terrible murders throughout the Arizona Territory. Suspected in countless other dastardly crimes.' "

"Busy little bugger, isn't he?" said Presto.

" 'The most dangerous man alive,' " read Doyle, darkly amused. "At least they resisted the impulse to hyperbolize. And a five-thousand-dollar reward. That explains the volunteers."

"Good God, could one man have done all this?" asked Presto, looking out at the slaughter around them.

"Not by himself. These men were caught in a crossfire," said Doyle, pointing to two sides of the clearing. "From here and there, behind the rocks. Four men, at least."

"With repeating rifles," said Innes, from behind the rocks. "Shells all over the place."

"And they all still have their heads," said Presto. "Hardly this Chop-Chop's traditional *modus operandi* . . ."

The flier was snatched out of his hands; Jack had walked up behind them and now held the paper, staring at the picture intently.

"What is it, Jack?" asked Doyle softly.

"He knows," said Walks Alone.

"Knows what?"

"That man is in the dream," she said, pointing to the flier. "One of the Six."

Jack looked up at her, agreement shining in his eyes.

"Then we can conclude these men were tracking him toward The New City when they were attacked," said Doyle.

Jack handed back the flier and ran purposefully toward the horses.

"Let's go," said Doyle.

"We should provide them a proper burial first," said Presto, looking around at the vultures gathering again at the perimeter.

"The desert will take care of it," said Walks Alone, moving back to the opening in the rocks.

"Bad form, don't you agree?" asked Presto of the Doyles.

"Yes," said Doyle, starting after her.

"Haven't you seen this fellow in the dream yourself?" asked Innes.

"Suppose I have, now that I think on it," said Presto in his peculiarly indifferent way, staring at the drawing. "Not much of a likeness, finally."

"Hope the bloke's half as good with that sword they say he's carrying as you are with your rapier," said Innes, running after Doyle.

"Let's hope he's on our side," said Presto quietly. He crossed himself, intoned a silent prayer for the dead, and left the scene of the massacre.

Jack was already on his horse by the time the group returned, and he galloped off to the west with Walks Alone close behind him before the others mounted. No one said a word as they scrambled to keep up with them; the secret delight Doyle felt at the signs of Jack's recovery was tempered by thoughts of what might be waiting for them in The New City.

*   *   *

The shirts made for a peculiar audience, thought Eileen. But why should that be different from anything else about them? Their attentiveness to the claptrap, Ruritanian melodrama bordered on reverent. Applause broke from a field of white in uniform bursts as unexpectedly as thunder. All their responses—laughter, sighs, gasps—came in a chorus, like one mind with the same thought expressing itself with a thousand voices.

Rymer had seemed irrationally pleased by the Players' lackluster rehearsal that day and he could not stop raving about The New City Theater. Was it only her imagination or was the man behaving even loonier than usual? For all his excitement, you would have thought the late Edwin-fucking-Booth was going to be in the audience that night.

She had to agree with him on one point: To her eye the theater's backstage facilities looked functional and well designed, if a bit rudimentary, but the auditorium itself was a stunner; plush and fancy as any she'd seen in New York or London, let alone the horse opera circuit they'd been haunting for the past six months. Perhaps the sight of such velvety opulence had thrown Bendigo into some fever-dream of Broadway; he was ripping through the text tonight as if they could hear him clear across the Hudson.

Eileen had played her first-act scenes—nearly deafened by Rymer's rampaging histrionics, most of them blasted only inches away from her face—but instead of retiring to the dressing room, she found a quiet spot in the wings where she could look out and study the audience.

Disturbed: Frank had not come back with news of Jacob, but he had told her it might take until after the curtain came down. Trying to silence her fears. She could depend on Frank McQuethy to keep his word, of that much she felt certain. In the presence of such a—there was no other way to put it—such a *man,* under any other circumstances it would have been herself she wasn't sure she could trust.

When Frank returned with Jacob after the show, the three of them would ride out of town and she would file Bendigo Rymer neatly in with the rest of her mistakes. Let the penny-pinching crackpot keep her damn salary; tonight was her last performance with the Penultimate Players. One more clinch with Bendigo and her prison sentence ended.

Then what? She would travel east with Jacob, make sure he returned safely home. Beyond that; well, yes, she loved the old man dearly, but be realistic, love: Is living with Rabbi Stern honestly the sort of life you see for your retirement, settling on the Lower East Side, doing the washing up in your babushka, seeing him into his declining years—and how far off can they be? Now Frank McQuethy, on the other hand . . .

A row of men wearing black caught her eye—the first she'd seen in anything other than white—above stage right, in the foremost of the mezzanine boxes. Standing around one man sitting alone in the first row of seats beside the rail. She shielded her eyes from the glare of the footlights.

Reverend Day.

Their meeting must have ended. She felt a dizzying flutter in her chest. But that should be good news. Frank and Jacob would be waiting for her. Why was her heart sinking?

The hard edges of the Reverend's face as he watched the play seemed lit from within by some wicked, hideous glee, radiating cold intelligence and cruelty, his head permanently craned to one side on that awful thrusting stalk of a neck.

Jacob was not safe and she knew it.

She heard a distant popping sound, like a string of firecrackers somewhere outside the theater, followed by faint shouts and the deep sounding of a bell—the actors suddenly looked silly; the real world intruding into their fragile, posturing make-believe, the illusion exposed as hollow and mildly ridiculous.

The guards in the box straightened up at the sounds; the Reverend spun around and gestured, two of them quickly exited. The Reverend's attention withdrawing from the action on stage—Bendigo strutting around, waving his sword, in the throes of heroism. None of the other actors aware . . .

A handful of black-shirted guards burst back into the box, led by the huge man in the long gray coat Eileen had seen on the street; Reverend Day turning to them, voice rising in alarm, competing with the actors now.

"No! NO!" shouted Reverend Day.

Heads turning in the audience, a buzz of confusion. Chaos in the box on the verge of boiling over.

"NO! NO! NO! NO!"

Reverend Day screaming at the men around him; they recoiled from his rage. The actors losing their way, falling out of character, staring out at the disturbance. Stagehands peering up from the wings. Bendigo dropping his focus in the scene, tracing the problem to its source, then marching impatiently down to the footlights.

Reverend Day wheeling around, limping to the edge of the box, shouting at the audience, all eyes turning to him, a desperate eagerness distorting his features.

"IT COMES! IT COMES! THE SIGN! IT IS BEGUN, MY CHILDREN! THE TIME!"

Instant a storm of terror sweeping through the white shirts below; moans, wailing, screams, men and women both. Terrible, piteous, abject.

"THE TIME OF THE HOLY WORK IS HERE! THE MOMENT OF OUR DELIVERANCE!"

The white shirts staggered out of their seats and up the aisles, crawling over each other, rushing to perform some unknown action at a station they needed desperately to reach.

"Excuse me!"

"TO YOUR STATIONS, EVERY ONE OF YOU, AT ONCE. THE MOMENT IS AT HAND—"

"Ex-CUSE me!"

Bendigo Rymer standing downstage center, indignant as a peacock, wagging his sword up at the box.

Ghastly silence. Reverend Day staring at the man in shock.

"Really, sir. We're TRYING to give a per-FOR-mance here. A damn GOOD one, if I DO say so my-SELF. I am sure that what-EVER this is a-BOUT is all VERY im-POR-tant. But I don't sup-POSE it is TOO much to ASK . . . if it could WAIT until AFTER we're FIN-ished."

No one breathed. Bendigo puffed up, staying his ground.

Reverend Day laughed. A chuckle, genuinely amused,

turning into a rolling, sustained guffaw that grew until its echoes rolled off the theater walls. The audience laughed with him; laughter building to a set of waves that roared and crashed down on the stage, shaking the scenery, knocking Bendigo's confidence out from under him. He took two faltering steps back, sweat dripping off his clammy made-up face. His sword drooped, he looked around desperately for support but instinctively the other actors onstage stepped away, avoiding his eye, smelling imminent theatrical disaster.

The laughter cut off suddenly. In the silence, Reverend Day leaned over the edge of the box and smiled at Bendigo Rymer.

"You're finished."

He gestured sharply with his right hand; the curtain plummeted to the stage, isolating Bendigo on the skirt of the proscenium. Fear putting the whip to his nerves, Rymer groped along the curtain to find an opening.

The Reverend bunched his hands into fists and twisted: The suspenders holding Bendigo's trousers broke away with a loud snap; his pants dropped and settled around his ankles. Reacting to the sound before realizing what had happened, Bendigo took a step downstage and crashed onto his chin.

Behind the curtain, actors and stagehands turned tail and ran, scattering out of the theater in a dozen directions. Eileen, alone, paralyzed with fright, watched from the left side of the wings.

Bendigo Rymer struggled to his knees, the uncomprehending look of an injured child in his eyes, a picture of dumb confoundment. Laughter rolled over him from the audience again; a harsh, disembodied, joyless pounding that never paused, never varied.

Reverend Day propped himself up on the edge of the box, waved his hands like an orchestra conductor; the buttons on Bendigo's blouse popped off and danced across the stage. The laces on his corset roped in and knit tightly together, stays groaning with effort, cinching his belly into an hourglass; she could hear the breath being squeezed out of Rymer's lungs. His wig rotated on his head, the absurd

Prince Valiant haircut falling over his eyes. He crawled blindly on the floor, then appeared to gradually lose control of his movements, until he was jerked abruptly upright to his feet, lifted by a dozen invisible hands.

Eileen looked past Rymer, saw Reverend Day manipulating his fingers in the air as if he were controlling a marionette. Bendigo danced, arms hanging limply in the air, a pathetic shuffling encumbered by his fallen trousers. . . .

And Eileen remembered where she had known A. Glorious Day.

His name was Alexander Sparks; she had seen him practice this same impossible nightmarish possession on another man ten years ago, a small, dear Cockney burglar named Barry. Inside the dining hall of a manor house on the Yorkshire coast. Along with six other lunatic, diseased aristocrats, Sparks had directed a plot against the Royal Family; she had fallen quite by accident into the outer tendrils of its web, but eventually found herself at its center, combatting the Seven along with Sparks's brother, an agent for Queen Victoria, and a young doctor who had gone on to become a famous author. Eileen left England for America hard on the heels of that experience and had never seen any of them since.

But Alexander Sparks had looked nothing like this Reverend Day and she could find no explanation for the discrepancy, unless over time the man's demonic heart had slowly wormed its way to the surface. If this was the same person, it certainly explained his iron grip on these people; she had seen him perform similar black miracles the last time. Yes; the idea that the revolting, twisted body and visage that bound him now reflected the man's true nature was only too easy to believe.

He had not recognized her for some reason. But why that was and for what purpose this misbegotten city had been born remained questions she could not begin to answer. Cold terror pinned her to that spot backstage as securely as a railroad spike.

With a manic smile carved on his face, Rymer's dance ended and he flopped to the stage in a deep curtsy; Eileen could hear the muscles in his legs ripping away from bones as his body contorted.

A flurry of gestures from Day: Bendigo flew to his feet again, his hand drew the saber from his belt, and he marched up and down the stage, sword raised, in a mockery of military high-step. Dead laughter from the audience doubled, deafening. For one terrible instant, Bendigo caught Eileen's eye; she saw conscious agony and horror bleeding through his eyes, but words could not break past the hideous smile that had stilled his voice before his body whipped around and marched away again.

She regretted every misfortune she'd ever wished upon the man; this humiliation was something no human being should endure. Tears in her eyes, she wished for a gun to release the poor bastard from this misery; the rest of its bullets she wanted for Reverend Day.

Bendigo came to a halt and gave a salute to the box. The Reverend raised his hands over his head and Rymer rose softly into the air, his bare spindly legs windmilling comically as if he were running up invisible steps. He soared up and over the audience, then hung suspended at the Reverend's eye level. The Reverend wiggled one hand; Bendigo's black wig flew off and scampered away in the air like a terrier. The laughter reached a hysterical crescendo, then stopped dead.

"Now do tell, Mr. Rymer; I hear that you have been harboring a secret desire to play Hamlet," said Reverend Day, in an exaggerated hillbilly twang.

Wheezing for breath, Bendigo nodded slightly; his own dim response. Eileen saw a twitch of excitement light up the pathetic fool's eyes, even a small stirring of pride.

"Well now, don't be shy, why don't y'all treat us to a little sampling of your melancholy Dane, you insolent, uncivilized cur?"

The audience applauded wildly, stomped their feet and whistled, egging him on to perform. Bendigo saluted Reverend Day with the sword, acknowledged his audience with a grateful wave. He took a step back in midair and lowered his head; a moment of introspection, the actor preparing for his entrance. The audience went silent.

Bendigo turned back around, in character now, bobbing like a cork in the water. With the pinched corset torturing his voice to a strangled parody of his rich baritone, he cried out, "To be, or not to be; that is the question."

Reverend Day leaned on the edge of the box, sly boredom, propping his chin up, the fingers of one hand drumming his cheek while the other waved idly in the air.

In response to Day's gestures, with each succeeding line of the soliloquy Bendigo raised the sword and ferociously slashed himself across a part of his body; nothing spared, arms, legs, back, chest, neck, face. Each cut opened gaping wounds.

"Whether tis *nobler* . . . in the *mind* . . . to suffer the *slings* and *arrows* . . . of outrageous *fortune* . . . or take *arms* . . . against a *sea* . . . of *troubles* and by *opposing* end them."

Eileen knew their blades were severely dulled down for stage combat; Rymer was striking himself with inhuman strength. Blood rained on the audience but the white shirts offered no reaction, looking straight up, not even raising a hand to shield their faces from the splatter as it pelted down.

"To *die,* to *sleep*—no more—and by a *sleep* to say we *end* the heartache . . . and the *thousand natural shocks* that *flesh* is *heir* to!"

A devastating blow nearly severed Bendigo's left hand at the wrist; bones shattered, hanging by a thread of flesh. Sheets of blood cascaded down his face from cuts along his scalp; agony informed every word he spoke, and Eileen thought she could hear an occasional desperate cry break through beneath the words.

" 'Tis a consummation devoutly to be *wished*. To *die,* to *sleep*—to *sleep*—perchance to *dream:* ay, there's the *rub*—"

Bendigo screamed as he thrust the point of the sword clear through his lower abdomen below the corset, straining with both hands to break its blunt tip through the resistant skin of his back.

Eileen sobbed and turned away, blinded by tears and rage, trying to pull herself to her feet.

Reverend Day stood in front of Bendigo and began to slowly applaud, banging his simian hands together; the audience picked up the rhythm and the clapping grew into a booming, rhythmic beat.

"—for in that sleep of death . . ."

Bendigo's voice failing, face collapsing, gray as ash, all the emotion breaking through, underlining his final words.

". . . what dreams may come . . . when we have shuffled off this mortal coil . . . must give us pause . . ."

Eyes open, Bendigo died, suspended limply in the air. The audience rose to their feet, applause growing steadily to a thundering crescendo.

"Bravo! BRAVO!" shouted Reverend Day.

The audience amplified the mocking tribute.

Reverend Day twirled his hand; Bendigo's body revolved and bowed low in each direction, dumb acknowledgement of the only standing ovation offered to him in a long and mediocre career.

Eileen stumbled blindly to the rear wall. A lantern burned on a hook near the door. She plucked it off and hurled it at the fallen curtain; the lantern shattered, the oil spread, ignited by the wick, and began to burn.

As the flames licked up the arch, she turned and ran out the back door of the theater.

Dante had never seen a play before. Frederick and he walked in late, after the show had started, settling into seats behind Reverend Day in a box above the stage. He guessed the actors were telling some kind of story down there, but he didn't feel much interest in trying to work it out. He liked the colorful pictures of the mountains and the pieces of a castle that rolled on and off the stage, and the uniforms on the soldiers were fun to look at, too; bright red with lots of shiny buttons.

But most of all he liked that girl with the black hair and her titties pushing out the top of her low-cut dress. He slipped a hand inside his briefcase and rubbed a thumb along the edge of a knife, daydreaming about how nice it would be to use it on her. The Reverend and Frederick had made him feel so free about his work that anything seemed possible. When it was over, he might even ask them to let him have that girl to play with.

Everything started to go wrong when that big fella Cornelius rushed into the box; he said shots were being fired and some guards had been killed; and when the Reverend stood up and started screaming, Dante could see a big, red cloud come off him like a barrel of black powder exploding.

Whatever the Reverend yelled at those people below made them real scared, even Frederick went a little pale, but as far as Dante was concerned, it felt like the real fun was about to begin. Then that fat actor floated right up into the air in front of them and began to cut himself, and Dante knew that he'd been right; this was better than freaks at a sideshow.

When the fire started, Reverend Day screamed at the people in the white shirts again, "TO YOUR PLACE, GO, GO! WAIT FOR THE SIGNAL!"

Whatever had been holding up the actor's body let go, and it plopped down onto the seats like a loose hank of rope. The people in white shirts were so busy rushing to the doors, shouting and screaming, that they started stepping all over each other; couple of 'em got crushed in the stampede. Dante leaned over the balcony and watched from his seat, rocking back and forth, laughing; this was a hell of a lot funnier than anything those dumb actors had been doing.

Reverend Day whirled round on the men in the box.

"Call out the Brigade," he said to Cornelius. "Everyone knows their responsibilities; follow the Plan."

"Yes, sir," said Cornelius, and he ran out of there.

"How many of your men are left to me?" he asked Frederick.

"Nearly sixty," said Frederick.

"Assemble them at the church for the Holy Work. Then you come alone to the chapel and bring me that book as soon as our visitors arrive. You have one hour before the Work begins."

"What about the fire?" asked Frederick, nodding toward the flames shooting up the curtains.

"Let it burn. Let it all burn."

Frederick gestured for Dante to follow him and started out; the Reverend clamped a hand on Dante's arm.

"No," said the Reverend. "He stays with me."

Dante could see Frederick's jaw working; he was mad. He clicked his heels, nodded sharply, and left the booth. Reverend Day held out a hand to Dante; he giggled and snuggled up under his sheltering arm as they walked out of the box and down the mezzanine hall. Smoke rolled in around them filling the air, temperature rising from the spreading flames, but they never hurried their pace.

"How do you feel, Mr. Scruggs?"

"I feel good, sir. I feel real good."

"That's fine, boy. That's just fine," said Reverend Day, holding him closer as they started down the stairs. "It's going to be a glorious night."

chapter sixteen

WHEN FRANK MENTIONED THE STOLEN RIFLES, KANAZUCHI told him about the machine guns and it occurred to both of them that the warehouse would be a good place to start. A wind had come up, swirling dust, thickening the air. Bells were still ringing in the church tower, and as they slowly crept back toward the main street, small patrols of white shirts occasionally ran by carrying torches and weapons, heading for the center of town.

A red glow lit up the sky above that area, and they realized a fire had started to burn.

"Looks like the theater," said Frank, seeing white shirts pouring out into the street. "Eileen's in there."

"She will move away."

"To where? It spreads to those shanties, the whole town'll go up like kindling." Jacob missing, Eileen on the loose; shit, his whole plan was collapsing. Frank looked over and saw Kanazuchi studying him. "What?"

"May I offer words of advice?"

"I guess we know each other well enough."

"Events move in a flow. Picture water in a stream."

"Okay." What the hell was this, a lecture on nature appreciation?

"More water means greater force. Harder to resist."

"Like a current."

"Like a flood. Takes away everything in its path. Now; here: We are in the flood."

Frank saw a massive number of armed men assembling near the House of Hope—the same militia outfit he'd seen running around in the dark last night. He could make out Cornelius Moncrief striding around waving a rifle and shouting orders.

"So once you got your feet wet, it's better to jump in, is what you're saying," said Frank.

"Once started, it is better not to worry. The river will carry you. Trust in a positive outcome."

"Okay."

Over Kanazuchi's shoulder, Frank caught a glimpse of a white shirt sneaking up the alley behind them. Frank stood casually and swung the butt of his rifle like a baseball bat around the corner, smashing the man against the wall. He fell and lay still.

"Damn; it's working already," said Frank.

No more waiting for the right moment to cross; Main Street was crowded now. White shirts heading for the church at the end of town; a hundred torches burned there already, lighting up its dark face. The brigade of militia marched down the street toward their position, platoons peeling off to search every side street.

Searching for us, both men realized.

They lowered their weapons, waited for a rush of shirts to congest the street, then walked calmly across through the mix. No one took a run at them; the militia was still a quarter mile away and the eyes of the people passing were all focused on the church.

Reaching the alley, they broke into a run; Kanazuchi drew his sword as he took the lead. At the next intersection, a white shirt patrol turned the corner ahead of them; Kanazuchi ran right through the four men, the sword in his hands a blur, and before any of them could fire a shot, parts of three bodies hit the ground. Frank killed the fourth man with a single shot. He saw a severed hand still holding on to the torch.

Lights and activity ahead: the warehouse. A long line of white shirts crowded its broad front entrance, black shirts inside at a stack of crates, passing out a rifle and a box of bullets to each man that passed. Frank followed Kanazuchi to the rear door and they entered the warehouse.

White shirts swarmed over the interior; a chain of them relaying crates forward to the distribution area. Taking cover at the rear, ahead to their right they saw teams of men in black loading the machine guns onto the back of caissons; two of the four guns already being wheeled toward the front.

"Gatling guns," said Frank. "Shit. You weren't kidding."

"This is bad."

"Bad don't quite cover it."

"Can you work one of these guns?" asked Kanazuchi.

"Yup."

As they turned to go, two guards in black came through the door, pistols drawn; they reacted quickly, raising the guns to fire. Kanazuchi rolled to the floor and as he came to his knees the long knife flew between them and pinned one guard's forearm to the door. His finger pulled the trigger before the gun dropped; the bullet shot harmlessly into the ceiling. Kanazuchi killed him with the Grass Cutter before he could scream.

The second man had the drop on Frank; no time to raise the Henry, Frank spanked out his Colt and fired. The man went down but his single shot creased Frank's face, skidding across his cheek, chipping the bone. Blood slipped from the wound in freshets; pain seared his nerves. Frank raised a hand to it and realized the damage was slight.

But at the sharp report of the guns, all work in the warehouse stopped, a hundred eyes searching for the source. Kanazuchi yanked the *wakizashi* from the dead guard's arm and they ran out of the warehouse, crossed the open plaza, and sprinted down an alley. Saw torches coming toward them from Main Street and veered right. Flames ignited the sky ahead; deep shades of orange and red, the fire spreading. Behind them men from the warehouse spilled down the side streets, the search intensifying.

Frank stumbled trying to keep pace with Kanazuchi; he had the night vision of a cat. Fifty steps ahead, Kanazuchi pushed him into a cramped chicken coop, hens scattering. Frank gasped for air; Kanazuchi closed his eyes, breathed deeply, drew his energy inward, and listened. One group rushed by outside, shouting to another. A minute later, a second group passed them, heading in the other direction.

The roar and crackle of the fire advanced on them; distant

screams twisted in the wind, crashes as a ruined building came down. Clusters of ash drifted, black snowflakes. A dim red glow lit the coop's interior; Frank could just make out the hard line of Kanazuchi's face, staring out at the night. Out of habit, Frank reloaded the Colt. He looked up at another sound, shocking, completely unexpected.

Children singing. A chorus of voices.

"What the hell . . ." whispered Frank.

Kanazuchi instantly alert. "Come."

They left the hiding place and followed the voices down the alley to the next street; ahead of them, marching together, herded by white shirts ringed around them, at least a hundred children, the ones Kanazuchi had seen in the holding pen, singing "Old McDonald Had a Farm." A few of the small ones crying, frightened; most of them skipping along, strings of them holding hands, laughing happily.

"Only kids I've seen here," said Frank.

For the first time, Frank saw anger in Kanazuchi's eyes.

"What are they doing?" asked Frank.

"Taking them to the church. They are all going to the church."

Miles before they reached the town, they saw the fire. The blistering pace Jack set in the lead spread them out over a quarter of a mile, but as he drew within sight of the guardhouse and gate, he slowed and waited for Walks Alone to catch him. Off to their right, strangled formations of rock glowed in the moonlight.

As she drew alongside, Jack whispered, "Three men."

"To the right," she said.

Jack nodded.

Doyle and the others still lagged a half mile behind. Jack and Walks Alone skirted the gate and rode on until the rocks were behind them, then doubled back, tied the horses near the entrance to a narrow passage, and entered on foot, drawing their knives.

In a clearing at the center of the formation, they found three horses and the cold remains of a campfire. Using gestures to communicate, they split up and stalked silently toward two openings at the guardhouse end of the clearing. Jack scaled a high rock to survey while Walks Alone waited below for direction.

Three men wearing loose black clothes stationed across a hundred-yard stretch at the edge of the rocks. Sniper rifles in hand. One held a pair of field glasses, watching Doyle and the others arrive at the guardhouse. Jack pointed Walks Alone toward the one to the left, jumped down softly, and moved in on the man in the middle.

Walks Alone tossed a handful of pebbles against the rocks to the man's left. As he turned, she ran in from the right and slashed his throat with one downward stroke of her knife. The man slammed her back against the rocks with a powerful blow, raised a hand to his throat, and realized the artery had been cut. Calmly pressing one hand to the spurting wound, he pulled his pistol with the other. She ducked under his arm before he could fire, plunged the blade in below the center of his ribs and ripped upward. Letting go of the handle, she covered the man's mouth with one hand and wrestled the gun from him with the other. He sank slowly to the dirt and died.

The guard in the middle heard faint sounds of the scuffle to his left, then something scraped the rocks behind him; all he saw was a deadly descending shadow.

Walks Alone joined Jack at the center position; together they approached the third guard. All they found was a pile of cigarette butts in the sand. Both sprinted back to the clearing; the guard was already on his horse, riding toward the passage. Walks Alone threw her knife; it clattered off the rock near the man's head.

They ran after him, losing ground; by the time they reached their horses, the black shirt was back on the road, riding low, heading for The New City. Jack pulled his rifle from the saddle, ran forward, steadied the barrel against a rock, and drew a bead on the disappearing figure.

Doyle and the other men were examining the telegraph key in the guardhouse when they heard two rifle shots crack the night. They ran out to the road; Jack and Walks Alone galloped toward them out of the darkness.

"After us," shouted Jack. "One of them got away."

Both of them covered in blood.

Jack and Walks Alone wheeled and took off down the road.

"Jack's back," said Doyle.

"I couldn't help but notice," answered Innes.

"Lionel," said Doyle, "perhaps you ought to wait here. . . ."

"By myself?" said Lionel, launching himself into the saddle like a veteran. "Are you crazy? Let's ride."

They followed Jack's hell-bent pace. The sky grew red; the violent bouncing of the saddles blurred their vision, giving the horizon a shimmering miragelike surreality, until The New City itself finally came into view; the entire southern half of the town was engulfed in fire, wind gusts fanning sheets of flame to towering heights. On the north side of Main Street, most of the buildings remained intact.

They heard church bells ringing, and at the far end of that street, for the first time they saw the black tower stark against the sky, lit up by the inferno, marbled in a dozen hues of swirling red reflections. A sea of torches swarmed around its base above an undulating mass of white that they realized was a crowd of people.

A second gate blocked the road in a fence that ringed the settlement; Jack and Walks Alone steadied their horses' strides on approach and cleared it with a jump. Two black-shirted guards jumped out of the guardhouse and took aim at their backs. Presto and Innes quickly dismounted and cut the guards down with a volley before they could shoot.

"This is it!" shouted Innes, running forward, opening the gate while Presto covered him.

"Leave the horses here," said Doyle, climbing down.

"But they've already gone on," said Lionel, pointing to Main Street where Jack and Walks Alone had ridden from view.

"We'll need a way back out," said Doyle, ending the discussion. "Tie them here."

They secured the horses to the gate and armed themselves.

"Lionel," said Doyle, "why don't you wait for us here as well. . . ."

"No, goddammit," said Lionel, cocking his Winchester as he'd seen the others do. "Stop treating me as if I'm some sort of inconvenience. It's my father who's in here somewhere, and I've a better right than anyone to be—"

A bullet whistled, knocking off his hat; Innes yanked Lionel to the ground, and the four scrambled to cover behind the guardhouse as another shot kicked off the gate.

"I do apologize," said Doyle to Lionel, who was nervously fingering the hole in his hat.

Halfway down Main Street, Jack and Walks Alone stopped in front of a large adobe house; the fire burning too intensely to risk taking the horses in any farther. They grabbed their rifles, turned the horses around, and spanked them back in the direction of the gate.

At the far end of the street through a thick haze of smoke and dust, they could see a column of people in white shirts moving toward the black church, where a large crowd moved slowly and steadily through its doors.

"There," said Jack, pointing toward the church. "That's where we're supposed to go, isn't it?"

Walks Alone nodded. They moved.

A patrol of white shirts came out of an alley; Jack calmly pulled his pistol and fired four times. As they stepped over the bodies, another figure stumbled toward them out of the darkness. Walks Alone raised the shotgun in her hand to fire, but Jack pushed the barrel aside.

A woman. Wearing a white low-cut gown with an Empire waist, a paste tiara fastened to her thick black hair. Face blackened with soot, dress shredded, arms raised in desperation.

"Help me, please," she said.

Jack stared at her. "Oh, my God."

The woman's eyes hit Jack and grew wide. "Oh, my God."

Walks Alone saw recognition lighting Jack's eyes as well. He moved right to the woman and she fell into his arms, holding on for dear life.

"It's you. It's really you, it's really you." Eileen opened her eyes, saw the Indian woman covered with blood over Jack's shoulder, and gasped.

"You're all right?" asked Jack.

She nodded, tears falling onto his shoulder.

"Where's Frank?" she asked, irrationally deciding they all must know each other.

"Who's Frank?" he asked.

"He went to look for Jacob."

"Jacob is here?" said Walks Alone.

"You know Jacob?" asked Eileen.

"He is here, then," said Jack.

"Yes, he's with your brother," said Eileen. "He killed Bendigo."

"Jacob did?" asked Jack.

"No; your brother."

"So my brother's here."

"Yes."

"Who's Bendigo?" asked Walks Alone, growing more confused.

"Who's she?" asked Eileen.

"A friend. Where's Jacob now?"

"I don't know; we came in with the Japanese man. . . ."

"Japanese man?" asked Walks Alone.

"*This* Japanese man?" asked Jack, pulling out the flier.

"That's him," said Eileen.

"Where is he?" asked Jack.

"I don't know; maybe with Frank."

"Who's Frank?" asked Walks Alone.

"Wait," said Jack, to both of them. "Slow down. Back up."

Jack pulled them into the shadows of the alley; Eileen took a deep breath and tried her best to explain.

At the guardhouse, shots peppered the logs around the four men. Their return fire had failed to flush out the sniper; Doyle looked through his spyglass and spotted a muzzle flash in the darkness of a shack to the northeast, a hundred yards away across open sand.

"We can't stay here," said Doyle.

"I'll have a go," said Presto.

The men looked at each other.

"Bit of the old tiger hunt," he said blithely. "Nothing to it."

"You're one of the dreamers," said Doyle. "You've some part to play in all this. Can't risk losing you off the board."

Presto reluctantly deferred. Doyle looked at his brother.

"Me, then," said Innes.

Doyle nodded. Innes edged to the side of the logs, looked left, and saw Jack's and Walks Alone's horses galloping toward him.

"Diversionary fire would be much appreciated," said Innes.

On Doyle's signal, the other three men rose up and emptied their guns toward the sniper. Innes dashed out from behind the guardhouse in front of the advancing horses. They reared as he approached; he grabbed one by the reins and used the horse as cover to take him to the nearest structure, a row of shanties north of the main street. By the time the sniper could spot him, the horse had run off again and Innes was in place; the shots cracked harmlessly through the wood over his head.

With the sniper firing at Innes, Doyle jumped out and grabbed the bridles of the horses, gathered them in, and tied them with the others behind the guardhouse. Presto spotted Edison's suitcase strapped to Jack's saddle and pulled it down.

Innes rushed silently through the back of the shanty, negotiating a series of empty buildings until he was directly behind the sniper's position. He picked up a rock, cocked his pistol, and closed in on the shack's rear door.

Through the glass, Doyle saw movement in the shack window and took off at a dead run toward the building.

Innes tossed the rock onto the roof of a lean-to on the right and kicked open the back door, ready to fire; the shack was empty. He heard a hammer cock to his left and dove to the ground; the first bullet cut through the meat of his upper left arm, the second kicked into the ground beside his head. His return shot went through the window wide, missing the sniper, a man in black outside the building. The sniper raised the rifle to finish him when three shots exploded in a burst and knocked the man out of sight.

Innes lay still, cocking the pistol, hands shaking violently. "Get him? Did you get him?"

Silence. Innes lowered the gun when Arthur appeared in the window, holding his smoking rifle.

"Got him," said Doyle, looking down at the man in black clothes.

"Is that the one?" asked Innes, feeling both faint and talkative. "Is that the one that got away? Out there, I mean. You know; the one they saw."

"He'll do for it. Not too bad, is it, old boy?"

"Not too bad," said Innes, gingerly touching his wounded arm. "Clean through, I think."

Doyle kicked down a wall of the shack to get to his brother and improvised a field wrap from a strip of his shirt to staunch the bleeding.

"Handy having a doctor along," said Innes, watching him work. "I should be good for an action medal now. Service ribbon, at the least."

"Victoria Cross, if I have anything to say about it. From the old girl herself."

"Younger brothers are good for something, after all," said Innes.

Doyle finished applying the bandage and patted him on the back, afraid that if he tried to speak he'd burst into tears. He helped Innes to his feet as the other two men ran up to join them; he noticed that Lionel carried the crate that contained the Book of Zohar.

"We must find Jack," said Doyle. "And then I think we'd better be getting you along to that church."

They returned to the horses and Doyle grabbed the medical kit from his saddlebag. Armed to the teeth, the four men walked down the middle of Main Street. The buildings to their left had already collapsed as the heart of the fire laid waste to the southern half of town. Red cinder and ash drifted toward them. The wind was shifting to the north; Doyle estimated it wouldn't be long before the other side of town ignited and began to burn.

As they neared the largest building left standing on their right, a solid adobe hacienda, Jack called out and waved them into the shelter of an alley.

"Someone here to see you, Doyle," said Jack.

Eileen stepped out of the shadows.

"Hello, Arthur," she said.

Doyle stared at her, stunned to his core, a thousand fragmented memories rushing into his mind at the trigger of her voice, riding a dozen colliding powerful emotions.

"Hello," he said.

She looked sheepish, relieved, bashful, ashamed, frightened, happy—in other words, the same violently oscillating range of feeling she had always managed to simultaneously convey during their brief and unforgettable romance.

"Someone you know?" whispered Innes, with the intuitive insinuation only a brother could manage.

Doyle nodded slightly, waving him away, unable to speak.

"You got my letter, I guess," she said when they were alone. The letter in which she'd said good-bye when she left England ten years before; the letter that had snapped his young heart in two.

"Yes," was all he could manage.

"How have you been?" she asked, then before he could answer: "What a stupid question, I know perfectly well how you've been; you're famous, for God's sake, probably fabulously wealthy, and married—"

"Yes."

"—I remember reading somewhere, with a lovely wife and three gorgeous children. And how have I been? Well, look at me."

"You look . . . beautiful."

She smiled ruefully and pulled the paste tiara off her head. "Awfully nice of you to say, Arthur."

"I mean it."

"If I'd stayed with you, I'd most likely own a real one of these by now. Really know how to back a winner, don't I. . . . No, I've been all right, it's been a fine life. I'm just not at the top of my game at the moment. . . ."

She burst into tears. Doyle put a comforting hand on her shoulder, then allowed her to hug him briefly before she pulled herself together. "Give me a moment, would you, dear?"

She walked off a short way without meeting his eyes.

The thousand things he had longed to say to her. All the experiences they'd never shared. He still wanted her, he knew that much. And it was impossible; not here, not now. And unless he wanted to destroy the life he'd worked so hard to build, not ever.

Jack had gathered Presto and Walks Alone at the edge of the street. He moved to where Doyle was standing. "We need to move on."

Doyle noodded wearily. Jack looked over at Innes, favoring his wounded arm. "Innes all right?"

"He'll survive."

"Will you?" said Jack, with a sly glance back at Eileen.

Doyle took him in. "That remains to be seen."

"Arthur, you're under no further obligation. Already far beyond the call. We'll carry on from here."

"But Jack—"

Sparks raised a gentle hand to still him. "We were the only ones actually invited to this party, remember?"

"What will you do if you find him? Alexander."

"I don't honestly know."

Through the net of his turbulent feelings, Doyle realized that standing in front of him was a man bearing an exact resemblance to his old friend Jack; light in his eyes again, life animating his gestures, a curl of amusement lifting the corners of his mouth.

How extraordinary to find him here, now, in this moment. Just when I might lose him again.

"My God, it's you," said Doyle, blinking in amazement.

"None other. Ever so faithfully yours, old friend," said Jack.

He laid a hand on Doyle's shoulder; Doyle covered Jack's hand with his and gripped tightly; the rest, a great deal, passed wordlessly between them. Doyle nodded in gratitude, wiping away the single tear that rolled down his cheek. Jack pulled away, snapped a jaunty salute, and with Presto and Walks Alone flanking him, started down Main Street toward the black church.

The bells in the church tower stopped ringing; the howling of the fire filled the silence.

"I'm coming with you," said Lionel, trotting after them, still carrying the Book of Zohar.

"We should follow behind," called Doyle to Jack. "Lay down some covering fire. . . ."

"Up to you, old man," shouted Jack over his shoulder. "I can't stop you."

"So," said Innes, who'd been slowly working up to speaking with Eileen. "Where do you know my brother from?"

Eileen, sitting on the steps of the House of Hope, resting her head in her hands, looked up through bleary eyes and gave the young man a once-over. "Church group."

"Shared the same pew, did you?" said Innes, with a knowing smile.

She smiled back; cheeky one, wasn't he?

"My dance card's a little crowded at the moment, junior," she said. "But thanks for asking."

"Sorry?" said Innes, thoroughly perplexed. For the first time, it occurred to him that there might be some women in this world who were out of his league.

Doyle walked back to them, holding a pair of rifles.

"Do you still know how to shoot?" he asked Eileen.

"I haven't forgotten much of anything."

"Good," said Doyle, handing her a rifle. "Then follow me."

As the city collapsed, so too did the white shirts' organized pursuit of the two intruders; Frank and Kanazuchi raced ahead of the fire through the southern side of town, shadowing the escorted group of children. They passed the workers' quarters where Kanazuchi had spent the night and drew within sight of the cathedral; the wide gap separating it from the shanties had acted as a firebreak, so neither the church nor any of its surrounding structures was in any immediate danger.

As the children marched over the open ground to the church, Frank and Kanazuchi realized they had no chance to attack and kill their escorts without endangering the children. They hung back at the supply shacks and watched as the children folded into the white shirts outside the cathedral, moving obediently along with the crowd through the entrance. With most of the town's population, including the armed militia, now secured inside, the doors to the cathedral slammed shut behind them.

"Wrong time for the Sunday sermon," said Frank.

The bells in the tower stopped ringing. As the echoes faded, they heard only the windborne moaning of the fire.

Kanazuchi gestured and led Frank closer, to a tool shed on the edge of the work area. As they ducked inside, an assembly of guards wearing black trotted toward the church from a number of different directions and fell into a defensive formation across its entire facade.

Frank counted nearly fifty of them.

The men in black lifted and slid thick wooden bars through brackets on the cathedral doors. Frank and Kanazuchi looked at each other, asking the same question: Why are they locking the doors on *this* side?

Cornelius Moncrief stepped around the side of the church. A squad of men in black rolled the Gatling guns on their caissons into position, facing out, protecting the cathedral doors; one at the front, one at either side entrance. Another team pulled the fourth gun around to the back.

Cornelius glanced at his watch, gave another order, and three-man teams who appeared to know what they were doing took their places at each of the gun positions.

"All this for us?" asked Frank. "I mean, we're good, but—"

"Not for us," said Kanazuchi.

"Maybe they saw something. Maybe the army's coming for its guns."

Frank saw an alarming idea enter Kanazuchi's mind.

"This way," he said.

They backtracked from the work area near the cathedral entrance and followed the men pulling the last machine gun to the rear. Frank and Kanazuchi settled in behind one of the high mounds of rocks and debris above the path and watched the men in black pass beneath them, stop and set up the gun twenty feet from the rear doors of the church. Frank turned to look at the sheer wall of rock rising in back of the mounds.

"Nobody's gonna attack from this side," he said, puzzled.

Moments later half of the black-clad guards they'd seen out front ran in and formed a line to either side of the Gatling across the rear of the building. Each man carried a repeating Winchester and an extra ammunition belt; they knelt in firing positions, loaded and cocked their guns. Then the team manning the machine gun wheeled the muzzle around and aimed it directly at the rear doors.

"Want to tell me what the hell you think's going on here, Hammer?"

"They are going to kill them."

"Who?"

"The people in the church."

Frank paused. "That's just plain crazy."

Kanazuchi looked at him and nodded.

"And I suppose you think we ought to stop 'em."

"Yes."

"That's what I thought. Shit."

Frank looked off toward the south, past the reddened horizon.

"Mexico," he said quietly.

"What did you say?"

"I said what part of the river are we in now?"

Kanazuchi smiled slightly. "Most treacherous part."

"Suppose you got an idea 'bout how we're gonna do this."

"*Hai*."

Frank lit a cigar. "You want to tell me or you gonna make me guess?"

He told him.

Reverend Day didn't loosen his fierce grip on Dante's arm the whole way across between Main Street and the church; about halfway there, Dante realized the Reverend was holding on to him so tight because he needed help to walk. Smoke and heat choked the air, making breathing difficult at best. The Reverend hadn't said a word for a while; his face looked gray in the red light and his breath smelled worse than some of the jars in Dante's suitcases.

After leaving the theater, they had gone to the House of

Hope, and Dante stood by as the Reverend rummaged through his desk, reading some papers real intently like he was trying to remember something; outside the office lay the bodies of four dead guards he hadn't even looked at. Then they'd gone down and out through a secret passage in the wall and started walking here. The Reverend had been getting weaker with every step. Dante felt scared; he didn't even want to think about anything bad happening to Reverend Day.

Ahead to the left, the last of a crowd of white shirts pressed inside the church; Dante even saw some little kids in the mix. The Reverend looked at the church, looked at his watch, seemed satisfied, then steered them to the right until they found two steel plates set in the dirt. Fumbling out a ring of keys, the Reverend dropped them on the ground.

"If you would be kind enough . . . to do the honors," said the Reverend, weary and strained.

"Sure."

Dante picked up the keys, the Reverend fished out the right one for him, and Dante undid the padlock. He lifted the heavy plates off their hinges, revealing a steep staircase descending belowground. The Reverend took his arm again and Dante helped him down the steps. Handing him some matches, the Reverend directed Dante to light a lantern hung on a bracket beside the black stone door at the base of the stairs. It reminded Dante of a bank vault he'd seen once. With the aid of the lantern, the Reverend used another key to unlock the door; he pushed it lightly with one hand and it swung silently open.

A blast of cool, refreshing air washed over them. The Reverend breathed deeply, leaning against the doorway for support.

"You okay, sir?" asked Dante plaintively.

The Reverend nodded, laughed slightly at his concern, tousled Dante's hair, and waved him inside. A clean room, carved out of smooth stone, as cold and welcoming as springwater. An earthy smell that reminded Dante of a graveyard in the rain. The Reverend lowered himself slowly into the room's only chair, fumbled out his watch, and checked the time again.

"You are to wait here, lad," he said, taking Dante's hand, speaking simply and directly. "Leave that door open. Frederick will be along with something that I need; when he does, ring this bell, here on the wall, and I'll come for it. Do not go back to the surface or follow me into that passage. . . ."

The Reverend pointed to a dark, curving hallway leading out of the room, carved from the same black marble.

"If anyone besides Frederick comes in, you are to kill them. Do you understand?"

"Yes, sir, Reverend."

"That's a good boy," he said, patting Dante's hand. "Help me up and we'll get started."

Dante pulled the Reverend to his feet; the man felt as insubstantial as a scarecrow. Reverend Day gripped the lantern in one hand and walked to the edge of the black hallway, smiled, and waved once to Dante. Dante waved back and the Reverend limped out of sight around the corner. Alone in the dark, Dante sat on the chair facing the door, laid his briefcase across his lap, and undid the clasps. He picked out his two favorite knives by touch, closed the case, and set it carefully beside the chair. His eyes adjusted to the dark, and soon a faint red glow lit up the outline of the open door.

He noticed that outside the church bells had stopped ringing.

Long before it reached him, Jacob saw the light of a lantern approach from the maze, reflecting off its smooth black walls; he'd been lying so long in total darkness, it took him a few moments to figure out which way he was looking: straight up? straight down? For some time he had been hearing the disorienting ghostly echoes of a thousand murmuring voices, the generalized hum of a crowd, drifting down from somewhere above.

He remembered he was on the floor, cold stone beneath him, hands and feet numb from the constrictions of the rope. When consciousness had first returned and Jacob found himself still breathing, he couldn't have been more surprised; surely the Reverend must have killed him by now.

Maybe he had. Maybe this was proof of an afterlife. If so, you'd think they could afford some lights over here.

Considering how lousy I feel, thought Jacob when he realized he was alive, I might as well be dead. But if this is Reverend Day I hear coming, maybe I won't have long to wait.

The shuffling footsteps; spurs jingling.

Yes, it was him.

Reverend Day entered the chamber, and by the light of his lantern for the first time Jacob saw the round room where he had been lying. In a slight depression scooped from the center of a round pattern, a detailed mosaic of some kind, set in the stone floor. Arrayed around him at the edge of the circle, he counted six silver pedestals. A squat coal-burning brazier stood off to one side. The cold wind he had felt issued from a rough gaping hole in the earth at the end of the room opposite the maze; a wide trough cut in the floor ran down to the lip of the hole from the hollow where he lay. Set in the ceiling above him, he saw a tight circle of grills that looked like manhole covers; the spectral voices he had heard were issuing from there.

The Reverend hobbled around the room, lighting a series of lanterns on the walls from the one he carried. He moved to Jacob, stood over and studied him a moment; when Jacob didn't move, the Reverend nudged him with the toe of a boot.

"I'm awake," said Jacob.

"Really? I would have settled for alive; *awake* is something of a bonus. I was afraid you might miss all the fun."

Jacob kept silent.

"I know how extraordinarily conversant you are with your Torah, Rabbi; how are you with Scripture?"

"Forgive me, I—"

"The Book of Revelation, for example."

Jacob's heart skipped a beat; he tried to adjust his position to jar it back into rhythm, and in doing so for the first time since the man entered, he caught a glimpse of the Reverend's face.

Good God. He looks worse than I feel. Like an exhumed corpse.

Caked blood encrusted his face, which had gone whiter than ivory. Blood vessels rimming his forehead undulated as if they had come to life and broken free of their moorings. His eyes looked as red and savage as raw meat.

"Let me refresh your memory," said the Reverend. " 'The blood of the innocent shall rain down into the wound that hath opened in the earth and the Beast shall ascend, which is the angel of the bottomless pit, whose name in the Hebrew tongue is Abaddon. And he shall make war against them and overcome them and kill them.' Ring any bells for you, does it, Rabbi?"

Jacob shook his head.

"Oh, it will," said Reverend Day, craning his neck to look at the grills overhead. "When the bells start to ring again and the Holy Work begins."

Dante saw a shadow creep across the wall outside the door; he stood up, holding his knives, ready to pounce. The door pushed open; Frederick. Dante relaxed, then saw the terrible look on Frederick's face.

"Is he in there?" asked Frederick, pointing toward the maze.

Dante nodded.

"Then we'll never find him." He looked furious, more agitated than Dante had ever seen him.

"Do you have the book?" asked Dante.

"No. Here is our situation, Mr. Scruggs: There is no more *time* and the Reverend has defaulted on what is owed to me, an enormous sum, and there is no *money*"—Frederick's face contorted in a spasm of rage—"anywhere in the town that I can find. Giving our lives without recompense is not part of my arrangement. Do you understand? No further service is required here; I am taking my leave. If you want to live, I suggest you do the same."

Dante looked toward the hall, thought for a moment, then shook his head. He liked Frederick well enough, but he liked the Reverend even more.

"Suit yourself," said Frederick, and he vanished up the stairs.

Dante walked to the center of the room: What should he

do? Ring the bell, have the Reverend come all the way back just to tell him Frederick didn't bring the book? That would only make him mad. Maybe he should go look for him. But the Reverend had said not to follow him into the hallway.

Dante stood paralyzed with indecision, until he again heard footsteps on the stairs.

As they neared the front of the church and saw the black-shirted guards rolling something on wheels into place, Jack directed them behind the cover of a stonecutter's hut. Presto and Lionel tried to make sense of the movement around the cathedral.

"What we're looking for is under the tower," said Jack.

"Right," said Presto.

Looking to her right about a hundred yards away, Walks Alone caught sight of a man in a suit climbing up out of the earth and sprinting off into the darkness.

"Over there," she whispered.

She led them to the spot from where she'd seen the man emerge; two steel flaps hinged back, stairs descending.

"This is it," said Jack.

Walks Alone led the way down the stairs.

"According to the dream, there are supposed to be six of them in total, whoever or whatever they're supposed to be, correct?" asked Innes.

Innes had hardly stopped talking since the moment he'd been shot; he's warding off shock, thought Doyle. He had led Innes and Eileen to shelter at the north edge of the shanties and was watching Jack and the others through his spyglass as they cautiously approached the church.

"Agreed," said Doyle.

"So Jack, Presto, and Mary what's her name, there's three of them," said Innes.

"Jacob and Kanazuchi," said Eileen, lying between them, rifle in hand.

"That's five," said Doyle.

"So my question is, if how many of them there are is so all-fired important—and it seems to be—"

"Who's number six?" said Doyle. "Not an uninteresting question."

He moved the glass right to follow their friends, as Walks Alone led them to a flat, featureless area where they stopped and studied something in the dirt.

"What are they doing?" whispered Doyle.

A moment later, he watched them disappear into the ground.

"What the devil?"

"What is it?" asked Eileen.

"Are you up to moving on?" Doyle asked Innes.

"Right; lead away."

"Eileen?"

"I don't fancy hanging back here by my lonesome, thank you."

They helped Innes to his feet and crept closer.

Dante withdrew into the blackness of the hall behind him as the door swung open, grateful the Reverend had given him permission to kill whoever came through that door. He gripped the knives tightly, flush with heat, poised to rush forward and go to work.

He stopped dead when he saw the Indian woman.

The shock delayed his attack long enough for the three men to step into the room behind her. All carrying guns; one with a small suitcase. His eye jumped to the chair where he'd been sitting.

Damn, he'd left his case sitting on the floor.

The lead man, a tall, thin one who vaguely reminded him of Reverend Day, went to the case, flipped it open, showed its contents to the others, then tossed it aside. They talked in whispering voices—Dante heard the word "Chicago"—then the tall man pointed them toward the hall where Dante was hiding.

Dante quickly felt his way along the wall to the first corner. He took a quiet breath, reached out to feel his way, and headed deep into the darkness.

Presto opened Edison's suitcase and took out the flash-a-light. Jack pulled from a pocket in his vest a handful of small square patches and the compass. Narrowing its aperture to a pinpoint, Jack turned on the flash-a-light, shined it briefly on the patches, took a reading off the compass, turned off the light, and led them to the mouth of the hallway.

"Do you remember this part of the dream?" he asked, voice low.

"Tunnels," said Walks Alone. "Twisted passages."

"Something like a maze," said Presto.

"Right," said Jack, attaching one of the patches to the wall at eye level; its back was coated with adhesive and it glowed a faint luminescent green. "We'll head north by northwest, towards the church."

Jack opened the suitcase and took out the night-vision glasses, handing the flash-a-light and the compass to Presto and Lionel. Jack slipped on the goggles and peered ahead into the corridor.

"Keep the light handy. Stay close," said Jack.

Wide enough to accommodate two people abreast, the hall gaped before them like a black throat. The other three followed Jack into the corridor, and its vast darkness instantly swallowed what little light issued from the room behind. Ten cautious steps on, they came to the first corner. Jack examined each of the three open passages.

"Compass," he whispered.

Presto turned on the flash-a-light; a minuscule beam hit the face of the compass in Lionel's hand.

"Northwest," said Presto, pointing left. He turned off the light.

Jack attached another glowing patch to the wall, and they inched their way down the left-hand passage. The red-tinged field of vision afforded by the goggles revealed little more to him than the crude outline of the walls; the glasses primarily detected objects that radiated heat. None were in sight.

Walks Alone caught the scent of something on a wind that blew toward them: chloroform, formaldehyde. The hair on the back of her neck stood on end.

Was it possible? She quietly pulled the knife from her belt.

*   *   *

Doyle, Innes, and Eileen crept down the stairs to the sanctum, entered the foyer, and waited for their eyes to adjust. Innes noticed a glowing green patch inside the hallway. He wanted to follow but on instinct Doyle held them back.

"Not yet," he said.

He led them back up the stairs where they stopped belowground, rested their rifles on the plates, and trained them on the church.

"I'm not trying to be critical, but what are we waiting for?" whispered Eileen.

"I'm not entirely sure," said Doyle.

"Did you miss me, Arthur?" she whispered a moment later.

"Not at all," he said. "Desperately."

"Good," she said. "Sorry."

Dead silence from the direction of the church; looking through the glass, he saw a huge man in a long, gray coat move along the line of men in black outside the front doors. The big man stopped to glance at his watch; he gave a signal, the bars across the doors were removed, and a team of men began turning what looked like a machine gun around to face the cathedral.

"Good Christ," said Doyle.

Another patch went on the wall; they were following the track of the compass, but Walks Alone could have led them on the air coming toward them alone. Jack stopped, his foot encountering an irregular shape.

"Light," he whispered.

Presto directed the light to the ground and turned it on; Jack pressed his foot down onto a slightly elevated patch of marble. A three-foot-square section of floor directly ahead of them dropped away. Shining the light into the pit that opened, they saw a field of gleaming spikes.

"Jump over or double back?" asked Jack.

"This is the right way," said Walks Alone, pointing ahead.

"Jump, then."

Presto opened the aperture and used it to guide the leap

across; Lionel carried the book and went first; Presto last, carrying the light. By the time they readied themselves on the far side and Jack had taken another reading of the compass, the light began to falter.

"Battery's fading," said Presto, switching it off.

They tested each step ahead. Reached another intersection that branched to the left and right; three passages from which to choose, all heading in the same direction. Jack stared down each of the corridors through the goggles. Presto thought he could make out a faint aura of light in each of the tunnels ahead.

"We're close," said Walks Alone.

Jack stuck a patch on the wall then handed the remaining ones to Presto and Walks Alone. "We'll each take a path a short way ahead. Lionel, with me. Call out at once if the light increases; we'll meet back here."

Jack attached a second patch next to the first.

They separated and edged up each of the three corridors. Presto widened the aperture and kept his finger on the switch of the light, a pistol in his other hand. Walks Alone gripped her knife and felt her way along the wall. Lionel held on to Jack's belt; Jack stopped when he heard a faint echo of voices ahead.

"Jacob!" Jack cried out.

"Father!" Lionel shouted.

Through the dim filtered screen of the goggles, Jack saw a line of heat and movement cross his vision in the nest of passages ahead and he realized his mistake.

Reverend Day's head twisted around as he heard the voices call out from the tunnel.

No, this was wrong, too close; the boy was supposed to stop them.

He pulled out his watch; two minutes before Cornelius gave the signal and the Holy Work began. He heard a laugh and whipped his stiff neck around to look at Jacob; the Jew was *smiling* at him.

"Expecting someone?" asked Jacob.

A low sustained rumble sounded from deep inside the pit. "As a matter of fact, I am," said the Reverend, returning the smile.

Here we go again, thought Frank.

His hands were in the air; Kanazuchi had the rifle pointed at his back.

What the hell, maybe Hammer's black pajamas looked enough like what these men were wearing to get them close. If they didn't, not much else mattered.

They marched down the embankment and across the space between them and the line of men, then along toward the Gatling gun. The first of the men in black caught sight and just stared at them. Word traveled fast down the line, reaching the gun well before they did, just as Cornelius Moncrief walked around the side of the church.

"Two minutes!" he called out.

Two of the men in black pulled the bar out of the brackets on the doors. They swung open, and the team manning the machine gun pointed it inside.

Cornelius saw the two men approaching and started straight at them, pulling a pistol; Frank could tell they were going to meet up right in front of the gun. He noticed that its safety was off and the feeder belt had already been attached to the mouth of the gun.

Good.

"What the hell is this?" asked Cornelius.

They came together and stopped three feet apart.

"One of the intruders," said Kanazuchi.

"Hi, Cornelius," said Frank. "Remember me?"

Cornelius stared at him, eyebrows wriggling like caterpillars. Frank saw the pupils in the man's eyes constrict: Cornelius's gun started up.

"You dumb fuck," said Frank.

Frank drew the Colt and fired six times, punching a circle around his heart.

Kanazuchi turned and emptied the rifle on the men at the Gatling, killing all three. Before the men in the line on either side could react Kanazuchi pulled the Grass Cutter and attacked to his right.

Frank jumped to the Gatling and swung it back left; he caught a glimpse through the doors of a sea of white shirts down on the cathedral floor, a splash of red moonlight shining on them through a round glass window. His hand found the crank and he let the Gatling rip; a stream of bullets kicked up a cloud of dust, hitting the ground to the left of the line—damn thing wasn't calibrated; fucking army didn't know how to fucking maintain its fucking equipment.

Men in black in the line returned fire. Frank found the balance in the gun as it continued to fire and wrestled it to the right. Now bullets ripped directly down the flank of their line, chewing it up, tossing men back and to the sides; ones in the rear ran for cover as they saw the others fall.

A shot smashed through Frank's boot; his left ankle shattered. He staggered but kept cranking; heard a bullet clip his ear. Another ripped clean through his right upper thigh.

Missed the bone, thought Frank. He kept his right hand glued to the crank and screamed through the pain.

Behind Frank, Kanazuchi barreled into the right side of the line; the Grass Cutter never stopped. The men had trouble distinguishing him from one of their own, and the ferocity of his assault drew their attention away from the machine gun. All they knew before he was on top of them was that this man had a sword and he moved like the wind. Their bullets struck each other as they fired wildly, others taken down by shots that missed the man at the Gatling. Highly disciplined soldiers, all of them, but their panicked cries testified that they'd never faced this hot a fight before. Their bullets whistled through the man but didn't seem to strike him. They saw limbs fly off their comrades. Heads dropped from necks, bodies opened, and the sword mowed through them as if it possessed a life of its own.

Ten men died before the others dropped their weapons and ran, and still the man with the blood-red sword came after them. One stroke apiece; he finished the assault with a terrible economy of violence. When the last man fell, without hesitation Kanazuchi disappeared around the right side of the church, zeroing in on the team stationed at the second gun.

Frank erased the last of the black shirts on his side with a burst that cut through a mound of dirt the man had sought shelter behind. He released the crank as the last cartridge fed through the gun. He reached down for more ammunition. His hand burned as it grazed the barrel.

A hail of bullets cut the air over his head; Frank glanced through the cathedral and saw muzzle bursts from the open front doors at the far end. Shit, the other machine gun, shooting at him clear through the church. White shirts inside screaming. They were being slaughtered down there.

A bullet bit a chunk out of his left shoulder and Frank went into the dirt. Most of their shots still going high. His shoulder wouldn't cooperate, so he stayed low, coaxed a cartridge out of the crate and up to the feeder with his good hand. He hit the crank and a burst shattered the window above the doors. Red glass rained down.

The shooting started. Doyle placed it at the rear of the cathedral: machine gun fire. The team at the Gatling in front of the church struggled to get theirs working; the rest of the black shirts took aim and shot their rifles down into the church. Desperate screams from inside reached them over the crack of the guns.

Innes had trouble steadying the gun with his wounded arm and he grunted painfully with each shot, but among the three of them, taking their time and shooting accurately they knocked out the team at the machine gun before it could lay down a steady field of fire. When two other men jumped in to take their place they picked them off as well, then began to direct their fire at the men with the rifles.

No one spoke, minds focused on the bloody business. As he reloaded, Doyle glanced at Eileen; she had definitely not forgotten how to shoot.

The first bursts of the guns from above echoed metallically down through the grillwork over Jacob's head. Reverend

Day wheeled around the circle, frantic, an open watch in his hand.

"No, no! Where are the bells? *WHERE ARE THE BELLS?*"

The gunfire steadily increased in intensity, deafening as it reverberated through the chamber. Jacob did not move or speak; he dared not draw the Reverend's attention now because he was almost certain that he had heard his son's voice calling his name out of the darkness of the maze.

He heard a sound above him like a rushing of water and raised his head to look. A trickle of blood seeped through the grills and dripped down around him.

With both blades in his hands, Kanazuchi charged the machine gun at the side of the church. Only three men stationed here, concentrating the deadly fire of the Gatling into the cathedral. They never heard him coming.

Kanazuchi cut off the hand of the man on the crank, back-handed the ammunition feeder away with the knife, and drove the Grass Cutter through the throat of the last man. He took control of the gun, raised the muzzle, and fired until the feeder emptied, wiping out the machine gun position at the opposite side door.

He looked down at the dark spreading stains on the arms of his tunic and pants; he had been hit three times. No vital organs struck, but he was losing blood rapidly.

Now all the Gatlings stopped firing; only rifles somewhere to the front.

Kanazuchi hurried to the edge of the church and looked inside. White shirts cowered and huddled together, horrible moans coming from every direction; a thousand bodies covering the stone floor. He could not tell how many had died; he did not know how long the guns had fired, but he could see a great deal of blood. Moonlight through the broken frame of the window illuminated the center of the room in a stark circle of white. He listened for the children. Heard them to his right.

He descended the stairs to the floor. White shirts moving now that the gunfire had ended, crawling over each other. Bitter sounds; shock, fear, and dreadful suffering. Kanazuchi saw many discarded rifles; the militia had been sent to the slaughter with the rest of them.

The children's cries led him farther right; he found them huddled behind a row of columns, a niche in the wall, a chapel. The guns could not reach this area; the hundred children were alive.

Kanazuchi walked into their midst, speaking softly, encouragingly, gathering the children around him, lifting stragglers to their feet, holding them together. He gently led them back to the stairs through which he'd entered. The children followed meekly, weeping quietly, stumbling and stepping over bodies that had fallen. The adult survivors they passed paid no attention, staring dully ahead with glassy uncomprehending eyes.

Walks Alone stopped when she heard the others call for Jacob, and then the sound of many guns began somewhere above. She reached another intersection, twenty steps beyond where they had separated, and realized that this section ahead was honeycombed with passages; ten more steps and she would be hopelessly lost. She headed back to the meeting place occupied with many thoughts, and when the smell of the one-eyed man and the rush of movement in the air reached her senses, she was a second slow to react.

Half-turned, she cried out as the first blade cut her left shoulder to the bone. She felt his other hand slash past her right, glancing off her hip; he had a knife in that hand too. She dropped to the ground, grabbed the handle of her knife with both hands, and thrust up into the darkness, felt the tip of the blade connect and enter, heard the man grunt in pain and surprise.

He struck down at her with both hands; the knives missed by fractions of an inch; one sliced her hair, sparks flew off the wall beside her head. She slashed back, felt the blade cut tendoned flesh on the back of his leg. He bellowed and fell to his knees.

"Here, Jack!"

Presto's voice, not far off, coming closer.

The one-eyed man whimpered like an animal and raised

the knives again; she wiggled to her right along the wall, parried the slash of one blade with her knife while the other scratched along her arm, opening a deep gash.

"You *bitch,* why won't you *die*?"

His face only inches from hers as their locked knives pushed against each other; blood and fear on his breath. Her arm began to drop under his weight.

A sharp beam of light shot through the dark and found his face; it lit up like a full moon, blinding his one good eye. Walks Alone slipped to the side and raised her knife. He fell forward and she drove the knife deep into the sky-blue sightless marble resting in its socket. Heard the marble crack against the blade. He screamed and staggered back, dropped his weapons, trying to pull out her knife by the handle.

She pointed her pistol and fired; two red holes appeared in the monster's head. He fell out of sight as the gunshots exploded in the tunnel.

Jack reached her first. Presto at her side from the other direction, holding the light for them to see.

"Can you move?" asked Jack.

"I don't want to look at him," she whispered. "I don't want to look at him."

They helped her to her feet and moved quickly away from Dante's body to the intersection marked by the two glowing patches.

Jack had run off into the dark without saying a word; when Lionel tried to follow, he stumbled ahead in the corridor and quickly lost his way. He heard a man shouting and bursts of remote gunfire coming from his left where the light was growing stronger, so he began to run and two turns later he abruptly entered the round room. Haunting screams from somewhere above underscored staccato gunbursts. Light in the room dazzled his eyes, and he raised his arm against the brightness; what he thought he saw in the center of the floor was a steady stream of blood pouring out of the ceiling onto a figure lying in a pool below.

It looked like his father.

"What's that you have there?" said a voice to his left.

He turned. A nightmarish figure that looked like a walking dead body gestured at him; the crate Lionel held flew out of his hands across the ten feet between them and into the arms of the ghoulish man. He ripped open the crate and laid his hands on the Gerona Zohar.

"I don't know how to thank you," said the man.

He seemed to lose all interest in Lionel. He rushed to his father's side and pulled him from the cascading stream of blood, flowing in volume down a trough to an open pit at the end of the room.

"You're alive," gasped Lionel.

"And I'm really very glad to see you, my son," said Jacob quietly. "Do you have a gun?"

Lionel took the pistol from his belt.

"Shoot him."

Jacob nodded at the man across the circle, the hump of his back to them, setting the Book of Zohar into the last of the silver caskets.

Lionel aimed the Colt with shaking hands. The man turned and waved his arm at them; the shot fired wide as Lionel's body was jolted. The gun flew out of his hand and into the pit. Lionel fell to his knees.

Paying no attention to them, Reverend Day walked to a brazier at the edge of the circle, took a handful of matches from his pocket, and tried to strike one on the brazier; the match broke in his hand. He tried another with the same result, then a third.

"Damn," said Reverend Day, laughing. "For the want of a match . . ."

A bloodcurdling scream and two shots boomed out of the maze. Reverend Day cocked his head, listened, tossed the matches away, limped over, yanked a lantern off the wall, and carried it back to the brazier.

Lionel worked furiously to untie his father's hands. Above them, the burst of gunfire died; they heard only occasional rifles and the rising, pitiful cries of the wounded.

As blood poured out of the grills and down the trough into the pit, the rumbling from deep belowground grew louder and more sustained.

* * *

The last of the black shirts left alive in front of the church dropped their rifles and ran shortly after the last machine gun quit firing. Through his glass, Doyle saw the first white shirts splattered with red crawling out of the open cathedral doors.

"Come on," he said.

Eileen and Doyle helped Innes up, and they hurried toward the church. Doyle broke into a run ahead of them. He passed the blackshirted bodies lying around the perimeter and stopped when he reached the doors.

A massacre inside. Bodies sprawled on top of one another. The cathedral floor red with blood and shattered glass. Numbed survivors staggering to their feet.

Eileen and Innes joined him; Eileen's breath caught, horrified.

"Good God, Arthur," said Innes, shaking his head in disbelief. "Good God."

There were many wounded, hundreds, and they needed help fast.

"Got to get them outside where we can see," he said. Doyle took Eileen by the arms, looked her in the eye, and spoke firmly. "I need your help. No time for tears now."

She saw the fierce compassion in his eyes and nodded. They entered down the bloody steps; they spoke to the ones who could still walk, directing them to help survivors to the front of the church. Many remained unresponsive, some needed to hear the instruction twice; the guns had nearly deafened them. It seemed to Doyle's eye that the deadliest casualties were concentrated in the center of the room, where blood was running down into a circle of drains.

The sound of children's cries outside drew Innes to the left side doors.

"Arthur, over here."

Doyle joined him on the steps, and they saw the circle of children sitting fifty steps outside, listening to a man in black who knelt before them in the dirt. Doyle and Innes walked past the dead at the machine gun to the man; he looked up at them as they stopped.

"Kanazuchi?" asked Doyle.

The man nodded; his face pale, ashen. Critically wounded.

"See to them, please," said Kanazuchi.

The man winced and with dreadful effort rose to his feet; Doyle helped him up. Innes tried to hold him back.

"You must rest, sir," said Innes.

"No," said Kanazuchi. "Thank you."

Kanazuchi bowed slightly, gathered himself, and walked slowly toward the church, grasping the hilt of his sword.

Innes and Doyle looked down at the small piteous faces staring hopefully, fearfully up at them.

"I'll look after them," said Innes in a husky voice.

Doyle clutched Innes and held him until their tears passed, bodies trembling with the effort to contain them.

"Dear God. Dear God in heaven."

"Mustn't show them we're frightened, too," whispered Innes.

Doyle looked away, gripped Innes's hand, then followed Kanazuchi back to the church.

As she reached the back of the cathedral, Eileen saw Frank through the rear doors outside, twisted around the machine gun. She ran up the steps to him, saw the blood pooled around him in the dirt, and went to her knees.

"No. No, please."

Frank opened his eyes and looked up but didn't see her.

"That you, Molly?"

"Frank, it's Eileen."

His eyes found her and focused. "Molly. Sure look pretty in that dress."

His hand reached out; she held it with both of hers, and the tears ran freely from her eyes.

"It's Molly, Frank. I'm here."

"Never meant to hurt you, Molly," he whispered.

"You didn't, Frank. You didn't ever."

"Sorry. I'm so sorry."

"It's all right."

"Nothing in our way now. Me and you."

She shook her head. "No."

"That's good."

"Yes, Frank."

Frank smiled; it made him so happy to see her again.

"Always love you," he said.

His eyes looked past her, then closed. His hand let go.

Eileen lowered her head and wept.

As he walked back down to the floor of the cathedral, Doyle could not accurately determine how many had died; perhaps a quarter of the thousand who had been inside, another equal number wounded. It was more than bad enough, but when he saw the deadly configuration of the machine guns, he realized how much worse it could have been; hundreds had been spared. He heard a deep rumbling in the ground far below the church.

Doyle found Kanazuchi in the center of the room, kneeling beside the open grillwork in the floor through which the blood of the victims still funneled.

"Help me," said Kanazuchi. "I must hurry."

Doyle moved instantly to his side; together they used the edges of his knives to pry one of the blood-soaked grills free from its rim.

Jack and Presto carried Walks Alone through the last turns of the maze toward the light they saw ahead. Powerful tremors shook the walls, rivulets of rock and dirt running down from the corners. When they entered the round room, they saw the Reverend Day pouring oil from a lantern into a small brazier; the coals ignited, Day picked up a long taper, lit it from the fire, and walked toward the nearest silver casket.

Jacob saw them; Lionel had untied his hands and was working to free his legs. Jack left Walks Alone with Presto and stepped into the circle, drawing his pistol. Sensing another's presence, Reverend Day turned to face him; Jack stopped a foot away. His face a grim, determined mask, he raised and pointed the gun directly at the Reverend's head.

The Reverend waved his hand sharply, as if trying to fend off a bothersome insect, a move that might have sent another man flying across the room. Jack did not yield or react but instead reached forward, touched the barrel to the Reverend's upper lip and coolly cocked the pistol's hammer, fully prepared to kill him. A quizzical look shaded the Reverend's features; fear had become such a stranger to him he seemed incapable of registering danger, but then fury erupted inside as he realized the affront this man offered him and he drove the power from his eyes forward into Jack's.

Jack appeared to stand his ground against the assault, but after a long silence the hand holding the gun wavered, then Jack slowly lowered it to his side.

"I'll deal with you presently," said the Reverend.

But Jack's move was not born of obedience. As the Reverend turned and again tried to set fire to the first of the Books that would trigger the summoning, Jack reached over and, oblivious to the pain, snuffed out the burning taper in the Reverend's hand. When Day raised his hand to strike at him, Jack caught him by the wrist in a steely grip, twisted hard, and the taper fell to the floor.

Blood continued to run down into the trough. The rumbling from the pit grew stronger until the walls and floor trembled steadily, but none of the others in the room dared to move, riveted by the confrontation.

"Let go of my hand," ordered Reverend Day, locking eyes with him again.

Jack dropped the gun of his own accord and let go of the Reverend's wrist. Again, before he could move away, Jack reached out, took firm hold of the Reverend's head with both his hands, pulled him close, and stared right back into his eyes.

"Look at me," said Jack quietly.

Enraged, the Reverend now brought the full force of his power to bear; the air appeared to bend around them, their forms wavered, warped by a savage expulsion of energy. Men had died under far less exposure to the sacrament than this, minds dissolving, their will slipping out of them in a runny stream.

Nothing happened. The man stared right back at him.

Blood poured freely out of the Reverend's nose; the effort had weakened him tremendously. Shocked, slowly realizing he could effect no control over this man, the Reverend searched this stranger's face with increasing desperation. The man's expression remained strong but infuriatingly neutral, without rancor, offering no purchase for the Reverend's influence to grasp.

There's no fear in the man, thought Jacob, watching Jack. Without fear there's nothing for the Reverend to seize hold of.

The standoff continued. Finally, when Reverend Day spotted a ghost of something familiar in the stranger's eyes, his own went wide with terror and he scrambled and clawed to pull away, but Jack held his head ferociously in place. Recognition was what he had been waiting for.

"No," said Jack.

Unable to escape, the Reverend tried to avoid his eyes, but Jack maintained his grip, exerted his own will, and pulled the Reverend's eyes back into contact with his own.

"What do you want?" the Reverend asked weakly.

Jack did not answer.

"Who are you?" said Day, his voice failing.

"You know who I am," said Jack.

The man's pitiful, ill face struggled against that suggestion until his last vestige of resistance melted and he sagged forward.

"You know who I am."

"Yes," the Reverend whispered.

"Who am I? Tell me."

After a long silence, the Reverend replied: "My brother."

"What's my name?"

Reverend Day looked puzzled again. "Jack."

"And what is yours?"

After an even longer silence, he whispered: "Alexander."

Jack nodded once. Every pretense fell away from the exchange between them, every mask. All enmity and struggle stripped away. Now they were only brothers.

"Listen to me," said Jack quietly and slowly, trusting that the words he needed would come to him. "Listen to me, Alex. We are all here, in this room; mother, father. Our little sister. None of us know why any of it happened, how you fell so far away from us, the darkness that took you and made you do the crimes you did to us or any of the others. None of that matters now. Do you hear me?"

Alexander Sparks stared at his brother with the rapt attention of a terrified child, praying for comfort and relief. Trembling, lost, the fear was in him now.

"They are all with us here in this room now; their spirits are with us and here is where it ends. I speak for them, their voices are joined with mine. Listen to me. . . ."

Jack found what he had come here to say, leaned forward, and whispered in his ear.

"We forgive you, my brother."

A quiet sob burst from Alexander.

"We forgive you."

Now Alexander sagged forward completely and collapsed into his brother's arms; Jack guided his brittle weight gently down to the floor, knelt beside him, and cradled his brother's piteous broken body in his lap.

"We forgive you," he whispered.

A heartrending wail rose from Alexander, a lifetime's mourning for a multitude of lost and stolen souls. He clung weakly to his brother as sobs jolted his fragile bones. The others in the room, despite their fears or anger at Alexander's crimes, could not look on with anything but pity.

With a grinding metallic ring, one of the grills above the center of the room lifted from its rim; Jacob looked up as Kanazuchi let himself down through the cavity and dropped to the floor beside them. The last of the blood flow followed and ran off into the pit. The rumbling from below rose again in pitch and power, wind from the hollow guttered the flames of the lanterns. Kanazuchi sat unmoving, stunned. When he weakly failed to lift himself to his feet, Jacob unsteadily walked the few steps to Kanazuchi.

"Come along, my friend," said Jacob quietly.

He extended his hands to Kanazuchi and helped him slowly rise; leaning on one another they walked to Jack and Alexander. Jacob helped Kanazuchi down and then sat beside him next to the brothers.

Walks Alone nodded to Presto; he wrapped an arm around

her. They moved forward and filled the last places in the circle. Walks Alone held Presto's left hand and extended her right to Jack. He grasped it tightly with his left, holding on to Alexander's in his other. While Kanazuchi held his right hand, Jacob leaned over and gently covered Alexander's right hand. Kanazuchi reached out to Presto and their hands completed the circle.

Alexander's sobs subsided; he looked up and his eyes found Jack's. Jack nodded to him, gentle and kind. Alexander nodded in return. Then Jack's eyes sought out each of the others and now a silent understanding, something pure and inexpressible, passed among them all.

Realizing there was no place for him among their number, Lionel stood up and moved deliberately around the circle, from casket to casket, removing each of the stolen books and securing them safely by the wall. When he completed this task and looked back at the circle, the sight that greeted him forced him to the ground, his back pressed against the wall in deep humility. Although he would never again be as certain of it as he was in the moments that followed, as the Six looked at each other Lionel thought he saw a penumbra of light extend into the air above them, a round transparent curtain that contained in the fabric of its weave a host of swirling forms and shapes and faces, each carrying within it the strength and beauty and compassion of a hundred thousand human souls.

In that moment this is what Lionel, a secular man, thought he had seen, but as the years passed he would never again be as sure.

As the light above the circle brightened, the deep rumbling in the pit below the chamber fell gradually away. No one in the circle moved.

When it was gone entirely, the light receded.

In the peaceful silence that followed, Alexander gave out a small cry and died quietly in his brother's arms.

Lionel helped his father to his feet, staring down in sympathy and horror at the broken, impossibly thin body of the brother still resting in Jack's arms.

"Whatever did he want the books for?" Lionel asked softly.

"He thought he wanted to destroy God," said Jacob.

Lionel blinked back his astonishment. "But he would have had to . . . end the world."

"He was mistaken," said Jacob sadly. "All he really wanted to destroy was himself."

Doyle had searched for and found a rope in one of the corners of the church after Kanazuchi went below. When the rumbling stopped—an earthquake or some sort of related seismic disturbance, Doyle decided, and no one later contradicted him—he secured one end of the rope around his waist, let the other fall down into the chamber, and called out to them to take hold. Then his powerful arms lifted the survivors and their rescued books, one by one, to the floor of the moonlit cathedral.

Jack Sparks was the last to ascend; after remaining below alone and committing his brother's body to the memory of their lost family, he grasped the line and Doyle pulled him up, up into the light.